MW00995841

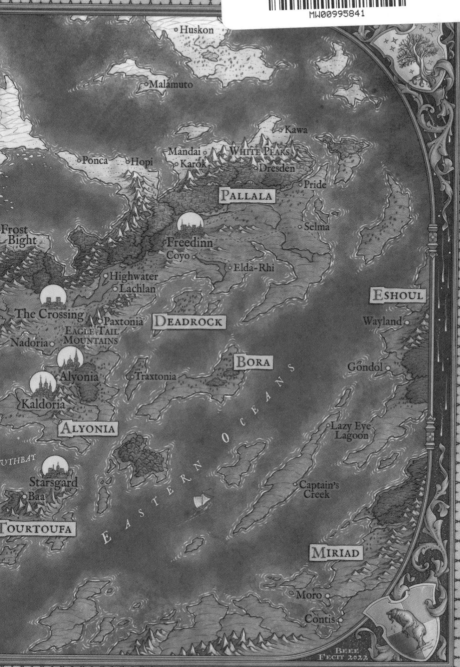

Huskon

Malamuto

Kawa

Ponca   Hopi   Mandai   WHITE PEAKS
Karok   Dresden

PALLALA   Pride

Selma

Frost
Bight   Freedinn
Coyo

Elda-Rhi

Highwater
Lachlan   ESHOUL

The Crossing   Wayland

Paxtonia   DEADROCK
EAGLE TAIL
MOUNTAINS
Nadoria

Alyonia   BORA   Gondol
Traxtonia

Kaldoria

ALYONIA

Lazy Eye
Lagoon

UTHBAY

Starsgard   Captain's
Baa   Creek

TOURTOUFA

MIRIAD

Moro

Contis

BEEE
FECIT 2022

DUST

DUST

A NOVEL

JOSH PLASSE

RESOLVE
EDITIONS

Published by Resolve Editions, an imprint of Forefront Books.
Distributed by Simon & Schuster.

Library of Congress Control Number: 2024920541

Print ISBN: 978-1-63763-354-0
E-book ISBN: 978-1-63763-355-7

Cover Design by Charles Brock, Brock Book Design Co.
Interior Design by Mary Susan Oleson, Blu Design Concepts
Map by @mistybeee

Printed in the United States of America

A SPECIAL THANKS to Brev Moss, for reading this book more times than anyone should. To my dogs, Jack & Teddy, for their relentless assault on my attempts to write in peace. To my friends and family who've provided feedback throughout the years. And to my dear friend Gannon, for reading a painful first draft of this book ten years ago, and having the courage to tell me how much it stunk. I needed that.

DUST

Book One

*More states have perished from the violation
of morality than from the violation of law.*

—Charles De Montesquieu

Prologue

PRIEST EROS stared up at the axe, eyeing its jagged, blood-stained edge. "You've taken the wrong priest!" he cried as he was forced to both knees.

The priest bled from every crevice, sweat from every pore. His sacred white gown had been ripped and soiled. Strong hands clutched his bony shoulders, keeping him pinned upon a rotting, splintery stage of pinewood. Still he howled, as if the twentieth shout would be the one to save him. "You've taken the wrong priest!"

Angry voices roared from below.

"On with it!"

"Maim him!"

Nearing death's door, Priest Eros barely heard the furious crowd.

"Kill the child-lover!"

That he heard.

Trumpets sounded abruptly—a royal arrival. The raging masses fell silent and searched for their beloved king as a group of house protectorates, clad in green and gold armor, cleared a path toward the execution stage, shoving sweaty tanners, butchers, and merchants aside. King Kaldor trailed these protectorates, walking between two standard bearers waving the green flags of House Kaldor high overhead.

Once free of the crowd, King Kaldor strode up a set of spiral pinewood stairs, each step draped with bits of shredded gown or bloodied skin. Priest Eros could do naught but watch as the king of Alyonia marched onto his infamous execution stage.

"Stand down," said the king.

Eros' executioner, a hulking figure by the name of Aypax the Honorable, stepped back, allowing the priest to release a breath he hadn't known he was holding.

"My king...I'm innocent," he coughed.

"To your feet." King Kaldor moved swiftly toward center stage, his royal surcoat of green and gold fluttering in warm winds.

Eros stood as a second captive was dragged beside him for all the city to see. He was a human, this captive, a rare sight for the city of Alyonia. The man appeared middle-aged. His dirty beard and haggard face hinted at a hard past. His once-golden hair had gone white with time, allowing his features to blend in with the priest and every Alyonian nearby.

Known for their disheveled white hair and slim tails, Alyonians were frequently mocked as "appearing closer to ape than man." Evolution had left them behind, at least according to the realms of men. Over time, the strong novas of the south had slowly changed Alyonian pigment from pale to various shades of bronze beneath their thin white fur, another source of repugnance for their human neighbors of the north.

"Today we charge two souls," continued King Kaldor. "Priest Eros Solanus, for the crime of youthful defilement... and Sir Henry-Fri, a prisoner of war belonging to our enemies of the north, the Rhi Empire. Both shall be put to the blade."

The crowd cheered, for they hated the Rhi Empire and every human living within it. And the priest...the priest had earned their fury. All went quiet as King Kaldor lifted his hand for silence. His muscular stature was imposing, even for an Alyonian. Lengthy white hair fell past broad shoulders. His forearm fur was well-groomed and his tail was concealed masterfully beneath a white belt. Nobility.

As noise from the crowd quieted, King Kaldor turned to his royal family lined behind him. They stood in single file among other political figures, each clothed in dark green tunics. "Prince Taaivetti, step forward."

Young Prince Taaivetti marched ahead proudly. He was a mere fifty-two seasons of age, no more than thirteen years by the count of men. Yet Prince Taaivetti seemed mature and always carried himself with the arrogance of a wealthy house patron or High-Lord.

"Two moons past, you heard both Priest Eros and Sir Henry-Fri's testimonies before the High Council," said King Kaldor. "It is now time to pass your judgment. By law, only you may pardon either."

Taaivetti stared up at Priest Eros, his bruised cheeks and pleading eyes. "No pardon," the prince said, his voice solemn. He turned to the human, studied him. "As for Sir Henry-Fri...freedom. Let him return home and tell the Rhi Empire of our power, but also, of our mercy."

The clustered masses clapped and nodded, content to heed the wisdom of their young prince.

"Well spoken, my son." King Kaldor shifted attention to his daughter, Taryn. She stood in line behind him, arms crossed, eyes fixed upon Priest Eros. King Kaldor watched her carefully, eyeing her with secret understanding. *My Taryn,* he thought.

Taryn's mother, Queen Lizabeth, also seemed worried about her. The queen stood by her daughter's side, swaying a crying infant in her arms. Baby Hendrix, the royal family's third and final child, had cheeks stained with tears as he teethed and tugged upon a small white book.

Hoping to drag her children's attention from the violence that lay ahead, Queen Lizabeth peeled Hendrix's fingers back and read the book aloud. "'Legend has it, the ancient comets struck down all over our world.'" Queen Lizabeth forced a smile toward her young ones as she recited the familiar words. "'These comets warped the men of old into all types of new beings…for you see, there was power in the dust of these comets.'"

"Bring forth the victim!" shouted King Kaldor, his labored breaths working to combat Alyonia's crippling heat.

The crowd began to stir, shielding their eyes from nova rays above and craning their necks until a young Alyonian gal emerged from below the pinewood stairs. She appeared no older than Taryn, even looked a bit like her.

"Please," King Kaldor said gently, "you've nothing to fear. Your bravery inspires."

The gal quivered as she ascended the stairs, taking in hundreds of inquisitive eyes. The fibers on her ragged dress snagged on the stage's splintery wood whilst she made for King Kaldor's side. Stepping in place beside him, the king gave her an approving nod.

"My fellow Alyonians," he began, "hard as this may be, it is law that Priest Eros be identified eye to eye."

King Kaldor kneeled to the tiny Alyonian's level and whispered in her ear. Her tail suddenly sprung from a loose under-belt and flickered behind, lifting the dress and exposing her bare backside. Taryn couldn't help but laugh. She nudged and whispered to a youthful Alyonian male standing in line beside her. "Kornilious, look."

Kornilious grinned. "Indeed." He hid his chuckles beneath the sweat-soaked collar of an expensive green tunic. "She ought to wear loincloths next time."

"Probably can't afford them." Taryn snickered silently, yet kept her eyes forward, her teeny tail stroking Kornilious' in secret.

King Kaldor pointed at Priest Eros. "Is this the Alyonian who defiled you?"

The young victim pulled her dress back into place, trembled, and blinked. "Yes…yes!"

The audience stirred once more, throwing shouts at Priest Eros as King Kaldor waved for the executioner.

"No! She lies!" Priest Eros' limbs shook as the executioner forced him back to his knees, axe in hand. "She *lies*!"

The tiny victim hurried offstage. Eros' eyes followed her as she walked through the raucous crowd and out past a road of alehouses, smithies, and inns. Time slowed, gifting him the moment he'd been dreading as his eyes alighted on the one face he'd prayed not to see.

Ellara, his beautiful bride-to-be.

Ellara could only watch as the executioner lifted his bloody blade.

"May you find peace," said Aypax the Honorable. His axe remained high in the air as red dribbled down its steel bit and splattered upon Eros' neck, drop by wretched drop.

Queen Lizabeth rocked baby Hendrix twice as fast, then gently nudged Taryn's head down, hoping her child's eyes would stay on the on the book's pages. "'The comet dust gave off strange powers, powers that bygone men were able to harness,'" she read. "'A great war arose over them, and eventually, the comets were locked away beneath an altar somewhere never known.'"

Still focused on his beloved, Eros somehow managed a smile. *At least she'll know of my honor,* he thought. *My truth.*

He closed his eyes, and everything went black.

The mob gasped.

Enraged as they were, even the masses stilled by such a sight. Eros' head rolled off the stage and landed with a wet thud before them. Citizens stepped back and held their breath, for the head itself might've carried some child-loving plague.

"'The men of old built this altar,'" continued Queen Lizabeth, now trembling. Shaky fingers flipped another page. "'They then crafted four keys, each needed to open the altar. The men of old rode off and hid these keys in four different realms across Adria...'"

Taryn rolled her eyes and twisted away from her mother, away from the story she'd heard a thousand times before. "Kornilious?"

Kornilious stared straight ahead as his parents had demanded, but he couldn't hide his smitten smile. "Yes?"

"Want to hear something funny?"

"I'm listening."

Taryn's hips moved, slightly touching Kornilious' for a brief moment of adolescent love. "My father paid that little girl to lie. I already killed the priest who abused me."

1

HENDRIX
Rain and Wind

Hendrix looked overboard at the powerful tides, at the swirling black abyss. A plunge into these waters would yield a harsh death, but then, so would being caught by his pursuers. He wondered which was easier. After all, it seemed a short jump...

Twenty-two moons with constant rain, he thought, glancing at the weathered white book in his hand. *Could* The Prophetics *be true?* It had been sixty-four seasons since Eros' execution, since Hendrix's mother began to read him the little white book of prophecies, yet still he remained unsure of the content's veracity.

"Bloody Perdition! Put that damned thing away and patch the leak!" shouted Aypax, before vomiting off the port side of their pitiful vessel.

Hendrix didn't hear his words, nor the chunks of undigested meat splashing against violent waves. Hendrix didn't hear much of anything, in fact. Perhaps due to the night's deafening winds, perhaps due to his severe intoxication. At sixty-eight seasons, or seventeen years according to the calendar of men, Hendrix wasn't quite old enough to drink, and yet the situation demanded it. *Twenty-two moons with constant rain...*

"Hendrix!"

Aypax wiped his pruned mouth and stomped toward his drunken accomplice. An incredibly large and intimidating Alyonian, Aypax wasn't used to repeating himself. But tonight felt different. Tonight, one had to earn the right to be heard. Heavy rain and echoes of furious thunder ensured that. Aypax shuffled cautiously across the slippery deck, exposing their pathetic ship. The miniature craft stretched no more than fourteen forearms in length. Worse, Aypax himself stood nearly half that in height. "We drift mere moments from the Tourtoufian beach, put the book away and help—"

A hefty swell assaulted their hull. Aypax gripped a slick railing as if life depended on it, and perhaps it did. Cold, dark water splashed high and engulfed him. Exhausted and drenched, Aypax appeared more primitive than usual. His archaic facial features and balding white hair often prompted the term *simian*, yet tonight, he looked particularly barbaric.

"Fine!" Unsteady on his feet, Hendrix swayed with the boat and tucked his book into a green travel sack as lightning illuminated the distance. Its bright shine revealed nothing but torrential downpour and seemingly endless miles of perilous sea. "Do you think I wish to read at a time like this?" Hendrix's thin white tail convulsed uncontrollably, a common sign of Alyonian fear. "*The Prophetics* are coming true!" He stood and untied a firm knot attached to the lower stanchion, finally helping his burly companion. "I must read! There could be warnings in these pages, Aypax—"

Hendrix felt a sudden flash of pain as the rope he'd uncoiled sliced through his hands and toward the bow like an angry snake, knocking over buckets of raw fish and potted meat. The disgusting cluster sloshed across the deck while Hendrix's palms bled. "Moons and stars and whor—" He stopped himself. The young Alyonian had long attempted to quell his cursing, at least in public. Blood dripped downward, mixing with the hideous scraps of food and washed-up kelp like a collage.

"The skies have pissed for twenty-two moons straight, Aypax." Hendrix pushed knotty white hair from his face. "We're in the Southbay! It hasn't so much as drizzled this far south in seasons. Now there's a monsoon?" His thoughts were interrupted by a drunken hiccup. "Don't you find this strange?"

While Aypax couldn't deny the strange confluence of events, he still refused to believe in the book's prophetic messages. "Vomit yourself to sobriety. I require your focus."

"I *am* focused!" Jarring gusts diminished Hendrix's words. "That's precisely why I'm afraid! Twenty-two moons of rain, Aypax... The sickness, a full famine across Alyonia. *The Prophetics* foretold all of this. It's too much to be coincidence."

Another wave rocked their vessel, forcing Hendrix to his knees. "Open your eyes!" The wet surface stung his open wounds. "You know my heart, my past. I'm the last Alyonian to ever believe in this prophetic nonsense, and yet...something is happening. I cannot deny it any longer." Finally giving in, Hendrix allowed his body to slump in defeat.

Aypax wished to do the same, to rest his aching muscles and throbbing headache. He couldn't; their pursuers were too close behind. To stop now would mean capture. Capture would mean much worse.

"My brother once spoke that any escapees seized beyond the borders of Alyonia would have their eyes plucked before their beheading," Hendrix said and burped. He'd turned over, now faced toward the night sky, though he couldn't see any of it. His brown eyes were closed as cold rain bombarded his lids. Temporary blindness only helped him imagine such a cruel punishment. "You know the laws of execution... Will that happen to us?"

Aypax finished patching the boat leak with a mixture of mud and cotton fibers. "Your help is appreciated," he said, mocking, as he rolled up the grey sleeves of his tunic. Adjusting their headsail, he heeled the boat toward defiant winds.

Hendrix marveled at his savior, thinking, *How does he keep it up? What motivates him?* As the vessel tilted, the young Alyonian rolled toward its edge like a lifeless ball. *No.* Catching himself upon a corroded rail, he stared down at the passing waters. *I shall not give in.* Now an arm's length away, he could practically touch the salty sea.

Hendrix lay there, nauseous yet enchanted by the ocean's soullessness, by the fear of what lurked in the deep. "Taaivetti also spoke of escapees who were ship-dragged, that a boat's barnacles and rusted underbelly would tear them to shreds before they arrived home for execution."

"Quite true!" Aypax remained focused on a flapping sail. "I've carried out both punishments myself. They're far worse in reality than thought."

Hendrix knew the brute never lied, ever. Aypax had been raised a warrior. He'd wedded brutality and slaughtered niceties long ago.

"But," Aypax furthered, "pain that doesn't kill you can be useful."

Hendrix studied his savior's eyes. It was then he understood what fueled Aypax. What kept him forging forward. *Revenge.*

"Your sister shall pay for what she's done." Aypax inhaled a deep breath, turning his pain to promise.

"I still don't understand how she could do such a thing…"

"It matters not. What's done is done. They're all dead, and they won't be coming back—"

"Taryn killed my mother!" snapped Hendrix. "Have some respect for her memory." The wind fell silent, allowing Hendrix to feel his agony free of distraction.

"I'll respect the queen's memory by removing Taryn's spleen and sending her to the same realm of torment she sent each of my brethren to."

That stopped Hendrix. "They died honorably…"

"Their bodies hang from the Kaldorian manor. They do not rest honorably."

Hendrix stared into the distance as their boat bobbed up and down. "Mother's image shall stay with me forever." A difficult truth to admit, gut wrenching to say aloud. "I can still see Taryn cutting her throat. The blood. The steel. The silent screams."

Aypax didn't hesitate. "Mental scars are far worse than physical."

"Do they ever leave you?"

"No." Aypax let out a horrific cough and pounded at his chest. Frightening, given the recent outbreak of sickness.

Hendrix didn't like that answer, nor the wretched cough. He changed topics. "Do we have any hope?"

"Hope is a disease. I prefer a plan."

"Do we have a plan?"

"Yes. Get our letter to Prince Taaivetti, and quickly. We'll need his royal decree of pardon before Taryn's assassins catch up to us."

"I thought you said you'd take care of the letter?"

"Patience." Nearly on cue, Aypax's eyes darted upward. A dark cloud burst open as he saw the very creature his "patience" referred to: an Askari. Tonight's skies came with a dim fog, but Aypax couldn't possibly miss his treasured Askari. "Pattar, *ramos*!"

"Patttttttaaaaaa!"

The Askari released a high-pitched screech to signal arrival. Seeing it up close, Hendrix gaped. Pattar was a majestic bird with three wings; its beak alone sharp enough to catch the dimmest light and shine through haze. Hendrix gawked as the bird, if it could even be compared to one, sliced through aggressive winds and circled overhead.

Pattar descended and landed on Aypax's muscular shoulder. A proud parent, the brute stroked his Askari's damp brown fur. Messenger birds were impressive enough, but the famed Askari doubled them in size, speed, and agility. "Pattar shall deliver our letter to Prince Taaivetti." Aypax kissed the Askari's forehead, ruffling its soaking feathers. "He should cover the distance within three moons. We'll need to evade Taryn for that long. At least."

Far too entranced with the Askari, Hendrix did not respond. Pattar had a bushy tail falling from its backside, and four stout limbs, each long yet well built. Its piercing red eyes returned Hendrix's curiosity.

"Did its mother hump a lion?"

Aypax chuckled, his first in seasons. "No." Rain rushed down his newly lit face, but the disease of hope had returned...even if only a sliver. "Pattar is a pure-bred Askari from the great trees of the eastern shore. They tend to be a bit...mean."

"You don't say." Hendrix grinned, momentarily rejuvenated. "I don't question the bird's origins so much as its methods of development. You strike me as one who might feed Pattar some...bird-enhancement herbs?"

Ignoring the boy's drunken inquiries, Aypax squinted ahead. "Quiet yourself and prepare the bow. I see Tourtoufa."

Hendrix nodded, then stumbled toward the pulpit. He gazed out at the island's beach and lost himself in its trademark mixture of black and purple sands, the first time he'd ever seen such a thing. Tall trees with orange and green canopies outlined the shore's opposite end. They spanned as far as one could see, a forest of unidentified proportions. The landscape was alluring to behold, but even its charm wasn't enough to shake the newest thought plaguing Hendrix's mind.

Will I ever see my beloved Madison Preters again?

2

TARYN

Love

Her room smelled of love. A new love, a passionate love. It smelled of sweat mingled with the finest perfumes the southern realms could offer.

One could say it reeked.

"Did you send the letter?" asked Bandano-Rhi, the illustrious emperor of the Rhi Empire.

Taryn's brown eyes looked up from his strong arms. "I did. Taaivetti should receive it any moment." She nestled her head into the curve of his neck, showing a side of herself Bandano-Rhi had never seen. A vulnerable side, a side he was growing quite fond of.

But as Bandano-Rhi scanned every freckle on the sun-kissed skin beneath her short, silky fur, he noticed something new: a small burn mark, a blister of sorts, scarring the back of her neck. The burn had been covered by Taryn's elegant, almost-silver hair, only noticeable from such an angle.

She rolled over and tucked her neck into a silk pillow. "My love."

Bandano-Rhi understood. He refocused on his surroundings. There were candles. *Far too many candles.* The sheer number of them went past the point of romance. It bordered on obsession…

Taryn pulled her eyes from Bandano-Rhi's and examined each flame lovingly.

The enamored emperor watched the flickering reflections in Taryn's chestnut-brown eyes. She was smiling, though perhaps unintentionally. Fire always brought forth the best in her. Or the worst, depending on one's perception. Regardless, flames had always shifted her mood, ever since her troubled youth.

"How is it that you grow more beautiful each moon we lay together?" asked Bandano-Rhi.

"I don't." She focused on the twinkling of yellow and red throughout her living chamber. "You're a man, and I'm nude."

"It is far more than that." He ran a callused hand down her smooth tan cheek. "I've seen many a nude woman. Never a nude Alyonian, I'll grant you this. But I know beauty when I see it, and you? You're one of a kind."

Taryn finally met his gaze. "That's merely your mind telling you to compliment me, so that you'll get the chance to see me nude yet again."

Bandano-Rhi chuckled.

"With men, it always comes back to lust," she continued.

"I prefer passion."

"Simply a fancy word for lust." Sensing that would end this game, Taryn rose from her ruby-red sofa.

Now standing, her body, curved and on full display, froze Bandano-Rhi. She hated this move, this power play. It seemed so simple, and Taryn was much too intelligent to be simple. Or perhaps much too intelligent not to be. Bandano-Rhi may have been an emperor, but he was still a man, and such a tactic always yielded exactly what she wanted.

"What am I to you?" she asked.

Her question felt honest. That made it powerful. For a moment, the emperor didn't feel like much of one. "You're my family."

Family.

Taryn despised the word. Yet in this moment, she wanted to kiss him, hold him 'til the eve was through. Taryn wished to say that she felt the same, that she'd never had a real connection to her own family. *Or to anyone.* Taryn wished to say that finally, after all of her one hundred seasons, she tasted a real connection now.

But that would be too intimate.

Sex. Love. Secrecy. Things were perfect as they were—safe, controlled. Taryn and Bandano-Rhi seemed unstoppable. From their recent political developments to their dark and delicate plans, dreams were nearing true. But family...family implied settling. *Settling invites weakness,* Taryn thought sadly, bitterly. And neither party could afford to look weak. Neither could show their true hand. Not yet.

"Why so many books?" Bandano-Rhi shifted the conversation, doing his best not to stare at the obvious. They'd been together many private eves, yet he'd never been to the city of Alyonia, and he'd certainly never been inside Taryn's personal chambers. The public would never have accepted such hybridizing. The Rhi Empire had recently struck peace with Alyonia, but such an ancient feud would not merely vanish overnight.

"I'm fascinated by them." Taryn sipped dark red wine whilst gesturing air quotes. "And you know, 'wisdom is power.' Or so they say." She swirled her wine round a sapphire mug, then walked toward a well-kept fireplace. "And do you know what is even more powerful than wisdom?"

"Yes." Bandano-Rhi pointed toward his longsword perched against a window in the corner. "Ten thousand men with spears and shields."

Taryn giggled, then peeked back at him, drinking him in. She loved his thick black hair, his glittering green eyes. "No. It is the controlling of wisdom." She nodded toward an incredibly large pile of burnt paper. Stacks of charred remains lay scattered next to her fireplace, a graveyard of parchment. Perhaps thousands of books had met their end here. "When you control what the masses remember, we can alter the past and curate the present. Thus changing the trajectory of our future." Taryn lifted a copy of a small white book titled *The Prophetics*. Another fifty duplicates sat upon a hefty bookshelf nearby, patiently awaiting their doom.

Bandano-Rhi grinned. "Just when I felt I couldn't love you more… Elo smiles down upon you. Praise him."

"Praise him." Taryn lifted a copy of *The Prophetics*, slid her hand over its title. "My father once told Taaivetti that *The Prophetics* would save Alyonia. That their prophecies and false god Balo would save us all." Her forearm fur raised ever so slightly at the thought of her father and his religious texts. She'd trimmed her fur perfectly for tonight, still, Bandano notice its movement. "That was the same eve I was forced over by a Balonian priest."

Taryn wanted the book to scream before she heaved it into the flames, to somehow beg for mercy the way she had that night. It did not. *Just as well*, she thought. Her old life had gone up in flames that night as well.

Bandano-Rhi watched her, speechless. "Taryn, I—"

"My queen. May I enter?" A quiet voice slipped through the front door, accompanied by an equally feeble knock.

Taryn walked behind a marble counter, only somewhat hiding her lack of clothing. "Come in then!"

Bandano-Rhi's look questioned her sanity. Too late.

An Alyonian male entered, clothed in a pricey beige tunic of heavy, luxurious fabric. His eyes shot straight to the nude emperor of man sitting mere forearms away. Taryn smiled.

"Hello, Trakkonious."

Trakkonious' thin tail slipped from a leather brown belt,

giving away slight nerves. "Taryn, my queen," he mumbled. "I have a message from Anaeous—"

"You may speak freely." Taryn turned to a curious Bandano-Rhi. "Anaeous is cryptic for Kornilious."

Trakkonious bowed. "Anaeou— Kornilious speaks that your brother Hendrix has been spotted in the Southbay. He is to be captured within three moons. Kornilious also relays that everything is in order for tonight. The eve is confirmed."

"Wonderful. Find him and relay the same. But make my words sound more pristine." Taryn simpered. "More queenlike. Do not say 'confirmed.'" Taryn couldn't hide her smirk, for she was only just getting used to her new title of interim queen. "And what of the story-papers? How did you detail Hendrix's treachery?"

"He murdered your mother, the queen of Alyonia." Trakkonious grinned. "Respectfully, this was the easiest story I've created in all my time as public heed. I even managed to dig up some of Hendrix's childhood offenses and had our scribes detail your heroic attempts to stop him during the murder. If it pleases, I would walk with a limp this week and accept condolences from each house."

Taryn nodded her approval, and Trakkonious slinked out.

Bandano-Rhi glared. "You've just set a fly on the wall to buzz about the city."

"Folks don't listen to flies, my love. They swat them. And my flies know better. Alyonia is full of spiderwebs."

Taryn sauntered back toward Bandano-Rhi, allowing his gaze to drink in her curves once more. *Lord, she looks like a woman, only better. Her bronze skin. Her soft yet muscular frame. Her breasts. Even the tail somehow...*

Taryn's tail danced with excitement, as if she could read the emperor's thoughts. Finally reaching her couch, she could still sense the unease swimming underneath his desire. "Relax, my love. Trakkonious is my family's High-Public Heed, and my image is now all that matters to him. He already knows of you and I."

Bandano-Rhi reluctantly accepted. "Whilst we are on the subject, have you had to...with Kornilious?"

"No." Taryn covered herself with a linen blanket before sinking onto the red sofa and reflecting upon her childhood lover. "Kornilious does as I ask. He believes precisely what we wish. And if he's reelected as Alyonia's Master of Defense, he'll be quite useful... Now, wipe away your jealousy. It isn't fitting."

Bandano-Rhi ignored the remark. He contemplated how best to say what was truly on his mind. Taryn's admission of this Balonian priest's actions had changed the course of the eve, shifted what could be said. *But this needs saying.* "Taryn...my son Maxoff, he's fled Pallala."

Taryn appeared struck. Her usually powerful posture changed yet again. "Go on."

"He married that whore from the Pallala countryside, the one I spoke to you of during our time in Nadoria. They ran away together. Sailed away, I should say."

"I'm sorry, Bandano."

And she was. Taryn cared. She actually *cared.* It was a new feeling. Her usual negativity replaced by compassion as her mind suddenly raced back to that damned word. *Family.*

"And he stole the key," continued Bandano, timidly, grievously. With these five words, he finally revealed the true reason for his presence in Alyonia.

Taryn's negative energy spiraled back in the form of deep worry and rage.

"I know." Bandano did his best to calm her. "I know." He took to his feet and retreated for the doorway, picking up his longsword and yellow armor along the way. "Maxoff is going to try and find the altar." Bandano let the thought sink in as he clothed himself and packed his things into a yellow and purple haversack.

Taryn's nose twitched; her anger rose. She leaped up and approached.

"Don't worry." He held his ground at the door, barely. "I shall see to my son after I've signed the peace treaty. When the Alyonian Peace Parade ends, I'll sail for him and take the key back myself." Bandano-Rhi's face appeared burdened with guilt and uncertainty. Even as a great conqueror, he was still a father.

"I know you'll do what needs to be done." Taryn lifted her hand for a kiss, then showed him out.

3

TAAIVETTI

The Heat of the South

It was hot. Far too hot.

Sweat dripped down the slope of Prince Taaivetti's nose as he stared out into a vast desert below. *Endless,* he thought. *Absolutely endless.* His sweat fell, splashing against warped wood beneath him, then fizzled into nothingness with a pained hiss.

"Two novas rotating over the same desert...a cruel joke," he murmured through cracked lips. Taaivetti had been here at the fortress of Hann for nearly fifty seasons, and even still, he had not adapted to such heat. No one had.

"My prince," said an Alyonian officer passing behind.

"Lord," exclaimed another.

The officers saluted their inattentive prince. Lost in thought, and severely dehydrated, Taaivetti looked nothing like his usual self, nothing like what many considered the most dashing Alyonian of them all.

Formalities continued as more exhausted soldiers marched across Hann's narrow wall walk in perfect unison, headed for a poorly built watchtower. This tower sat perched upon the north-eastern corner of the ramparts. Hann's wooden walls were at their highest and flimsiest here, a four-story heap of decaying wood.

Taaivetti didn't turn to repay his weary brethren's respects. Such a lapse in manners was unlike him, yet everyone has a breaking point. Everyone. Still gazing out into sheer nothingness, Taaivetti ran a hand through short white hair, then blinked repetitively, as if he'd seen a sparkle of life in the blowing sand. He hadn't. It was as red and dead as ever. The Red Sand Desert, it had come to be known… Not even tumbleweeds survived here. Even the surrounding volcanoes, resembling heaping mounds of red dirt, were long dormant. The sand's scarlet color served as a scathing and constant reminder of the bloodshed it so frequently played host to.

Lost in thought, Taaivetti failed to feel the flesh and fur burning from his forearm. Leaning against the metallic railing of a blistering merlon, it finally hit him. Not the pain, nor his body posture, but the answer to a long-pondered question.

To leave, or to stay?

Taaivetti walked away, leaving a bit of dead skin behind. As he paced the northern parapet of Hann, nausea gripped the prince. This wasn't new, for the heat made nausea a normality at Hann, frequent as daily meals for some. But this felt different, the kind of queasiness one gets from heartbreak, or the loss of someone dear…

"Your officers await you in the boardroom, my prince!" shouted the honorable Sir Rynn of Kaldoria. "They're eager to hear your decision." Sir Rynn wiped heaps of sweat from his thin white tail as he approached, then tucked the appendage beneath a brown belt. He had a rather tiny tail, a half arm shorter than most Alyonians.

Sir Rynn was also remarkably old. Truthfully, no one knew his real age. Some claimed he'd lived for more than five hundred seasons, others thought mankind had cursed him with immortality. Regardless, whatever the elder lacked in physical gifts, he made up for with an undeniable aura of wisdom and happiness.

As Rynn advanced, Taaivetti noticed the Alyonian's green and gold battle armor shifting from side to side. Blistering heat had turned his stomach's perspiration into lubricant. Having also lost a bit of weight, Rynn's plates were comically loose.

"Thank you, brother." The prince opted not to embrace his sweat-soaked companion.

Sir Rynn studied him, quickly noting that Taaivetti's uncertainty was about far more than sweat. "You have made your decision, my prince?"

"Yes." Taaivetti's word came out harsher than ever. "Though the truth is, we're damned if we stay, and damned if we leave."

"Aye…forty-thousand Gorsh." Rynn stroked his thick white beard. "I still can barely believe it. The desert beasts have never amassed such a horde. Not ever. But for us to withdraw now, to retreat back to Alyonia—"

"I shall not retreat."

"Tactical withdrawal, I should say," Sir Rynn corrected himself, knowing Taaivetti's hatred for such cowardice.

"I must stay," stated Taaivetti. "We've given too much to this desert…too much to let it all go. Besides, this war is my legacy. I've waited patiently for the opportunity to earn my place amongst the warrior stars. I must convince Hann's defenders."

Sir Rynn nodded, though something else remained on his mind. "My prince, where have you gone off to these last few eves? Some of the brethren have begun to worry."

Taaivetti eyed him sternly. "To prayer."

"With all my respects, we do have a…prayer hall."

The words stung Taaivetti. "I prefer the tranquility of the desert mountains. I hear more clearly there." Even the prince himself knew his claim stunk of rubbish.

Sir Rynn knew not to push. "Well, if you are to stay and fight, might I put forth a stratagem for the boardroom?"

"Speak."

"Cancel the vote entirely. Why give the brethren a chance to leave if you've decided we must stay? You have the power, Taaivetti. Use it. That is, if you truly believe we must stay."

They began strutting down Hann's wall walk. "I can't force my own soldiers," said Taaivetti, his blue earrings bouncing with their fast strides. "I simply can't. But yes, I do believe we must remain at Hann because…"

Sir Rynn stopped the prince with a hand on his shoulder. "Because why, Taaivetti? What have you been doing in the night—"

"Because we've given too much! Too many Alyonians have paid the ultimate price for us to leave this place now. The desert would resort to what it was before we ever arrived."

"Ripe with potential?" Rather annoyed, Sir Rynn spoke his truth.

"Careful, Rynn," said the prince. "Sure, the desert tribes had more wealth here than they ever discovered. But without our protection from the Gorsh, they may've died long before finding it on their own." Taaivetti sounded truthful, yet he was still hiding something.

Sir Rynn held his tongue. As they moved toward Hann's boardroom, the old Alyonian ran his hand over a row of decaying wooden chests. Similar chests were visible along the top of the wall, each holding precious minerals, grains, and jewels taken from the many starving tribes of the Red Sand Desert. *Without our protection the savage Gorsh may have killed the desert tribes indeed,* thought Sir Rynn. *But have we remained for their protection?*

"I do wonder something," said Taaivetti. "The Gorsh hordes have never unified, not since our elders discovered them. They've always pillaged the desert tribes or fought one another in the desert, clan against clan. Why change that now? Why join forces now?"

Sir Rynn didn't pretend to have an answer. For all of his good-natured humor, Rynn allowed no nonsense when it came to advising his prince. "I know not. A bit of good news, however. Scouts have informed us of a few supply ships just three moons out. Wood, food, and water."

"Send a bird and have them hold those ships. Should the

brethren vote to leave, we'll need them." Taaivetti turned, leaving the overflowing chests as he quickened his pace.

"I shall," said Rynn. "Though it's a three-moon ride through the desert if we're to retrea—depart. The supply ships could not fit us all, and many would not survive the journey. Perhaps such a horrific trek is another way you might convince the soldiers to stay?"

They continued in silence. Taaivetti's long legs were hard to keep up with. "I can't force my own. I won't."

"You've a heart of gold," said Sir Rynn. "But the hard head of a mountain ram."

Taaivetti nodded, though he wasn't listening. "I'll stay true to the vote. Let fate decide."

"Fate tends to be a fickle thing."

The duo descended into a reeking courtyard and quickly reached the boardroom door. Sir Rynn locked eyes not with his prince but, in this moment, his friend. Taaivetti looked haggard. Rynn wished to tell him that his prince's charm had vanished. That he could see the stress in his ocean-blue eyes, the swelling of his lips and bronzed ears…*or the hidden stains on his normally fresh tabard and chainmail.* He didn't. Friend or not, Taaivetti was royalty. A chasm would always exist between them.

"My prince!" A voice echoed from afar as an exhausted Alyonian scout ran down the bailey, sweating from head to tail. The scout slowed his run and knelt.

"Rise," said Taaivetti.

He stood and extended his hand, gifting the prince a letter. "From your sister, Taryn, of the royal family."

Taaivetti thanked his messenger before unraveling the parchment. Only then did he notice his burnt and scabbing forearm. *What a morning.* Taaivetti read the letter, and finally, his vomit came. Whatever he was reading brought worse news than anything Hann had ever given him.

House Kaldor

Letter type: Urgent, Informative
To: Taaivetti Kaldor
From: Taryn Kaldor
343 A.B, Windy Season, 92nd Moon, Double Novas

I do not know how to begin this letter, Taai. By now, word may have found you, so all I can do is say that I love you and spit it out.

Our parents are dead. Murdered. Hendrix put a knife in them.

I do not know what befell him. He was completely different. Possessed, almost... Hendrix has always loathed our parents. We've known that since he was forced to cover for father's abuse. But this was something different, something else entirely. You know how I've always felt of him. Why I've never trusted him. Yet, no one listened. You didn't even listen. And now...

Hendrix was not alone. Your dear friend Aypax "the honorable" (though he no longer holds this title) was an accomplice in our family's murder.

I'm struggling to pen this, Taaivetti. I'm so angry that you weren't here to stop them, though I know that isn't fair. I do.

Hendrix and Aypax escaped the catacombs and fled the city. I don't know why they did this. Why they're still doing this. I don't even care why. I just want it to be different. I want the pain to stop.

I know this shall be hard to swallow, though it is all true. Word shall spread faster than the sickness, so I wanted you to hear it from me first. Please come home, brother. I need you.

All the love I have,

Taryn

4

TARYN
Well-Kept Secrets

"Oh, quit your pouting, Kornilious."

Taryn sighed with frustration as she walked slowly across a dark and spacious hall of her family's ancient catacombs. "The peace treaty has been finalized; there's nothing left to say."

The Alyonian Master of Defense didn't reply. He'd always been better at erecting emotional walls than real ones.

"You're envious of Bandano-Rhi, this much is clear," furthered Taryn. "But you and I have long agreed to use him for creating a two-realm function. So what's your real fear here?"

Kornilious ignored that remark too. He concentrated on the catacombs' thick brown walls and ceilings. Normally a cloistered space, the catacombs of Alyonian royalty were tall and wide, ever arching overhead. Built primarily of cobblestone and Balonian forest mud hundreds of feet beneath the Kaldorian manor, the final resting place for members of House Kaldor was a wonder. Kornilius pondered how long this place could—and would—stay intact.

"The treaty may have been agreed upon," he began, "but it isn't yet signed… I fear you haven't thought this new alliance through, my dear. If we sign the proposed peace treaty with the Rhi Empire, we'll have to stop aiding their enemy, the Wayland Empire. But Wayland pays us great coin for our arsenal. In fact, I dined with Alyonia's Master of Coin just yesterday, and he's more than worried over our realm's current state. Our sending of elite weaponry to Wayland is one of the few consistent streams of coin we can rely on."

Taryn grinned. "I do love how your mind reasons, Kornilious. But you're thinking only one step ahead."

"Indulge me."

"First, the treaty with Rhi merely states that we must stop supplying the Wayland Empire with Alyonian weaponry. It *doesn't* say we can't sell them to the republic of Gondol, for example, who, in return, may choose by means of their own free will to then sell such weapons to Wayland. Don't forget, it greatly behooves Gondol to see Wayland fend off Bandano-Rhi."

Kornilious released a long exhale. "You're unbelievable—"

"Second, our agreeing to such a stoppage was contingent upon Rhi allowing Alyonia to keep mining steel and other resources in our territories just outside of the Wayland Empire. For their lands are ripe, even during our winters here at home."

The Master of Defense raised an eyebrow. "Go on."

"If and when Rhi defeats the Wayland Empire in battle, he will give them a choice: die by the sword, or surrender their territory and agree to pay him seasonal tribute." Taryn shrugged, passing walled lanterns and pesky moths floating about the muddy halls. "And as we know, Wayland is a realm reliant upon the weapons and strength of others. They will undoubtedly surrender. And guess who will be sitting right next door with the very resources they'll need to rebuild everything they lost during the war?"

Kornilious smiled as Taryn continued, "Rhi depletes his forces against Wayland while we continue building our own treasury by secretly manufacturing the very weapons depleting him. When the war is over, I request the contracts for rebuilding Wayland lands as a part of Rhi's empire. Given our proximity and resources conveniently placed outside of Wayland, Rhi will agree to our terms. Thus we'll be paid twice, at the expense of our enemies, and we keep our own presence in Wayland forevermore."

Kornilious stared, impressed, yet worried. "Brilliant, if not risky." *Too risky*, he thought, but Kornilious would shelve that discussion for now, for he was busy admiring his incredible surroundings.

The colossal space was lit by hundreds of torches and lanterns hanging from wall mounts or hiding behind statues of stone. Others sat upon rows of wooden tables spanning far as the pair could see.

These tables were red and green in color, all freshly painted. *Not exactly Alyonian colors…* Kornilious noted that these tables had been painted well, and recently. Positioned just beside the cold walls, the tables rested beneath a collection of shelves hanging above. The wooden shelves hung from stout green vines tied to rusty ceiling rods. This, too, seemed a recent development. *Odd*, Kornilious thought.

The wall mounts showcased glorious relics of times past. Scrolls, precious jewels from the Red Sand Desert, maps, garments, battle armor. There were weapons too. Ancient axes and shields, longswords and great bows. Deprived of their once glimmering steel, most of these weapons had long rusted.

Taryn's voice shattered the quiet. "I will interpret your silence as an agreement with my position on Wayland and Bandano-Rhi."

"Taryn, please." Kornilious adjusted his beloved silver chaplet. "I'm merely taking in my surroundings." They reached a four-way intersection of connecting corridors. *How had this possibly been dug?* "I never thought I would live to see anything like this. It's remarkable."

Kornilious walked toward a towering glass case, which held the bones of an ancient Askari, twice the size of Kornilious himself. Rats climbed in and out of the primitive bird's rib cage, ever blinking judgmental eyes in Kornilious' direction. "If I may be honest, my queen, I'd hoped my first visit would come in a more respectful manner. It's not exactly pleasant what we're doing here."

"Few great things begin pleasantly." Taryn scraped dirt and mud from beneath her black boots. "Why so unnerved? Where has my eagle of Alyonia gone?"

Kornilious knew not where his unshakably powerful demeanor had fled to. "He's right here, beautiful." He smiled. His large neck and broad shoulders almost covered a passing shadow on the walls behind. Almost. Taryn did notice it, however, as she had one hundred times before. She deemed it best to stay quiet.

"Good. I was beginning to miss him." Taryn kissed his cheek before turning down the hall. Captivated, he followed her like a moth to the flame.

* * *

"I must admit," Kornilious shivered from a passing breeze, "this place gives me a feeling of unease."

Taryn knew. His best attempts at covering fear had failed miserably as they'd descended deeper. There were fewer lanterns here, and more rats. Far more rats. The halls had also narrowed, exposing Kornilious' fear of tight spaces.

"I know that, dear," she replied. "But don't fret. I only think slightly less of you."

"Please. It's natural to feel uneasy when surrounded by the dead."

Surrounded they were. This deep, the catacombs had changed rather abruptly into a burial hall for her family's past generations. This was made obvious by the many coffins positioned on either side of them.

Taryn ran her hand along the top of a particularly dusty plinth, causing Kornilious to scold her. "Show some respect, my dear." The Master of Defense may have colluded with Taryn of late, even bypassed a few laws at her request. Still, he considered himself an

Alyonian of respect and dignity.

The coffin's dust flung about, dirtying Taryn's dark-green corset. She cared not. The interim queen seemed more interested in poking the bear, in repaying Kornilious for his irritating silence. Taryn raised both brows, then swept her hand atop another coffin, knocking a glass jar of sentimental letters from the plinth. She rolled her eyes whilst it crashed and shattered.

Then something snapped.

Not inside Kornilious… but Taryn. Something snapped inside Taryn. She dropped to the ground on both knees. Her eyes darted to one of the letters, a piece of parchment lying on the hardened floor. She unfurled it and found not a letter but a child's drawing.

Taryn ran her fingertips across the parchment's surface. Its illustration was simple, a family of four, happily holding hands with two puppies at their feet. This family gathered around the coffin of King Kygos. The very coffin lying before her.

"Grandfather died honorably," she said in a very high-pitched voice. A surprising voice, a voice that wasn't her own. "He was one of the good ones. That's what my daddy always told me and Taaivetti when we came down here."

Kornilious halted, watching Taryn's posture change drastically. She suddenly acted like a young girl at the local pastry stand. Happy as can be. Excited even. Taryn turned to Kornilious with a child-like smile. She stood, adopting a new stance, a new walk. Her neck hung differently, slightly tilted. *And that smile,* thought Kornilious. *Unexplainable.*

"Grandfather died protecting Alyonia. He was truly one of the good ones," she repeated. Her voice remained that of a small child's as she recalled her father's words, words he'd spoken to her and Taaivetti so many seasons ago. "He fought loyally for what he believed in. To die for Balo is to live forever by his side in the warrior stars."

Taryn lowered the drawing and looked directly at Kornilious.

Her eyes even seemed anew. "Then I said, 'I don't know, Daddy, to die is to die, and dead is dead!' He-heeee!" Taryn jumped with excitement at the notion of death. Her leap forced Kornilious a full step backward.

"My queen!"

A voice sounded from a narrow doorway farther down the hall. Kornilious moved his hand toward a miniature dagger. The tiny blade rested beneath a tight belt concealed by his tail.

"Trakkonious!" Taryn offered a welcoming smile. A new smile. Kornilious didn't know this side of her even existed. Trakkonious opened a hefty metal door wider, revealing more light behind, and the dim image of his cloaked face.

"All things are in order, my queen."

"I love it when things work out," snapped Taryn, still behaving oddly.

Kornilious didn't understand; her very body moved as if she were someone else entirely. Taryn grinned and grabbed Kornilious by the forearm, then led him toward the open door, toward Trakkonious, toward whatever lay waiting on the other side.

* * *

Kornilious stood amongst the company of others, yet he'd never felt more alone. He'd followed Taryn through the door, fighting his instincts with each step. This side of the door played host to the most bizarre room he'd ever witnessed. A room below rooms, presumably unknown to even the Kaldorian family themselves.

He entered Taryn's room. Her secret room. The moment he'd stepped inside, he found himself greeted by six Alyonians standing in a curved row, a crescent-moon arrangement. Each of the six wore matching robes, all woven with beautiful fabric, all colored in a captivating ruby red.

But the splendor of these robes went unnoticed, for Kornilious could focus on one thing only. *Neck burns?* Six of them, shared by the entirety of this group. *Why do they share such burns?*

"You think this is it?" Taryn appeared even happier than before. Her childish voice had doubled in energy.

"Yes," said a tall Alyonian lady, standing beside an Alyonian male who looked a mirror image of her. Twins. They stood in the center of this oval, an underwhelming vase filled with beige clay at their feet. "It lies inside the soil."

Kornilious studied the unknown Alyonian. She looked quite lean, yet muscular. Two lengthy ponytails of white fell behind her bronzed, wrinkled face. Such wrinkles seemed odd, however, because to Kornilious, she appeared both young and old. *Her brother shares the same features. Youthful traits, as if my own age, yet the wrinkles of my elders. Perhaps familial flaws?*

The twins' red robes were slightly different from their companions: tighter, more flexible. Kornilious' veteran eye spotted daggers and other masterfully hidden weapons beneath them. *Assassins,* he presumed.

"I can barely believe it." Taryn began sweating with excitement. "Taryn is going to love this!"

Kornilious shifted his attention from the neck burns and enshrouded weaponry. Had he heard Taryn correctly? He scanned the room more intently as a new set of chills drifted up his spine. The space was cluttered with old toys. Children's toys. Dolls, dresses, and marbles. There were playing cards and more sheets of parchment covered in childish drawings. He noticed a bed to one side, fully made, with a lone red book resting atop its sheets. The book appeared ancient, yet well-kept, a green key as its cover art.

Wooden torches in every corner would've revealed the contents of the room long ago, but one doesn't notice their surroundings when presented with six robed strangers. Kornilious observed something else. An utter lack of cobwebs and dirt. The room appeared perfect, as if cleaned this very morn.

"Are you not concerned with what's in front of you?" questioned the Alyonian lady with ponytails.

Kornilious returned his attention to her, irked by such aggression. He glanced at Taryn, half expecting her to reprimand this assassin. But Taryn wasn't present, at least not in the sense that he'd ever known her. She simply stared back at Kornilious, hands on her hips, feet tapping the floor.

"Well? Come now, siwwy, it's not powite to ignore others."

Taryn's youthful voice had gone too far. Kornilious was either the center of a rather unfunny joke or in the midst of something unexplainable.

"My concerns are my concern only." He glared at the Alyonian lady, subconsciously clenching his fists. "State your name?"

Her eyes seemed void of life, black and empty. She smirked, no intention of telling him anything.

"This is Kantis! And that's her brother, Kantor!" said the childish Taryn. "They're our family's keepers of secrets. That's why no one knows who they are. But keep it a secret!" Taryn giggled. "'Cept me, of course. I know them well!"

Kornilious felt cornered, though he remained calm and investigative. There would surely be a clue as to what was happening. *Somewhere.* He squinted at the red robes. *Nothing.* No markings nor insignias revealed their affiliations.

"Kantor," said the Alyonian lady known as Kantis. "Let's send Lizabeth the Second home. This meeting is to be with Taryn. We need her present for the time being."

Kantor shuffled to a nearby torch, shocking Kornilious with his speed. The Alyonian wasn't running, yet he covered impressive distance. Kantor diminished one torch, then moved to the next.

Kornilious looked back at Kantis as the room grew dim. Her eyes blended in with the growing darkness. She smirked once more as any remaining light faded all around her, a sight that would remain with Kornilious forever.

"Taryn, come forth!" Kantis screeched loudly.

The lights were out now. Complete black.

* * *

Kornilious found himself back in the hall of coffins. Ten minutes had passed since they had left that room. That *unforgettable* room.

"I feel it." Taryn appeared her typical self, voice and all. Her hand dug deep into the vase's soil, a full forearm inside. Kornilious stared, anger building inside him. Taryn acted as if nothing had happened, as if the entire experience were a dream of his. He felt betrayed, mocked, furious.

"We had to wait 'til you were officially the interim queen before we could share such a secret." Kantis watched Taryn dig. "I do hope you understand. Should Taaivetti return, we shall make him aware of the key's position. Our loyalty to your house and your family comes before *anything*."

Kornilious noted the emphasis on *anything*. Kantis was sly with her words, but he was a politician. No form of deception would ever creep past.

"So be it." Taryn continued digging. "Should he come back, I'd expect nothing less. But on the off chance that he does not return…" Taryn pulled a hefty key, blue and weathered from the dirt. She held it in her hands, let a finger trace the etchings deftly carved on its surface. "This is one of 'the four' keys?" She danced it through her fingers.

"Yes."

"And the whereabouts of the Kaldorian Map?"

"We have it safely in our possession." Kantis smiled. "Hidden in the Forest of Balo."

Kornilious' eyes lit up as Taryn shook her hands clean. "Good," she said. "That puts us one step closer to the altar. Lead us."

Kantis bowed before heading down an extensive hall. Kornilious, however, took Taryn by the waist and held her back. After what he'd just witnessed, he was beginning to believe in a new realm of possibilities. But this…this he could not believe. "The Kaldorian Map? The four keys, the altar? These are myths, Taryn. Legends and tales."

Taryn faced her skeptical accomplice, then lifted the strange key to eye level. "Sometimes, the truth is more peculiar than any legend or tale."

House Kaldor

Letter type: Urgent, Informative
From: Hendrix Kaldor
To: Taaivetti Kaldor
343 A.B, Windy Season, 93rd Moon, Single Moon

Taaivetti, I find myself rowing across the Southbay, fleeing Alyonian law for crimes we both know I didn't commit. I don't think I must convince you of this, but nevertheless, I'm innocent.

Taryn lied. I was falsely accused.

YOU MUST ACT QUICKLY.

I write this letter in the midst of a storm, a severe one at that. My ink runs low, and as such, I must be precise. Aypax and I are fearful that we'll be caught and put to death within a few moons. You are our only hope.

There are three points you must know, brother.

Taryn killed our parents.
Kornilious aided her.
They are planning something.

Please send immediate aid. A royal decree of pardon. We are innocent, and I can prove it through a trial with the High Council. Send the pardon back with Pattar only. Trust no other flier.

Hendrix & Aypax

5

HENDRIX

Tourtoufa

Hendrix watched as Aypax sealed their letter for Prince Taaivetti, then prepared to run ashore. Their battered boat slid smoothly over rippling shallows before carving its way into the dark grains of Tourtoufa's beach, dragging clusters of seaweed and clouds of foam with it.

Aypax whistled Pattar to his shoulder and tied the letter to its abnormally large leg. Patting his Askari, he sent him off. Hendrix watched the magnificent creature fly high into the night sky before the duo leapt from their boat and sloshed through ankle-high water, fighting toward the colored sand. Thankful to be aground, Hendrix sat on the beach, decompressing, gazing out at the black shallow waters. He could hear the rain colliding with the sea more easily here. A steady rhythm. Majestic. Time itself seemed slower onshore.

Twenty-two moons with constant rain... Hendrix found himself unable to accept recent anomalies. Raised in the royal family, he'd always been forced to study *The Prophetics*, always heard these times would one day come. He never believed he would live to see them.

"Wait," said Aypax. "The bags—"

"I got it." Hendrix waded back through nasty tides reaching into the boat to retrieve his green travel sack. Riffling through its

contents rather obsessively, he exhaled with relief at the sight of
a half-empty bottle and a secret pouch of seeds. If the end times
were truly afoot, he was going to numb them one way or another.
Grabbing Aypax's bag next, Hendrix struggled back to the beach
with laden arms.

Aypax pressed his dirty boot against the ship's weathered wood,
then kicked her away into clouds of fog. "The tides shall pull her
offshore. That'll grant us a bit of lead against whoever Taryn has on
our heels." Aypax reached into his pants, revealing a palm-sized blue
box. "Put this in one of the sacks." He tossed the box to Hendrix.

Hendrix stored Aypax's box, then swung the wet bag over his
shoulder. It was a short walk before they reached the forest edge,
where a wall of monstrous trees towered over them. Daunting as they
were, the trees reminded him of those on the tiny plot of land he'd
only just purchased in secret with Madison Preters, the land he felt
he may never see again.

* * *

The rain never eased, though the canopy above shielded the forest
floor from most of the storm's wrath. The ground still drowned,
but at least the treetops provided Hendrix with relief from what he
suspected was an infected eardrum. His ear throbbed as he picked
at it.

"Stop," cautioned Aypax. "It'll worsen." Alyonian ears were a
near-perfect circle, at least by the standards of men. This allowed for
superior hearing but came with an added risk of infection. Water
easily pooled in such a vessel.

"It hurts."

Aypax's patience wore thin. "We'll tend to it once we arrive at
Starsgard."

Aypax examined a cluster of stars visible through canopy

openings, a navigational trick he'd learned during his many moons of service leading the Honorable-Six. Such a position carried extreme prestige, but also the great weight of acting as the king's executioner. "Should be two hours north."

Hendrix sighed and followed. It wouldn't be an enjoyable journey, but at least his buzz from the seeds and booze helped combat the intimidating forest. The ground was an odd mixture of dirt and displaced beach sand; Tourtoufa's aggressive winds could be thanked for that. The tall trees displayed lemon-tinted bark, others a dirty orange. Worst of all were the constant shadows moving in his peripheral. Hendrix was unsure of these shadows, however, as forty hours without sleep had drained his senses. "When we arrive at Starsgard, how shall we afford a boat? You don't have much coin, and you're not exactly the type to mug."

"We'll purchase travel from pirateers. I hate their kind. But they're our only hope of sailing undetected."

"Yes, but how shall we pay them?" Hendrix was carrying few valuable items. But the ones he *did* have, he needed to know would remain safe.

Aypax appeared reluctant to answer. "I shall sell them something."

The blue box. Not wishing to upset, Hendrix dropped the subject of coin. "How can you be certain we'll find pirateers in the city?"

"Starsgard is the slave trade capital of the known world. Filthy kin from every realm flock there. It's a rare moment when pirateer ships aren't docked at bay. More often than not, there are at least fifty."

Aypax hated the ignoble thought, but this is where they'd been forced; it's where fate had dragged them. Besides, pirateers were the only way he could ever return home to settle things with Taryn. "Once we have our ship, we sail straight for Hann."

The need for vengeance burned in Aypax's eyes. His High-Lord father had raised him to seek justice, never vengeance. Though the two were easily confused of late.

"We must get to Prince Taaivetti before Taryn gets to us," Aypax continued. "I would've rowed to Hann immediately, but our boat would not have lasted long in the Midline Tides."

Hendrix wanted no part of any storm ever again. "A fair assessment." Disheartened, he looked down at a pink bracelet choking his swollen wrist. The initials *M.P.* were carved into its leather surface. He would *survive*...if only to return to his betrothed.

Hendrix breathed through the pain of his eardrum, through the pain of a broken heart. He refocused. Madison was all the motivation he needed.

* * *

Three hours passed, darkening the forest further. Hendrix stared daggers at Aypax as they hiked in silence. They were not in Starsgard, nor had they seemed to cover much ground at all.

"I need to lay down." The bags under Hendrix's eyes had swollen, and worse, his eardrum pounded more painfully by the minute.

"We'll arrive soon, stay true." Aypax kept pressing their walk, though it had slowly changed into a climb. The terrain became more hazardous with each mile. Fallen logs and dense brush produced a maze of bark and brambles. Alyonians were excellent climbers by nature, but in this moment, the fatigue and wet surfaces proved too much for the pair.

"The clouds' piss has doubled." Looking up at the increasing rainfall, Aypax released another horrid cough. "This means the canopy is thinning. We're almost clear."

"Your cough." Hendrix tried to keep his balance on a wet log.

"How can we be sure you don't have the sickness—" He stepped on a damp branch, snapping it, and fell for the second time in three hours. It wasn't a long plummet, merely five forearms down to the forest floor. Still, the branch wasn't all that broke. Laying on his throbbing side, Hendrix remained still, demoralized.

Aypax looked down at his companion. "We cannot be sure. Though if I am infected, we can be sure that you're also doomed. So shut your lips about it."

Hendrix allowed his head to fall back on the ground. Cheek and lip to moist dirt, he stared sideways, watching the soil turn to mud as raindrops pounded all around. He watched the bugs and worms feeding and crawling. In something of a trance, he noticed his travel sack resting a short length away...

It, too, had taken the fall and seemed filthier for it. Though the bag wasn't what stole Hendrix's eyes, no. His attention shot to what rested inside. *Fitting.*

The miniature white book hung from the opening of his sack, half in, half out. Hendrix felt the nagging pain of his mother. "It was the first item she ever gifted me."

Aypax stared at the youngster and his book.

"Growing up in my family, I was forced to study *The Prophetics*," said Hendrix. "Forced to memorize every damned page. No matter how much I complained. Mother always told me I'd thank her one day. And I always told her to piss off..."

Hendrix fought back the coming emotions. "The eve she died, we'd just returned from a speech, well dressed and fragranced, fake... Mother asked if I would study with her before bed. I was to come of age the next morn, an Alyonian grown, so I told her I was done studying. I said I intended to wed Madison Preters and leave Alyonia for a different life on our own lands. I told her I was tired of lying to the public, tired of her suffocating me, of constantly hiding my father's true self. Those were the last words I ever spoke to her."

Hendrix scooped a bit of mud into his hand and squeezed it through each finger. His skinned palms still ached from the ship's ruthless rope. "Now she's gone! She's gone, and I'll never get to apologize. It's not fair! We're innocent, and no one believes us!" Hendrix had proven strong up to this point, but he'd held in far too much. "Nothing shall ever be the same. You know it, Aypax. Admit it. Even if you aren't sick, Taryn won, and she's going to kill us. The realm will believe I killed my own mother…"

Aypax leapt down from his position atop a fallen Yellowwood tree. The jump tugged at a painful quad injury he'd been hiding. "Do you know of the quasi-bug?"

"The quasi-bug?"

"It's a bug that searches for sad creatures, crying creatures. Turtles are their favorite prey. The quasi-bug is abandoned at birth and lives its life alone. Saddened, the quasi-bug lands on the eyelids of crying animals and drinks their tears to consume its need of salt. But three seasons ago, a Pretorian academic found groups of quasi-bugs sipping from a salt pond in the east, proving they had no true need for tears. They simply enjoy preying on the weak."

Hendrix looked up. "What's your point?"

"Quit your crying, or you will indeed become Taryn's prey."

Hendrix sniffled worse from the words as his forehead hit the mud again.

Aypax appeared fed up. "*Bloody Perdition*. Listen, Taryn will send the most vicious Alyonians she can muster, yes. She may even call upon Bandano-Rhi's men. He'll wish to impress her after the Peace Parade, and as such, shall dispatch his finest assassins. They'll be fast, well-equipped, and well-fed. They'll have scent hounds on the ground and hunting birds in the sky. We'll be outnumbered and outclassed, but not outwitted. The known world is big, Hendrix, and we are but two little Alyonians." Aypax referenced his height. "Well…by the time her assassins arrive for us at Starsgard, you and I shall be halfway across the Midline Tides, ready to dock at Hann and join with Prince Taaivetti. With Taaivetti at our backs, and a proper trial held, we'll take down Taryn together. I promise."

The words lit Hendrix ablaze, springing him slowly to his feet with a second wind. If Aypax promised something, then he meant it. "My brother told me you were the most righteous Alyonian he'd ever known," said Hendrix. "If you truly believe we'll reach Hann before it's too late, I believe you."

Aypax wasn't used to lying. It simply wasn't something he did, and it certainly wasn't something the Honorable-Six did. Honesty was a part of their creed, a creed Aypax had branded on the back of his shoulder.

Honesty. Heart. Honor. 6

But this is different, he thought. *The situation demands it.* It was a small lie, a lie that he half believed. "I do."

Another thirty minutes passed before the fugitives finally reached the forest's edge. Angry rain raged yet again, though it now marked the end of the forest and the outskirts of Starsgard. They had arrived.

Aypax led Hendrix out of the woodlands and into a vast crop field. Soaring rotten cornstalks stretched far and wide, swaying back and forth, creating an irritating sound as they collided in furious winds.

Aypax could see a good ways ahead. He peered over the stalks and marveled. There she was, the behemoth city of Starsgard.

In ruins.

6

TAAIVETTI

Pain

Taaivetti's tears had been shed, his anger released. Sir Rynn had spent the better half of the evening embracing his dear friend, the prince, over the loss of his mother and father. Taaivetti had delayed his commanders' voting and withdrawn to his favorite room: Hann's smithy. But even that birthed little comfort. Try as he may, the prince was unable to make sense of his dead parents, his weeping sister, his brother and best friend Aypax on the run.

Sir Rynn sat silently, lacking the words to aid, wise enough not to force them. Keeping his eyes downcast, Sir Rynn sharpened a weighty longsword along an oily whetstone. Present.

"Sir Rynn..."

Taaivetti tried voicing his pain on occasion, though nothing ever came of it. He'd always returned to pacing, ever pacing. Both Alyonians had cried all the tears they could muster, neither caring for appearance nor judgment. Such behavior was rare among royalty, but if the prince had one friend he could lower his guard with, it was Sir Rynn of Kaldoria.

A knock sounded from outside.

"Enter," mumbled Taaivetti.

A youthful scout heaved open the heavy smithy door. "My prince." He bowed. The scout wore a thin and presumably nimble green surcoat, white hair braided and sweaty, saddlebag in hand. "We've located the Gorsh horde. Their numbers are true…forty thousand, perhaps more—"

"No word from Hendrix or Aypax?" Taaivetti asked.

"None. I've even put extra eyes on watch. The heat took a few of our birds, others are missing entirely. With so few in the skies, I'd know if anything came in."

Sir Rynn didn't like the sound of that. Missing messenger birds usually meant they were intercepted, a skill the Gorsh hordes had never displayed in times past. Rynn glanced down at the edge of his blade. It was sharp, yet recent news made him think that perhaps not sharp enough.

"Forty-thousand Gorsh?" said Taaivetti, as if saying the number aloud would somehow make it smaller, or help him decide what to do.

"Aye, my prince." The scout lowered his posture and raised the saddlebag to eye level. "And another severed head, my lord." Dried red tainted the bag's color.

"Who now?" questioned Rynn.

"Brother Deliss, of the Honorable-Three," mumbled the scout. "Our finest attempts to assassinate this new Gorsh warlord have failed yet again. The desert tribes are more than questioning our ability to protect them any longer. Word spreads as quickly as their fears."

Taaivetti nodded, his eyes on the bloody saddlebag, his mind elsewhere. "Forty-thousand Gorsh…"

"Aye, my prince," repeated the tired scout. "Forty still holds the majority report. Though some of my eyes say more. Sir Olivorio claims he'd reckon them for sixty thousand. Most of our forward bases have evacuated or been slaughtered, and the desert tribes have fled north to the river. Some even risked the heat and tried walking here to Hann. Tried and failed…I should say."

"Sixty-thousand Gorsh under one banner." Taaivetti could barely accept his own words. The Gorsh hordes had always pillaged the Red Sand Desert and any life within it. But spawning from the mountains of the far west, the beasts had primarily killed only one another until the fateful day they ventured far enough east to discover life outside of their clans. From then, it was merely a matter of time before unifying. Exhaling, Taaivetti passed a dirty hearth, various weapons and tools rested atop its charcoaled surface. The prince ran a hand over them, blackening his furry fingers. "How many moons before the beasts arrive?"

"Ten. Or so we guess. Though that's playing by normal standards. These things were born here, and if I may, their hides are built for this desert. They don't need water. Balo knows if they even sleep." The scout clocked tired bags beneath Taaivetti's eyes. His time was running out. "You ask me, I'd say their horde could do it in seven—"

"Thank you." Taaivetti curtly dismissed the scout, who bowed before taking leave.

Sir Rynn could do nothing but watch his prince writhe around the dark room, muttering to himself. "This new Gorsh warlord…," Rynn began, "if he can unify the clans into one, he can likely inspire them too. My guess is he's a truly big and nasty one. Probably has half a brain, even. At least enough to talk some sense into the other clans. He likely promised them blood, and fast."

The prince lifted a small axe, inspected its poorly crafted handle. "Forty thousand, sixty, it makes no difference. We cannot win in our current state. Not with piss supplies like this."

Sir Rynn sheathed his sword, then stood and hovered over a wooden barrel filled with dirty water. Greasy water. But lands, he was thirsty. *I shall pay for this later.* Rynn cupped his hands and scooped a small drink through the creases of two sweaty palms. He winced. "You are correct of that. We cannot win as things are, which brings me to my point. If we do stay, High Commander Bolden is our only option."

Taaivetti winced at the name. "We've spoken of this. I shall not be associated with such scum. It's impossible with so little time anyways."

"I know how you feel about him. But I also know that Bolden's ranks are twenty-thousand strong—"

"I said *no*—"

"My prince!" Rynn shouted, clearly struggling to remain submissive. "Bolden has countless stables filled with Naomi bred to run in this heat. He'll ride to our cause, and fast, if we call to him. Do it in secret if you must—"

"Such a move is unlawful," countered Taaivetti. "It's treason! I will not lie to the High Council again. Bolden's forces are reservists. To call on them is an act that must go through the next voting cycle, and be seen by all of Alyonian parliament—"

"To the realm of torment with parliament! Moons and stars and whores, Taaivetti, you're about to be king!" Sir Rynn paused, a sudden realization filling his face with red. "I'm sorry. May your parents rest peacefully. But Bolden is our only choice. Piss on the High Council." Sir Rynn lowered his temperament. "I understand he dislikes you, and I understand this isn't lawful. But let me ride to him. That simpleton is perhaps the most notorious law bender in all the realm, and he despises the High Council as much as we. By the time he arrives, you'll be the official interim king. With his ranks, this would mark the greatest battle of our time. Ballads would be written, stories told. If you're so keen on staying and fighting, fine. But let us do it wisely. I can convince him to help, I know it."

Sir Rynn kissed his source of certainty, a beautiful golden pendant in the shape of the divine tree god known as Balo. Nodding, Taaivetti clutched his own necklace. It shared the same golden pendant but lacked the luxurious silver chain of Sir Rynn's. The prince's necklace had instead been woven with dark green vines from the Forest of Balo. Named after the ancient god, the forest's vines were thick enough to use on nearly anything and had long become a staple of Alyonian goods, weapons, and architecture.

"Bloody Perdition, *fine*, ride to him." Taaivetti grabbed a small travel sack in the corner. "You've my permission."

Sir Rynn's brows rose in surprise. "You're sure?"

Taaivetti began stuffing the sack with supplies. A blade, a canteen, and two pairs of heavy white gloves. "Sure enough." He made for the door.

"Where are you going?"

"To prayer."

"Damn it, Taaivetti! The prayer hall is that way!" Rynn's words fell short, for the prince had already exited.

* * *

Taaivetti strode through Hann's courtyard, passing a poorly lit butchery and an even darker arrow range. This late, scarcely anyone lingered. No sounds other than the wind wrestling with torch flames and the occasional lizard scurrying past. Heading for Hann's stables, Taaivetti nodded toward a few lookouts on the wooden ramparts above. They bowed as he entered a foul-smelling stall.

"Hello, beautiful." The prince lifted a hand toward his Naomi. The creature nuzzled its fluffy white mane against him, her neck protruding over a wooden rail. "You know me well, Sindria." Taaivetti willed away his coming tears and returned the Naomi's nuzzle. But as he slowly pulled a saddle into view, the animal reared.

"I know, I know," he said. "One more night. Just one more."

Sindria released a neigh, a high-pitched utterance. Similar to the northern horse, the Naomi were tall and known for stubborn love.

58

"One more night…" repeated Taaivetti. Opening a wooden drawer beside Sindria's pen, the prince grabbed a small pouch and fingered out a thin strip of meat. The Naomi sniffed, rubbing her snout against his palm.

"That's my girl."

Preparing the saddle with one hand, and clutching Taryn's letter with his other, Taaivetti readied himself for an unpleasant journey.

* * *

Kicking up red sand beneath her hooves, Sindria galloped hard, covering impressive ground. Gripping both reins, Taaivetti had an easy go of it, for the desert presented no obstacles. With faint moonlight as their guide, the duo held a straight course toward a cluster of mountains ahead. The peaks were difficult to see in the poorly lit sky, but Taaivetti could make out their outline rising high, with blood-red coloring that matched the desert itself.

Perhaps an hour passed before the mountains became clear. As they closed in on a second hour of riding, Sindria's gallop turned to a trot, bringing them to the base of these red mountains. Scarce villages came into view all along the mountain's base, only noticeable by smell for some time. Squinting, Taaivetti could see tents flapping in hot wind, tendrils of smoke dancing up into the warm night.

"Pull." Taaivetti slowed Sindria, then surveyed the shoddy villages and dangerous mountain terrain.

Sloping upward, the crimson sand was now accompanied by boulders and desert shrubs, a welcomed sight after miles of pure nothingness. "Slow…" The prince stroked Sindria's curved horns. She had two horns, bony and encircling both ears to protect her tiny lobes from passing winds.

Looking ahead, deep caves pocketed the mountainsides, pitch black and unnerving.

Taaivetti dismounted and led Sindria to a hidden cleft beside the largest boulder. "Stay." He dug into his travel sack, then dropped a rugged bone on the sand. Sindria laid down and gnawed. "That's my girl."

He paced up the steep mountainside. Jagged rock formations protruded in every direction overhead, blocking more of the weak moonlight. Still Taaivetti pressed on. Ledge after ledge, foothold after foothold, the prince climbed expertly. Finally, he arrived at a long row of caves, no less than fifty. Passing ten or eleven entrances, he focused his gaze ahead, swallowing deep pain.

You're one of the good ones, Taaivetti… One of the good ones.

He continued his search, nearly tripping on his own boots.

You're one of the good ones.

Spotting an array of rocks beside a peculiar entrance, he'd found what he was looking for. The cave's entrance stood twice Taaivetti's own height of seven feet from the ground, with odd etchings on the mountain surface surrounding. Taaivetti stared at these markings, contemplating, exhaling.

One of the good ones.

Entering, darkness engulfed him and silenced any distant sounds of civilization. Unable to see his own hands, Taaivetti dropped and rummaged through warm sand. Then he found it. A rope. Withered and old, ancient, even. As soon as he grabbed the rope, the familiar sensation sliced through his hand.

Every time.

Tiny thorns and handmade glass had been woven into its fibers. Swinging his small sack around, Taaivetti pulled forth the hefty white gloves and secured them. Placing hand over hand, he followed the rope farther into the blackness.

7

HENDRIX

A Short Night

Hendrix awoke alone. He'd slept for thirty minutes at best. Having seen the ruined city of Starsgard, Aypax had led them back beneath the forest canopy for a few hours of sleep and strategizing. Yet strangely, Aypax seemed nowhere to be found.

Hendrix searched, rubbing his bloodred eyes and picking his aching ear. The woods were nightmare black, though he could hear the sound of owls and ever-present rain pattering above. The thick canopy kept the rain at bay, but also withheld any starlight. Sighing, he did his best to stay strong, to suppress the memories of his mother's screams and his betrothed's radiant laughs. Hendrix knew he would never see either again. He stood and squinted in each direction. *Do I call out to him? No. Shouting would draw attention; attention would draw death.*

Snakes, abogos, hilliots. Hendrix imagined all sorts of horrid beasts, almost welcoming them, anything to keep his mind moving.

He lingered, nearly collapsing from sheer exhaustion and a painful hangover. He'd hoped last night's booze would quell his heartbreak, though it had only amplified his swell of emotions on the comedown. As he shuffled, his foot grazed Aypax's bag, reminding him of what rested inside.

No…don't do it.

Hendrix fought against the unshakable visuals of his mother's death, of his twirling Madison Preters in the air as she accepted his proposal. He slowly recalled Aypax's words.

Mental scars are worse than physical.

He plopped down and reached inside the bag. Retrieving Aypax's miniature hatchet, Hendrix rolled up the sleeves of his wet tunic and held the blade over his veiny forearm.

Do they ever leave you?

Scared breaths grew deeper, harsher. His eyes watered. The blade hovered over Hendrix's skin, ready.

No. Aypax had answered him so simply, as if warning Hendrix of the grief-stricken life to come.

Eyeing the hatchet, Hendrix wondered if such a life was worth living. He fought against himself, against his own thoughts, until he felt a pull of sorts, something deep within beckoning him toward life. Dropping the hatchet, he rushed to open his own travel sack. Pushing aside his bottle and the little white book, he pulled forth the bag of seeds. Hendrix poured a few into his wounded palm and stared at each seed dreadfully. The young Alyonian had many new enemies, though none newer than this.

"I'm sorry," he whispered, looking up. But it was better to numb the pain and live another day.

Hendrix tossed the seeds back and munched violently. They were tough and chewy, each bite tasting worse. He swallowed in one foul gulp before falling back onto the cold, mushy mud, knowing how quickly the seeds would soon take effect.

A few moments later, the bitter taste ferried his mind away. He reflected upon the Alyonian prisons he'd spent a pair of nights in some three moons ago. Sentenced to five full eves, he and Aypax had been preparing to face the High Council after their minds were beaten into submission in the dark, dank cell. But their cellmates had other plans…

Hendrix smiled as the face of Brendann Brackwater, the ever-pleasant farmer, swam into view. Even in the darkness of Alyonia's catacomb prisons, Brackwater had always managed a grin. It wasn't 'til Hendrix asked how that he learned of the rare and infamous dalli-seeds Brackwater had snuck in from his farm.

Young Hendrix felt guilty for keeping such a secret, for having withheld his seeds from Aypax. But he needed something to ease the heartache, so he'd held on to Brackwater's seeds ever since their escape.

Hendrix's body suddenly shook. Slightly at first, then aggressively. His limbs contorted, muscles spasmed. His smile became a harrowing frown as the seeds drew him deeper in, the perfect blend of pain and pleasure. Opening his mouth and shivering, Hendrix exhaled, then fell into a deep sleep.

* * *

"Save some for me!" Madison Preters laughed and extended her hand, subtly grazing Hendrix's arm.

Hendrix smiled and passed her a lit piece of brown bark, blowing smoke through coarse lips. His hair was short and pristine, his age perhaps twenty-four seasons younger.

"My thanks." Madison puffed the bark as she swept her short white bangs out of the way. "Question two. Did you finish your Balonian studies?" She grinned sarcastically while eyeing a stack of white books on a desk just across Hendrix's personal chamber. *The Prophetics.*

Hendrix rolled his eyes and blew a ring of smoke through a square window. A few years younger than Madison, he was desperate to appear mature.

"I joke, I joke." She coughed into her hand before she

continued. "Question three. If you could be anything in the realm, what would you choose?"

"I, uh...I don't know." Hendrix shifted uncomfortably atop his bed, ruffling the blanket of wool beneath them. "Never thought much to it."

"What?" Madison laughed, her green eyes holding him captive. "It's easy. You can choose anything you wish!"

"Well, suppose I don't know what I wish?" Hendrix hid his uncertainties behind another drag of bark. Having spent his life beneath the shadow of Taaivetti and the wrath of his notorious father, Hendrix had grown up doing all he could to help his mother keep the royal family's image intact. He'd never given thought to his own ambitions. "My turn. Question one. What—"

"Get inside!" A loud and powerful voice interrupted as the front door swung open two floors below.

"Don't touch her!" shrieked another voice.

Hendrix winced as he recognized a familiar pain in the second voice. It belonged to his mother, Queen Lizabeth.

"Close your lips, Lizabeth!" King Kaldor's slurred command boomed through the Kaldorian manor. Hendrix peeked over the railing as his father shoved Taryn to her knees in the doorway.

"You're drunk!" shouted Queen Lizabeth.

Suddenly, Hendrix found himself floating in the doorway beside her. He was close enough to touch her silk gown, smell her perfume and the scented olive oil hairpin tucked into her long white hair. He reached out a hand but watched it move through his mother as if she were a puff of smoke.

He was dreaming. Seed dreaming.

"Of course I'm drunk!" shouted King Kaldor. "I was to give the damned king's speech at Preem's ball before Captain Crimson found Taryn being Taryn yet again."

Hendrix's attention shot to his sister, still writhing on the floor.

Rose petal eyeshadow had been smeared across her adolescent face, staining her cheeks, and she was spilling out of a rebelliously tight red corset. Seemingly drunk and scared herself, Taryn hid behind a chuckle.

"And thank Balo he did!" continued King Kaldor. "He found her with her head in between Kornilious' legs in a ballroom closet!" The king drove his fist into a wooden wall, bruising his white, hairy knuckles. "Why waste my coin on her studies with new Priests if she's just going to sneak out and raise the realm of torment each night?" Kaldor paced to the bar and poured himself a hefty drink. "By the stars, Lizabeth, Alyonia's biggest patrons were at Preem's ball tonight. All of them! We need their coin, not their judgment."

Queen Lizabeth knelt beside Taryn, partially to consult, partially to avoid King Kaldor's drunken breath. "Await us in your chamber. We'll speak later of this, and of your unwedded actions with Kornilious."

8

KORNILIOUS

Of Legends and Tales

Kornilious stared ahead, his vision limited by darkness and merciless rain, ever-present rain. Alyonia hadn't seen such a downpour in all its recorded history.

"Taryn."

Kornilious tried to whisper, though she heard him not. A few feet ahead, Taryn walked shoulder to shoulder between Kantis and Kantor. Kornilious didn't like that, nor the four others following closely behind him. He could hear their footsteps in the mud, their robes sloshing through water. He could practically feel their breath tickling the back of his neck. "Taryn," he repeated, much louder.

"Yes?" She turned and waited for him as their group trekked on through the moonlit Forest of Balo.

"I'll only ask this once." Kornilious moved a circular sunshade comprised of animal pelt overhead, covering them both from the rain. "How does searching for an imaginary altar help us forward our plan? How does it help me win reelection? We're wasting valuable time, dearest. We must return to the city."

"What makes you so sure it's imaginary?" A silence followed, ruined only by the drumming of rain upon their sunshade and the howls of far-off creatures. Taryn nodded toward Kantis and Kantor.

"They've served my father longer than I've been alive, their sole purpose to find the altar. Do you think the late King Kaldor would've tasked them with something he didn't believe to be true?"

The Master of Defense hadn't thought of that, nor wished to speak of the dead king. "I do not."

Taryn wrapped her arm around the sleeve of his dark green tunic as they walked, hand in hand. Slipping her tail from her green dress, she lifted it slowly and caressed Kornilious' lower back, a move she'd frequented since their youth. Pressed against one another, Kornilius found the warmth of their embrace a welcomed distraction from such cold drizzle. Yet Taryn seemed to ignore the night's elements, keeping her focus on the woods. Even in the rain, Balo looked breathtaking. Known for trees so tall they pierced the clouds, and trunks wider than small ponds, its beauty knew no end.

"Magnificent, isn't it?" Taryn gazed about, stunned. "Legend has it, these trees have lived since the dawning of time. But what is legend? And who exactly spoke such things?"

Kornilious smirked. "The Alyonian elders, I suppose. Or perhaps the men of old."

"The Alyonian elders," she repeated. "The men of old. Interesting."

"I know what you're playing at—"

"The men of old also wrote that a forest existed with trees so enormous they dwarfed Billow-Balo trees..." Taryn gestured toward the trees in every direction. "They wrote of this very forest on parchment so old it's no longer legible. For hundreds of seasons, Alyonia thought this place to be mere legend. Yet, they eventually discovered it. And now here we stand, seeing it firsthand. If this forest exists, why is the altar so improbable?"

A chilling breeze pushed against them, seemingly from nowhere.

JOSH PLASSE

"A forest with large trees is perhaps the product of overzealous soil." Kornilious dug his boot heel into the mud. "An altar with magical power? This is a tale for toddlers and storybooks."

Taryn pinched Kornilious' side flirtatiously. He smiled and flinched. By the stars he hated how she made him smile and flinch.

"The men of old did not claim the altar has magical power," she corrected. "They claimed it contains the last of Adria's original comets beneath it."

"Which are rumored to be magical…"

"I believe they used the term *mystical*." Taryn laughed before pointing toward the stars. "Kornilious, there is so much we don't know of this life."

"And we never will. I believe those of us most hungry for knowledge can do no better than fully comprehending our own ignorance."

"I like that," Taryn said, grinning. "But I've seen things, my dear. Seen them personally."

Finally. Kornilious had been waiting for Taryn to get serious, for her to speak of whatever had occurred in the catacombs. But the sight of his love—his *addiction*, if he were honest with himself— grinning beneath their sunshade shifted his mind from concern to admiration. He elected to hold his many questions. For now.

"The men of old wrote that the comets were real," she continued. "That the power of their dust was real and that the altar existed. They wrote they'd built the altar with their own hands, and buried those comets far beneath." Taryn seemed to enjoy the thought. "They went so far as to forge the four chests, the four maps, and the four keys, then ride thousands of leagues to separate them across Adria. Would they go through such trouble for something they didn't believe in? Something that was simply a tale?"

Taryn had a valid point, again.

She lifted the blue key from her pocket. It glimmered despite the darkness. "Even if we are wrong, is it not worth making sure? I need you on my side, love. Indulge me."

*　*　*

Temperatures fell with each hour as Taryn's party trudged through the forest. Kornilious felt a few shivers along their journey. Familiar shivers. He wondered why his body allowed them of late. He'd certainly weathered harsher winters. His concerns were brief, however, for Kornilious appeared far more alarmed by his current whereabouts.

He saw blood. Much more than should be present. It stained moss-covered rocks and logs, even changed the color of nearby puddles. Bewildering, as it meant the blood had been shed recently. Even the trees were marred by red.

Kornilious hadn't the time to speculate, for he noticed a strange symbol painted upon the bark of a Billow-Balo tree.

Where are you leading me, my love?

Just ahead, the same marking colored another tree, then another.

Where have I seen such a symbol?

"Syntrilla, Stralli, one union," mumbled Kantis.

"Syntrilla, Stralli, one union," replied Kantor.

Their hands grazed these symbols as they passed each tree, slowly making their way from the forest floor, speckled with leaves, onto a dirt path. Small forts were scattered along either side of the path, composed of timber twigs and dirty linen. The juvenile forts looked to be built by children.

Kornilious ignored their strange chants as he noticed various toys sprinkled round these primitive forts, though such rapid rain made it impossible to see clearly. *Toddlers' toys?* He killed the thought as their group entered a small clearing, void of trees entirely. A drop-off lay twenty forearms ahead, a clear edge sloping down.

"Ten score southeast." Kantis moved to the edge and inspected a meadow below their position. "Give signal."

Kantor obeyed. Stepping beside her, he untied two knots from a ruby-red haversack, then revealed an old lantern. Hunching over to block a harsh breeze, he lit the flame inside, then lifted his lantern. Kornilious stood perfectly still, eager and terrified to see what came next.

A second flame flickered in the meadow beneath them. Everyone descended slowly.

* * *

"Stay to the tall shrub. Avoid any vines to your left. Poisonous." Kantis' voice sounded less commanding as she led everyone down a long, congested hill.

She appears frightened, thought Kornilious, feeling slightly better of himself. The group found themselves surrounded by towering, slippery shrub. These shrubs covered the entire hill, excluding a narrow path cut down the middle.

"Do not wander nor look too far to your right. The woods begin to…" Kantis searched for the proper word while everyone formed a line behind her. "Change."

Change?

Kornilious couldn't help himself. The shrub stood tall indeed, but he stood taller. His eyes darted right, scanning the woodlands. A dreadful, strange, and misty fog engulfed them. It lifted and swirled seemingly by its own accord. Some of the trees had fallen where they once stood, others were slanted and deformed, still hanging on for dear life. Heavy rainfall masked the foggy terrain, yet no amount of drizzle could hide the passing shadows.

"Taryn," snapped Kornilious.

She didn't turn. Not this time. Kornilious' eyes watched the moving shadows. Too distant to make out, the shadows resembled silhouettes. Pure black, with the shapes of unknown things. They leapt across open woodlands, from crooked trees to black mud below. Kornilious stared on, like a beast to its prey, or perhaps prey to its beast. At first there were so many, he couldn't count their number. Dumbfounded, Kornilious watched as the last few shadows disappeared in the muck.

What are you? Kornilious wondered. Another shiver took control of his spine.

Suddenly he realized…in the midst of tonight's cold, his feet were growing increasingly hot. Taryn peered down at her own boots, another unhinged grin spreading across her face.

Kantis threw a hand over her shoulder lace, stealing attention. "Everyone is just ahead." She pointed north, then led Taryn away.

Kornilious watched his addiction leave him yet again. Life itself slowed.

Now incredibly cautious, he began to notice the tells he'd missed before, such as Kantor's quivering and the shortened breath of those nearby. Next came the stench—a known smell, the smell of death.

"Careful," said one of the red-robed Alyonians.

She warned Kornilious just in time. A baby Naomi lay mutilated in the weeds below, inches from his mud-soaked combat boots. The Naomi had been torn to the bone, with nearly no flesh nor fur remaining.

"Kantis! Welcome!"

A familiar voice lifted Kornilious' eyes from the dead beast. He glared ahead toward the path's end, where an Alyonian stood beneath a wooden archway, awaiting everyone's arrival. The arch spanned overhead and led to a hidden clearing just behind.

Kornilious studied this newcomer, recognizing him from the catacombs.

Trakkonious.

He was leaning against the dreadful arch, dark green vines dripping down all around him.

"And you've brought company," continued Trakkonious, bowing. "Syntrilla, Syntrilla."

"Syntrilla, Syntrilla." Their entire group passed beneath the arch, avoiding poisonous vines along the way.

On the other side, they came to a circular clearing of the shrubs. This far beneath the forest's ground level, the area had been concealed to perfection. Kornilious stopped in his tracks at the sight of all that surrounded.

A circle. A circle of Alyonians surrounding a tree, each kneeling and holding opened chests filled to the brim with sugar.

No, not sugar. It's grey...

Taryn stepped beside him, her eyes on the chests and the grey dust within. "You no longer need to comprehend your own ignorance, Kornilious. From here on, you are enlightened."

9

TAAIVETTI

Visions

Taaivetti's gloves were shred down to bare flesh. His dry palms now bled as he reached the spiked rope's end. Finally through the tunnel, a light revealed its opposite side.

You're one of the good ones... he thought, releasing the painful rope.

He found himself at the bottom of a new path—marble, tall, shiny, well-constructed. This path shot upward, stair by marble stair. Colossal mountainsides surrounded him, pushing high into a crimson sky and creating a narrow alley in between. An alley he'd become quite accustomed to.

"Back so soon?" said a voice from the top stair. "You promised this to be a one-time arrangement. Remember that?"

Taaivetti gazed up. The voice belonged to an old woman, a human much shorter than he. She wore naught but a silk strap around her sagging breasts, barely covering either nipple. Dark gold was the strap, tied in a flimsy knot behind her. Such gold demanded attention, as did the golden chair she sat upon, yet both paled in comparison to what rested just behind. A stone, well more than his own height, weathered and worn. A stone possibly as old as the dawn of time. Strange dust and red sand filled its crevices, discoloring a natural grey surface.

"Though that promise was, what, six visits ago?" continued the old woman.

A chorus of female laughter filled the alley as hundreds of women poked their heads from small caverns on both sides. The women had turned these caves into tiny homes, spacious enough only for a body or two. The chuckling women stared down at him, all wearing the same golden straps over their bare bodies. They did don some covering, however. Red sand had been pasted to their lower torsos, as if stuck there permanently. Taaivetti had always wondered how it stayed on…

He looked to the stars. *You're one of the good ones.*

"Oh, don't fret, Prince," continued the woman on high, her sandy legs dangling from the golden chair. "All our visitors do the same. 'Tis nothing to be shamed over. We know your heart to be good. You are a rare soul." The woman stood slowly, her ancient figure now brightened by the garnet-red sky and piercing moonlight. "Bow."

Taaivetti did all he could not to lose temper; he'd never gotten used to being spoken to in such an imperious way. Shaking from a cocktail of anger and sadness, he could practically feel Taryn's note burning a hole through his pocket. Swallowing pain and pride, he knelt.

"Good," announced the woman. "Now. What is it you seek of the sibyls?"

"You *know* what I seek!" he shouted, still on one knee.

"Ah, your future," she said, nodding. "We've tried to see Hann's fate many times, Prince. Each time, we've failed."

"Then might I suggest that perhaps you are a piss sibyl?"

The women in the surrounding caverns gasped. A few even stepped out of their caves, their gazes burning with insult.

"No, no," said the old woman. "His anger is just, for I have failed him these past visits. The future is much harder to glimpse than the past, for the past is already within you."

Taaivetti stood and glanced up at her. "Just once more. Show me what I want, and I shall be done here—"

"Oh yes! Yes, of course!" She laughed aloud. "'Just once more!' How many times have we heard that, my sibyls?"

The women chuckled as their elder took a step away from her treasured chair.

"'Once more.' Please, you are addicted!"

Taaivetti ignored the taunts and instead stared at a stone table halfway up the marble path. Flanked by shelves carved intricately into the mountain itself, this table was surrounded by herbs, jars, and bowls of powder. He'd been there so many times before; he knew what was to come. Taaivetti shivered, his body quivering from withdrawal and fear.

"You'll find what you seek," said the woman, stepping down each stair. "But this gift takes time. Let us hope your heart still cares about Hann's future when you see it."

"Today is different." Taaivetti's hand moved to Taryn's letter.

"Oh?"

"I'm no longer interested in the future. I wish to see the past."

The woman studied him from afar, then lifted a wrinkly finger and pointed toward the table. "Then you know what must be done."

Taaivetti's quivering continued as he loosened his copper belt and dropped his trousers. Red filling his cheeks—from embarrassment or fury, Taaivetti could not say—he removed his gold chainmail and green tunic, tossing both aside. Now fully disrobed, Taaivetti paced up the steps, his tail moving restlessly behind his chiseled frame.

The old woman scanned her many caves on either side. "Redbird, who amongst us is in season?"

A slim and starving woman crawled out from one of the lowest caves. "Redriver is in season," she announced with a raspy, desert accent. "I can feel her fertility. She shall produce a powerful sibyl."

The crowd shouted angrily, each wishing their own name had been called.

Taaivetti stepped up to the stone table, waiting for the sight of Redriver. For a moment, he simply took in his strange surroundings. Lengthy strands of beads ran overhead, strung from caves on both sides. Skulls, shells, plants, and glass combined to build skinny pillars outlining the marble path. Even the mountain itself had been drawn and painted upon.

Finally seeing her, Taaivetti struggled not to vomit. The woman stepped from a cave and stood even larger than he, telling, given his immense Alyonian stature. Knotty hair fell to her waist, where its tips had been stained by patches of red sand pasted to her flabby torso. He looked up to Redriver's face and saw she had two piercings in both ears, where golden jewelry lined her lobes that hung down to her chin. He closed his eyes and inhaled a deep breath, steeling himself for the task before him.

"Sibyls!" announced the elder, her own earrings and wrist jewels flashing. "Feast your eyes upon beauty. Even with our own men dead and gone, Elo provides us with means. A new sister shall soon be born!" She walked down the steps as her followers began to smack the mountain in unison. She arrived at the opposite end of the table. "Are you ready, Taaivetti, son of Kaldor?"

"Just give me the concoction," he groaned.

"I cannot. Your members must be unharmed upon leaving you. You shall get your mixture soon enough."

Redriver joined them at the table, her fast pace marking an excited arrival. Taaivetti could smell nothing but her.

"I am in season," she purred in a low and surprisingly alluring voice. Sliding onto the table, she opened herself to him. "Begin."

Taaivetti stared down at her, ignoring hundreds of glaring eyes and the subtle sounds of cave drums and wind chimes surrounding them. Exhaling, he nodded an apology to the cold stars above, then climbed onto the table.

* * *

Taaivetti laid flat on his back in a pile of sweat and defilement. The stone table was masterfully crafted, yet always contorted his spine. *Or lack thereof,* he thought.

"Elo, god of creation, has sent us another male…and graciously gifted us with a daughter!" shouted the old woman. "We shall greet her in three short seasons. As Arch Sibyl, 'tis my honor to name her Redmoon, daughter of Redriver. Let us all give thanks on the morrow." She looked down to Taaivetti, somewhat breaking character and whispering, "Six children…our future thanks you."

"Just begin," he spat, knowing the process.

The Arch Sibyl turned and made her way back to the top of the path. Walking behind her gigantic stone, she vanished for a long while as Taaivetti waited, thinking, breathing. The longer he lied there, the angrier he became. Staring impatiently at dim stars, a tear slipped from his eye.

The Arch Sibyl suddenly walked back down her path, clutching a wooden box. "What precisely do you seek?"

Taaivetti sat up. "My brother, Hendrix. I wish to see him on the first eve of the Alyonian Peace Parade. I wish to see his actions."

"Describe him."

"Hendrix is half my size, with long hair, white in color like the rest of us. A handsome youth, seventeen years of age by the standards of men. He wears a tired smile and shall likely be found beside my mother, the queen."

"How long ago?"

"Less than three moons."

"This shall suffice." The Arch Sibyl walked to her shelves and grasped a jar of liquid that contained a floating, slimy, brown flower. "Lean back and open."

He obeyed as the Arch Sibyl removed this dead flower and shoved the bottleneck down his throat. Gripping her flower, she rubbed it over his chin while he drank.

"Good, good…"

The Arch Sibyl opened her wooden box and drew scared breaths, as if she herself were preparing to endure something awful. Digging both hands inside the chest, she grasped a palmful of grey dust… then lifted it high for all to see. "Elo, protect me!" she shouted as she lowered the dust onto her face. It fell into her eyes, nose, and mouth. She snorted and swallowed, blinked and inhaled. "Taaivetti, prince of Alyonia, son of Kaldor! Give me your permission to enter!"

Taaivetti laid back as she made her way behind him, her ancient eyes turning dark grey, whites and pupils disappearing.

"You've my permission."

She reached out her hand, then dropped it down upon his forehead.

* * *

Taaivetti awoke in the corner of a private room. Having felt the sibyl's power before, he was beginning to feel the difference between reality and dream. Taaivetti attempted a smack on his nose, though his hand merely passed through his face. The prince may as well have been air, and maybe he was.

"Taryn!" shouted a voice from behind.

Taaivetti swirled to the sight of his mother, Queen Lizabeth, entering through a wooden door. She looked beautiful, her blue eyes and majestic white hair falling to bronzed shoulders. Even at her mid age of two hundred and fifty seasons, Queen Lizabeth stunned. She

78

wore a green robe and wooden sandals woven with vines from the Forest of Balo. Young Hendrix entered beside her in his royal surcoat of green and gold, eyes red with exhaustion.

Then there was Taryn, blessed with her mother's looks, cursed with her father's stubbornness. Wearing knee-high boots and a daring red corset, she wouldn't be caught dead in royal attire if she didn't have to. Realizing she'd yet to answer, Taaivetti studied his sister. She leaned out over a windowsill, gazing down at the plaza below. Slight drops of rain pounded, dampening her silver hair and a pair of green window drapes beside her.

"Taryn?" repeated Queen Lizabeth. "I know it's a bit chaotic down there, but I could use your aid. These humans, they expect so much of us. You know it's a direct insult to their emperor if our family does not, at the very least, make an appearance?"

Taaivetti watched his mother cross the room toward a sickbed in its center. The bed seemed oddly placed, surrounded by greenery, stones, and mounds of well-wishing letters strewn across the floor.

Father, he thought, as his mother leaned her head over the king's sickbed.

Queen Lizabeth's face contorted at the sight of her husband. "Hendrix...Taryn..." she mumbled, staring down at her husband. "Call for the apothecary!"

Taaivetti's eyes grew wide, for he was about to see the truth of whatever took place—

* * *

Taaivetti came to on the warm stone, shooting up and nearly head-butting the Arch Sibyl.

"No! No!" he roared. "Why!?" The prince leapt to his feet but quickly collapsed.

"'Tis out of my control!" replied the Arch Sibyl, eyes still grey, vision still blinded. "Something interfered!"

Taaivetti's eyes burned, his heart pounded. Sweat seeped from every pore on his face. Pushing up to both elbows, he fought with all he had, desperate to see the faint glimpses of his mother...but they didn't last.

The vision had ended. It was over.

10

HENDRIX

A Forgotten City

Two novas rose slowly over the desolate city of Starsgard, shining boiling beams of mockery down upon Hendrix and Aypax. The fugitives stood, barely awake amidst the cornfield's sea of gold as they stared at the city's broken ruins rising before them.

The night had come and gone, and seemed the hardest Hendrix's body had ever faced. The drugs had gifted him a short slumber. Four hours, perhaps.

Aypax stared at the city, motionless. "I led us the wrong way." Displaced beach sands swirled overhead with fury, covering the shattered tops of every building. Constant rain did its best to wash the colorful sands away, a fruitless cause with such aggressive winds replacing sand by the second.

"Then where are we?" asked Hendrix.

"Baa."

Aypax stood still, thinking. "What's left of this place will not be kind to us. But if we're to find pirateers, this will be a start."

Hendrix stared at the ruined city, at the debris and blood-stained craters embedded within the ground. "What happened?"

"*We* happened." Aypax took off, making his way forward through the gyrating cornstalks.

Hendrix followed, trailing close enough to dodge itchy stalks bouncing off the big brute. "What's that mean?"

"This city was once beautiful. But the Tourtoufian parliament began taxing their citizens too heavily. Eventually, the poor banded together and fought back, killing tax collectors, city guards, and elected officials. The poor grew in numbers rather quickly until they became a ruling class all their own. They officially became known as the Bintonns."

"What's that have to do with us?"

Aypax eyed the cornfield's boundary; they'd soon arrive. "When the Tourtoufian parliament fought back, they sent highly trained forces to kill the Bintonns before they created a full-fledged uprising. But Alyonia caught word and did what we do best. Seeing an opportunity, Alyonia funded the Bintonns in secret, never letting the Tourtoufian parliament know. We helped the Bintonns grow, even provided them with superior weapons to gain the edge over their rulers."

Hendrix stopped in place, forcing Aypax to do the same. "Wait, what? Why? I don't understand. Surely I would've heard about this?"

Aypax scoffed, placing a hand on the youngster's shoulder. "Secrecy is the first essential in the corruption of large parliament. It's what we do and have always done. For as long as I've been in this wretched game of life, Alyonia has subtly expanded their empire by putting one foot into wars, usually through a back door, yet never risking the other. It's a brilliant, albeit damned, strategy we stole from the Rhi Empire."

"But why? What did we gain from helping the Bintonns? You're saying my father ordered this?"

"Hard to say regarding your father. What goes on behind closed doors is a luxury only for those in attendance. But I do know this. By funding the Bintonns, Alyonia not only weakened the Tourtoufians, a potential enemy to our south, but also gained a natural foothold here on the island. A foothold with ports and perpetual novalight to help grow crops. Baa is merely one of perhaps ten desolate cities, and when the fighting was at its worst, Alyonia offered to help rebuild the city using superior materials. Naturally, what was left of the Tourtoufian parliament agreed to our terms, and our empire has been 'rebuilding' here ever since."

"I see."

"But we're wiser still. Why do you think I was stationed here so many seasons ago? Alyonia was not only paid by Tourtoufa to help rebuild the city we ourselves helped crush, but we also demanded our own protection from the Bintonns while doing so. We built a port and two fortresses here on the island, and to this day, they're flourishing."

"Parliament," sighed Hendrix. "The High Council. The Vetusian and Novellusian parties…diplomacy, I hate it all. Every last bit—"

"You and me both. Moons and stars, you and all of Adria at that. But for now, our knowledge is our strength. Alyonian fortresses here on the island will receive word about us from Taryn at any moment, so we'll need to stay as far away from them as possible. Follow."

Aypax made for the rubble city. Once clear of the cornstalks, he could see the ruined city's outskirts some eighty paces ahead. "Without any stalks to protect us, the blowing sands will be unpleasant." The brute squinted, noting old alleyways would supply refuge soon enough. They were a long sprint from cover. "Good luck." He dashed off.

"Wait!" Too late. Hendrix followed Aypax into the open, allowing sand to pelt the bubbly wounds on his hands like a swarm of hornets. The stinging pain was brief, for they reached the rubble city quickly.

The streets were eerily quiet, as most of the ruins stood multiple stories high, blocking the wind's angry voice. Collapsed stone, wood, and steel vomited down from buildings, sprinkling smaller stones about. Trash and dead carcasses littered every street.

Hendrix examined the area, awestruck, but Aypax seemed to hardly acknowledge their surroundings. His attention rested solely on the second floor of a nearby ruin.

"What?" Then Hendrix saw it too.

A dark orange hat, round and tightly fitted, half covering someone's face. Flurries of sand blended them with the abandoned ruin. Though hard to make out, the stranger was undoubtedly glaring down in their direction.

"*Bintonns*," Aypax said under his breath. "Place your back to the wall beside me."

The Bintonn stranger puffed a thick cigar, then stubbed it on a grimy orange vest. Aypax's body stiffened, his fists clenched. The orange hat and vest...they triggered something in him.

"Ay-yay-ay! Howdys!"

Hendrix turned and saw five creatures approaching from an adjacent street. They, too, smoked but sported no orange. At least six feet tall and skinny they were, waiflike, with smooth yet battle-scarred green skin. Webbed fingers and curled tails distinguished them from any race he'd ever seen. They weren't Alyonians, though they weren't men either. Hendrix raised a brow at the small group's outfits. Tattered farm hats, overalls, and sandy boots.

"Tourtoufian cattleboys." Aypax ignored these cattleboys, never taking his attention off the Bintonn above. The big Alyonian looked like a rabid dog, salivating. It had been seasons aplenty since he last saw the unforgettable orange hats or the ruthless gangsters beneath them.

And whatever his last encounter, Hendrix noted, *Aypax seems to have no taste for these Bintonns.* "What's a cattleboy?" he asked aloud.

The Bintonn in orange slid its way into the shadows. Satisfied, Aypax shifted focus to what Hendrix feared may be a more serious issue, considering their weaponized belts. As scrawny as these cattle-boys appeared, they seemed fans of sharp items.

"Farm thugs." Aypax stretched his neck and tried to calm himself. Failed. "Looters. Wannabe Bintonns. I met one of them thirty seasons ago, the first time I ever stepped foot on this island." Aypax removed the small blue box from his pocket and handed it to Hendrix.

When did he take that from my bag? thought Hendrix. *Last night I suppose, but why...*

"They're of Tourtoufian blood, hence their green skin and curved tails." Aypax assessed the group. "They raid farms and cattle from ranchers who can't defend themselves."

"Ay-yay-ay! You folks gots anything on yous—" The cattleboy leader coughed, cutting himself off.

That cough. Hendrix stared. *Perhaps the sickness has traveled here.*

A nasty scar smeared the thug's left cheek, easily noticeable thanks to aggressive hacking and slim facial features. Steeling himself, the cattleboy took a bite of Tourtoufian chewing seed. Hendrix nearly vomited.

"That's quite a pretty bag yous gots over your shoulder," spat the leader.

Aypax grabbed Hendrix's bag and tossed it to the ground. "Yes, it is. Quite expensive too. You fancy it?"

The cattleboy leader disliked this response. Though unedu-cated, he seemed no fool to reading body language. "Yous a pretty big un'," he spat, fingering a knife pressed firmly to his belt. "But big oaks crash hard. Just looks at the forest behind yous."

Aypax nodded. "Oaks do not strike back."

Hendrix wished to help but remained glued to the wall behind his protector. *They look like me...if I were a lizard.* Hendrix knew what Tourtoufians supposedly looked like, for he'd read many a book describing them. But face-to-face, they were so different, yet so similar. He recalled his mother's words, *The Prophetics'* words.

"*These comets warped the men of old into all sorts of new beings… pained beings, for there was magic in the dust of the comets. Wicked magic.*"

The leader hawked his wad of chewing seed. "Well, no use talkin' abouts it." He drew the short blade and stepped forward. His followers angled, giving them better positioning on Aypax. There was no getting behind him, however. The ruin saw to that.

Aypax remained still as each thug closed in, lulling them. In a flash, he darted toward their leader. The lanky thug wasn't expecting such a courageous move. Aypax parried a poor strike before kneeing him in the liver, a crippling blow.

Aypax moved immediately, avoiding two swings from unrelenting cattleboys. Their cheap blades sliced through muggy air. Three more strides and shuffles, slips and weaves. Accurate punches downed another foe. The big Alyonian was near perfect 'til a random slash gashed his forearm.

"Ahhhhh!" Aypax pulled his miniature hatchet from the side of his combat boot.

Hendrix couldn't blink before two cattleboys felt the agonizing bite of sharp steel. Two strikes to two throats, both cattleboys fell, never to rise again. Blood spurted as the ferocious Alyonian locked eyes with the only remaining bandit. *Well?*

The final thug glanced at his fallen comrades, then decided it would be best to run.

* * *

Thirty minutes passed as Hendrix and Aypax stuck to alleyways, hugging the walls of old buildings to avoid the swirling sand and relentless rain. The occasional dog shuffled past, drenched and bone-thin. Stenches lingered. Old linens and torn blankets hung from shattered windows and rusty laundry lines above.

"Aypax." Hendrix had many questions, but as his ear throbbed, he focused on his most pressing fear. "That Tourtoufian's cough, do you believe it possible for the sickness to have traveled this far alrea—"

"Going fors one hundred! I'll takes one and a half!"

He stopped, as did Aypax. They turned and listened.

"Going fors one and fifty!" The unknown voice boomed again.

This time, Aypax pinned where it was coming from. He led Hendrix down another series of roads 'til they came to the noise's source: a public square filled with hundreds of Tourtoufians pressed shoulder to shoulder. Impoverished tents encircled the square, each selling pitiful portions of meat and grain.

Has the famine also made it this far? wondered Hendrix, reflecting on the state of his homeland.

An immense tarp had been strung overhead from two ruins. It stretched across the entire square, shielding everyone from intense Tourtoufian nova rays and the constant pattering of rain. The heat and drizzle amplified odors tenfold, creating a stink beyond anything Hendrix had ever smelled.

"What's the commotion about?" Aypax approached a starving local toward the back of the crowd.

Hendrix observed the local, his seared green skin and long neck. *Just like the cattleboys.*

"Everyones just tryings to get to the fronts," replied the local, speaking in the ever-frustrating Tourtoufian accent. "These tents wills run outta food in a hot flash. And that means yous hungry for another week!"

Now realizing Aypax wasn't able to help, the local shoved his way back into a vying crowd. Hendrix lost himself in its chaos, its violence and urgency. Growing up as royalty, he'd never seen anything like it. "Wow. This is som—"

"Not all folks come from Alyonia," Aypax said. "This is common life for most."

"Wahhhhhh!"

A horrid, muffled cry stole their attention. Hendrix saw a frantic Tourtoufian lady rushing toward a separate tent with a screaming child in her arms. This tent was different, empty and positioned quite far from the others. A lone box rested in the sand beneath its shade, with no tables nor goods surrounding.

Aypax grabbed Hendrix. "Look away."

"Wait…" Hendrix broke free and refocused on the green-skinned Tourtoufian. She was crying tears of her own, barely visible given most of her head and body were wrapped in cheap linen. There was something about her, something torn. Her very movements howled for help as she rushed toward this box, doing her best to quiet the child.

"What is that?" Hendrix pointed to the lone box. There were no lines for it, not a single customer.

"A mercy box," sighed Aypax. "They're all over Tourtoufa. Usually at places of worship, but you'll get the occasional good doer."

Hendrix marveled as the mother and daughter reached this box. "I don't understand."

A fat Tourtoufian clothed in loose overalls sat behind his box on a flimsy wooden chair. He nodded toward the mother lovingly.

"As I said of this island," said Aypax, some past memory paining him. "You're in the slave trade capital. Here in Baa, there isn't much, but Starsgard may be the most heinous city to ever exist. Familial inbreeding, no laws, whorehouses with more coin than your family. Many children are born lame or mind challenged, others missing limbs altogether. Many families cannot afford to keep these newborns."

Hendrix's opinion of the mother shifted quickly. "Where do

the boxes go?"

"Back home with whoever sets them out."

The mother took a final moment with her child, staring down into its sweaty, blinking eyes. Slowly, she lifted the baby and placed her into the box, displaying the motion as some sort of necessity for the arrangement.

Bloody Perdition. Hendrix shook to his core.

The heavyset Tourtoufian in overalls handed this mother a slip of parchment and embraced her. Embarrassed and distraught, she fled the square.

Hendrix felt a strange pull to this box, to the incredibly virtuous Tourtoufian behind it. Leaving Aypax, he rushed toward the Tourtoufian. "Hello."

"Howdys." The fat Tourtoufian perked up. A long dribble of sweat slid down his nearly amphibious forehead. Hendrix still couldn't believe one could appear so human and yet so reptilian. "What's cans I do for yous youngin'?"

"Do you have a family?"

"Surely," he replied. "In facts, we just grew by one."

Hendrix nodded with admiration. He dug into his travel sack and revealed an expensive, albeit weathered stone with a *K* engraved into its surface. "Take this, and go to them. A Kaldorian family Riverstone. It's worth more than legends say. You deserve this, friend."

The Tourtoufian grabbed Hendrix's beautiful stone. "Sirs, I...I...cannots accept this."

"You *must*." Hendrix folded his webbed fingers around the stone.

The Tourtoufian swallowed, stunned. He looked to the clouds and lifted one hand, a quick prayer of sorts. "Thank yous, thank yous," he said, sweating more profusely and storing the Riverstone in a bag of his own. "Blessings to yous."

"Greetings." Aypax appeared and gestured Hendrix aside.

Hendrix obeyed, slyly hiding what he'd just done.

Now alone, Aypax surveyed the clerk, then leaned into a whisper. "My friend, how much for the little one?"

The amphibious clerk's demeanor changed instantly, his sweet eyes morphing for serious business. "Yous a buyer?"

"Aye."

"Yous wants her for the slave trade, or personal funs?" The Tourtoufian couldn't help but grin.

Aypax held his stare, trying not to break. "Personal fun."

"I'll sells her at ten thousand condits to the Rhi-Empire standard. Fifteen, if yous needs me to raise her of age. I'll haves her begging to do whatevers yous please—"

Aypax punched him square on the nose. The Tourtoufian collapsed backward as Aypax hovered over him. "Do you know my favorite thing about this island?"

The Tourtoufian stared up, quivering with cowardice and palming his broken nose. "What…what's yous want?"

"It breeds the worst crimes but the sweetest justice." Aypax slipped the still-bloody hatchet from his weathered boot, using a free hand to hold the coward by his throat. "There may be no one to save the child…but there's no one to save you either."

Hendrix stood back, awed. Gazing about, no one in the war-torn, hungry square so much as turned in their direction.

"Please, pleases!"

Aypax leaned closer, his forehead mere inches from the sweaty Tourtoufian. "Where will I find the Bintonns whorehouses?"

The Tourtoufian peered around stealthily. "I…I truly don't knows. They's own so much it's hards to say. They's one of mys biggest buyers. They hurts folk, though, kills 'em too."

Aypax deemed him truthful. "Good. Now, where might I find the nearest pirateers?"

The clerk lifted a brow. "Yous mean you're looking for thems?"

"Yes."

"Wells..." he mumbled. "Most of 'em are over at Starsgard, being the capital and alls." Desperate to live, the Tourtoufian kept rambling. "Don't goes arounds asking about the Bintonns or pirateers. Yous won't be happy what yous finds. But I can tell yous this... There's an old saloon about ninety score east of here. It's the onlys place in all of Baa that still has the good drinks. It's a rough crowd, if yous never been. But yous might find a pirateer in the establishment. Or two..."

"My thanks." Aypax dug his hand into the coward's bag, pulling out the Kaldorian Riverstone, then released his grip and stowed the tiny hatchet. "Hendrix, let's go."

Hendrix had yet to move, still disgusted. "What...what of the child?"

Aypax referenced the droves of starving locals fighting toward food stands. "At least its master will feed it."

* * *

The Tourtoufian sands felt the brunt of fifty boots. Fifty yellow boots. Stout boots, with purple laces, and dangerously sharp lips. The sands felt the pain of multiple ships sliding into the coastline. These ships' paint shared the boots' coloring. Dark yellow. Dark purple.

Hunting birds screeched a few hundred feet above, watching the sands sink beneath large paws and claws. Scent hounds...all of which dug holes, burying their noses into the multicolored beach. Such fierce hounds were unaffected by its hot temperature.

They howled and barked as more dogs made their way toward the forest edge. Those fifty boots followed closely behind.

Whoever was here was hot on the track.

11

TARYN

A Large Crowd

"Taryn cannot go out on that stage; she mustn't! It's political self-slaughter!" yelled Orani, a dedicated member of the Alyonian High Council.

The interim queen watched quietly as Orani stood from his seat at a rectangular oak table. He was surrounded by five additional High Council members, each clothed in forest-green robes with gold *HC* insignias, each palming the dread from their own faces.

"Look at this crowd!" Orani screeched, his long hair bouncing as he walked toward an oval-shaped window. He stared down at thousands of bodies gathered in the streets of Alyonia below.

Positioned on the highest floor of the Kaldorian manor, the High Council's chamber of discourse had been built to view the entire city. But today, its members cared only for the anxious masses congregating directly beneath. Yells and cheers rang out as droves of citizens approached a wooden stage below, the Kaldorian theater stage.

"Taryn must be perceived as mourning the loss of our king and queen, not delivering a speech mere moons after their murder." Orani flicked an irritating fly from his green robe. "We must cancel the event and announce our alliance with Rhi later!"

"Cancel?" Trakkonious leaned over one of the many empty seats. Dressed in his impressive beige tunic, he strode toward the head of the table where Taryn sat beside an incredibly old and bald Alyonian. "Nonsense. Now is the perfect time for such a speech."

Orani began to retort, but Taryn's steely eyes silenced him.

"The public is crippled with fear," continued Trakkonious. "Their queen and king are dead, Taaivetti is away at war. They need leadership now. Sure, Taryn cannot appear unaffected by the tragedy, but by the stars that's what onion juice is for. I'll spray her eyes before she walks onstage if I must, allow her to fight the tears. This will show strength through times of grief. Let the public believe she's putting their problems before her own personal issues, then yield the stage to Bandano-Rhi. The perfect blend of future strength and lovable weakness."

Trakkonious looked to Taryn, as did the High Council. She gave a sweet smile.

The meeting adjourned.

* * *

The crowd was large, and looked even larger from where Taryn stood. Nightfall had brought her atop the Kaldorian theater stage. Its position elevated her slightly above the wet, clustered masses. She liked that. It made her feel powerful. Such an audience might terrify most, but Taryn wasn't *most*. Like her brothers, she'd been raised in the limelight. The thousands of curious eyes staring up at her only magnified the joy of lying, only intensified the rush.

"And without further introduction," she yelled, limping away from the podium. "I present to you the leader of the Rhi Empire, and more importantly, our new ally...Bandano-Rhi!"

The bundled crowd roared with a mixture of emotions as the once-infamous Bandano-Rhi paraded across the stage and hugged

Taryn, an odd sight for the crowd of Alyonians.

Looking out, the interim queen watched as Bandano-Rhi surveyed the thousands of bodies huddled together beneath wooden sunshades, all ready to hear tonight's news. Diverse groups had traveled from all over Adria to attend the evening's hearing. There were humans from Oblia, Kios, and Selma. There were even a few Jordzillians; they'd made quite a trek. He also noticed a surprisingly numerous attendance from the timber trade city of Myre.

Taryn smiled and waved in their direction. So many desired to witness the signing of "the most important treaty ever proposed." At least that's what the whispers named it. Regardless, this was a night that would change Alyonian history forever. Change all history, in fact. Two powerful empires combining forces: economic, military, political. It was astounding. Unprecedented.

It was . . . Taryn's crowning moment.

"Thank you! Thank you!" Bandano-Rhi waved and gestured bows of love. "Please, there's no need!" A man capable of anything faced a hefty task of taming this group. "Myre! Marvelous to see you all!"

Proud to be singled out, the Myrian representatives raised their voices, prompting the Alyonian locals to follow. Taryn wasn't surprised at the outpouring, given the sheer magnitude of recent events. Alyonia's peace treaty with the Rhi Empire, an upcoming election, the sickness…not to mention the murders within the royal family and endless gossip over Alyonia's standing within the Pallala-Accord. Tonight would surely affect the entire continent of Adria. No wonder so many had shown up.

Alyonia's Peace Parade had ended three moons prior, yet its commotion roared on. Drunkards still filled the streets, beggars roamed, and more messenger birds covered the skies than ever. So many, in fact, that the city's sanitation forces were called into work, tasked with combating the ever-present smell of feces.

Bandano-Rhi took center stage, replacing Taryn. "Before I press on with official statements, I must first pass my condolences to each and every Alyonian. The events that transpired during the Peace Parade are the exact atrocities we now set out to ensure never happen again. Senseless murder. Royal treason. Never again!"

Bandano-Rhi thrusted an overly muscular arm into the air. "Our treaty today will end the long hostility between Adria's most powerful empires. We will begin a new era. An era of peace and prosperity. I vow to do everything in my power to stop the issues plaguing our societies."

Thousands of Alyonians cheered loudly, all with white hair, all with smiles. But there were others present. The weary travelers from all over, the representatives of Adria's surrounding free countries. These representatives belonged to the long-held but teetering Pallala-Accord. They were here for one reason, here fearing one thing: the Rhi Empire.

Just as well, thought Taryn. *Keep fearing them.*

"Alyonia has served as a model society for more than a thousand years," continued Bandano-Rhi, though it was hard to tell if he meant it. "We've had our many differences and conflicts, sure. But the Rhi Empire has always admired this great land. It's time we return the favor. Together, we'll put swords in the hearts of the hideous Gorsh. Together, we'll create an herb for the deadly sickness. Further, my coastal farms have pledged seasonal shipments of grain and corn, putting a cease to your southeastern famine!"

Waves of starving Alyonians fought toward stage, replacing their hatred of man with an urge to touch the hero who might end these times of hardship. *Sheep are so easily led,* thought Taryn.

"And I personally swear to avenge the loss of my new, but dear friend, King Kaldor. And my most admired Queen Lizabeth." Bandano-Rhi looked over at Taryn, tears gathering in his eyes. "Your loss will not go unpunished."

Bandano turned to his acclaimed honor guard standing behind him. Ten in all, each clad with flashy yellow and purple armor. One of the guards stepped forward and handed Bandano-Rhi a long scroll. He unraveled it, then extended the scroll toward Taryn.

Wasting no time, she seized it, admiring its surface. The curious common folk wanted nothing more than to see this scroll. What it said, what it looked like up close.

As Taryn read silently, a hulking Alyonian began clapping from the opposite end of the stage. He rose from his position amongst a long row of other political figures.

Kornilious, thought Bandano-Rhi.

Now donned in his parliamentary attire, Kornilious wore dark-gold combat boots with a dashing green robe to complement. A silver chaplet clung tightly to his head, as if he himself were the king. "Wonderful! Wonderful speech!" Kornilious' fellow politicians were seated in fashionable chairs. They stood and applauded the monumental moment. "I'm honored to share the stage with such a man!" Kornilious walked arrogantly toward the podium and extended his hand. The emperor gave him a sturdy shake, though he didn't seem to share the same affection.

"Today, two great military factions shall unite." Kornilious peered out across the audience. "With the aid of the Rhi Empire, we can finally withdraw our forces from Hann and concentrate our seasonal tributes on home-front spending!"

The crowd loved this. They'd grown tired of seeing their money funnel toward a never-ending war in the desert. More importantly, the act would grow Taryn's popularity. *And further our plans in the Red Sand Desert,* she thought.

"We should not be wasting precious Alyonian coin on our troops at Hann or the Bolden Barrier. The Gorsh have never made it to the Barrier! Not once!" Kornilious patted Bandano-Rhi's yellow shoulder plate. "Thanks to Bandano-Rhi, we can now afford to allocate funds on more pressing issues. We can even bring home Prince Taaivetti!"

Kornilious stole a fast look toward Taryn, nearly impossible to catch, unless one were waiting for it. Which one member of the crowd certainly was...

Tiannu Preters stood shoulder to shoulder with thousands of commoners. Holding an umbrella, she blended in to perfection. Tiannu studied Taryn's and Kornilious' every motion, their every word and move. It had been challenging to see, sure, but something was there. Something electric.

"The Vetusian party misunderstands me!" Kornilious' words carried a hint of derogatory compassion toward his opposing political party. "We love our warriors. We simply don't wish to watch them squander their lives away in the desert! And we certainly don't wish to continue wasting our own seasonal tributes on a perpetual war."

Even Bandano-Rhi nodded. He, too, was a proponent of withdrawing the Alyonian military from the west. *But for much different reasons*, Taryn thought.

"And so it is with great honor, and the weight of all those who've graciously elected me, that I sign off on the combative clause of this historic treaty." Kornilious put his ink pen to the massive scroll and after the briefest hesitation...he signed.

"And now for the two primary signatures," said an incredibly tall and bald Alyonian. He'd previously sat next to Kornilious and obviously shared Taryn's interest in wasting no time. The imposing Alyonian, High Council-Lord Preem, leader of Alyonia's High Council, wore a familiar forest-green robe with the golden High Council insignia woven into its sleeves.

"With the witness of all those you see before you," Preem continued, his old limbs trembling, "and with the presence of the High Council, and all members of Alyonian parliament, excluding the Prince Taaivetti." Preem referenced the politicians resting comfortably behind him. "We elect Taryn, the interim queen, to sign this peace treaty on behalf of our entire realm. This includes, but is not limited to, the great cities of Kaldoria, Pretoria, Nadoria, and Traxtonia. If any members wish to appeal a final objection, let it be heard before the interim queen now."

Not a one objected, though they wouldn't have had the time if they wished.

"Wonderful!" Preem placed an exorbitant silver bracelet on Taryn's signing wrist, then withdrew a blue box from his robe's pocket. Opening it, he revealed a magnificent ink pen.

Taryn bowed respectfully before delicately grasping the Alyonian relic. Her hands quivered, for this pen had been rumored to have existed for thousands of seasons. Arrogant as she was, even the best could fall victim to the body's nerves.

Taryn collected herself. Then, using the bracelet hand and historic pen, she signed away the borders of Alyonia.

She signed away the free city of Nome, the fields of the east, the Eagletail Mountains, the books of old. She signed away an unknown number of long-held laws and regulations. A new era had indeed begun.

"To peace!" Bandano-Rhi raised his arm again, signaling his honor guard.

From behind, they hoisted Rhi Empire banners for all to see. Bandano-Rhi's house crest swung about as his tapestries flapped in brisk winds. The notorious yellow and purple bear, claws at ready, dead fish in mouth. An aggressive and powerful sigil. The most known in all of Adria.

Anticipating the moment, Taryn's house protectorates marched across the stage and turned face-to-face with Bandano-Rhi's honor guard. Not to be outdone, her green armored protectorates lifted their own Alyonian flags. These banners were expertly woven with green and gold, and flaunted a pristine drawing of the tree god Balo. An equally beautiful sigil. Balo stood in the flag's center, surrounded by bright stars. A breathtaking, but perhaps outdated, trademark.

Both groups remained still as the impressive tapestries collided against one another. The true sign of a new house alliance.

"Before we adjourn, let us take a moment for the beloved late king and queen of Alyonia." Bandano-Rhi cupped his hands and looked to the sky. "I've been informed they will be honored in three moons. Their bodies are to be pushed into the Southbay, and their hearts buried in the Forest of Balo, as they'd wished. Though I do not share their adoration of Balo, I will pray to Elo for a successful passing into the stars."

With that, he turned and exited the stage.

12

TAAIVETTI

Hard Choices

Taaivetti's head throbbed as he descended the mountainside, finally reaching his beloved Sindria. Hours had passed in the alley of the sibyls, yet the moon loomed high and darkness maintained a hold of the desert. The repugnant smells of nearby villages assaulted Taaivetti's senses as he reflected on his honor. Or what was left of it. *You're one of the good ones, Taaivetti… One of the good ones.*

A rustling stole his attention. The prince drew a whip from Sindria's saddle, relaxing his weary eyes to focus his hearing. The nearly utterly black concealed his adversary, but Taaivetti had long mastered desert warfare. Kneeling low, he felt the sand for Sindria's tracks. *She moved west…enemy came from the east.* Using his whip, Taaivetti searched the air around him, ensuring his foe was out of striking distance. "You move, you die," said Taaivetti, halting the footsteps of someone or something nearby. *No growls…*

Silence followed as the prince continued twisting and twirling his whip, closing the area quickly. Drawing a blade with his free hand, he prepared to kill whatever his whip would soon feel.

"My sorrows! Sorrows! Many sorrows I send you!" The voice sounded youthful.

Taaivetti stopped a few feet from a young one, still unable to see him yet knowing precisely where he stood. "You're out far too late. This only comes with purpose in your tribe—"

"Mother smelled your horse, and I was sent to bring it back. I will leave you now, you've my sorrows—"

"She's no horse. You would've soon discovered that the hard way." Taaivetti straightened his posture and scratched his chapped lip. "Boy, does your mother give you wax for your lips or elbows?"

The child stepped a bit closer, looking somewhat confused as he crept into view. "Yes. Yes, it comes from the black bees—"

"I know. Take me to her."

The child stepped closer still, now exposing his tanned desert features. Long, knotty hair fell to narrow shoulders where a tunic, so loose it could've been a dress, hung on him from neck to toe. "Follow," the boy said.

Mounting Sindria, Taaivetti followed indeed. A few moments passed before they reached a row of flapping tents, the first of perhaps fifty others along the base of the mountain. Taaivetti surveyed the dark village, lit only by moonlight. It wasn't long before he noticed a few Naomi positioned outside of these tents, each clad in recognizable saddles from Hann's stables. Whispers, drunken laughs, and subtle moans drifted from the tents beside these Naomi. *To discipline my soldiers,* thought the prince, *would be hypocrisy.*

The young boy made his way inside as blowing sands pelted the tent's exterior. He returned with a skinny desert woman wearing the same style of dress.

"The hour is late," said the desert woman, yawning yet seemingly used to being awakened. She stopped when she saw Taaivetti, recognizing she was in the presence of an Alyonian. "I, I am filled with sorrows—"

"No." Taaivetti stepped forward and handed her his canteen of water. "Don't be. Will you trade for wax?" He pointed to his lip. The woman nodded and rushed back inside her tent. A brief moment passed as she rummaged through her modest home. Taaivetti glanced around, then spoke to the desert child. "The warriors who stop here from time to time, those who look like me. Have they ever traveled into the mountain?"

The boy thought. "Never that I have taken sight to. They mainly...well, I am not to say."

Taaivetti nodded; his soldiers' unlawful actions poured coals atop the flame of his own remorse.

"For you." The mother returned with a tiny glob of wax and handed it to Taaivetti.

She smells different, he thought. *A perfume of sorts.*

The mother rubbed the wax on her lip slowly and somewhat sensually, showing Taaivetti how to use it or perhaps subtly pleading to exchange herself for coin. The motion crushed him.

In that very moment, one of his soldier's Naomi released a neigh as if signaling for his attention. Taaivetti turned to the beast and noticed four wheelbarrows filled with iron and various jars of dye beside it. He stared at the wheelbarrows, at this season's shipment from the starving villagers in return for Alyonian protection. Then another thought struck, one he'd faced one hundred times over.

Were we ever really the good ones?

"Thank you." Taaivetti accepted the woman's wax and turned toward Sindria. "Stay safe," he called.

"Wait." The woman stopped him, reaching her hand out but not touching the large Alyonian. "Is it true...what the desert whispers? Have the red beasts truly gathered as one?"

Taaivetti inhaled, unsure how best to respond. "Are you... happy my kind protects you?"

The woman forced a confused nod. "Happy. Very happy. You have my gratitude."

The prince stared, his eyes demanding truth. "Speak truly. You've nothing to fear."

"Happy. Happy we are for you—"

Taaivetti put his large, gloved hand on her quivering shoulder. "Please. Only the truth can be tolerated. I am not with the soldiers. In fact, I may take them away forevermore."

The words softened her. "I…" She paused, now thinking quite earnestly. "I truly am. Happy. Happy."

Taaivetti nodded and lifted his hand. "Okay, if—"

"But…" she furthered. "I do wonder what the stars might have done in a different life." The woman looked up at the night sky. "Without you there is no protection from the Gorsh, the red beasts. We may all be dead. But without you, we could have kept our grain and jewels, metals and colors from underground. My people may've grown rich, wise and strong…time will never tell."

Taaivetti lingered, digesting her honesty. After a moment, he reached into his belt and revealed the same blade he'd nearly slain her son with. "The red beasts have united indeed." Taaivetti placed the blade in her hands. "Their new warlord, he'll skin you alive if he ever shows up. Don't give him the chance."

* * *

Taaivetti's wrists burned with exhaustion, his ass chafed. Barely gripping Sindria's reins, he galloped beneath Hann's center gatehouse. Today's first nova rose over the Red Sand Desert's distant peaks, pushing rays of morning orange over the fortress. Identifying himself as he had many nights before, Taaivetti removed his hood for a few sentries above. They gave their usual nod of discretion as the prince slowed his way into a quiet courtyard. Taaivetti buried his afflictions and dismounted Sindria as they neared Hann's stables.

"Morning," said Sir Rynn, conveniently awake and waiting beside Sindria's stall.

Had he not been in such horrid agony, Taaivetti would've

laughed. With no sleep, no food, and no honor, the prince was powered by one thing: his need to see more.

"I presume you were off at prayer?" Sir Rynn studied a slight blemish developing on Taaivetti's lower lip. "Must've been a desert house of worship I haven't heard of. Have the Gorsh converted?"

Taaivetti led Sindria inside. "I prayed through the eve—"

"Spare me." Sir Rynn took a more sincere tone. "Hann's officers have gathered in the boardroom for our vote. Time to make your choice, my prince."

"My choice is made."

* * *

Taaivetti pushed open the boardroom's weighty door. Perhaps twenty of Hann's finest stood and bowed with respect. They used traditional Alyonian bows, a slight nod and tilting of the head, one hand over the heart.

Taaivetti needed no honors. "All may sit," he said, gesturing to their chairs.

A simultaneous dropping of bodies exposed the small room and a number of strategic corkboards hung about. These boards featured desert maps and hand-drawn patterns of war, most marked with a dismal red X. In the center stood a colossal desk with a hefty piece of bark upon its surface. The emerald-colored bark had been sanded down skillfully and played host to various pieces of pottery.

"Forty-thousand Gorsh!" shouted Commander Zo, running his hand through a sweaty white mohawk. "Under one banner! Let that sink in, brothers. We cannot stop that magnitude of assault. Hann simply isn't built for it. Further, consulting High Commander Bolden and his reservists without approval from the High Council is treason!" He stood and placed his family crest down onto the board's left side. It was a wave, the crest, a piece of hard clay painted light blue and molded into the shape of a powerful wave. The sigil of Zo's house, a well-respected one at that.

The commander had made his decision, but many others had not. Sighs clashed with nods of approval as Zo set down the model crest.

Sir Rynn peered at the bark board. There were an even number of votes on either side of a dividing line—*to leave, or to stay?*

A balding officer kicked a withered chair, angry with Zo's decision. "How shall you sleep at night, you coward?"

Zo met his gaze. "Coward? I was killing Gorsh when you were at your mother's tit!"

"Enough!" Taaivetti approached. "Only constructive arguments are to be heard. Commander Zo, you've made your decision. Tell us why."

Zo nodded, then glanced upon his comrades. They all shared two distinct features. The first were faces so bronzed they bordered on black; this feature was common, given Alyonian pigment and the strength of two desert novas. Some faces were freckled, others bland, yet every face appeared the same beautiful shade of bronze. This would've seemed angelic in fact, had the Alyonians around the table not also shared a second feature: an exhausted and terrified look of worry.

"Brothers." Zo squeezed moisture from his tall mohawk as he spoke. "Some of us have volunteered to serve at Hann for ten seasons. That's nine too many, if you ask me. We all know what this place is. We all know what we're fighting."

The room's tension had been palpable since Taaivetti entered, but this comment sparked a different kind of fear.

"I've served our great home of Alyonia as long as I can remember," continued Zo. "I've fought since most of you lot were snuggled in your mother's womb. So I can say to you in the most honest of manner, I have not made the decision to abandon this post lightly. I do not vote to leave due to our conditions. I do not vote to leave out of demoralization, thirst, or hunger."

Zo lifted a copy of yesterday's Alyonian story papers, exposing a headline to all:

High Council signs seasonal tribute cuts to Hann and Bolden Barrier in effort to combat rising famine.

"I vote because of *this*!" he shouted, slapping the headline. "I vote because Alyonia has changed. We no longer fight for a homeland that deserves our bodies, our lives. Look around you. We send precious materials home every season, yet we barely have enough supplies to keep ourselves outfitted. And we're supposed to defeat the most aggressive horde our history has ever seen? I grow tired of watching my brothers die, moon after moon, for a bunch of prissy, unappreciative twits back home!"

Murmurs erupted around the room, echoing in agreement.

"I've always been proud to fight. Bloody Perdition, we all strive to a glorious death for Balo, for a place amongst the warrior stars!" Zo beat his green breastplates proudly. "But now, things have changed. Alyonia has no honor. Worse, with the election looming, if Kornilious retains his position, and the Novellusian party wins the High Council majority, I fear we'll receive less aid than ever."

Had there been a shred of hope in the room, it fled.

"My brothers." Zo sighed. "I see a tight vote, and I understand both positions. Truly. But we must remember, Hann is not a mandatory fortress. You are here this season by choice, and the Windy Season is merely a few moons from ending. If you volunteer for another season, the Bright Season at that, well, we all know firsthand what lurks in the desert. And this time, we face forty thousand of them." Zo pointed toward the X-marked corkboards.

Taaivetti nodded in approval at Zo. "Well spoken. Thank you."

The prince was right, Zo had delivered a powerful speech. Moved by their leader's words, a few hesitant voters walked forward and placed their family crests to the left of the line, then nodded respectfully to Commander Zo.

Only five left, thought Taaivetti, as he watched more soldiers cast their handmade ballots. Taaivetti stood and approached the board with increasing nervousness. But the prince had been trained to never show weakness. A childhood full of Kaldorian theater and combat was responsible for that. "I look around this room and see fear." He let his statement settle before continuing, "But I also see greatness. I see some of the hardest, sweatiest, nastiest Alyonians our realm has ever known. I see a group I'd sooner die next to than send home with our tails tucked between our legs!"

Half the room roared.

"Perhaps this is my flaw. I see the good in those around me. A dreamer, as many say. But believe me, I've done little dreaming of late. In truth, I've lost what precious sleep I can afford, pondering what to do. The unrest in Alyonia, the upcoming election, the Gorsh horde…and now the loss of our king and queen. I came here today intending to end my service at Hann."

The soldiers began to buzz, fiercely whispering in confused gossip.

"I, too, grow tired of watching good folk die. I, too, share your anger for Alyonia's ungratefulness. I miss my loved ones. I miss the smell of…grass."

The room bellowed unusual laughter. Contrary to nausea, humor was a rarity in the Red Sand Desert.

"However, it is only in this moment that I see my flawed reasoning. It is only now, with my parents' blood still splattered across my mind, that I envision everyone we love back home. They're sitting in their cozy manors, snuggled beside a fire. But this time, they're not waiting for us. They're *counting* on us." The prince raised his voice. "They're counting on us to protect them! For we're all that stands between them and death! Believe me, I dream of the day we can return home. But, brothers, we must renew our stay for the upcoming Bright Season. If we don't stand now, we'll just have to stand later. So let us rise and carve out our place amongst the warrior stars!" He rose his fist. "Who's with me?"

The boardroom roared louder than ever, nullifying the entire voting process with one simple speech. As Taaivetti laid down his own crest, it became apparent what the rest of Hann's defenders would do.

13

HENDRIX

The Saloon

"Is this it...?" Hendrix failed to hide his disappointment. They'd trekked the entire day *for this*?

"Must be," said Aypax.

Aypax had said the place would be a dump, yet even he seemed underwhelmed. Hendrix watched as his companion eyed the strange saloon, craftily built into the side of a crumbled three-story ruin, perhaps utilizing the building's destruction as decor. This could've been a creative ploy, though it appeared more of a lazy attempt to cover a lack of funds.

"If pirateers are anywhere, we'll find them here," Aypax concluded.

Open ceilings allowed night air to funnel through the saloon, presumably to help quell an intolerable stench. But tonight, it also welcomed light rain.

Hendrix pointed to a notch in the building. "I see a sentry out front. I shall likely not be allowed in."

"Have you heard anything I said about this island?"

They walked toward the saloon's front deck, carefully surveying their surroundings. Clumps of stone debris had been halfheartedly crafted into benches and tables out front. Dubious patrons filled them, most of whom wore cloaks or cheap raincoats. The locals sipped drinks, passed cards, and played a multitude of games that resembled death wishes, if not an unpleasant time. Hendrix saw blade juggling, arm wrestling, bug fights, a few fistfights, and even a rope-pulling contest in the side alley.

"Is that for the losers?" Hendrix referenced a pile of dead animal guts, blended with bar trash and spread out on the sand in between both teams as a rancid punishment for the losers.

Aypax barely looked. "Yes."

They're just asking to spread the sickness. Hendrix observed this barbaric game, subduing his need to puke by concentrating on the participants themselves. All types of unusual folks tugged. Tourtoufians, Jordzillians, even a few men from realms he'd never heard of. An abundance of race. Perhaps most surprising, however, were the Alyonians he spotted on the front deck.

"You're confused?" Aypax sighed. "I already told you of Alyonia's expansion. Those confined to this island have to entertain themselves somehow. Aypax approached the sentry. "Is there a front charge?"

The hefty sentry eyed Hendrix. "He's too youngs." His tongue and green skin inferred he was a true native. "Can'ts permit you twos in. Parliament rules."

Aypax laughed and nodded through a bar window. "Oh? That's interesting, considering the ten females standing in the corner who are young enough to be your daughter."

The sentry shrugged. "You knows what to do."

Aypax revealed a tiny bag of coins. The sound of expensive clinking changed everyone's tone.

"Twenty of fifty to the Rhi Empire standard," said the sentry. "That's the front charge."

"Twenty of fifty?"

The sentry smiled. "Each."

DUST

Aypax paid him with an Alyonian condet. The sentry examined the coin, then swung open two wooden double doors.

Stepping inside, the saloon was surprisingly expansive, even well decorated. "Wow…" Hendrix gaped.

Aypax, however, had already scanned the entire area, and luck hadn't taken his side. More than one hundred bodies moved all around them, yet not a single pirateer in sight.

"Bloody Perd—" He stopped, more frustrated than expected. Aypax clutched his veiny forearm, which showed signs of quick infection. "This needs cleaning. Wait here. Don't move."

Hendrix heard him loud and clear. Aypax needed him to stay put, and he would, but that didn't mean he couldn't look…

His eyes drifted to a live band positioned on a wooden high-rise hung between the ruin's first and second stories. The unadorned wooden stage was as bare as the ropes holding it in place. The band's instruments were equally ragged, as was their high-pitched melody.

Hendrix wasn't used to such a sound. Upbeat. Far too upbeat. The kind of music that caused hundreds of bodies to dance atop one another, even through falling rain. He looked up. Holes the size of boulders pocked the roof, exposing long poles of metal running horizontally overhead. *Old floor joists?*

Dancers, scarcely dressed, expertly maneuvered their way around these poles. Hendrix watched in awe as they twisted and twirled. Masters of their craft, the dancers somehow managed to wave foggy incense over an energized crowd. His will broken by exhaustion, Hendrix couldn't help but feel enticed. He glanced down at his promise bracelet. *Look away…*

There were narrow torches in every direction, dying slowly. Still, they lit the place, even exposed a few passing shadows near the ceiling. Hendrix found the fast-moving shadows rather odd, though he was merely thankful he wasn't near any flames. It felt hot enough already. In more ways than one.

* * *

Aypax approached the bar and stopped, halted by his own peripheral. Six Tourtoufians drank at the opposite end of the stone bar top, harassing female patrons. Looking closer, the Tourtoufians all wore the same orange vests. Bintonns.

"What's can I gets ya?" shouted the barkeep, a middle-aged human with long blonde hair and a cheap vest of white cotton fibers. A piece of parchment had been woven into his vest, inked with the name *Joel*.

"The purest drink you've got." Aypax kept his eyes on the vested Bintonns. Their very mannerisms annoyed.

The barkeep returned with a potent liquid in a brown mug. "Purple sand tornado, the purest I have. Yous won't find this anywhere else on Tourtoufa, my friend! Only heres! I don't recommend consuming mores than two." He reckoned Aypax's size. "Well, yous could perhaps have three. But don'ts push it."

Aypax paid before grabbing the drink hastily; he wouldn't be tasting it anyway. Spinning to find a seat, he stopped suddenly, staring with his mouth agape. "Have I gone mad? Delirious?" Aypax counted his fingers, blinked rapidly. Repetitively. No. He wasn't going mad…There was, for certain, a squirrel jumping from seat to seat beneath the bar.

The squirrel moved with the grace of a master thief as it robbed travel sacks from everyone seated at the bar. Aypax raised a brow whilst the animal scurried with its new wares to a back room. *Leave it be. Leave it be…*

* * *

Aypax led Hendrix across a slimy dance floor. Five minutes had yielded a clean wound and an increased desire to catch the thieving squirrel. There wasn't time for such distractions, but Aypax had grown tired of the unjust.

The task wasn't easy, though. As the pair crossed the dance floor, incessant bugs hovered. Drinks spilled. Toxic fumes and smoke mixed with soft rainfall, filling the muggy air. Worse, they had to fight off the constant assault of wet bodies thrusting against them.

Hendrix had never seen such a place; his eyes wandered as a hand pawed his shoulder, hoping to lure him away. He stayed diligent, however, keeping a grip on Aypax's wrist and his mind on his beloved Madison. What was she doing right now? Would she believe Taryn's lies? Had she fled Alyonia too? Perhaps to their newest sliver of land... So many questions unanswered. Finally escaping, the duo rounded a jagged wall, taking them to a poorly kept and poorly lit sporting room.

"You..."

Aypax stopped a few forearms from the brown squirrel, looking around for another figure. Surely the rodent's owner would be close by, presumably collecting his stolen funds.

The squirrel sat nestled inside one of the pockets of a cornerstable, its bushy tail popping out. "Yea?" it said, plain as day.

Hendrix dropped his belongings on the disease-ridden floor. "Did it...speak?"

Aypax peered at the thing curiously. He'd traveled most of the known world, but this, this he'd never seen. *Could it be?*

Growing up in Alyonia, Hendrix and Aypax had heard legends of talking animals from their tutors, tales of mutated beasts secluded to one horrific island. Whispers said the island had been bombarded by the original comets, leaving soil infused with traces of *the dust*. "Speakers," as the animals came to be known. Rumored to be vicious and wise. But even those legends were nearly lost, as was any trace of belief that Speakers still existed anywhere today.

"*It?*" The squirrel stood and snapped its tail back and forth. "*It* has a name, ya skweek." The furry rodent sniffed the air and studied Hendrix, its voice feminine yet aggressive. "The youngin' smells like he just squirted his pants."

"What?" Hendrix gasped as he looked down at his crotch.

The squirrel let out a wicked snicker. "I'm foolin'," it said, before sitting back into the corner pocket. "But I saw you eyein' those broads on the poles. Keep your snake in its den, pal."

Neither Alyonian knew how to respond.

"Okay." The squirrel inhaled. "Now you're angerin' me. Ya never seen a talkin' squirrel, I get it. That's why I hang here. It's a bar, and folks usually think they're hallucinatin'. So. You're hallucinatin', havin' a vision, that's all. Now walk away, and enjoy your eve—"

"I saw your actions." Still shocked, Aypax recognized the need to adapt. "Return the items you stole from my family."

Family? Hendrix turned, surprised by the lie, though it paled in comparison to his stupor regarding the squirrel. His heart pounded and forced him to inhale a deep breath as he wondered if the animal had a point. *Am I hallucinating? Could the seeds still be working?*

"Your family?" The squirrel's voice raised twelve notches as it burst into peals of high-pitched laughter. "First, I wouldn't return these items if I'd snatched 'em from your mother. Second, callin' anyone in your little gang 'family' is comical. You're a buncha dead-beat, mulch-for-mind skweeks! Ya want your money back? It's in that pouch right there. Try takin' it!"

The squirrel pointed to a camouflage pouch before crouching into a defensive stance.

The Alyonians had no words.

Aypax swept for the small creature, missed. The squirrel hopped off its table and dashed across the room before scurrying onto the shoulders of a much bigger friend.

Hendrix stopped, nearly frozen in his own skin. *Skweek... Family...* He sat upon a barstool and searched frantically through his bag for the small white book. Fishing both hands through his seeds, spare garments, and liquor bottle, he found it. Hendrix flipped over the pages until landing on chapter 9.

Prophetics 9 — Family

1. The heat overbearing,	2. The rescue daring,
3. Success arranged,	4. Hearts forever changed,
5. A new family bred,	6. Six souls long misled,
7. When animals speak,	8. Snap to it, you skweek,
9. Dark times to come,	10. He must never succumb,
11. From the forest they'll rise	12. Underground, holds demise,
13. Upon understanding,	14. You, I'm demanding,
15. Warn the one you love most,	16. Avoid the forest, be a ghost.

"Aypax!" yelled Hendrix.

But he'd already made it halfway across the room, furiously following the squirrel toward a much larger, and far more intimidating, companion.

14

BANDANO-RHI

A Dark Past

Taryn straddled Bandano-Rhi atop her bed. She felt strong, empowered with every thrust of her hips, invigorated by his every submissive quiver. She could hear his teeth grinding, feel his pelvis shaking beneath her. Taryn stared down into the emperor's usually stern eyes. In this moment they appeared anything but.

"You were great today," she whispered. "You belong onstage."

Bandano-Rhi spoke between breaths. "Where were you tonight? I spent half the eve here waiting."

Taryn thrusted a bit faster. "Am I not making it up to you?"

Knowing this wasn't the time for confrontation, Bandano-Rhi conceded. "Let's switch. I don't wish to end this way."

Even his words were fragile. *Weak.* She grinned. "You do not sound like my emperor."

That did it.

Bandano-Rhi clutched Taryn's sides, turned her over with ease and lifted her tail. Taryn snickered as she rested her elbows on the ruffled sheets. The emperor pulled her silvery white hair aside and began to—

"Get off! *Get away from me!* Stop! Help!" Taryn's abrupt screams rang through her bedroom before echoing down the stone halls.

Bandano-Rhi lunged backward, cutting his shin on a bedside table. He caught himself on the stone wall as glasses of wine crashed to the floor. His blood mixed with wine, staining an already red carpet. Shocked and confused, Bandano-Rhi stared at Taryn like a mouse cornered by a snake.

Taryn paused, looked back at her lover. "I'm sorry," she squealed. Her voice had changed...into that of a small child's. A young Alyonian female. "You scared me. I thought you were the priest. I don't like the priest." She frowned, then crinkled her face in terror. "He hurts me."

Bandano-Rhi stood, speechless. Taryn's entire demeanor had shifted. Here he gazed at one of the realm's most powerful Alyonians, but listened to a helpless child.

"Taryn...what in Elo's name are you doing? This game does not please."

"A game!" Taryn giggled uncontrollably, perhaps trying to appease. "I love games! But no one ever plays them with me." Her frown returned, and for a moment, the sight of it broke Bandano-Rhi.

"I don't understand." He studied her. "Please, stop."

"Sometimes Taaivetti plays with me," said the childish Taryn. "But that's only because he feels sorry for me since I have no friends. He doesn't like my only true friend." Taryn plopped on the bed, hanging her head.

Bandano-Rhi gathered himself. *Perhaps it was the dalli-seeds.* His shin pulsated. *Perhaps the wine, even.* He dabbed his wound with a nearby cloth. No longer aroused, Bandano-Rhi retrieved his purple undergarments and concealed himself. *A new strategy,* he thought. "Who is your only true friend?"

"My friend in the fire." Taryn focused on the many candles burning around them.

Bandano-Rhi allowed the thought to sink in. Something *did* make sense here. Candles were always burning all over...always.

Candles consumed the tops of shelves, filled bedside tables, and illuminated her many walled paintings as if part of the art itself.

"My friend says he'll help me kill the priest," she furthered. "He says the priest is a baaaaad Alyonian who deserves a painful death."

Bandano-Rhi felt his resolve slipping. "What else does your friend in the fire tell you?"

Taryn twisted her torso playfully, then patted her bare thighs with sweaty palms. "He says if I let him in, he'll protect me!"

"What do you mean let him—"

"My queen!"

"Taryn!"

"Open the door, now!"

Her guards slammed against the entry of Taryn's living chamber. Even safe inside her personal room, their sudden presence was troublesome for Bandano-Rhi.

"I'm fine!" she called out. "Just bled my shin is all. Leave me to my duties!"

Bandano-Rhi spun toward Taryn. Her voice had suddenly snapped back to normal, as had her posture and awareness.

The guards took a long moment before shouting back through the door. "Yes, my queen!"

"As you command! Shout if you should need us."

Bandano inhaled the deepest of breaths before sinking into a small couch in the corner of Taryn's room. Pulling back a red tapestry, he peeked out a window. Five bodies hung beneath a connecting skywalk, two stories above. They blew in the night's rainy wind, dangling over Alyonian streets for all to see. Bandano stared at their limp bodies, at the mortal wounds he himself had helped inflict upon them. *The Honorable-Six were heathens, but they deserved a proper burial.* He looked back at Taryn, then stood powerfully. "Taryn, you will tell me exactly what is—"

"I'm *fine*." The interim queen sounded normal. Still, Bandano remained unsure if she was mentally present.

Taryn looked down, saw her nakedness, saw the wine and blood discoloring the floor. She curled into herself, embarrassed, then covered her breasts to the best of her ability. "I presume you are now acquainted with Lizabeth the Second."

Bandano-Rhi felt a river of emotions. Love and compassion for his flustered Taryn, curiosity and fear over her changing personas. "Lizabeth the Second?"

Taryn put on a nightgown and wool sandals. She observed her room. The messy sheets, Bandano-Rhi's lack of garb, the wine and candlelight. Her tail fell limp with humiliation. "As I feared," she began. "Bandano, didn't I warn you when we started this to never take me from behind?"

He sat still, recollecting and swirling with guilt. "You did. But in the moment, I simply thought—"

"*Never* again."

Bandano-Rhi nodded as Taryn moved toward the small couch of black quilt and nestled beside him. "As I've already confided in you, I was forced over in my youth by a Balonian priest named Gypsis. I was only forty-four seasons young. Eleven years by your count..." She paused, struggling to find the words. "He took advantage of me for a very long time. I never told my family. I simply watched them favor Taaivetti, watched them mold him into the next great king. My brother was 'one of the good ones' as father so often said." Taryn drifted in her mind, both eyes going dark with memories. "They loved him so dearly. My father barely spoke to me. I was the second born and happened to come with breasts and a wet spot between my legs."

They shared something of a laugh, though there was nothing truly funny.

"Mother and Father demanded I continued my Balonian

studies with Gypsis. They were, of course, unaware of his actions, I must grant them that. The priest knew I'd never tell a soul. I was damaged goods. Public knowledge would ruin me, and thus the family name. So he continued teaching Taaivetti about Alyonia's god, Balo, and teaching me about a very different world."

Bandano-Rhi sat quietly, rage simmering. "I will kill this priest."

"Long dead, my dear." She gave an assuring chuckle. "The point is this: Every night that he used me, I withdrew into myself, into my mind. When he was done, he'd lock me in his private study. He granted me pens and parchments to pass the time, so I began drawing happy places. Drawings of Taaivetti and me, of our family. I imagined us all as happy and free of public judgment." Taryn fought back rising tears. "Now, whenever my mind gets lost in childhood drawings or abusive pleasures, something deep inside me comes to the surface...My inner child, I believe."

"And your inner child is named Lizabeth the Second?"

"Yes. I am truly named after my mother, Queen Lizabeth. Taryn is the name my father bestowed upon me once he caught wind of the abuse, once he no longer considered me fit to carry mother's name." Taryn's expression shifted with shame. "Father beheaded the priest publicly. But he could not allow the realm to know that I was the one he'd abused, that I had been tarnished. Father needed me pure, should a need arise to make a marriage pact between potential allies. So he forced a young Alyonian girl to come forth and pretend she was the one who had been violated."

"She obliged?" Bandano-Rhi couldn't believe it.

"Of course. She'd been approached by the king himself. But ol' King Kaldor was wise. He changed my birth name to Taryn, then told the realm that the priest had cursed the name of Lizabeth the Second, cursed me because father ordered him executed. Father spun the story as if he were protecting me by changing my name, but truly, he was simply disgusted by his damaged goods."

Bandano-Rhi wished to tread carefully, but the words poured out. "Then I'm glad he died the way he did." The duo sat in unpleasant silence. "This Lizabeth the Second…she comes when you see things that remind you of the priest's private study?" Bandano-Rhi paused. "But you know this. You are aware of her existence. So are you conscious when you are her?"

"That is difficult to answer. When I am Lizabeth the Second, it's as if I am riding in the front of a carriage, but not steering or holding the reins myself. I'm simply sitting next to the coach. I can see everything around me, but I'm not in control. And if I reach out to try and take the reins, my hands are slapped away."

"Elo's truth…" muttered Bandano-Rhi.

Taryn ran her fingers over his hairy thigh, squeezed his muscle. "But you see, my love, I don't look back on those eves as tragedy. No, quite the contrary. I look back on them as destiny." Taryn smiled. An odd yet addicting smile. "Once Father changed my name, I knew I was worthless to him. I could see it in his eyes. When he looked at me, he looked deeply…and he saw pain. He saw darkness."

Taryn placed Bandano-Rhi's hand over her heart. "So I decided to embrace this new me. The new 'Lizabeth the Second,' the Taryn. I decided to harness the emptiness and solitude everyone so believed they saw inside me. I rebelled as most youth do, sure. But I also spent seasons all alone, educating myself on life, on true light, on true happiness. That's when I found Elo. That's when I was transformed."

"Amazing," whispered Bandano-Rhi, enthralled by the force in front of him. "Praise him."

"Elo was not worshipped in Alyonia, so I stole books of devotion from sellers I'd been warned of. Met with strange folk in stranger basements. The more I read, the more I realized there was something to this god of creation." Taryn leaned in. "Most importantly, it led me to you."

* * *

Bandano-Rhi sat with Taryn. No longer in her room, she had brought him to the highest of heights, the peak of the Kaldorian manor: its bell tower. Their feet dangled over a daunting edge, daring fate.

"What a view," he said, looking down over the city of Alyonia. Thousands of manors and roads stretched endlessly, a maze of wet wood and green painted stone.

"I used to come up here and conjure ways of making Father see me. The real me."

"Funny." He kept his eyes out over the city. "I used to try and conjure up ways of having my father *not* see me."

Taryn laid her head in his lap, undaunted by any fear of heights. "Tell me of him."

"A hard man. He loved Elo more than life. Loved his wife, his kingdom, and me. In that order. He instilled strength at any early age." Bandano-Rhi gazed toward the stars, listened to the pattering of raindrops upon the bell's golden brass. "He would strike me, frequently. But so long as we were in the combat pits, he'd always guised it as toughening me. Maybe he was true in this, I'll never know. I do know one thing. I was never good enough. No matter what I did, no matter how high I climbed. Never good enough."

Taryn caressed his stubbly chin. "'Never good enough.' I understand."

He kissed her softly.

"Bandano, I brought you up here for a reason." Taryn paused, reached her hand into her pocket. "I have it. Alyonia's key."

Bandano-Rhi lifted her, then sprung carefully to his feet and away from the tower's edge. "No. This quickly?"

Taryn grinned as she revealed the ancient blue key. "Once we took care of Kaldor, it was easy."

Bandano-Rhi gaped at the priceless artifact. "You've done it."

"*We've* done it," she corrected. "Father wouldn't have died of 'natural causes' if it weren't for you...Shortly after he passed, my most trusted searched tirelessly for the key. King Kaldor was quite resourceful in his hiding of it. But ultimately, they found the damned thing."

Bandano-Rhi took the key, marveled. "Did you find the—"

"The Kaldorian map? Yes. Father hid it in the Forest of Balo."

"And?"

"It leads to the final key." She smiled. "It's in the far north. Just beyond the Lookout."

"The final key..." he repeated. "We must double our presence in the north. Once we have the fourth key, we need only my son's." Bandano-Rhi appeared torn. "I shall send my finest men north at once. With the Kaldorian map, they'll find the key by season's end. I must send word."

Taryn stood. "And your son?"

Bandano-Rhi made for a spiral staircase. "Being dealt with."

"My love," she said. "We are close...Do not fail."

Bandano-Rhi rolled up his sleeve and referenced his forearm brand: E-L-O. "I can't fail. It has already been foreseen."

15

HENDRIX

Sir Edmund Drake

Talking animals, skweeks, thought Hendrix, still questioning his sobriety. *It's clear.* He held the book in hand, an open passage before him. The pages were here. They were physical, proof he was not intoxicated. *This can't be coincidence.*

Aypax stopped short of the squirrel and its comrade. Seated upon a dirty couch in the corner of the sporting room, they awaited. Moonlight shined through open crevices above, silhouetting the rodent's tall friend. *Of course,* thought Aypax. *The only damned pirateer around.*

"Name's Sir Edmund Drake." The pirateer stood, displaying his lean physique; middle-aged and haggard, human. He wore a dashing grey double coat. His black tricorne hat was weathered and damp and matched a long beard of the same color. Sir Edmund Drake's rugged facial features hinted at wisdom, or perhaps just a hard life at sea. "What be yur quarrel?"

Aypax stared, vexed. Here stood his only hope of sailing to Prince Taaivetti, and his temper had already ruined it. "Your accomplice has stolen."

Sir Edmund Drake drew an annoyed breath, suggesting this to be a common occurrence. "Eh…" He shrugged, whilst toking a slow drag from a greasy smoking pipe. "Yur a member a' the Bintonns?"

"What?"

"Your friends!" interjected the rambunctious squirrel. "Your 'family' you just accused me of stealin' from."

Aypax killed his stupor. "I'm no member, no. I thought you to be."

The squirrel scurried about frantically, struggling against natural instincts. "Do ya see an ugly orange vest on either of us?"

Aypax held his ground. "Regardless of your affiliations, you stole, and that's unjust. Return the items."

Sir Edmund Drake rose and stepped forward beneath hazy light. Only now did his outfit sparkle. Black stitchings were woven into the grey double coat, creating emblems and nautical insignias: anchors, squid, sharks, and flapping sails. Beneath his coat, Drake wore a white toga that wrapped tightly round a thin body. Two black cavalier boots made him appear taller than he truly was. "Who'r you ta' tell us what's unjust?"

Aypax slid down his grey tunic, revealing a scarred Honorable-Six shoulder brand. "An Honorable." Aypax knew the pirateer would care not for such a title, but at least he'd know its truth.

Drake grinned. "Live long enough and that'll change." He returned to the grimy couch. "Anyone willin' ta' become a Bintonn deserves much worse than theft—"

A group of Tourtoufian ladies shouting at the bar interrupted the pirateer.

"You're disgustings!"

"Screws off!"

"Settles it downs!" yelled a drunken Bintonn, grabbing and groping.

The Tourtoufian females looked mortified, but Hendrix saw something else in their posture. Something in the posture of everyone. "Why is no one helping?" he whispered to Aypax.

Aypax knew the answer. Fear. Fear and respect. He returned his focus to Sir Edmund Drake. "I see the Bintonns have only grown more power hungry."

Drake gave no answer. He and his squirrel appeared furious. Not with Aypax, nor Hendrix, but with the belligerent gang at the bar. "Yea," replied the rowdy rodent. "They've got all the power now. You two've obviously never been to Tourtoufa."

Aypax's hand tapped his pocketed blue box yet again. "I've passed through. Do either of you know a Tourtoufian lady by the name of Katrin?"

Drake spoke for them both. "No. No Katrin."

"What's *your* name?" Hendrix asked the squirrel. His harmless nature seemed to ease the animal's sass, though it didn't seem keen on yielding identity. "Hear me fairly. You clearly hate these Bintonns, and we certainly don't love them." Hendrix looked toward his enigmatic protectorate. It was becoming increasingly clear that Aypax had a history with this island. "So it seems to me that an alliance could benefit all."

"Sammy," said the squirrel. "As in Samantha. Ya want my undergarment size too?"

Hendrix laughed through severe fatigue as Aypax revealed the trusted sac of coins and flashed it before Sir Edmund Drake. "I'm willing to pay heftily for a well-sized vessel, or a cabin aboard your own. We must sail for The Red Sand Desert by morn."

"The Red Sand Desert?" Drake nearly choked. "I've no need a' coin. And if I did, it'd take a'lot more than that—"

Another scream echoed from outside the saloon. The four of them walked toward an opening in the rubble bar and searched for its cause. It didn't take long.

Glaring out, they saw a lengthy line of slaves in the dirt, all chained to one another by filthy hands and feet. Twenty Bintonns surrounded them. Focusing, Aypax noticed an abundance of plated armor beneath their orange vests. *Alyonian-crafted armor.*

The scream had come from a young girl. A human girl, who appeared no older than Hendrix. Her clothes were torn and muddy, as were those on the rest of the slaves. She'd been shoved to the dirt by an overweight captor and now held herself up on all fours, spitting dust, no doubt yearning for water.

"I'll kill 'em." Sammy's tiny claws extended. "I'll bleed 'em all out. I'll gut 'em from head ta' toe!"

Hendrix didn't hear a word.

His eyes had met the young girl's. She, too, stared, enthralled. Even while hacking harmful dust, the pair remained locked on one another's gaze.

Aypax noted their connection, an immediate and rather strange connection he recognized. *The fire,* as he called it. The kind that burns forever. *No matter how hard you try to put it out...*

"Me ship ain't here." Drake looked away from the slave girl. Her inevitable beating was just another night on Tourtoufa. "She's docked at Starsgard with me crew." Drake stroked his hefty beard, contemplating. "But I think I can lend you twos a hand. If I were ta' help ya, though, I'd require somethin much different than coin."

Aypax listened. Hendrix however, kept staring at the young girl. "Whatever your ask, I'll triple it if you save her."

Aypax slapped him hard. "Shut your lips—"

"Done and done!" said Drake. "You've got yurself a' bargain. Payment'll be due once we reach me ship."

The pirateer shook Hendrix's hand before Aypax could retort. "This Bintonn convoy'll be headin' down ta' the Ratna River. They got a' dock there where they transport slaves to Starsgard. Plan is...we help the gal, then sail up the river toward me ship. That way, you both win. We help the girl, then we get my ship and sail for the desert."

Everyone looked to Aypax for an answer.

"Backs in place!"

Another Bintonn suddenly forced the slave girl upright. His hands were intrusive, feeling much more of her than necessary. Once she'd been secured in line, the captor saddled up onto a skittish horse. The hungry beast's ribs nearly protruded its rain-soaked skin. It tugged and fought, sharing the girl's hatred for its rider. "Let's moves!" the captor shouted.

The remaining Bintonns followed his lead, each mounting a different stallion. Most of these animals were also malnourished and unsettled by such rainy nights. Nevertheless, they carried their slave convoy into the dark streets of Baa.

"Well?" Drake appeared desperate to receive his unknown form of payment.

Aypax watched these slavers disappear into the black, his mind completely ignoring them. Instead, his mind was playing that damned memory on repeat. The Tourtoufian memory. The one he'd spent countless seasons locking away. He felt the eyes of those surrounding him, the brunt of his untold secret. He felt the ticking clock of Taryn's pursuers and the unpleasant sting of his brand pulsating behind his shoulder.

Honesty. Heart. Honor. 6

But he had already lied. Now the past was attacking his heart. All eyes were on Aypax the Honorable.

16

HENDRIX

Ava

"So be it." Aypax peered out into the drizzly eve. He'd made his decision; he needed to do what was right, what was just. "If it gets us to the boat, let's move."

"Wait." Sammy stopped his exit. "We need to let a little time pass. The Bintonns ain't stupid."

Sir Edmund Drake nodded. "They'll take smoke breaks every fifty span. They pretend ta' be chattin', engaged in conversation. But really, they're observin' their surroundins. Just waitin' ta' see if they've been followed." The rugged pirateer stowed his canteen and began packing a black leather pouch for travel.

"Followed?" Hendrix tied his own bag, eager to move.

"Angry family members," said Sammy. "Usually fathers who saw their daughters taken. You'll get the occasional ma and sister too. Tourtoufian ladies tend to be fearless."

"But havin' no fear ain't always good." Drake looked at Aypax. "Strength won't get ya far on this island. The Bintonns may look weak, but they're used ta' dealin' with folk like us."

"Not folk like me."

Drake studied him. "Maybe. But it don't matter."

"How do you know so much about them?" asked Hendrix.

Sammy leapt onto Drake's shoulder. "Keep your enemies closer than your wife—"

"—and your wife won't know where to find ya!" Drake finished the saying and bellowed laughter. "But enough of that. For now, let's toss back a' shot of somethin' sinister and play a nice game'a corners!" Sir Edmund Drake gestured toward the room's sporting rack. "Grab a stick."

Hendrix obliged reluctantly as Sammy dashed for the bar, stopping occasionally to smell spilled liquids along the stone floor.

Aypax maintained his position, having no time to waste on games. Assassins were surely close. The slave girl moved farther away with each moment. And his shoulders grew heavy from the weight of his own Tourtoufian past. He watched as Drake relit his smoke and clutched a wooden stick. Leaning over the table, he concentrated on the game's opening shot. Focused, Drake kept one eye on the circular ball and one eye on the big Alyonian.

* * *

An hour passed before the game concluded. Sammy had spent most of her time sharing a stolen bottle of purple liquid round the table, common with any game of corners. "A shot for a shot! Courtesy of Joel," she'd said and laughed.

But Aypax's feet tapped incessantly. Drake had guzzled his fair share throughout the game; still, he noticed. "'Tis time," he proclaimed. "When we get outside, search for any clothin' that might 'a ripped off the slaves. Me dog'll pick up the scent."

Hendrix stopped. "Dog?"

Aypax cared not; he simply led everyone out of the saloon. Reaching the front deck, Hendrix noticed the squirrel's behavior. Sammy acted peculiar; peculiar in that she was acting quite normal. The tiny rodent sniffed the damp ground and moved about in abrupt spurts of energy.

"What are you doing?" Hendrix asked.

"Blendin' in." Sammy kept her eyes to the dirt. "Bein' normal. Do you know how much folk would pay for a talkin' squirrel? We ain't in a barroom no more."

Hendrix hadn't thought of that. Nor Aypax, admittedly.

"Jakko!" whistled Sir Edmund Drake.

On cue, a furry dog lifted its head. It had been tied off by a thick leash around a wooden hitching rail in the alley. Rain drizzled down all round the pup, doubling its beauty.

"Wow!" Hendrix smiled. "Gorgeous."

"Looks like a' wolf, eh?" Drake seemed quite proud of his pup. Its black and white fur did resemble the traditional northern wolf. But this creature appeared far too small, a canine through and through.

Hendrix noted the rain had driven some patrons inside, yet many others had grown used to the recent downpour. The front deck still buzzed with life. "How is it no one steals him?"

Drake walked into the alley and untied his pup. "I'd love to see someun' try. Jakko ain't so friendly." The pup popped up and nuzzled Drake, then sat, awaiting orders.

"Come, come." Drake led his new team a few paces south. It wasn't long before he came across muddy footprints, barely visible thanks to relentless rain. "Jakko, sniff sniff!"

His canine darted ahead, following the tracks. "Woof!" It discovered more footprints and a long line of trails carved by slave chains and horse tracks. These trails led toward a dark alley.

Aypax squinted, yet visibility vanished after twenty forearms. Then there was only darkness.

"Woof!" Jakko's nose led where they needed.

Drake chuckled. "Looks like our gal was smarter than we thought."

Hendrix hustled over, glancing down at the area Jakko circled and pissed upon. He'd found where the slave girl had fallen. The spot was marked by tracings in the wet and sandy dirt, barely legible.

Ava-14

"She wrote that while kneeling," muttered Aypax. "Clever."

"She knew we'd come for her." Sammy dug a hole beside the name, dropped a twig inside. "That's probably why she stared at this doofus"—she cocked her head at Hendrix—"for so long."

Hendrix looked away, insulted. Sammy buried her twig whilst speaking. "Make 'a fella fall in love, fella suddenly thinks he's a prince. Prince thinks he's a hero, hero goes after the gal. She played you like 'a deck of cards. Classic. Makes me sick."

"Well, technically," Hendrix said and coughed. "One day I could be a prin—"

"What does the fourteen mean?" Aypax silenced him, examining the girl's message and protecting the young royal's identity.

"'Tis her slave number," replied Drake. "Each captive is assigned a 'number. They usually match with the keys ta' their handcuffs and chains."

"That's how the Bintonns keep track of high slave counts," added Sammy. "Could also be her cell number, but that's only if these prisoners came all the way from the Bintonns' holdings."

"Holdings?" Hendrix felt fearful for Ava.

"They bring most 'a their slaves to Stadium Starsgard." Drake stared down at the footprints, calculating. "There's an underground prison beneath it, thousands of cells. The Bintonns auction their ladies to high buyers, and sell the males as field-workers to dirty Tourtoufian establishments. Which consists of pretty much all of 'em. Anyone left over, they send into the arena."

Hendrix readied himself to ask, but Sammy interjected. "Yea, the arena is as bad as it sounds."

Aypax approached Drake. "How long do we have?"

"Depends. The Bintonns'll take their slaves to a'dock just south. When their boat arrives, they'll sail down the Ratna River toward Starsgard. They get on that boat, 'tis over."

"But the boat comes at different times." Sammy buried a new twig. "Usually first thing in the mornin', sometimes in the middle of the eve. If we leave now, we can get to the river within an hour, then we play the waitin' game."

"Then let's hurry up and wait." It seemed a clever maxim, though Hendrix had simply recalled his brother's favorite saying. The youngster took lead, sprinting forward with a reinvigorated spirit. No one had a chance for rebuttal.

* * *

The stone walls on both sides of Hendrix were grey, though tonight's darkness had rendered them colorless, even from a mere five forearms away. "Slow down." Hendrix began to fatigue.

Sammy and Drake were fast, Jakko uncatchable. Their well-timed movements informed Aypax that this was a path they'd taken before. The city of Baa was void of all life, yet full of demolished buildings, a maze of stone and sand that only a dog's keen eyes could navigate without light.

"Gem Street!" Drake pointed to a wooden sign illuminated by moonlight. Sammy took her cue and ascended the side of a three-story ruin.

Finally catching them, Hendrix bent over and dry-heaved, nearly puking a stomachful of seed residue and booze. Even Aypax held both hands overhead while taking in the vulgar stench from Hendrix's breath...a stench he recognized. Aypax ignored that for now.

Sammy reached the building's peak and scanned a vast horizon.

"No boats!"

"Thank the tides." Drake sat on a piece of stone and took to his pipe whilst Sammy descended.

"How can you see them from such a distance?" Aypax held back another cough.

"The docks have a long row of torches and lanterns," said Sammy, landing beside them. "I can see just enough."

"They'll camp about a' hundred span from our position." Drake held his hand over the pipe's flame, blocking wind and drizzle. "Let's set up here and keep an eye on 'em. Given there's no boat, they'll stay put for awhile. We make our move when they sleep, or get too drunk ta' function—"

"Paaaaatttttttaaaa!" A mewl erupted from above.

Aypax searched the skies. "*Ramos, Pattar!*" Once visible, he waved Pattar to his shoulder, but the bird missed and crashed hard into wet sand. Sammy and Jakko jumped back instinctively, both taking animalistic positions. Hendrix calmed them as Aypax made for his Askari. Pattar's torso bled. Its feathers were torn and scratched. The creature nestled into Aypax's chest as he knelt and held it in both arms.

"Patttaa," it screeched, much quieter than before. Pattar released a letter from its talons.

Aypax took the letter, fighting tears. He scanned its contents, then quickly understood what had happened to his beloved Askari.

17

TAAIVETTI

The Basement

Taaivetti roped his way through the dark tunnel once again. Funneled winds assaulted his chapped lips, stinging a growing blemish. Worse, an ugly rash had taken root upon the bottom of his chin. The prince hated both, having glared at himself in the mirror of his personal quarters some two hours prior, wondering how best to get rid of them. But as time drew on, his mind was on one thing and one thing only.

The truth.

This particular journey through the tunnel felt longer than ever, but Taaivetti did arrive at its end. Tossing a new pair of gloves and the spiked rope aside, he entered the alley of the sibyls.

"I cannot say I am surprised," announced the Arch Sibyl, sitting in her usual position high above. "Our visitors, they always return. Now, bow."

Bow.

Taaivetti had once despised the word and all that it stood for. He'd nearly left this place and thrown away his chances at gaining any answers upon his first visit, just over the sheer audacity. But then, he cared far less these days. Dropping to one knee, he obeyed.

"Disrobe!" she shouted, never bothering to stand.

The many sibyls took to the edge of their caves as Taaivetti followed instruction. Looking down at his forearm fur, the prince could see each strand rising with discomfort, or perhaps withdrawal. His skin itched, his muscles ached. He wondered if he was tired… or truly addicted.

The women pulsed with energy, eager for a view and the calling of their name.

"Redbird, who amongst us in in season?" asked the Arch Sibyl.

Redbird stepped out of her cave, licked her palm and lifted it toward the sky. Closing both eyes, she announced, "Redheart! Our beloved Redheart has come of age. She is in season for the first time. She shall produce a woman."

This time, the ladies did not moan nor groan. Instead, they seemed pleased by such a decision, understanding.

Long past honoring their traditions, Taaivetti stepped up the familiar marble path, exhausted. He noticed a few fires deep inside caves with lizard meat cooking on sticks. Tongue salivating, he almost wished he could crawl in. The sound of drumming overtook his ears as the sibyls began their ritualistic patting of the mountain. Taaivetti waited for the inevitable sight of Redheart, the inevitable feeling of disgust.

"Hello."

A voice came from behind. It wasn't exactly alluring, though it wasn't off-putting either. Taaivetti spun round and took her in.

She was *beautiful.*

At least as beautiful as one could be coming from such a place. The red sand pasted to her lower body sent heat flowing through his, and her long red locks framed an attractive face with creamy skin almost as bronzed as his own. A spray of freckles painted her nose.

The prince tried to speak. Failed. Redheart walked toward him, a mixture of excitement and nerves strewn across her rosy, nova-burnt cheeks.

"You know what we require," said the Arch Sibyl, already

stepping down with her wooden box. "It is a simple exchange."

Taaivetti stared at the box, then slowly moved his pupils toward the shelves of liquids and herbs. His lip quivered, lusting for the hallucinogens. The herbs and flowers were blackened and old, yet something about them appeared tasty, enticing. Taaivetti grinned stupidly as he thought of the high he'd soon feel and the knowledge he'd soon obtain.

The Arch Sibyl gave a smug smirk and removed the grey pouches of dust from within her box. "What do we search for tonight? Or are you merely here for other reasons?"

"Show me the rest of that day. The Peace Parade. Taryn, Hendrix, my mother." Taaivetti's chin began to itch. He reached up to scratch the sores. "Pick up precisely where we left."

His itchiness could've frightened Redheart, yet she walked forward unaffected, having seen this before from Taaivetti and the few others to ever make their way into the alley of the sibyls. She gave him a simple smile and tugged at the fabric across her chest, letting her nipple covering flutter to the floor as she moved onto the table.

* * *

Taaivetti blinked and pinched himself, his usual to ensure this wasn't real...

The air was thick, the commotion imminent. No longer in the room's corner like last time, he found himself in its center, beside his father's sickbed. Soon, he would finally see the truth of his parents' demise, the authenticity of his sister's letter.

Taryn still leaned upon the windowsill while Hendrix lingered in the doorway. Everything seemed precisely how he'd left it. Then there was the queen. Motionless, looking down into the oval sickbed, wearing an expression Taaivetti could not describe.

"Mother!" shouted Hendrix.

Taaivetti spun toward his younger brother.

He paused.

Everything in the room stood still. It seemed time itself halted as he began to feel a slight pain in his chest.

"Taaivetti!"

The Arch Sibyl's voice…seemingly from above, or perhaps everywhere at once.

His pain doubled, forcing him to the ground.

"Something's wrong!" she cried, her tone more worried than he'd ever heard. "There is a blocking, Prince, a blocking to my gift. Speak of another time. Do so now and do so quickly! *Speak of another time!*"

The prince raced through his memories as fast as he could, his mind swirling for any moment that could possibly be of use. "As a child…" he mumbled. "I—I was near her, Taryn. We were above the basement. I recall a voice, a horrible dreaded voice, but I couldn't see who it belonged to!"

* * *

Taaivetti opened his eyes yet again. Peeking down, he noticed both hands. They were smaller, much smaller. His entire body was. *I'm me,* he thought, taking in his youthful limbs.

He found himself in an Alyonian alleyway. Cobblestone, wide and dimly lit. Candles and lanterns protruded through the occasional window, illuminating a group of Alyonian girls some twenty paces ahead. Even now he recognized them immediately.

"You're weird!" shouted the eldest of them. She was a leggy Alyonian, at least for her age. Flanked by four other adolescents, she likely led this group. "Give me that!"

Taaivetti focused his eyes beyond them where he saw young Taryn sitting alone on the highest step of a small staircase leading down to a basement. No older than forty seasons, Taryn had yet to even bleed. Her hair seemed shorter, her posture less confident. She was innocent, sweet—and surrounded.

"No, it's mine," young Taryn pleaded.

The long-legged Alyonian shoved Taryn and grabbed a small notebook from her hands. "Let's see." Her accomplices laughed as the bully read Taryn's diary aloud, ripping and tossing the pages aside one by one. "At prayers the priest takes me in his chambers for private instruction; this makes Mother glad, that I am receiving such attention. When the door is closed, he reaches in his trousers and pulls out his fleshly grey worm, wriggly then stiff, and stuffs it up inside me. It hurts and hurts, and once I cried, but he struck me and forbade from shouting."

"Stop! Give it *back*!" Taryn squeaked, clawing for the notebook. The bully snickered, shoving her down with ease.

Holding the book out of Taryn's grasp, she kept reading. "He'll butcher me if I tell, he says. Chop off my tail—"

Taryn shrieked, reaching for the diary as one of the other bullies grabbed her by the tail.

"This tail?" she said. "I wish he *had* lopped it off."

"Oh, this is rich," the ringleader said, flipping through the diary. "Look, drawings of Daddy—obsessed with Daddy, are we? And candles, so many candles. Odd. You poor Alyonian. These drawings are dreadful. You're ugly on the outside and in. No talent, no looks. Pity." The others chuckled.

Taaivetti fumed. On one hand, he'd begun to suspect his sister might be responsible for his own nightmarish reality. But now, he felt his stomach drop, his heart going out to her. He yearned to quell her pain.

"Hey!"

Taaivetti swirled to the sound of his own voice. For a moment, he'd forgotten he wasn't truly here. The dreaming prince watched his younger self sprint down the alley, fearlessly headed toward the commotion. The older Taaivetti smiled as the bullies scattered. He'd acted honorably back then...

Taaivetti followed his younger self through this vision, this memory, getting closer to little Taryn with each step. But as he neared, she retreated down the unlit stairs.

"Taryn!" shouted both Taaivettis simultaneously. A weird moment, one that stripped his breath away. The prince swallowed, watching his younger self descend these cobble stairs. He recalled the sinister voice that came next, the voice and moment that tore he and his sister apart.

He was *mere moments* from an answer.

Taaivetti trailed himself down the stairs but stopped intentionally at their midpoint, just far enough to glance through a barred window of the basement itself. Young Taaivetti did not stop, however; he pounded at the door far below.

"Taryn! Open up! Open up! Let me help you!"

But the old Taaivetti had grown wise, or at least he fancied himself as such. Having been caught in the moment, his younger self had never thought to check this window, not 'til it was too late. Pushing his face to the glass, Taaivetti spied on young Taryn, doing all he could to search her surroundings. *Who was there?* his older self wondered. *I heard you...*

Taaivetti watched his young sister collapse in the basement's center, knees to its cold cement, hands palming her tiny face. He watched her cry. The basement door was thick, and as such, he'd never heard her tears. He only heard what came next.

The voice arrived right on cue.

"Tarrryyyn... Syntrilllla..."

Even the old Taaivetti felt his nerve slipping. *Come on, Taaivetti, you're not to be unnerved.*

"Taryyyyn..." The voice sounded slow and whispery, yet so

very loud. "Syntrillllllla."

The prince eyed his young self, who'd suddenly stiffened, terrified by such a voice. He placed his little ear to the door and eavesdropped.

"Taryyyyyn..." continued the voice. "I will rid you of the priestttt..."

Young Taryn's tears doubled as she fell over and curled into herself.

"Syntrillllllla..." hissed the voice.

Taaivetti could take no more. He punched the glass, but his hand went straight through. *I see,* he thought, before walking right through the wall.

The prince dropped a short ways and fell to the chilly basement floor. Unlit, aside from one chandelier hanging above Taryn's head. Its lights flickered as the chandelier itself began to sway and shadows moved quickly overhead. There were barrels in each corner of the room, tables too. Taaivetti squinted, trying his best to identify this voice.

"Tarynnnnn...I will rid you—"

The voice stopped. Taaivetti held still, careful not to move a muscle. His eyes shot back and forth, surveying every crevice of the room. They darted past the barrels, behind them, under the tables and many boxes of stored grain. He could see no one, no more shadows either.

What's happening? he thought. *I recall the voice speaking much more. It spoke much more! It spoke of my father and summoning some—*

* * *

Taaivetti shot up on the warm table once again, his deep breaths nearly choking him. The Arch Sibyl stood behind, as she usually did. But this time, this time she didn't move. Her grey pupils had returned to normal and her body aches did not occur. The Arch Sibyl, it seemed, was confused.

"What happened?" asked Taaivetti, feeling much of the same pain he'd grown accustomed to.

The Arch Sibyl did not speak nor look up, keeping her gaze on the table.

"I asked you a question!" Taaivetti fumed. "We had an agreement!"

"There is a blockage," she whispered. "Powerful. I have lived for one thousand years."

Taaivetti stared, unsure how to respond to the claim. "And?"

"And I have never seen such a thing."

18

AYPAX

Things Untold

Jakko laid flat on his back, sprawled out awkwardly upon the warm floor of an old ruin's kitchen. Located on the fourth story, time had turned this kitchen into a mess of debris with walls shattered from the outside, creating broad openings for everyone to look out far and wide. The group had been here for some time. Sir Edmund Drake thought it four hours, though Aypax disagreed with that estimate. He claimed the booze had distorted Drake's judgment, a claim he immediately regretted.

"And just so ya know." Drake stumbled against a chipped wall, bottle in hand. "Me senses only increase as I get more and more drunkeden." Drake knelt beside Sammy and gave her a tiny sip.

Aypax glared from across the barren room. "It would be best if you were clear of mind during this." He held Pattar's letter; it was his own letter for Taaivetti, returned. *Pattar never even made it to Hann.*

"Don't judge us." Sammy finished her little guzzle.

"Aye," burped Drake. "We work best this way."

Ignoring them, Aypax evaluated Pattar. "He must have been intercepted by a few Askari. One alone could not stop him."

"Could've been arrows?" Hendrix nodded to the creature's cuts.

"No, the scratches are too small. Someone did not want our letter reaching Taaivetti. We know who. But how did she find Pattar?

Taryn has no Askari in The Red Sand Desert, nor Kornilious. And Pattar knows to fly undetected." Aypax stood and walked toward a rusty stairwell. Worn steps of jagged iron led down the side of this once inhabited complex. "We must find another way of getting word to Taaivetti. I must think. Whistle when it's time."

Drake gave Aypax a sarcastic salute, then plopped beside Jakko. The dog's eyes remained fixated on the Bintonns.

Hendrix's eyes, however, hadn't left the pages of his little white book. Not for hours.

Prophetics 3—Rain

1. The enemy is real, the war is to come,
2. What better time for martyrdom,
3. When the rain does stop, it shall be time,
4. For the king's son to end his line,
5. Thirty-three moons it shall continue to pour,
6. The rain's end shall start the war.

The rain's end shall start the war.

Hendrix reflected upon the troublesome passage. "*Thirty-three moons it shall continue to pour.*" *That would leave ten moons 'til thirty-three consecutive passings. Is 'the king's son' Taaivetti?* The prophetic puzzle was rapidly becoming another brain ache, though holding the book somehow comforted him. Perhaps a subconscious reminder of his mother.

Forget it.

He shut the book, then made for the eroded staircase. "Aypax?"

Hendrix stumbled to the stairs, tired and tipsy from hours of sharing Drake's bottle. Stepping carefully, he peered down at the unstable steps. A single door had been swung open from each story below, presumably bringing old residents out onto the raggedy stairs as they fled their homes during the Bintonns' uprising. Ripped from their hinges, these doors now dangled from their frames, each painted with smeared emblems of the Bintonns anarchy.

"Careful." Aypax's head stuck out of a doorway below and stole Hendrix's attention.

A good thing. For Hendrix looked down to see his right foot lingering in midair, preparing to step out onto a missing stair. He refocused. Placing one hand over his promise bracelet, he descended cautiously. It wasn't long 'til he arrived at Aypax's door. This one seemed different from the others. The wooden door was completely intact, perhaps modern. Hendrix inspected its knob.

"In here!" roared Aypax from farther inside.

Hendrix entered the room. This floor was quite dissimilar from the fourth. Newer. *Or at least not in total ruin.* More strange, was the room's lack of clutter. The furniture remained untouched by sand, dust, or debris. A few tapestries hung, depicting odd images. Flames, books, frightening creatures with wings and claws. Hendrix turned away and kept searching. "Aypax?"

"Do you need a map?"

Hendrix followed the voice, quickly noticing a stack of children's clothes and a tattered red robe hanging from a rack near the door. *Strange.*

Next came a few finger paintings on the stone walls. He leaned in, had to, given such intense darkness. Moonlight pressed through the room's open walls and windows, lending him barely enough to see. Hendrix ran his bruised hand along a particular painting, spooked. The painting showed a tall and mighty shadow, black as the deepest depths of sea. The shadow looked down upon hundreds of worshippers. Some knelt at its feet, others erected an incredible temple of gold and marble. Dreary clouds parted in the red sky behind as flames sprang from the ground beneath. Green smog filled the backdrop.

"That is the Shadow God known as Stralli." Aypax stood in the hallway, watching. "Stralli is the ruler of night, king of the realm of torment—"

"I know who Stralli is. He's all over *The Prophetics*. He's all they talk about in Balonian churches." Hendrix stared trancelike at this painting. The illustration looked masterful, an absolute beauty in all the wrong ways.

Aypax stepped closer. The room's shadows made this painting even more intimidating. He'd grown used to all kinds of iterations when it came to Stralli. Many depicted him as a dark being as large as the Great Trees of Balo. Others had painted Stralli as a mere human. One thing was always a constant however. *Those unforgettable red and green eyes...*

"It's as if his eyes are scratching my stomach." Hendrix grimaced. "Dark. Depressing."

"We live in a dark and depressing world."

"And is that...Elo?" Hendrix pointed to another finger painting done in a different style. Peaceful, loving. A simple rendition of a winged god floating beside the stars.

Aypax examined it. "I believe you correct. Elo, the god of creation. Man's interpretation of our own god Balo. You know the stories. The comets, the magic, the gods who came down with them. Balo, Elo, it's all the same shit."

Hendrix snickered. That much they could agree upon. "Oh, I know Elo. The Rhi Empire have stated their intent to murder anyone who doesn't worship him. Mother told me they believe Elo created the sickness to deal with the city of Coyo's unclean heathens. They believe he's punishing them for their iniquities." Hendrix shook his head. "And yet they also deem him a merciful god."

"She spoke truly," said Aypax. "Though it isn't only Coyo. Bandano-Rhi's holy order has been secretly slaughtering unbelievers all over, hoping to appease Elo. Their gaining of land and riches along the way is a happy coincidence."

Chuckling, Hendrix moved to a connecting corridor. "Whilst we speak of disturbing topics, I've a question."

Aypax followed. "Shocking."

"Where were you last night? I awoke, and you were gone."

Aypax exhaled as they came to a final room and looked out through a surprisingly unscathed window of glass. "When I thought you asleep, I traveled a bit deeper into the woods to a cabin I knew of." Aypax shifted, pained. "I was searching for someone very special to me. Katrin."

"Katrin?"

Aypax revealed the blue box. "She was the most beautiful soul I've ever known." He opened it. A golden bracelet rested tightly inside, with red and blue crystals embedded onto its surface. It glimmered a radiant sadness, aching to be worn. "A Tourtoufian of unmatched beauty. I met her many seasons ago while I was garrisoned here on Tourtoufa. The Honorable-Six were given a few eves off duty, so she and I shared food and ale. Even Taaivetti met her."

Hendrix's eyes widened. Everyone loved stories of the esteemed prince, even his own brother.

"She adored him," continued Aypax. "Your brother saw something between us and immediately changed my assignment. Without telling the High Council, he elected a new executioner and ordered the Honorable-Six were only to return home once I'd learned to sail a five-mast high-deck by myself, or wed Katrin. Whichever came first."

"That sounds precisely like Taaivetti." Hendrix laughed.

Aypax smiled sadly. "She and I spent countless moons together, growing close and falling in love. I felt it the moment I saw her. She silenced the voices in my head, Hendrix, the voices of all those I'd sent to the warrior stars. War is wretched enough, but the execution stage, those who squirmed in their final moments…I still hear them in my head every night. Eventually, I purchased this bracelet and extended my invitation for marriage."

"She sounds wonderful, Aypax. Though I'm surprised she saw anything in you..." They both laughed a bit before Hendrix continued. "Equally surprised Taaivetti ever lied to the High Council."

Aypax closed the box and killed his emotions. "Yes, Taaivetti's taken the Council rather seriously ever since. With enough time to fester, a harmless lie becomes a harmful dagger to your conscious."

"I suppose so." Madison suddenly flashed before Hendrix's eyes. "Well, what happened? To Katrin?"

"She said yes." Aypax closed his eyes and exhaled a heavy sigh. "Then I caught her on her knees, swallowing another Tourtoufian. I couldn't believe what I was seeing, and in a rage I struck her and butchered him. She screamed and fled...never returned." Aypax drew a deep breath, reliving the pain. "I sailed home the next morn, with the sound of her screams replacing the dreadful voices that once inhabited my head. It wasn't 'til many seasons later that I received word from her and discovered it was her husband I'd killed."

Hendrix's eyes widened.

"Her son took his life shortly after. Then her sister. They say self-slaughter is contagious..." Aypax trailed off, as if the horrible thought had perhaps crossed his own mind in times past. "Somewhere along the way, without friends or family to take her in, Katrin became a brothel gal...selling herself at a whorehouse in the woods."

"Bloody Perdition. My brother knows of this?"

"No. When Taaivetti inquired, I told him that Katrin denied my invitation for marriage. It was the first time I ever lied, and to the very prince I'm sworn to protect. Perhaps Sir Edmund Drake was right."

Perhaps my honor already changed.

A long silence ensued. "That's why you took us into that forest? Why we were 'lost'? You knew we'd wind up in Baa."

"Some three seasons ago I received my bracelet and a letter

from Katrin's matriarch. She wrote that Katrin had intended to leave her husband before I killed him, but feared his wrath, for he was a Bintonn. She then wrote that Katrin had been taken from their cabin in the midst of night, stolen by the Bintonns after hearing what took place. Apparently, I was her only remaining acquaintance. She pleaded for my aid."

"After all she suffered, why turn to a brothel? Coin?"

"Perhaps she became what she felt she truly was…The mind can be an awful thing. I've yearned to mend my relations with her ever since. I requested two trips of leave during last Snowy Season. Both were denied by the High Council. Kornilious runs Alyonia's branch of defense. Seems he wanted to keep the Honorable-Six in Alyonia during the Peace Parade. Now I know why."

Drake whistled from above.

"I left you last night so that I might go and ask Katrin's matriarch for any clues on how best to track her," Aypax continued. "When I arrived, their cabin was burnt to the ground. No bodies."

Hendrix heard the scuffling of paws and boots as their companions came down the stairs. He looked Aypax in the eyes. "She's out there. I feel it."

19

HENDRIX

A Thief in the Night

Drake led the group toward the sleeping Bintonns a few blocks ahead. "One more crossroads an' we arrive. All clear on jobs?"

Everyone nodded, then crouched behind a broken carriage and surveyed their enemy. Well over twenty Bintonns there were, with twice as many enslaved laying in a field beside the Ratna River. Horses, tents, and a few guards surrounded the bonded group. Hendrix didn't like being so close, even with the night rendering his companions nearly invisible.

"Those torches an' lanterns'll light us up the moment we get near, so do your part fast." Drake pointed out the torches. "There's about twenty Bintonns in total, but I'm only seein' three or four guards awake. Let's keep it that way." Drake turned to Jakko, then pointed down an alleyway. "Jakko, grrr, grrr."

The dog took off.

Drake nodded a *good luck* to Sammy, then led both Alyonians toward the Ratna's waterline.

"Gggggrrrrr…" Jakko's growl sounded aggressive but not loud. "Gggggrrrr…" His second was loud indeed.

"Perfect." Sammy grinned as three Bintonns stood and moved toward Jakko, drawing blades and raising lanterns. With the guards now gone, Sammy sprinted straight into the heart of their camp. *Come on, come on,* she thought.

Sammy ran by sleeping captives and sleeping Bintonns alike. This low to the ground, her enemies were finally eye level. Smiling, she leapt over a few torsos and sidestepped expensive Bintonn bags.

I know you're here, ya little skweek.

Weaving under an unheated pot of water, she expertly avoided spots of light from sporadic torches along the way. Finally, she saw it. *Bingo.*

Sammy's eyes locked onto a hefty set of keys attached to a wooden stake between a group of snoozing Bintonns. The keys were ripe for the taking. Well, almost. There was one problem. One very large problem.

"Scent hounds," Sammy said and sighed, loud enough to realize she was still intoxicated. "Oh no."

The hounds raised their ears, opened their eyes. Necks lifted as two sets of black pupils peered straight in Sammy's direction but found nothing. She'd managed to scurry behind the leg of the nearest sleeping slave.

Calm down, calm down. Sammy's concern seemed justified. Bintonns could be outran; scent hounds could not.

"It's a mutt! Ain't no feral dogs to worrys overs!"

The scent hounds' attention shot to their masters closing in on Jakko. Leaping to their feet, the hounds darted toward the commotion.

Sammy moved for the keys but caught something on the periphery. Turning back, she squinted at the leg she'd just hidden behind. Slowly, she inspected two rusty shackles tied round the slave's skinny calves.

Sammy smiled. Sweet destiny had shown her face tonight, and she was *beautiful.*

"Slap me with a sack of coins." The shackles couldn't be more clear.

14

Sammy crawled alongside the sleeping captive's torso, sniffing up toward her face. *Ava.* Using Ava's head as cover, Sammy gazed out at the key chain, making sure her path remained clear. *Ale gods be with me.* Sammy bolted for the keys.

Sliding by a few snoozing Bintonns, she sprung onto a wooden stake, attaching herself with the grace of an acrobat. Sammy scanned the keys, carefully reading each. *10, 8, 22, 36, 33.* She was almost reading aloud. *42, 14, 11, 29, 7—*

"Aha! Fourteen!" she exclaimed too loudly. Sammy dropped from the stake and landed on all fours. She looked up, but no one seemed awake. No sign of the hounds.

"Gggggrrrr…" Jakko's low growl again. This time it sounded different, a warning to the other hounds.

Fearing for her comrade, the drunken squirrel doubled pace. *I'm comin', Jakko. I'm comin'!* Following scratches she'd previously made in the dirt and the scent of her own foul odor, Sammy found her way back to Ava. The difficult part came next.

"Ava, Ava," she whispered. "Wake up."

Using the key, Sammy began unlocking Ava's shackles as quietly as possible. A tough task, even for trained fingers. The key slid in, metal on metal, but a slow insert couldn't stop its inevitable *screeeech.* Sammy cringed as she twisted the key inside a rusty lock. Ava's shackles opened with a sharp *clink,* then fell to the soft dirt. A bit of dust flew up into Sammy's eyes, though she was thankful the coastline's dirt was soft. *That could've been loud.*

Ava's eyes opened, then fixated directly on Sammy, who scratched at the shackles on the ground. Ava's eyes grew wide as she recognized she was free. Sammy made a second gesture, equally calm. She put her nose to the dirt below Ava's jawline. The girl lifted her neck, then read the scratched dirt.

AVA-14

Sammy had cleverly re-scribbled her writing. Ava's cheeks lifted. A smart girl, she said not a word. Her eyes drifted back to Sammy, awaiting orders. Ava knew whoever she'd seen back at the saloon would surely be close. Such a well-trained animal obviously belonged to someone.

Sammy stayed in character, aware that speaking would undoubtedly frighten the young girl. From all fours, the squirrel contorted her body in the direction of a long wooden dock. Three torches were now visible beside it, placed far from the dock itself. Ava nodded, a silent confirmation she understood the signal.

The girl dropped down and began to crawl, slowly following Sammy across camp, across a hot mixture of mud, dirt, and cigar ashes. A full minute passed as the pair inched along in silence. Then Sammy heard scuffling, followed by barking. Far off, but ferocious. Jakko had likely been caught; he was likely in a dogfight. Sammy quickened her pace. *Come on, Jakko.*

Reaching the camp's end, Sammy and Ava made for the river, careful to stick to the darkest path possible. Then Sammy realized the harsh sounds of fighting had ceased. *One dead Jakko, or many dead scent hounds.*

Drunk as she was, Sammy spiraled. The inebriated squirrel may put on a carefree facade, but deep down, she had an itch for family. An itch to fit in. And Jakko was part of her pack.

* * *

"Over here!"

Hendrix watched Sammy and Ava sneak toward his position, his torch acting as a beacon. *They made it.* The duo became clear as they neared his flame, which wavered in the slight rain. Hendrix squinted as Ava approached, then felt a sudden pull. Another fire kindling inside him whilst Ava neared. Shadows and fluorescent glows danced across her face as the torches flickered in the wind beside her. Two chocolate-brown eyes pierced the night itself and found their home in Hendrix's heart. He gulped nervously, then thought of the tasty chocolate Mussa back home in Alyonia. He thought of the deep chocolate eyes of his dearest Madison Preters.

"Have you seen Jakko?" Sammy doubled over with a stomach full of liquor and panic.

"No," said Aypax. "Though I did hear him."

"He ain't back yet," Drake said, clearly troubled.

Ava went straight to Aypax's side, assuming him in charge. Now up close, she didn't smile nor pierce Hendrix's heart. She didn't even notice him. His ego wounded, he tried remaining an enigma.

Drake knelt and pressed the tips of all three torches into the rushing river. Their flames died a quick and painless death. "Quiet." He forced his ear to the ground, occasional waves from the choppy river nearly touching his lobe due to harsh winds. "Listen."

His group heard the rapid pounding of dirt. The incredible pace that could only be set by a hound, a hound they were eager to see. "Now!" Drake jumped to his feet and ran for the dock as fast as he could. "To the boat!" His companions followed.

"Ggggrrrr!" Jakko was indeed closing in. Fast. The thunderous stampede of paws belonged to four scent hounds no more than twenty paces behind him.

Ava followed everyone down the dock, seemingly unafraid and easily keeping pace. As they moved, she noticed four Bintonns floating face down in the shallows, bloody foam surrounding them. Their group came to the end of the small pier, where a maroon vessel drifted— a thirty-foot cog. Tied only to a single cleat, one trusty rope was all that kept this boat from fleeing down the rough Ratna River.

"Get in!" Drake motioned everyone aboard.

Hendrix and Ava obliged, but Aypax drew his axe, choosing to stay on the wooden dock.

"No!" Hendrix pointed to Aypax's pocket, to what they both knew rested inside. "Get in!"

The hounds' loud barks and ferocious sprinting likely woke every Bintonn nearby. Any attempt at subterfuge had perished.

"The boats!" screamed one of the Bintonns, waking and standing. "Gets to thes boats!" The commotion heightened as angry thugs scattered about in a confused frenzy.

Only then did Ava notice the rest of the Bintonns' small vessels floating away down the Ratna. She observed every cleat nearby. They all shared the same remains of bloody, shredded rope. Aypax's hatchet had been *quite useful* this evening. She'd remember that for later.

Jakko let out a sudden squeal, and as he rounded onto the dock, it became apparent as to why.

Rows of torches on the pier illuminated white wood beneath his paws. The white turned pink as Jakko's blood poured down and stained its splintery surface. The blood created a trail, a nasty trail that widened Drake's eyes. It froze him, in fact. Hendrix too. *Jakko's hurting. Bad.*

The horrific sight of his new friend in such pain stirred Aypax's insides; it made him hungry for the vengeance he pretended to never seek. The big Alyonian gripped his hatchet tightly, then lunged toward the incoming pack of scent hounds.

"Ggggrrrr."

Jakko's final growl came out weak and unsettling…a plea. His piercing blue eyes haunted Aypax, perhaps warning him. The bleeding dog was a mere forty forearms away, but slowing…

Aypax felt as though he knew what Jakko wanted. As though

he knew what had somehow been asked.

But his blood boiled as his muscles tightened for combat. "Agh!"

With a ferociously angry swing, Aypax cut the rope from its cleat, setting their cog free. The boat drifted quickly, thanks to the river's powerful current. Fighting one final urge to taste Bintonn blood, Aypax stepped aboard and shoved off.

"No!" Sammy leapt and scratched violently at Aypax's forehead.

"What in the sweet maiden's name are ya doin?" Drake punched Aypax square on the chin, barely missing his own rodent. The big Alyonian fell backward, nearly slipping overboard. He caught himself while Sammy scurried onto a railing, desperately trying to regain her balance.

"Jump!" Hendrix held his hand out over the same railing, and to his surprise, Ava joined him. But as the boat drifted away, Jakko became more blurry with every second.

Sammy regained her balance and now gazed out at the foggy dock. The distance had become much too far, though she'd certainly jump if it meant even a chance at saving Jakko.

She didn't have to.

The gang marveled at what seemed to pass in slow motion. Fur raised, blood flying through brisk winds, legs spread wide, Jakko appeared to fly.

He hit the deck with a bang, clearing the railing by a full arm's length. Aypax looked toward Jakko's pursuers, blade at ready. It wouldn't be needed. The scent hounds pulled their run, stopping short of the dock's edge.

The hounds appeared more fearsome than ever. Those eyes were all anyone could see as their boat moved along the Ratna. Stray arrows descended as shouts of anger and revenge filled the humid air.

But Jakko's gang didn't hear a one of them. They knelt beside the dog, focusing only on his wounds.

House Kaldor

Letter type: Secret, Urgent, Informative
From: Hendrix Kaldor
To: Madison Preters
343 A.B, Windy Season, 94th Moon, Single Moon

INTRO
Madison, my love, my heart goes out to you. I'm safe, and under Aypax's protection. Please do not worry of me. Though I'm sure you already know of my innocence, I write to explain the truth of my situation. More importantly, I write with the hopes that your mother shall look into things and publish my truth in her library's seasonal story papers.

WHAT HAPPENED
When mother and I returned from the Peace Parade, we made our way to the Kaldorian manor sick bay. We were visiting father, who was fighting a severe illness, as you know.

Mother and I arrived at the door, only to be met with two sentries. We'd never seen either sentry in our lives. Upon reflection, this should've prompted suspicion, but in the moment, it did not.

BOTH GUARDS HAD BURN MARKS ON THEIR NECKS.
(This could be important for your mother's work.)

Mother and I entered the sick bay, only to find Taryn leaning against a windowsill. Then it happened.

It's odd how fast our lives can change in a single moment and how our minds react when it does. I don't even remember seeing Taryn cross the room, yet she was there in a flash. Her left arm wrapped round mother, and wielding a sharp blade in the other, Taryn cut her throat.
It was silent. Mother had no chance to scream. She rose two hands to her neck, hoping to stop the blood, but that exposed her chest, allowing Taryn to dig the blade into her heart. She withdrew the weapon as mother fell to her knees, lifeless.

I couldn't move. Quite literally in shock 'til Taryn's harsh screams unfroze me. She tossed her bloody blade on the carpet and ran out the opposite door. Just like that, my limbs functioned once again. I leapt as fast as I could to mother's side. I held her in my arms, but she was gone. And yet, I felt closer to her than ever. I knew I was far too late. Nothing could be done. No last words.

A moment later, the door swung open just as quickly as Taryn had closed it on her way out. Guess who came running in? *The burnt neck guards.* Right then it all made sense. Taryn was framing me for the murder, Prince Taaivetti was gone, Mother and Father were dead, and I would soon be imprisoned. There was no one else. This would make Taryn our new ruler, the queen of Alyonia. Brilliant.

I was dragged into a courtyard below and put to my knees for immediate execution. Then Aypax and your father arrived. Your father saved us, Madison. We owe him our lives.

I lack the ink to continue, but I shall find it and write you again. Have your mother locate Priest Yalino and the blacksmith Justillian. Aypax believes they have more information. Also know that Kornilious is an accomplice of Taryn's, though I am not sure how or why just yet. I can prove all of this, Madison. Don't believe the lies. You have all my love.

Return word only with Pattar. Trust no other flier.

Speak soon,

Hendrix

20

TIANNU

The Preters

Tiannu Preters stared at a clock on the wall. Rows of dusty bookshelves sat beneath the ticking device. These shelves spanned across a very antiquated and perhaps, based on the many walled portraits, family-run library. Silence reigned as the clock glared back at Tiannu, judging her. *Am I doing the right thing?* she wondered. What was right after all? No one seemed to know of late.

"I knew it!" said Madison Preters. The young Alyonian gazed up at her mother from the library's white carpeted floor. Madison sat cross-legged, with Hendrix's damp letter laying flat across her thighs. "There's simply no way! No way Hendrix could ever do such a thing." Madison's sage-green eyes pierced Tiannu's soul. If she hadn't already agreed with her daughter, these would have done the trick.

"Kornilious and Taryn, I knew it!" continued Madison. "Hendrix does not have that in him. It's too terrible, too ruthless." She stood and brushed her bangs out of her eyes. Madison's white hair complemented her light-beige blouse, a milk-and-cream combination. She'd always favored simplicity and preferred to attire herself the same, having no interest in dresses.

"These are ruthless times, love." Tiannu took the wet letter. "Though I agree, Hendrix could not have done it, and Aypax would

159

not lie about what he saw. I believe this letter to be true. And if it is true, the question remains: Why would Kornilious help Taryn? More importantly, how do I approach Priest Yalino? If I'm going to write about this case, I'll clearly need to start with him."

Tiannu gazed down the long and dreadfully empty aisles of her library. "Worse, if it is true...if Taryn killed Queen Lizabeth with Kornilious' aid, we're speaking of the highest crime in Alyonian history."

"All the more reason for you to hurry and publish a story!" Madison chewed her fingernails.

"All the more reason to protect ourselves," countered Tiannu. "If Taryn is willing to go through with such an act, then killing two Alyonians far lower in stature shan't mean much to her. We must keep our own tracks covered. If she or anyone else discovers this letter, they'll string us up by our necks."

Tiannu thought of burning the letter here and now, of forgetting this ever happened. Uncovering the truth of such a horror would certainly mean risking her life, perhaps even the lives of her loved ones. Yet if Hendrix's words were true, they needed to be shared with all of Alyonia. If Taryn could kill her own parents, what *wouldn't* she do? For the sake of the realm, the interim queen needed to be stopped.

"Mom, you must help him." Madison stood. "Think about it—" The ticking clock struck midday, causing them both to jump. "We need to relax. We've been on our toes all day."

"It is a fair thing to worry over." Tiannu began writing on a separate piece of parchment. "What we're contemplating is dangerous, my daughter. Spying on the interim queen, on Kornilious. We shan't worry, you're correct of that. Worrying does no good. Though we do need to make sure we're perfect in our execution. Flawless."

"I know." Madison sat upon a wooden bench. "In truth, something feels off. What if you're caught? What if the High Council is a part of this?" Madison grasped her well-trimmed tail, picked at its fine white furs. "I hate that he's gone. He'd know what to do."

Tiannu knew Madison missed her father, Captain Crimson, who'd been deployed recently. Unfortunately, there wasn't a thing she could do to bring him back. Crimson had been sent to the infamous Lookout. A place farther north than most Alyonians would ever go voluntarily. A nightmarish place. Moreover, Crimson had only just departed, and the travel alone would take weeks, never mind the long duration of his stay.

Tiannu decided to lighten the mood. "Hendrix, or your father?"

Madison's cheeks grew bright red. "Father, of course."

Tiannu pointed at Madison's *H.K.* bracelet. "You'll see him again." She walked around her work desk and hugged her daughter tightly. "Listen carefully, love. You're one of the wisest young Alyonians I know. But don't overestimate yourself. If we're to help Hendrix, we must be smart."

Tiannu walked to a separate workstation covered in parchment and writing utensils. Quills, chalks, gels, even coal. "If I accept this case and publish our library's story paper on it, everything shall change." She lifted a small jar filled with chunky black ink, then returned to her desk. "With the election so close, it's likely the candidates will try to cover up past wrongdoings. Especially Kornilious."

Madison squirmed at the name. It'd been said one too many times today.

Kornilious had a reputation in Alyonia, for better or worse, and was officially up for reelection in nine moons. Adored by his party for multiple terms, the Novellusians loved him with every fiber. The Vetusian party, however, were more than ready for a change.

"If Kornilious is truly a part of this murder..." Tiannu kept scratching her parchment. "He shan't go down lightly. I cannot begin my research unless you promise to be wise and careful. If anyone inquires of this library, or of your father, you know what to say. You must swear to never overstep."

Madison gulped. "I don't think I could, even if I wished."

Tiannu chuckled and rolled her letter, then bound it with thread. "It's settled then. I shall send this letter to your father. He must know of our actions."

Madison gazed at her mother, knowing the consequences should their letter be intercepted.

"The election is in nine moons." Tiannu's voice revealed the gravity of the situation, yet it carried a hint of excitement. "That means Kornilious and his team shall act fast. I must act faster. If we're correct, then I'd guess Taryn and Kornilious' plot doesn't end at royal assassination. I'd guess it is bigger than we can imagine. And that means they'll stop at nothing to achieve it."

Madison felt a sharp and sudden stomach pain. Their situation was worsening. "Where shall you begin?"

Tiannu opened a library window, revealing a long wooden railing running along its outside edge. This railing was covered in dried bird poop, scratches, and dents; messenger birds tended to land aggressively. Looking out, Tiannu's family library appeared even larger than usual. The building played home to far more than books and letters, however. It had become a hub for information, a place of local study and prayer.

Tiannu whistled. In mere seconds, three birds flocked from nearby rooftops and landed upon the railing. "We begin here." Tiannu attached her letter to a strong yellow-winged Askari. "Tonight, I'll go find Priest Yalino and these burnt-neck guards."

21

CRIMSON

A Long Ride Home

Captain Crimson's dark green eyes scanned back and forth across the letter, his frown growing deeper with every line. *Why? Why would she do such a thing?*

But that seemed a foolish question. Crimson knew precisely why Tiannu Preters needed to risk her life, why she needed to heed Hendrix's letter and discover the truth for herself. He loved her even more for it. *The purest of hearts.* A fitting nickname he'd given her long before they were even wed.

Tiannu's secret letter had found its way safely to her husband. Her handwriting exquisite, her prose wise. Subtle jokes and marital puns were woven through each shocking paragraph.

Finishing the letter, Crimson exhaled, then looked up at a cloudy sky. Dreary, yet alluring, with light patterns of snow peppering the scene before him. The northwestern landscape had always been breathtaking, even after twenty-three moons of constant rain.

Crimson's company hadn't made it very far from Alyonia, for it had been a hard trip. The surrounding mountains created a deep gorge, a long basin of slippery snow and rock. Trekking on Naomiback had been undeniably beautiful, though a slow way of travel. Snowcapped trees and boulders filled this gorge, and the ground itself rose and fell often. Rapid rivers streamed in each direction, pleasant to look at but difficult to navigate.

Crimson knew the terrain would change for the worse shortly, so he enjoyed the gorge's tranquility. His followers, however, were already quivering at the notion of their destination, at the thought of missing their families, at the growing cold.

Snowflakes grew thicker with each mile, sticking to the surface of Crimson's letter, dampening his wife's lovely work. That was fine; he'd have to burn the letter anyway. Crimson crumbled the flimsy parchment inside the palm of his brown leather glove. He only wore the one, however. His right hand remained bare, always. "Lukon!" shouted Captain Crimson.

"Yes, Captain?" Lukon called as he kicked the side of his Naomi and galloped to catch up with the company's point rider.

Crimson always took point in the group's riding order, a wise strategy. While riding ahead, his thick shoulder fur and dark green hood masked any facial expressions from those riding behind. This allowed him to never break his steely character. He could gaze at a lily, tilt his head and bask in the rare nova light. He could even hide the occasional smile, should any fond memories of Tiannu strike. He could read in peace— maps, news, perhaps even a letter…

"Add this to the burn pile, but do it yourself." Captain Crimson handed Lukon the crumpled note. "We'll stop at the foot of Roderic's Ridge and make camp. Have the new recruits set out for timber."

Crimson trotted ahead, reestablishing his preferred position and letting everyone know he was not to be disturbed.

If Taryn or Kornilious discover that Tiannu is investigating them, they'll have her head before I could possibly return. And with Kornilious' renomination, he'll have someone protecting him in secret, perhaps even covering his tracks. Crimson inhaled a breath of cold air. *But I can't go home now. To do so would be obvious. Too obvious. I've only one option.*

Crimson's attention was stolen by a thunderous sneeze, the

type that could only belong to one creature. A Naomi. A sick one at that.

Crimson turned to find the ill beast, but his company had grown perhaps forty strong, each mounted on a different Naomi. The animals were tough, far more resilient than the horses of man. Still, even they would struggle through the coming elements.

"Report to the front!" Crimson frowned. A terrible thing needed doing. Strong as the Naomi were, they were doubly susceptible to sickness. One contagious creature could mean forty Alyonians on foot, and that wasn't an option where this group was headed.

"Report to the front!" Crimson sounded more aggressive.

The harsh command worked.

A skinny Alyonian pulled his Naomi from behind a few black wagons toward the rear of their ranks. The Alyonian recruit galloped around all of Emerald Company. Steering his sick beast skillfully, he halted beside Crimson. "What are your orders, Captain?"

The skinny recruit stroked his ill companion's fluffy mane. Crimson wondered whether the act was genuine, or a subtle way of asking for mercy.

"How bad is she?"

"Hard to say." The sad recruit's Naomi whimpered but remained strong. They were born for long journeys, and as such, made perfect escorts for Crimson's company.

But the road ahead shall be tough, thought Crimson. *And this batch hasn't ridden in some time.* "We'll set camp shortly." Crimson looked his recruit in the eyes. "Our apothecary shall take a look. If it's a no, bring her two leagues south and bury her. I don't want wolves smelling her at night."

Crimson studied the gorgeous Naomi. Her white mane flowed down the animal's graceful neck and shined bright. *It blends perfectly with the snow.* Her posture remained powerful, even while ill. He wondered if she knew what was happening and gave her best efforts to impress. She twisted her head in circles, showing off two perfect horns. *So symmetrical, so pretty.*

The Alyonian recruit saluted, then rode back to his position.

"Moving!" shouted Captain Crimson.

"Move!" a handful of rugged Alyonians responded. They were positioned on every side of the expedition. Two in the rear, one to the east and west. These were older Alyonians, battle hardened, with nasty scars to prove it. They encircled Emerald Company like cattle herders.

"Point check!" Crimson roared again.

"Check!" echoed the same group.

One might expect these riders to be wearing boisterous armor. But their stocky furs hid any evidence if they did, as did their matching pine-green capes flapping in the wind.

Crimson was merely testing his leaders' awareness, a great way to keep cold minds sharp, and sharp they would need to remain.

* * *

Night fell quickly, hardening the once flowing rivers into blocks of ice that surrounded Crimson's camp. The camp's location was no accident; the frozen water made Roderic's Ridge a perfect place of rest. Ice is tricky, and even wolves can lose their footing.

Five fires were lit throughout the encampment, attempting to lighten a thick and frosty mist. Frigid riders snuggled closely to these flames, some on logs, others wrapped around their travel sacks. Two wagons were positioned in the back of camp, resting beneath the soaring ridge itself.

Lukon sat inside a wagon, his legs dangling off its edge. With both brows furrowed, he took vicious bites from a flabby chicken breast. Bone in mouth, Lukon sneered, angry with the shivering recruits.

"This might be the most worthless lot yet," said Gable, one of the green-caped Alyonians. The others flanked him, as did Captain Crimson. These leaders leaned against their hefty wagon holding chicken and ale. There was even some salmon and rock-hard potatoes.

"You're tellin' me." Lukon's northern accent sounded thick, even for this group. He held his glare upon the recruits, more annoyed with each bite. "If they believe this to be cold, they're not gonna last a day at the Lookout. I oughta go out there and smack some toughness into 'em."

"It's the damned standard testing," added Gable with an equally hard inflection. "No one in their proper minds would ever sign up for this job anymore. So those bastards in the High Council lowered the standards."

"They aren't signin' up." Lukon brushed snow from atop his cold chicken breast. "They're being forced in. Look at 'em, absolutely miserable. I'm surprised we haven't had to track down any deserters yet."

"Give it time." Gable's crooked teeth ripped at a bite of uncooked salmon, half of which fell into his white beard. "We had six last Windy Season. And that was before we even made it to the Lookout. I miss the ole days, when we had a real reason to be doin' it."

"We still have reason." Lukon spoke to Gable but appeared to be convincing himself. "What we don't have are decent recruits."

Crimson shared Lukon's feelings, though he also knew the value of proper training. Anyone could be taught anything; these prospects were no different. Crimson had become a renowned trainer, even to his own displeasure. "Don't forget how far you've come, Lukon." Crimson smirked at his youngest green cape.

"Aye! You were a proper shit squeak when we took ya in," echoed Gable. "If I recall, I had to knock some sense into ya once or twice!"

Lukon leapt from the wagon's edge and took to his feet. "I'd like to see ya do that now, ya fat lard."

The Green Capes cheered. These Alyonians were close, and

banter was the only way to stay sane out here.

"I may've put on a few pounds." Gable patted his stomach. "But it's only to keep me warm. I'll still put your arm on its prissy little side!"

Even Crimson joined in. "Now that I'd like to see. A proper arm grapple."

Lukon locked hands with Gable, preparing for the contest of strength. "Count of three," said Lukon. "One, two—" Before finishing, he slid around Gable with an arm-drag and tossed him to the ground. Everyone laughed as the two wrestled playfully.

"I said arm grapple! Not proper grapple!" Gable still chewed a mouthful of salmon while foolishly attempting to defend himself.

Loud howls bloomed in the distance, freezing the group to a halt. Lukon stood. "They're close."

"And we're many." Crimson pulled his green hood overhead. "They're smart animals. They won't come near this crowd." Crimson meant what he said, but even he had never been sure. "Let's get some rest. Watch is set for the eve. We make for the Crossing at first light."

The group moaned. "Aye yai yai, the Crossing…"

Gable roared with them. "If any of those men so much as *look* at me in the wrong manner, they might just find this boot of mine shoved up their ass!"

"They're gonna stare, and they're gonna try to demean ya. Ya look like a damned snowman." Lukon referenced Gable's fat stomach and white beard. "It's who they are, naturally hateful. 'Specially at the Crossing."

Gable lifted his mug into the air. "Agreed. I'll need a clear head for that. The men there…sometimes I'd prefer the Gorsh."

"You've never seen a Gorsh!" spat Lukon.

Gable nodded. "Other than your mother! And cheers to her, aye!"

The Green Capes laughed before smashing their silver mugs together, then downed the remainder of their ale.

22

TARYN

Cunning

Taryn flanked Trakkonious in the back seat of a modest open-top carriage. One hundred Naomi-mounted riders surrounded, trotting alongside, their green and gold armor flapping as they escorted the interim queen out of Alyonia's southern farmlands. A dirt road below made for bumpy riding, yet Taryn remained unfazed, her attention resting solely upon hungry crowds of farmers clapping on either side of the road.

"I'm glad you heeded my choice of carriage," said Trakkonious, waving out to the cheering masses. "Past reports have shown the public's struggle to resonate with the crown flaunting their wealth, particularly our farmers. I believe this approach to be a winning strategy. The more they share in common with you, the more they empathize. A fancier carriage would've portrayed us as out of touch with their many issues."

Taryn waved to her Alyonians, subtly whispering to Trakkonious between smiles. "Such strategies are why I keep you around, Trakkonious."

The High Public Heed gave a laugh. "And a brilliant choice to leave soldiers here in the farmlands for protection. Not a soul would ever guess the crop fires were your doing in the first place."

Trakkonious waved to a group of soldiers dispersing bread baskets and preparing the beginning woodwork for lookout towers.

"The crop fires will continue," said Taryn. "So long as our realm relies upon Bandano-Rhi for grain and crop, our public will support an eventual withdrawal from the accord...With limited harvest of our own, we can also force trade with the Rhi Empire and easily provide an empathetic reason to increase our citizens' seasonal tributes. Preem is already aware."

Trakkonious nodded. "Then disperse the newly levied coin between Rhi and our wealthiest house patrons? They above all, must be kept happy."

"Our patrons have seen the beginnings—and benefits—of the societal changes they wish to usher in. This alone keeps them happy. Have you arranged the pirateering of our supply ships?"

"I have." Trakkonious opened a bag of cheese and ate, ensuring the crowd saw his choice of affordable meal. "I've ordered four supply ships pirateered on their way back from Gondol. Tomorrow's story papers are ready to pen the tragedy."

"And you're sure this to be the correct move? I fear the public will think I'm incapable of defending my own ships."

"Have trust, my queen." Trakkonious grinned. "As our enemies grow more brave, the public will see such hostile acts as our rivals attempting to take advantage of Alyonia's fallen king and queen. The transition of power is always a great time for adversaries to strike. But you see, that is precisely when we will insert you. With Taaivetti absent, our citizens will witness you taking action against our would-be attackers; they'll see you hanging these pirateers you so brilliantly captured. And with Bandano-Rhi's aid to our famine, they'll follow you into a stronger alliance, and in time, support our withdraw from the Pallala Accord."

"I indeed trust." Taryn gazed out past the masses and into a green pasture some distance off the road. Heaps of finely crafted lumber and fishing nets created a playground surrounding an old barn, filled with squealing Alyonian youth. "Alert the Night Raiders of this town. Have them visit in a few moons."

"Understood. Speaking of the Night Raiders, does Bandano-Rhi know of the children?"

"Of course not." Taryn smiled outwardly, yet her tone went harsh. "Don't be a fool. He knows the Night Raiders burn our crop fields and raid our realm's caravans. That's all he knows."

Trakkonious bowed, though he had trouble forgetting Taryn and Bandano-Rhi's unclothed encounter. *I surely hope.*

"That said," she continued, "I have begun to mark a few humans as my own. They're quite traitorous by nature, and many have already joined us underground."

"You've my caution," said Trakkonious. "Bandano-Rhi is rather wise, and many of his traitors could yet be insiders. If he discovers our true intentions, the greater plan is lost."

Taryn turned to him, her eyes forcing another submissive bow. "Anything else, Trakkonious?"

* * *

Taryn's royal party had been escorted through the southern gates of Alyonia, then made their way past lively markets where a few performers on stilts entertained in the gloomy rain. Taryn's carriage had passed pottery mills on the city outskirts as well, wisely built a safe distance from the town's inner wooden structures. Eventually, they arrived at Alyonia's heart, the Kaldorian manor.

"Bloody Perdition," whispered Taryn. "This will not be short."

As they came to a halt, she could see no less than fifty affluent Alyonians waiting, all donned in black condolence tunics.

"Patience." Trakkonious mimed the flipping of a coin. "Some of the finest houses are here to pay their respects. Don't be cold or they'll withhold the gold."

Ten Kaldorian house protectorates took to the side of Taryn's carriage, helping her down beneath an umbrella and ushering her toward the droves of wealthy patrons.

"My queen."

"Our sincerest condolences."

"The farmlands have never known such support. Blessings upon you and your heart."

Taryn smiled demurely in every direction, distributing bows and hand kisses as each house patron tried showing the others how close they were with their interim queen. "My thanks, my thanks," she said.

Trakkonious did his part, exchanging words with the leaders of house Zo, Bartellus, and Arrevon. These Alyonians reeked of wealth and status, never allowing so much as an inch of spinal slouch. A slew of house servants stood on their tiptoes beside them, laboriously reaching sunshades over their Lords' heads in an effort to fend off the rain. Lord Bartellus himself gave whistle to an adjacent street where a group of tanners finished polishing leather gifts: wineskins, belts, and shoes. Animal skins still stretched upon timber canvases beside them, freshly urinated upon and preparing to undergo the next stage of crafting. These tanners turned and rushed in Bartellus' direction, eager to pass his many gifts to Taryn.

She welcomed these gifts, even smiled at the soaking-wet servants, though it wasn't long before Taryn noticed Kornilious lingering outside of the Kaldorian manor's front door, talking with its many sentries. She grinned.

* * *

Taryn sighed. "By the stars, I thought it might never end."

Kornilious laughed and followed her up a winding set of stairs within the Kaldorian manor. "Agreed. And what of Bartellus' gifts? Shadow and light, he's desperate."

They chuckled as they turned down a hall.

"Ah, greetings, mortician Edelly," said Taryn, bowing to the approaching mortician.

Edelly nodded his old and feeble head as Taryn studied the hefty wooden box he carried. There was a painted label atop: *Taaivetti*.

"My queen," said the mortician. "I would return your bow, but..." He shrugged, gesturing toward the large box in hand.

"What's this?"

"From your father's study. He requested this be passed to Taaivetti in the event of his demise."

"I see." Taryn lingered a moment, processing. "Nothing for me?"

Kornilious squirmed behind her.

"Nothing." Edelly's expression soured. "Nothing yet, I should say. We've only just begun the funeral arrangements. I suspect we'll uncover a box or two with your name soon enough."

Taryn forced a smile and continued down the long hall, passing warm lanterns that somehow felt cold, magnificent paintings that now appeared hideous. "A fool he was," said Kornilious, catching up. "I'm sure your father has something—"

"Close your lips." Taryn opened a glass door and walked out to a balcony. "You know my father's feelings of me."

He joined her by the balcony railing. Rain now scattered everywhere, soaking a courtyard of gardens below and drenching a great awning overhead. Water poured down the awning and fell before them like a waterfall for two.

"My apologies, love." Kornilious wished to hold her, but such actions were forbidden in public, and eyes were everywhere of late. "I've been meaning to speak privately, and I suppose now is as good a time as ever."

Taryn turned to him, listening intently.

"I signed off on the combative clause of our peace treaty with Rhi because I believe in you. I believe in your vision for Alyonia, and I believe in greater peace through two empires, not one hundred realms constantly bickering and forcing others to take sides during conflict. This was a clear part of our agreement. But what you showed me in the forest, this dust…incredible as it is, I'm unsure how this plays into our plan? And I certainly do not understand my role in it."

Taryn nodded and stepped closer, her breath silenced by pounding rain. "Bandano-Rhi is needed for the two-realm function. You and I have long agreed to this. But what I've shown you now is how easily we could one day overtake him to create a one-world function…*That* is the only way to true, lasting peace, Kornilious. That is how the dust plays into our plan. Without it, we lack the strength to challenge his armies. And your role? Quite simple. A future king must know everything going on in his realm."

23

TAAIVETTI

Preparations

"Keep climbing!" Commander Zo clutched tightly to a thick rope held between both hands and legs. Blood oozed from his calluses, making the rope harder to grip. Moans and groans traveled from beneath him as exhausted soldiers cried out in agony. Their feeble whimpers ascended faster than any Alyonian was climbing.

"Fifteen count! Test yourselves!" Zo fought against the unbearable heat and his own body's desire to faint. He managed a quick glance to his right; ten additional ropes hung from the wall's many merlons. One hundred of his brethren ascended these rugged ropes in groups of ten, each team fighting to reach the top first.

"Soft points, let loose!" Sir Arrevon's voice boomed from a wooden battlement above. One of Hann's most esteemed defenders, Arrevon belonged to the Honorable-Three, having earned his spot in the legendary trio during the bloody battle of Mordikic. Today however, he merely watched countless arrows zip through Hann's hot air. Training arrows. "Another!"

Many arrows found their marks: the heavy sandbags strapped to the back of every climbing Alyonian. Sir Arrevon had long maintained that pure body weight wasn't enough for this exercise. And the bags made better targets than spleens.

"Nine count!" roared Captain Tigan. "We're closing in!"

Tigan found himself in the midst of pulling both legs toward his torso. The athletic captain re-gripped his rope and locked two feet together expertly. His team was in the lead and readying themselves to mount Hann's wall walk. Their hopes were quickly crushed, however—not by practice arrows, nor Sir Arrevon's many defensive techniques, but by a pile of feces falling downward from their rope's team leader, Sir Olivorio. The vile excrement splattered onto Tigan's already disgusting team, dropping many to the red sand below.

"By the stars, Olivorio!" Tigan swung but held on, then used one hand to wipe his shoulder clean.

It was all the time Zo needed. His unit quickly passed Tigan's, finding their way to the wall walk first.

"Time!" shouted Arrevon.

Everyone froze. Even those mid-ascent. Even those covered in dung. "Let every Alyonian breathe this moment in and calculate our many mistakes."

There were more units behind Arrevon, farther down in the bailey. They carried thick barrels filled with boiling water and blistering sludge. These groups were desperately racing toward the western wall walk, but Zo's unit had arrived first. They'd won the game.

"If this were a real siege, our walls would be breached, and the beginning of the end would be at hand." Arrevon's tone needed no harshness; his soldiers were plenty disheartened. "Tac-company, how did you falter?"

The ten Alyonians in Tac-company seemed surprised, for they'd easily held their assigned opponents from ascending the wall. Zo's group had not been a part of their orders.

"I know not, sir," said a gallant member of Tac-company, hoping his humility would suffice.

Arrevon stepped toward him. "Knowing your company was

winning, you should've concentrated your arrows on commander Zo's unit, and on captain Tigan's. Instead, you took the shots closest you, the easy shots. You did this to win today's challenge, but what good is your victory if even a single group fails?"

Tac-company dropped their heads, shamed. "We must all be of one mind, one singular unit if we hope to stop what comes from the desert," continued Arrevon. "Release!"

Hundreds of grateful sighs filled the humid air, all thankful, all relieved.

"Rest up!" called Arrevon. "We resume at nightfall."

*　*　*

True to his word, Sir Arrevon had Hann's soldiers back in action the moment he caught a glimpse of the moon. Leaning over a bartizan railing beside commander Zo, he stared down at well more than five hundred defenders working tirelessly in the dark desert. Line after line, his Alyonians dug long trenches and erected defensive ploys. This high up, Hann's western bartizan gave him a wide view of all below.

Taaivetti approached from behind. "They look strong. Working fervently."

Zo and Arrevon turned.

"Your boardroom speech inspired them, my prince," said Zo.

"Perhaps." Taaivetti walked toward them both, his legs moving slower than usual. *In fact,* thought Zo and perhaps even Sir Arrevon, *everything about the prince seems unusual.*

Exchanging a subtle glance, the duo watched Taaivetti. His eyes were red and heavy, his green tunic dirty and unkept. Even his aura felt different, uncertain, unclean.

"Though there is no doubting their loyalty to you, nor their respect," said Taaivetti. "It was apparent today and apparent in the boardroom." Taaivetti forced a smile. His teeth even looked different, mildly blackened.

Zo lacked a response. Not long ago, he'd been angry with his prince's decision. Now he was worried.

"It is acceptable to be upset with me." Taaivetti stopped next to Sir Arrevon. "I've news. Ill news."

Arrevon turned, sensing. "Brother Deliss?"

"Dead."

Sir Arrevon shifted, the news nearly crippling.

"I'm sorry," said Taaivetti, preparing to quote his father. "But as an Honorable-Three, he fought loyally for what he believed in. To die for Balo is to live forever by his side in the warrior stars. I can feel Deliss shining down upon us as we speak."

Arrevon leaned over the bartizan rail, half balancing, half collecting himself. "When?"

"Hard to say. Our eyes broke the news some three moons ago."

"Did he finish the job?"

"No. The Gorsh Warlord remains."

That sentiment lingered as Taaivetti came closer and placed his hand upon Arrevon's broad back, nearly touching his branded crest.

Honesty. Heart. Honor. 3.

"Then we will finish it." Arrevon paced toward a set of decrepit wooden stairs. "I'll be in my quarters."

Arrevon disappeared into the night, leaving Taaivetti alone with Commander Zo.

"A tough loss," murmured the prince. "I worry our forces will lose heart at the news."

Zo did not respond.

Desperate to provide some alleviation from the news of the Honorable brother Deliss, Taaivetti changed course. "Do you know how the Honorables came to be?"

"I do not," said Zo, his mind elsewhere. "Such knowledge is a privilege."

"The privilege is now yours." The prince passed his comrade a canteen of whiskey, suggesting he'd come for a serious talk. "Long before the first Great War, Alyonian legions were led by a warrior named Acchus. He was said to never tire, spawning whispers that his heart was twice the size of others' and was so pure that he was incapable of lying. The great warrior never refused a challenge, and evidently, he never lost. So great was his skill that our legions began proposing single combat to their enemies, hoping to limit bloodshed on all sides. For some time, Acchus achieved peace through his own sword, and so bore the title of Acchus the Honorable."

Zo nodded, intrigued yet unsure why Taaivetti was telling him such things.

"Our enemies grew privy to his skill, however, and eventually stopped accepting such combat. So our legions adapted to Acchus' abilities and sent him running through the night, his mission solely to kill opposing commanders while they slept. After a few successful assassinations, Acchus refused the job, saying it went against everything his title stood for." Taaivetti took the canteen and sipped. "So Alyonia dismissed him from their ranks and replaced Acchus with a new warrior. Some say Acchus was a light-god, and he's still out there, running."

"Why tell me such secrets, my lord?"

"I'm nominating you for the Honorable-Three." Taaivetti let that linger. "Sir Arrevon and Brother Clark will, of course, have to accept, and you'll have to pass the Honorable training, but you're one of the few warriors who possesses the other requirements."

"You honor me," said Zo. "No play of words intended."

They stared out over the desert, over their warriors building relentlessly.

"Tell me," Zo said, breaking the silence, "if the Honorables began as one Alyonian, how did they grow into six different groups?"

Taaivetti took another swig. "Although our enemies no longer accepted single combat, Alyonian leaders yearned for the same result that Acchus had so brilliantly provided. Once he was replaced, a new assassin took his role, but he could only kill so quickly. Naturally, Alyonia created a second group of two assassins, and as a means of stroking their ego, military leaders bestowed them the same title, birthing the Honorable-Two. The two became so prestigious that young warriors trained solely for such a role, and soon the Honorable-Three were born, giving Alyonia three units of highly trained assassins and warriors."

"I see," said Zo.

"The true genius rests with the Honorable-Six."

"So I've been told." Zo spit over the bartizan, watching his saliva evaporate in the dark. "Do tell."

"By the time the first Great War showed its ugly head, Queen Pallala had caught on to the Alyonian Honorables, making it nearly impossible to penetrate her camps. Not wishing to waste our Honorables' talents, their groups slowly turned into a more generic fighting force on the front lines. But one eve, our legendary Commander Kadd selected the six greatest warriors in all of our realm and created the Honorable-Six." Taaivetti nearly chuckled from the thought. "He sent the group to Queen Pallala's front lines, ensuring her leaders saw and made note of them. All six of them."

"Interesting."

"It's said that the great queen remained hidden in her fortress for half a season after such reports."

"I don't understand," said Zo, watching Taaivetti full on chuckle. "Out of fear for the Honorable-Six?"

"No. Out of the fear for having never found the Honorable-Four and Honorable-Five!"

Finally understanding, Zo joined him, cackling louder than he thought possible for such a time.

"The four and five didn't exist then, and they don't exist now!" revealed the prince. "But legends claim that old Queen Pallala spent more time checking behind closed doors than she did commanding her forces. Mankind says she died of friendly fire, but Alyonians say she died of worry."

The duo laughed harder still, gifting a rare moment.

"Tell me, my prince," said Zo. "Do you truthfully believe we can hold off the Gorsh?"

"I do." Taaivetti grew quiet, his eyes gazing out over the desert. "On the condition that Sir Rynn arrives with Bolden's force. Without their aid, well, I believe we both know how that ends."

"I value your honesty."

Taaivetti referenced a few birds soaring high above. "Have we received word from Sir Rynn?"

"A letter arrived mere hours ago," said Zo. "He and Bolden are no more than three moons afar. Sir Olivorio's scouts have reported the Gorsh hordes to be somewhere around the same. It should be a close race."

Taaivetti nodded as he watched his loyal Alyonians work ceaselessly. "The Gorsh are untrained and unwise; they shall attack the moment they arrive. This usually works in our favor."

"Not this time," replied Zo.

"Not this time," repeated the prince. "If only they'd try to starve us out, or spread disease."

"Spread disease?" Zo asked in surprise.

"My father used to tell me of harsh times. Thousands of seasons ago, when Queen Pallala's ancestors waged war on all of Adria, they were known to have catapulted sick animals over their enemies' walls. Hundreds. Quite effective during long-term siege. Naturally, Alyonia adopted the practice."

"Naturally," mumbled Zo, squeezing his irritated calluses and blisters, draining their blood.

The prince never took his eyes off the desert below. "King Kaldor put an end to such techniques. Though the fact remains, we can be just as primitive as the Gorsh. Dare I say, we'll need to be when they arrive."

Zo plopped upon a flimsy bench when loud screeches sounded overhead. Groups of messenger birds flocked toward Hann's eastern stables, grabbing the attention of everyone working below. "If I may, my prince?"

"Speak."

"I've noticed a few Askari soaring by recently, some late in the eve. I thought nothing of it, originally, but now I'm sure. These creatures have been arriving from the far west and leaving Hann in many different directions."

"You believe they've come from the Gorsh? The Gorsh do not speak; they certainly do not write."

"I'm not sure what I believe. Yet I've seen it continuously, and these Askari have moved well, dare I say, stealthily…"

"Who would communicate with the Gorsh? Especially here at Hann?"

"A question I was hoping you would know." Zo scratched his itchy tail. "I suppose it matters not, given I've no evidence. I'll continue to keep watch on the skies."

"Send out interceptors tonight," said Taaivetti. "Use our best Askari. Do not send any birds nor hawks."

Zo bowed and took his leave, shuffling down the crooked bartizan stairs before turning back to his prince. "One final remark." Moonlight cut his face and white mohawk in two. "I received word from my wife two moons ago. After hearing my decision to renew my stay here at Hann, she's decided to sever our ties. She sent back my proposal bracelet."

Taaivetti stood eerily still, unsure how to proceed. "Zo…you should have merely blamed me—"

"Our problems run deeper than my absence at home. The warrior's life comes with sacrifices, as you know. I do not seek your pity, only your understanding." Zo took a long breath. "I've truly enjoyed our discussion, my prince, and I am humbled by your offer to join the Honorable-Three. But I must reject it. I intend to return home and fight for my wife's love. After this is over, if we're still standing, I shall request your permission to resign, elect a new commander for Hann, and, of course, a new member of the Honorable-Three. If I must choose between family and the warrior stars, well, I shall choose family."

Taaivetti winced. He couldn't help but feel responsible for Zo's wife. The commander had stayed at Hann due to a majority vote. A vote Taaivetti's presence had undoubtedly swayed. "You shall have my permission," he said.

24

HENDRIX

The Ratna River

"Morning," said Hendrix, in a tone so foolish he wished he hadn't spoken at all.

Ava jolted upright, removing her head from beside his leg. She'd fallen asleep in the tight space of their boat's cabin, and needed to be clear that was all. "Morning." She turned away shyly.

That inflection. Hendrix deemed it the most beautiful eastern accent he'd ever heard. Such a simple word, *morning*…but this was the first word, the first she'd ever spoken to him. Hendrix suddenly envisioned the morning in a new way. Quite peacefully. There would be no more Alyonian traders or loud street cleaners staining its image.

"How is he doing?" she continued with far too much emphasis on the *D*. Clearly not from the continent of Adria, Ava had a difficult time pronouncing the common tongue.

Jakko!

Hendrix stood quickly and smacked his head upon the low ceiling of their tiny cabin. "Jakko's great," he lied, fully aware he hadn't checked on his new pal since being forced to join Ava below deck. "He's healing. We drenched the wounds with strong liquids while you slept. Aypax bandaged him well." Hendrix hoped with all his heart that Aypax had, in fact, bandaged the dog. But such a lie was a gamble he was willing to take, so long as it meant another moment here with Ava.

They locked eyes, neither sure what to say. She spoke first.

"Many thanks to you. I cannot tell you how much—"

"No need for thanks." Hendrix hid his excited tail behind him, desperate to look as human as possible. "It was the right thing to do."

A true statement, yet Ava couldn't help but wonder whether Hendrix's obvious feelings had spurred his heroic decision to free her. She pushed her black hair from the sides of her tanned face, doing what she could to appear less fatigued.

"I'm Hendrix." He extended his hand for a shake. It felt sweatier than it should've. His entire body did.

"Ava." She returned a firm grip, shifting Hendrix's attention to his *M.P.* bracelet resting inches above their embrace. He paused for a beat too long.

"Did I grip you too hard?" she asked.

"No, no…" Hendrix noticed a heinous branding of letters along her wrist. As if a full sentence had been burned into her flesh long ago. But that wasn't all. Hendrix caught a whiff. A familiar stink.

Ava's face grew solemn; she smelled it too. She closed her mouth as Hendrix glanced toward his travel sack.

"Wait!" She clutched his hand. "I'm sorry, I needed them. I haven't slept, and my body hurts. The aches…" Her eyes welled, pleading. "Please, do not send me away. I will never do a steal again."

Her broken verbiage softened him. Everything about her did. Hendrix sighed. "How many are left?"

"I took only two." Ava's red eyes betrayed her.

That's why she fell asleep so deeply.

"I shall not tell," said Hendrix, secretly protecting them both. He felt angry, though truly Ava had done him a service. He'd tried ditching the seeds more than once. "Next time, simply ask."

She smiled, then followed him toward a ceiling hatch.

* * *

Hendrix led Ava up the small hatch toward the cog's deck. Surfacing, rainfall poured all around, dampening their sail and a makeshift blanket tied over the tiny cockpit.

"Stay low," Aypax said. He steered their ship with one hand and stroked Pattar with his other. The wounded Askari had regained a bit of vigor.

"Mornin'!" Sammy had wrapped herself around Sir Edmund Drake's smoking pipe, desperate to spark it.

Ava crouched low, concealing herself in the cockpit. "I had a feelin'. Feeling." She corrected herself while staring at Sammy. "When you rescued me, your movements…your brain. I had a feeling you were a Speaker."

"A Speaker?" Sammy looked at her quizzically. "You sayin' there are more of me?"

Aypax lifted a brow.

"Yes." Ava struggled to find the correct words. "A few."

"Well, tickle my ass with a Moronian long-feather!" chirped Sammy.

Ava laughed an incredibly contagious giggle. "Long-feather! Do you come from Moro?"

Hendrix tried not to stare, though his eyes felt magnetically locked onto Ava. He'd never seen anyone so beautiful; even Madison paled in comparison.

"No, I'm from Gondol. But I've spent plenty 'a time in Moro, hence my knowledge of their long-feathers. Those things'll get you zonked!" Sammy mocked her accent, but Ava wasn't fazed. She'd been through much worse.

"Does he speak too?"

All eyes shifted to Jakko, who lay fast asleep in the arms of Sir Edmund Drake, both unmoved by the endless rain. Drake, too, was out cold, snoring at the ship's bow, a canteen leaned against his pant leg. For all of it, Jakko was, as Hendrix had hoped, bandaged.

"Nah, he don't speak," Sammy said as she puffed her chest, bragging.

"But he shall live," Aypax said, a warmth in his eyes as he noted Ava's genuine care for the dog. "He requires rest aplenty. Thankfully, his wounds were not mortal."

Mortal.

The word showed Hendrix how terrible his bandaging lies had been.

"Wow." Sammy pointed over the starboard side. "Look."

An array of farmlands dawned east of the river. Breathtaking plantations and vineyards. Luscious fields and gardens, pastures and meadows, each beautifully colored and masterfully tended. Workers were scattered through these fields, putting axe to wood, shovels to dirt, trimmers to exotic greenery.

"They're at it early." Hendrix noted that Tourtoufa's first nova had yet to fully rise.

Then it clicked. These weren't workers. They were Bintonn captives. Staring closer, they saw that their owners patrolled on horseback with whips and jugs of water in hand.

Fury filled Ava's once delicate eyes. "I am grateful for my rescue. And my heart aches for the pains of your dog." She stepped toward their ship's railing and focused on the starving workers. Even this early, they were drenched in sweat. She knew how they'd feel by midday. "But I must request that you leave me in Starsgard on your way to wherever you are goin'. Going. My sister Adora is locked under Stadium Starsgard. The Bintonns have her, and she will perhaps get tossed into the games."

Hendrix glanced at Aypax, silently asking the same question he'd asked at the saloon.

"*No.*" Aypax held firm. "We shall drop Ava at Starsgard, nothing more. The Bintonns will have alerted the entire city soon enough. Not to mention the more prevalent enemy close behind."

Hendrix understood. Sammy, however, had a few questions. "The more prevalent enemy?"

"Ggggrrrr."

Everyone turned to see Jakko, awake.

"Jakk-Jakk!" Sammy forgot her question and leapt onto her furry friend. "How are ya?" The squirrel ruffled back and forth, unknowingly scraping Jakko's injuries.

"Easy!" beckoned Drake, coming to. He yawned a series of horrid-smelling breaths. Still, the pup and squirrel showered him with love. Sir Edmund Drake rose. "Let's help the gal."

"You heard?" asked Aypax.

"Aye." Drake rubbed his temple and burped, his brown eyes colored with a tired and sickly pink. "Some. I just awoke from a dream, see…I was layin' in me cabin bed when everything stopped." Sir Edmund Drake palmed his forehead, battling a brain ache. "I saw somethin' standin' in the corner of me cabin…shadowy, mean. I tried to stand but couldn't move, and as it got closer, it took the form of me ma…I couldn't make out her face, but I knew it was her, I knew she was tryin' 'a talk to me. I heard her words clear as day, but it felt like someone else was sayin' 'em. She said two simple things: '*Rescue. Family.*'"

Everyone remained silent. Entranced, Hendrix could almost feel the dew dissipating into an increasingly hot atmosphere.

"I don't understand," said Aypax, as an enormous vessel passed by their port side. The ship took up half the river. Her impressive sails had been repainted over in black, perhaps covering a prior symbol. "What's the point of your dream?"

"I feel like me ma was speakin' 'a me from the afterlife," said Drake. "Tellin' me to rescue somethin'. Seems a strange coincidence to wake up next to this beauty talkin' 'bout a rescue."

Rescue. Family.

Hendrix's mind travelled even quicker than normal. He recited those damned lines in his head: his mother's favorite passage.

Prophetics 9 — Family

1. With the heat overbearing,	2. The rescue daring,
3. Success is arranged,	4. Hearts forever changed,
5. A new family bred,	6. Six souls long misled,
7. Marked when animals speak,	8. Snap to it, you skweek,
9. Perilous times to come,	10. He must never succumb,
11. From the forest they'll rise,	12. Underground, holds demise,
13. Upon understanding,	14. Yes, you, I'm demanding,
15. Warn the one you love most,	16. Avoid the forest, become a ghost.

Hendrix looked around and counted. There were precisely six souls…

"Why should you care?" questioned Aypax. "You're a pirateer."

"Not sure." Drake blew snot from his nose. "I's never given a shit 'bout anyone other than these two." He nodded to his hairy pals. "But I feel we met this gal for a reason. Feel we're suppose 'ta go and save her sister Adora."

Drake's words moved young Ava to tears, as if she, too, sensed this premonition.

But Aypax had a different thought. *Adora's name was mentioned when Drake was fast asleep. How does he know it?*

"They killed my mother," admitted Ava. "They stabbed her right in the front of me. They took my father to work the fields and butchered my youngest brothers. My sister is all I have left."

"Shadow and light..." Hendrix wished to take her hand, to console her. "My apologies, Ava."

"And mine," added Sammy. "I know what it's like to lose family—"

"Aye," interrupted Drake. "Me too."

"And I," Aypax chimed in, still suspicious of the pirateer.

Hendrix nodded. "I also watched my mother fall, right before me."

Sir Edmund Drake nodded at his scarred accomplices. "I suppose we just found our reason."

"Family..." said Sammy. "Destiny be a fickle bitch, but everyone needs kin, and that's one throat-punchin' gang name! I declare us 'The Family' from this moment on!"

Aypax drew a deep breath, knowing this conversation wasn't going his way, knowing precisely what they'd end up doing. "Drake, how far to Stadium Starsgard?"

"Fifty score, as the bird flies. Well over two hundred score if we're goin' through the city."

"Any shorter paths?"

"'Fraid not." Drake pulled forth a soaking map from his pant pocket. "I can get us in and outta the city safely, but there's no avoidin' how long it'll take. And if the Bintonns know we're in Starsgard, 'tis over."

"And breaking into the cells beneath the stadium?"

"That we can do." Drake pointed to a stitching in his coat, a circular emblem showing a fist inside a heart. "I know some folk in Starsgard. That'll be the easy part."

"How long a sail?"

Drake thought. "A full day. We'll arrive at the docks tomorrow morn."

Ava lit at the prospect of hope. "I cannot ask you all to come.

You have done so much of enough."

Hendrix looked around. "Ava, I think we need this just as badly as you."

Though he disagreed with such a notion, Aypax accepted heading into Starsgard, accepted delaying their sail for Hann. If Starsgard was good for one thing, it was *an abundance of brothels.* And that meant he just might find Katrin after all.

"Get below deck, Ava," Aypax said. "And don't surface 'til tomorrow. If we're to do this, we do it my way."

25

HENDRIX

Allure

A full day had passed. Both novas set over the Ratna River, stunning Aypax with magnificent shades of yellow and bluish pink.

Hendrix and Ava, however, weren't able to see such wonders. Ordered to stay hidden, Ava had been contained to the clustered cabin. One thing was nice, however: company. Hendrix hadn't left her side, for better or worse. Without room to move, things were confined. Sweaty.

They'd talked nonstop, laughing, growing closer.

Aypax checked in on occasion, though his lack of care surprised even Hendrix. For hours he'd found himself alone with Ava, immersed in her words, her stories. Only a small meal of bread had broken their conversation.

"No, no," chuckled Ava. "You must answer me now. I'm tired of answering to your questions always. I thought we each had three? I do not understand this game." She leaned back upon a dusty pile of bags and clothes, exhausted.

Though weary himself, Hendrix's dimples raced to his skull, ignoring his guilt over playing Madison's favorite game. "Okay, okay. Answer one more, then I will give you four turns. What is your favorite animal?"

"The bird. Any kind. For they are free."

"*Boring*. The bird is everyone's answer!"

"Not where I come from," she countered. "My culture pities the bird. It is easily killed, and it lives not long. It has many predators and no real home. It is always on the move."

"Then why is this your favorite?"

Ava locked eyes with Hendrix. "The bird may die quickly, but it loves madly and flies about each moon as if it could be the last."

Hendrix nodded, doing all he could not to stare at her lips. His face was that of a giddy schoolboy. How had he become enamored so quickly? Madison's smile suddenly filled his mind. That same smile she wore as she accepted his proposal for marriage. *A marriage*, he thought, *that had technically not yet been sworn over.* "I think you give the bird too much praise."

She grinned, her eyes now drifting to the ceiling above. "Hendrix?"

"Yes?"

"I hurt." She waited before continuing her thought. "I see that you hurt also."

Her voice soothed him. Hendrix watched a bead of sweat roll down Ava's forehead, down her cheek. Thinking his days numbered, he wanted to follow it down, down, down. "I don't understand—"

"I want to do seeds with you." Her eyes returned to him, focused, full of life and pain.

"Hendrix!"

Aypax's voice rang out from above. The brute pulled open the tiny hatch and poked his face into view. "Time to sleep. Shut your eyes, shut your mouths, shut everything. We reach the docks in seven hours, give or take winds. Be ready." He closed the hatch, leaving them alone once more.

The pair lay in silence. Shifting awkwardly. No more than two feet apart, it became difficult to get cool or comfortable.

I can't do seeds with Ava. I can't. The face of Madison Preters assaulted yet again. Her contagious laugh as they visited their little plot of land far enough east to run away. Her deep breath as they secretly paid the owner a deposit. *The seeds couldn't possibly lead to anything good…*

Hendrix turned to Ava. "I want to do seeds with you too."

* * *

"Do you feel it?"

Hendrix sat cross-legged across from Ava as they looked deeply into one another's eyes. Their faces were close. Far too close.

"It's creeping." Her torso swayed slightly, nearly falling backward. "My bruises feel better."

"There are spiderwebs around your eyes," whispered Hendrix. "And your eye circles are changing colors."

"Yours already have."

"I feel relaxed. I feel lovey."

Their sweat increased. Their tongues dried.

"Hendrix," she said. "May I tell you something?"

Oh no. "Of course."

"Today, when we were up top of the deck, I caught the pirateer sneaking many looks at me." They sat in silence, contemplating. "Not as the sex," she continued, "but, how do you say… evilly? I feel I know him. Though I cannot say from where."

"Why do you feel his looks were evil…ly?"

She grinned as both their bodies swayed. "Instinct. Heart."

Hendrix imagined her grabbing his hand and placing it over her heart—*no.* He wasn't imagining. Ava held his hand over her heart. He felt its steady beat as he brushed the side of her breast, feeling the firm but gentle curve. "What would you ask me to do with the pirateer?" Hendrix drooled slightly, half seeds, half smitten.

"Ask your friend, Aypax. Ask him to keep watch. I fear the pirateer may be lying. I fear he may wish me ill."

"Done." Hendrix pulled back his hand, though he wasn't sure why. It suddenly felt cold and angry with him.

"I saw you writing a letter earlier. Who was this for?"

Hendrix thought as best he could. "My friend. A good friend. Very. Very...good." His words slurred.

"Is that friend...*M.P.*?" She put her fingers on his bracelet, rubbing dust from its surface. Defiling it.

Hendrix didn't know whether to curse or kiss. "Yes."

She leaned in, nearly touching her nose to his. "Is this friend a lady?"

"Well—"

"What part of 'close your mouths' was confusing?" Aypax lifted the hatch, yelled down.

The youngsters jolted. Hendrix had hidden the seeds back in his bag, though the smell lingered. Aypax whiffed and sighed. "Hendrix...be ready." He closed the hatch.

House Kaldor

From: Hendrix Kaldor
To: Madison Preters
343 A.B, Windy Season, 95th Moon, Double Novas

INTRO
Madison, as promised, I continue my prior letter. Aypax and I remain safe and currently sail down the river. We rescued an elderly woman last night, a human. She was a Moronian slave; her sister remains captive. We shall attempt to break her free as well. Do not fear, I shall return home the moment Taaivetti grants us a royal decree of pardon. I miss you more with each moon. I yearn for all that is to come.

WHAT HAPPENED: PART TWO
I was on my knees in the courtyard, blade above my neck, when Aypax arrived with his famed Honorable-Six. He fired a warning arrow near my captor. Needless to say, things heated up. Aypax announced for all that he himself witnessed Taryn commit the murder from a nearby manor. Tensions arose quickly as a large crowd gathered to hear his claim.

That's when Kornilious arrived and put a real arrow in Aypax's quad. Kornilious declared Aypax a liar and said that he himself had seen me murder my mother. An obvious lie and the sole reason I know Kornilious to be aiding Taryn. We seemed doomed 'til your father and his Green Capes showed up. Your father quarreled with Taryn and Kornilious for a just trial on our behalf. The crowd turned again, this time in Crimson's favor.

That's when Bandano-Rhi showed. With no less than twenty of his honor guard, and when things got truly scary.

I am again running low on ink (my apologies for rambling). So I must shift focus to something else that's been pulling at my heart.

The Prophetics
Please do not judge me, but ever since the moment I fled Alyonia, I've begun to notice strange events, too strange to be considered coincidence.

You know I despise worship and creeds, Balonity in particular, but I am hard pressed to deny recent happenings.

Many of them have been foretold, it seems, and last evening, I had a dream of one. Feels many folks tend to be dreaming these days.

I saw you standing in a forest, reading Prophetics 44. Something spoke to me, and I immediately felt compelled to write you this letter.

Read the below and heed its warning, I suppose?

Prophetics 44 - Sacrifice

1 At night at night, the three of three,
2 The time shall come, for two to see,
3 What's to come, without the key,
4 Feast they shall, on skin and bone,
5 The Captain's journey, for he alone,
6 Must forge through the cold and harsh unknown,
7 One hundred and one moons,
8 Not an eve too soon,
9 The childrens' souls were already doomed,
10 Questions and fears,
11 Concerns and tears,
12 Their wrinkles show truth and lies and years.

Yeah...I know.

Speak soon, dearest,

Hendrix

26

MADISON

Madison Preters

Young Madison laid in Hendrix's arms, her loving eyes fixed upon a bright moon, her soft lips pursed round a lit piece of bark. Smiling, she blew a sensual waft up into Hendrix's mouth.

"Keep your clothes on, will ya?" laughed Stennis, Hendrix's best childhood friend.

"Don't be jealous," said Bree, Madison's closest friend to match.

"You could change that right now, sweetheart." Stennis winked at Bree, then stood and looked out at hundreds of young Alyonians surrounding. "Why must all the ladies be courted?" Scanning for potential mates, Stennis took in the infamously rocky shoreline of the Lukonite Lake. Jagged rocks of grey and white filled this beach, forcing inhabitants to lay down blankets or thick surcoats before enjoying the view. And enjoy they did. Most of the young males smoked, drank, and gambled whilst their ladies danced or dove into shallow waters.

Seeing others dance, Bree stood and swayed herself, allowing the bark's high to move her limbs freely.

Stennis laughed. "Your dance classes are really paying off..."

"Dance is an art you couldn't possibly understa—" Bree stopped, noticing. "Hendrix, your sister is here. And she's with Kornilious."

Hendrix popped up, squinting across the party-ridden shoreline. He rolled his eyes. "Just my luck."

Madison lifted herself beside him. "Love, you don't have to—"

"If my father hears she's out with Kornilious again, after the last few times he already caught her…" Hendrix took Madison's bark and inhaled. A long drag, far too long for one his age.

"Slow down, love," she urged.

"When your father is the king, and your sister is Taryn, you may judge my decisions."

And with that, Hendrix made for his sister.

* * *

Madison awoke, frightened and breathing rapidly from the dream. Coming to, she slowly recalled the task at hand.

An open copy of *The Prophetics* lay before her. Exhausted, her green pupils danced across its dusty pages. She stopped on *Prophetics* 44 - Sacrifice. Hendrix's dirty letter lay beside, and had traveled quite far since being penned this morn. But the day had long passed. It was now late, much later than Madison was used to—unless she were sneaking out to meet Hendrix, of course. Those nights felt ancient, unlikely to ever return.

A knock sounded. She looked up, torquing an already stiff neck. *Who would knock at such an hour?*

The library's front door struck repeatedly, an urgent entry.

It must be mother, which means her task has gone horribly wrong.

Madison hid Hendrix's letter, then hurried toward the door of her family's library. *Stop it, Madison. Do not allow your worries to control you any longer.*

Long windows welcomed moonlight down upon the carpeted aisles, permitting Madison's shadow to form. She felt a friend in that, at least.

"Mother?"

No answer.

A few more strides brought her to the large door. The heavy metal door was painted a combination of black and blue.

"Mother?"

Still no response.

Has the rain drowned out her voice?

Madison crept toward a window and pulled back a beige curtain, then peeked into the rainy street.

"Greetings!" said Taryn from outside.

Madison shuffled back, nearly falling to her bottom. *What is she doing here!? She must've caught Mother...*

"My apologies for startling you!" shouted Taryn. "But I should think you'd now open the door for your queen?"

Madison rushed for the knob, allowing Taryn to shuffle inside. The interim queen tossed her umbrella on a desk of dark pinewood and wiped two tiny boots on a furry white mat below.

"How are you, my dear?" Taryn patted rain from a wet green gown, her tone immensely difficult to dissect. "Where's your mother? One would presume she'd be here so late in the eve, closing up herself?"

Madison's mind moved swiftly, for it seemed impossible to know what Taryn knew and what she didn't. A single lie detected would incriminate her.

"Mother has left me in charge of closing. She's set out to the westside in search of a very rare book. She hopes to add it to our collection."

Taryn nodded along. "I see. What book is that?"

Madison had repeated her cover-up story one hundred times. "*On the Cultures of Moro.*" She annunciated each word in the book's title, steadying her nerves. "As rumor goes, it is supposedly a very well-crafted collection of Moronian stories and tales. Moro is an interesting realm, if I may say." Madison smiled.

Taryn nodded. "An interesting realm, indeed. While we are on the subject, I've come in search of a few books myself."

What is she playing at? wondered Madison.

"The Kaldorian High Librarian has been sent to the country-side for a season of containment. He showed severe signs of the sickness, poor soul. I'm here in his position." Taryn gazed up at the high vaulted ceilings. "I knew this library to be impressive, but I've forgotten how large it truly is. Guide me to your history aisle."

Madison knew not how best to respond. Perhaps Taryn really didn't capture her mother. Perhaps she was truly here on her own reasoning. *But why?*

"Of course. Follow me."

Madison led the interim queen down the library's center walkway, ever sure to keep her distance. Rain pounded against colossal glass windows on either side as they passed aisle after aisle. Finally, she landed at row H. "Here we are."

Taryn had already moved ahead and begun to slide her still-wet fingers over a few titles. "Ah…" She pulled out a particular book, grinning whilst reading its cover. "'*The First Great War: And How Its Ripples Formed the Pallala-Accord.*'" Taryn shoved the book between her armpit and scanned the painted blue shelves. "Now, where are you?" she whispered.

Madison could barely take her eyes from Taryn, which was surprising, given the aisle. Aisle H had always been her favorite. She and Hendrix used to laugh at the walled portraits of ancient Alyonians deemed influential enough to be hung in the prestigious history section. The Alyonians in these paintings always appeared so uptight, as if competing for the most dull and emotionless rendition. She and Hendrix loved to chuckle at each other's impersonations.

"Did you hear me?" questioned Taryn.

No. She'd gone completely blank, lost in the memory. "It

appears my mind wandered off, my queen, I apologize." Madison bowed. "Repeat yourself, if it please you."

Taryn held up a thick and rather old book. "I asked if you've ever read this lovely text?"

"I cannot say I have." Madison looked at its side engravings. *The Pallala-Accord.* She furrowed her brow, willing herself to comprehend what the queen might want with it. *A clear topic...but what is the meaning?*

Taryn flipped toward the book's end, landing on a wordy page. "I've always admired this text. Father used to read it to Taaivetti and me during study, and even now I recall the scribe's gifted ability to make us empathize with the realms of the Pallala-Accord. Those poor, pitiful realms who were bullied and beaten, nearly destroyed by the ancient Pallala Empire." Taryn trailed off. "When you truly reflect, those old realms deserved the beating they received. They should've been ready for war. They should've known their neighbors and thought ahead. But alas..."

Taryn put her finger to the page, referencing a long paragraph as she read aloud. "'Queen Pallala sent her armies across the lands, killing and conquering everything in her wake. She submitted one realm after another, forcing kings and emperors alike to their knees.' As this book reads, young Madison, Queen Pallala was nearly unstoppable. Her armies were strong, well-trained, and full of passion for their cause and their queen. It is amazing to think what one soul can do. What one single soul can achieve...if others simply believe in them."

"I agree," said Madison. "My father always taught me that even the smallest of deeds from the smallest of Alyonians can have lasting effects."

Taryn simpered. "I like that. Your father is wise." She continued reading. "'As the Pallala Empire conquered all of Adria, the dying realms sought to form a union. To form one pact upon which they could band together and fight against the vicious men of the Pallala Empire. And so they formed the Pallala-Accord.'" Taryn shut the book. "And can you guess who they asked to lead this new Accord?"

Madison knew the answer; still, she could only shrug.

"Alyonia," exhaled Taryn. "They called upon Alyonia. And what did our ancestors do? Well, they marched out and saved the defeated realms, of course. 'The keepers of peace,' my father used to call us. Alyonia has always stood for lesser empires, always risked our own well-being to maintain a peace that never lasts. But why?"

This time Madison had no answer, though she wasn't sure if Taryn were truly asking.

"Your silence speaks volumes, young Madison. You are wise like your mother and father. The correct answer is, in fact, silence. There is no good reason for Alyonia to play hero any longer. The realms of the Pallala-Accord have taken advantage of us since the First Great War. We supply them with free protection, goods, modern herbs, and advanced methods of construction. And what do we receive in return?"

Madison's heart beat faster, her palms began to sweat.

"The answer, sweet girl, is silence once again. They've drained us of valuable resources, and now worse, the men of Coyo have brought forth the worst sickness Adria has ever known. Can you imagine, sweet girl, if Alyonia had chosen to side with the Pallala Empire? *Or Queen Pallala's newest descendent, Bandano-Rhi?* There would be but two realms today. Two realms working together, building each other into forces of greatness. Instead, we have hundreds of societies bickering and suckling at our power, slowly diminishing everyone into nothingness."

Taryn reached into a pouch tied to her girdle and removed a letter. "Leave this for your mother. A royal order. Seems there are a few books upon your shelves the High Council has recently deemed dangerous and inaccurate. See that your mother takes care of them."

Madison grabbed the letter. "Yes, my queen."

Taryn stuffed both books into her pouch, then made her way down the hall.

"My queen," began Madison, "if I may...why do you seek these texts in particular?"

Taryn continued her walk, never turning. "Names and bloodlines, sweet girl. Names and bloodlines. Oh! I almost forgot." Taryn swirled abruptly, excited. "I never expressed my apologies over Hendrix's betrayal. You must forgive me, it's a hard subject to speak of. But I always thought you two were an adorable young couple. I'm sorry he turned his back on you. On us." Taryn approached and placed her hand on Madison's shoulder.

Madison's insides heated, begging her to stand up for Hendrix, knowing she could not. Not here.

"My brother didn't deserve you," continued Taryn. "He's a traitor...a murderer. I find the best way to move past a tragedy is to accept it and scream it into the wind."

Madison met her eyes.

"Say it," whispered Taryn. "Get it out, sweet girl. Say Hendrix is a traitor. A murderer."

Madison's limbs tightened, her anger rose. *No.*

"Say it, sweet girl. Say it now and move forward."

No, she thought. *Never. I love Hendrix. I shall wed him soon.*

"Did I stutter, young Madison Preters? Say it aloud! Scream it!"

Madison fell to her knees and wept.

Taryn glared. "I see." She moved for the door but quickly noticed Madison's desk. There it was, that disgusting book, resting on an open passage. "Seems you're unable to let go of my little brother. Shame. You're a darling Alyonian."

Taryn grasped her umbrella and opened it. "Though I of course understand, the wound is fresh...You will need time. I have

a thought that might help. Yes, a splendid idea. I know a young
Alyonian. He, too, is darling. Given you're far too sweet to be alone,
I'll arrange for marriage. Your father's house would do well to ally
with this boy's. And besides, I've been meaning to speak with your
father about allegiance."

Madison wished to scream. *An arranged marriage.* Nothing
could be worse.

Taryn smiled and opened the door. "Enjoy your eve, Madison.
And close up quickly, it's getting late for someone your age. Our
streets have never been more dangerous."

27

TIANNU
The Silent Priest

The streets of Alyonia were silent, eerily so. Yet Tiannu Preters remained unnerved. She'd worked many a night shift in the past, perhaps too many, for darkness and late hours now barely affected her. Still, these nights past there was something in the air, something troublesome. It seemed to follow her everywhere.

Tiannu leaned against the frigid, slippery stone of a towering grey statue. Shaped as a tree, the statue seemed ironic, given hundreds of real trees surrounded the stone replica. She found herself in the middle of Bergeron's Plaza, one of Alyonia's most frequented areas of prayer and meditation.

Bergeron's Plaza stretched ten blocks in length, half in width. Grassy meadows covered the plaza, excluding the cobble roads crossing through in all directions. Billow-Balo trees spread about with benches or wooden altars resting beneath. Tiannu noted the plaza's condition. What used to be considered holy ground was now covered in muddy footprints, hoof tracks, and garbage.

Three minutes, she penned on a wet notebook in hand. *343 A.B, Windy Season, 95th Moon, Double Novas. Still no sign of Priest Yalino. Still endless rain.*

Tiannu focused on a green door at the bottom of a modest

brown manor situated across this plaza. Hundreds of similar manors surrounded Bergeron, connecting with one another by balcony and creating a complex of forestlike homes looking down upon her.

One minute, she wrote. *Yalino has yet to be spotted. Little activity in the area.*

A mucky canal ran through Bergeron's heart, long overflowed from incessant rain. The unclean waters spilled over onto once charming meadows and benches, slowly drowning them and adding to the plaza's degradation. Two stone bridges spanned over the canal. Green Kaldorian banners stemmed from their rotting, wooden railings.

Time's up. Two separate watches, no Yalino.

Tiannu closed her flimsy notebook and moved covertly toward one of the bridges, careful not to let tonight's winds remove her hood, mindful to stay amongst shadows. Tiannu's black tunic snuggled tightly round her athletic limbs. An even darker rain cloak rested over it.

Tiannu paced over the bridge, but passing by, she noticed something strange about those banners. They'd been painted over with an abundance of red and green symbols. Throughout her life she had seen her fair share of vandalism, though never so boldly. She splashed her way out of the plaza, then ran for a wide alleyway. A wooden sign hung overhead, lettered with golden paint: **BRON'S ALLEY**.

Tiannu entered the alley nimbly, hurrying past dark windows and closed sales stands filled with story-papers along the way. Leaning over to block chilly rain, she jotted a few notes. *Bron's Alley, no sight of any tracks, no sign of Yalino.*

A brief journey spat Tiannu out of Bron's Alley and landed her before an intersection. She chuckled at a few paintings depicting a regal Kornilious on the sides of nearby armories and smithies. Political ads were abundant, as were alehouses, granaries, and impressive watchtowers.

Crossing the intersection, she avoided a few drunkards roaming the otherwise silent streets. Finally, Tiannu came to a row of oak trees, common even for Alyonia's inner city. A colossal church lay hidden behind. Sapphires and rubies had been implanted upon the church's freshly painted stone, no match for the decay she knew rested within.

Failure is no option. I shall enter the church at any cost. I shall find Yalino.

* * *

Sneaking around back, Tiannu peeked in through the chapel window. She saw no one, not a soul, though she couldn't shake the lingering feeling of being followed. Tiannu paused, checked behind her, double-checked. Nothing. She soon arrived at a secluded side entrance.

"Yalino?" Tiannu took another look in, then noticed…

The side door's window had been shattered from the outside. She reached her arm through its jagged hole, heedful to avoid sharp glass. Twisting a bronze doorknob, she shoved her way in. Pews, altars, and statues stared back, enhancing her unease. There were tiny trees inside too, scattered about the chapel. Copies of *The Prophetics* rested beneath them, accompanied by worship pamphlets. Tiannu passed a few before looking up. Glass chandeliers loomed perilously overhead, casting strange shadows on the ceiling, but still no Yalino; she was alone yet again… Such solitude wasn't a new feeling, however, for she'd attended this very church by herself on countless past occasions. Try as she may to convince her loved ones, Crimson and Madison had never quite shared her love for the Balonian faith after the infamous scandal of Priest Eros and Taryn Kaldor. Priest Yalino had long taken over in Eros' wake, and done what he could to salvage the church's image. Though in truth, the damage was done, and local story papers had further driven the youth away from Balonian religion for over a decade since.

A bang sounded from behind.

"Hello?"

Tiannu shouldn't have responded, she knew that. There would be no valid excuse for breaking into holy grounds at such an hour.

She knelt behind a pew, gazed round the chapel. Another bang sounded from above. This time, she spotted the source.

A bird colliding with the outside window. Repetitively. Aggressively.

"Just a bird," she whispered. "There's no one."

The bird finally flew off, leaving a smidgeon of its own blood upon the glass. Tiannu moved quickly to a stairwell, maneuvering down its winding, unlit stairs. "Yalino?"

Reaching the bottom, she saw a door was half open. She removed a small blade from her cloak pocket. Stepping forward, Tiannu glanced at the ground.

Blood ran from beneath the door. *Fresh.*

She kicked it open and moved aside. Nothing came for her. No arrows nor swinging blades from either corner. "Bloody Perdition…" Nausea rose up within.

Priest Yalino laid below, covered in a puddle of red. His office desk had been overturned, his many books and plants shredded. A trail of muddy footprints led up a separate stairwell. *Equally fresh.* Tiannu knelt beside him, surveyed his grotesque wounds and torn papers. She searched for a clue, then pulled out her notebook.

Yalin —found dead in his church office, cut wounds and deep impaling, she wrote, hands trembling. *Office—ransacked, papers shredded, mainly from books and personal journals. Plants of worship —ripped and thrown round the space.*

She continued her hunt for clues, nothing.

Assassination occurred recently, perhaps within the hour. Culprit shattered the glass of a side entrance located out back.

Tiannu stopped scribbling, for her attention suddenly shot to a yellow booklet resting in a secret compartment of Yalino's dismantled desk, barely noticeable. Tiannu grabbed it, flipped through.

Entry #22 – Yalino

I have prayed fervently over the situation. I can no longer ignore what is blatantly in front of me. I feel them all round. I see them in the shadows. I fear the real enemy has returned.

I have tracked them into the forest. Into the heart of Balo.

It is real. It is happening. They must be stopped.

They?

Tiannu closed his book and stashed it away in her cloak. Taking one final look around, she suddenly felt more alone than she ever had in the empty pews above, praying her family would one day join her. Now she merely prayed for their safety.

28

CRIMSON

The Crossing

"Take it in, ladies!" shouted Lukon. "This'll be the last decent view ya have for the next few seasons."

He wasn't wrong. There wouldn't be another sight like this for some time. Captain Crimson halted Emerald Company in place. They'd finally peaked Roderic's Ridge and were beginning their descent down the northern side of the Eagle Tail Mountains.

This high up, the altitude created fascinating conditions. Harsh, freezing, and yet somehow, the very air itself seemed lighter. Perhaps it was their being a bit closer to the stars...or perhaps just delirium. Whatever the feeling, it was undeniably contagious.

Emerald Company could see for leagues in every direction. From Alyonia to Freedinn. From the Crossing to the Damascus Mountains. Meadows and rivers, grand lakes and salt mines. Even the never-ending El-Road glimmered from dazzling valleys below. It contorted like a snake, connecting cities and paths of trade.

"More snow than ever, Captain." Gable leapt down from his Naomi, giving it a much needed break. "Never seen such a fallin' this far south. Nearly as deep here as the Lookout."

"Rain," replied Crimson, fighting a lingering headache. He turned his palm over, allowing snow to pile atop his brown glove.

"This land has never seen so much. And as such, she's never seen snow like this."

Gable inhaled a deep breath of fresh air, then gazed down upon a clearing of trees, a crooked path leading to the ground. "The clearing is frozen over. She'll make for a perilous descent with the wagons and this untried lot."

Lukon agreed. "Aye. A plan for the way ahead, Captain?"

"Yes." Crimson ignored the hazardous path of ice and grass, thinking only of his wife. "We tread carefully."

* * *

The frozen clearing kept true, breaking chariots, limbs, and flipping a wagon entirely. Two Naomi ran free from the crash, but up here, freedom led to a cold death.

"Captain." Lukon pointed west. "Look there. Tracks."

Crimson had already seen, though he didn't care, given his relentless headaches. "Noted. I'm unsure what could've caused them."

They stared down at an incredibly large set of tracks in the deep snow some distance beneath their position.

"Tracks head west," continued Lukon.

Gable mounted his Naomi to gain a better vantage point. "What, did they drag a boat through the snow? Ain't an animal in all the lands big enough to make tracks like that."

"Other than your mother," replied Lukon.

Crimson smirked, then turned away from the tracks as his company fought downward, eventually making their way to the bottom of the Eagle Tail Mountains. Craggy ground leveled out here, as its frozen path began to connect with the illustrious El-Road.

"Ahoy! Finest greetings to you folk."

A small caravan of humans shouted from the El-Road. There were three families, each dressed in poor, thin pelts. Starving horses pulled their carriages along the well-paved road.

"Our blessings and prayers toward the peace treaty!" said the caravan's leader. "Tonight, we'll raise a mug to harmony and prosperity!" He appeared tall for a man, even carried a powerful demeanor. Still, one could easily see his intent.

Sad how far we've fallen, thought Crimson. *Such fear…and with no reason.* "The same to you, friend." Crimson bowed, signaling the humans to move ahead untroubled.

"Didn't like his tone," spat Lukon.

Crimson watched them flee. "He was scared."

"What are we gonna do, rob him?" asked Gable. "He ain't got nothin' worth takin'."

"Man's youth are taught that Alyonians are defilers and cannibals. He likely thought we fancied his family."

"Even with peace, we'll never truly get on." Gable sighed. "Though I suppose fear is better than disdain."

"Both are better than war—" Another headache stopped Crimson, viciously stabbing his brain. "Shadow and light…I need a proper cup of ale."

"Captain!" An Alyonian rider pulled short of Crimson and his Green Capes. "I've scouted ahead. No ambushes, no robbers, at least none to trouble us. Some strange news, however. I found groups of dead just northwest, likely dead awhile, every one of 'em by bow and arrow. Arrows still inside 'em, in fact. Bodies lined beside the El-Road, on display."

"Scout ahead farther, report back by nightfall." Crimson's tone was harsh and dismissive. "Bring Tartarri and Fruvallo with you. Ride hard and alert the Crossing of our early arrival. I'd prefer to let our birds rest."

* * *

Another four hours yielded impressive gains for Crimson's company, as they fast approached the city of the Crossing. Its signature stone pillars shot high into brisk air on both sides of the El-Road, marking Adria's official meeting point of the north and south. Snowflakes latched onto each pillar, painting them a stunning shade of white. Hundreds of families shivered in endless lines beneath these pillars, waiting. They waited all along the road, in fact, all eager to arrive at the city gates, all eager to find refuge or pass into Adria's far less crowded northern cities.

"These folk must 'a heard the rumors," stated Lukon. "No sickness up north."

"None yet." Crimson scanned the sad lines of citizens. Oddly, there were a few regiments of human soldiers as well, patiently standing in separate lines. *They're surprisingly equipped for a simple pass through the Crossing. Could they have been involved in the reported arrow deaths?*

Lukon also stared down these soldiers, challenging them with stern eyes. They were tough men, hardened warriors wearing the yellow and purple armor of Bandano-Rhi's renowned army. Standing in perfect lines, they were unfazed by such biting weather. "Why are they so heavily outfitted?"

Crimson paused to think. "Perhaps they're heading north to dispose of Huskon raiders."

"Ayyyyye." Gable shoved his flask back in its saddlebag. "But Bandano-Rhi already has defenders up north. Shit sakes, we've had to talk our own way outta a brawl or two."

Crimson looked ahead at two vast cities surrounding the Crossing. They spanned in both directions of the pillars, clearly separated by the El-Road. Two cities. One dividing line.

"I'm just happy to see some new faces for the eve." Gable shot snot from a single nostril. "The Alyonian lads here may be humdrum, but our ladies have always craved drifters!"

"Drifters, not cows." Lukon chuckled, avoiding a smack from Gable.

Their group rode toward a pair of iron city gates. Wooden fencing spanned in both directions of these gates, further fortifying the Crossing.

More archers on guard than last time, noted Crimson. To his right was the Crossing's city of man. It belonged to the Rhi Empire; well built, well kept, and beautifully painted in dark shades of purple and yellow. To his left, the Crossing's city for Alyonians. Much less pristine, and clearly lacking the funds or artistry to compete. Straight ahead were two menacing guardhouses in the center of the El-Road. A few men holding parchment exited their guardhouse and approached.

"Captain," said Lukon, "do we still need penned approval from both sides? Given the treaty has passed? Or can I tell these lads off?"

Gable laughed as the humans closed in.

"Travel permits and regiment paperwork," stated one of them.

"No 'please'?" Lukon smirked whilst adjusting his reins.

"Enough." Crimson presented his company papers.

The men scanned them as heavy snow fell across their surface. "Heading to the Lookout?" bellowed one of them. "You simians find anything up there yet? Or still just freezing your breasts off?"

"Should've gone with 'tails,'" said the other.

Lukon and Gable swallowed their pride, barely following Crimson's wishes.

"We've found nothing." Crimson observed a well-concealed burn behind one of the men's neck. "May we move on to the Alyonian guards?"

"You certainly may." The man cast a disgusted glance at Crimson's tail hanging beside his Naomi's. "As a matter of fact, I beseech you."

"It means to beg." The other guard winked at Crimson, then spat a wad of dark chew.

Crimson did not return the gesture, nor counter with his own. He simply made note of the burn mark, then steered his company forward.

"Apologies for their behavior." A skinny Alyonian emerged from his own guardhouse. He wore the light green tunic and heavy chainmail of those who hold the Crossing. "We're more than outnumbered here, and they aren't worth the bickering."

"No apologies needed." Crimson grinned. "It's good to see you, Nario." The captain extended his paperwork, an unnecessary gesture. Crimson had passed through the Crossing fifty times before.

"Enjoy your stay." Nario bowed. "The Rommani manors are empty and prepared for your company."

Those close enough to hear cheered loudly.

"Our gratitude." Crimson returned his bow, then rode for the city.

"A thought," said Gable, catching up to his captain. "Given there's a new treaty an' all, I say we stop in for that proper cup of ale over on their side of the city!" Gable glanced at Lukon. "What say ya, little one?"

Lukon nodded. "I say I'd like to put this peace treaty to the test."

The duo awaited Crimson's inevitable answer, and for once, they got what they wished.

"I said I needed some ale, did I not?"

29

TAAIVETTI

Days to Come

Taaivetti had never been so torn. He found himself deep inside a new sibyl by the name of Redwind, taking her over the slimy table, and yet he wished to vomit. Good as she felt, very little of this pleased, and the act could not distract from his growing face sores. Worse was the embarrassment. Even after his many nights in the alley, he'd never become accustomed to the hundreds of eyes staring down upon him.

At least she's moaning, he thought.

This Redwind…her noise did distract from the sound of flesh against flesh. Taaivetti tried to hurry, a difficult task, given so many eyes were glued to his pleasure. The morning's nova also shined particularly bright, exposing every sore and blemish upon his body. He'd always fancied his appearance rather perfect: tanned muscle, white hair, chiseled jaw, and magnificently kept tail. *Dashing,* he'd once thought. But now…

Taaivetti lifted his gaze from Redwind's bare back and stared ahead. He immediately regretted it. Redheart sat in the nearest cave, looking right back at him. She appeared hurt, betrayed even.

This was the way of her sibyls, and yet, Taaivetti couldn't help but feel traitorous.

* * *

The prince lay flat on his back, staring up at the desert sky. He'd come to know the sky here, developing a sort of understanding, a type of unspoken forgiveness. His back ached, per usual, contorted upon wet and sticky stone. He shifted for comfort, only to irritate the worsening sores.

The Arch Sibyl laughed. "At this rate, you'll sire me one hundred sibyls." She walked toward Taaivetti with her liquids and herbs. "If you don't perish first."

Taaivetti's face grew sweaty, though his mouth and eyes were dry. Staring at the herbs, his extremities shook on their own accord.

"Where shall we pick up?" she asked. "The Peace Parade, the basement? I've grown rather curious as to what stopped our vision…"

"The basement," he replied, sternly. "Bring me back to the basement."

* * *

Taaivetti awoke to loud noises. Horrible noises. Blood-curdling screams and cries, arrows zipping so close he could feel them. He heard the clashing of steel and iron, the breaking of glass and tile. Above, the skies themselves seemed to plummet downward, closing in on bloody cobblestones beneath him. It appeared red and starless, the sky…with touches of ghastly green fog. Fires ravaged countless buildings and manors in every direction, allowing strong winds to blow ashes where they pleased.

What…what happened?

Taaivetti was not in the basement, nowhere near it. This vision had gone awry. Terribly awry.

Studying his surroundings, the prince found himself in Alyonia, though an Alyonia he'd never known before.

"For Balo!"

Taaivetti turned toward the shout. Perhaps forty Alyonian soldiers charged down the street nearest him, each donning his army's green and gold.

"No prisoners!" bellowed a deep voice from an adjacent road. There were far more soldiers here, and strangely, Taaivetti noticed a few men amongst their ranks. Their group sported the traditional Alyonian green but with red trimming opposite their enemies.

His heartbeat raced as they closed in from both sides. Taaivetti began to move, but gazing down at two misty hands, his very essence was naught but a dream. The soldiers were a few strides away now, their weapons shadowy in the low light. "For the queen!"

His resolve broke as bodies collided all around; one even passed right through him. Whatever Taaivetti was, he could feel the heat and speed, the blood splattering through warm air as sharp steel tore and pierced skin. He smelled the foulness of guts and bowels spilling out onto uneven cobblestone. He heard the cries and whimpers as adrenaline faded and pain throbbed. The prince ducked as more arrows passed overhead, felling a few citizens behind. He tracked these arrows to a rooftop, where groups of archers popped up and down.

"Ahhh!"

Yet another cry demanded Taaivetti's eyes. He looked to a separate roof, where twenty red-robed Alyonians stood behind a line of frightened commoners, all forced to their knees and blindfolded. One by one, the red robes slit necks, then kicked lifeless bodies from up high. In disbelief, Taaivetti watched their corpses descend upon droves of families fleeing burning homes just beneath.

Bloodied remains had been stacked everywhere, sometimes piling overhead. Alyonian ladies and children poured from flaming or collapsing homes. These children wept, many alone and searching for dead parents. More soldiers fought in the distance, swinging blades and dying as fast as Taaivetti could spot them. Thick clouds of green smoke slowly descended upon the manors nearest him, plaguing the area with choking odors.

"Do it, then!"

A body burst through glass windows above, then plummeted two stories to a withering garden below. Taaivetti recognized this body. *Jackkdon Religos*, a friend and famed Alyonian warrior.

The prince ran to Jackkdon's side and gazed up at the shattered window. More red-robed Alyonians came into view, staring down at Jackkdon and tearing clothes from his struggling wife. Taaivetti sprinted toward the building's entrance, desperate to help. Arriving at the door, he noticed a sign nailed to its front.

Article seventeen — on bows and arrows.

Taaivetti reached for the handle only to have his hands pass right through. "No!" Fuming, he looked about. Nearly every manor in sight had peculiar markings painted across their sides, red and green in color. Symbols. Keys. Eyes.

"Up high! Cover your ears—"

Taaivetti obliged. Though not truly present, he heard the unforgettable screech. It drew nearer, forcing him to both knees from sheer pain. His eardrums pounded, nearly popping.

Taaivetti fought the pain and stood, searching foggy skies for a cause. *Balo, help me*, he thought as a group of winged beasts descended upon the Kaldorian manor bell tower. Landing fiercely, one nearly shattered the bronze bell entirely. The bell rang out over Alyonia, announcing the creatures' arrival. They were difficult to see, even squinting, but Taaivetti could make out their bony structures. They must've been *twice* his height, with wings spanning another full Alyonian in width. Sharp talons glimmered from occasional moonlight, a single one *nearly half* the prince's size.

Taaivetti was lost; lost in it all. Focusing, he made out the distant image of a window cracking open beneath the singing bell tower.

Taryn?

The beasts extended long necks in her direction, as if listening to the window or whomever resided inside—

* * *

Taaivetti shot up, awaking to his familiar position on the familiar table. Only the Arch Sibyl seemed different... She stood still, her features completely normal. Her pupils weren't grey, her body didn't tremble.

"Interesting..." she murmured. "Sibyls! Prepare yourselves. Tonight, we gather. There is a disturbance, a blockage. We must discover its identi—"

"Was that the future?" asked Taaivetti.

The Arch Sibyl slouched, deep in thought. "I cannot say for certain. Though I believe so."

"I did not see myself."

"No. No, you did not."

Taaivetti inhaled slowly, no longer troubled by his sores or addictions. "How do I go?"

"How should I know?" She walked to her marble stairs.

"Balo..." he mumbled, trembling.

"I'm unsure of your god, Prince. But if you are to meet him soon, might I suggest you align yourself." She nodded to his nakedness, his utter lack of everything.

That did it.

The prince's trance was broken. Somehow, someway, his circumstances suddenly became clear.

Look at yourself, he thought.

But the words weren't his. No, they seemed to come from his

father. Taaivetti surveyed the alley, though the deceased King Kaldor was obviously nowhere to be found.

"Return to Hann," said the Arch Sibyl in a more hopeful tone. She'd already shimmied back into her golden chair. "A glorious victory awaits you. I've seen it."

The prince stood and walked slowly for the exit. "You won't see me again."

The Arch Sibyl nodded. "I hope not, Prince. I hope not."

30

HENDRIX

The Docks

The morning's first nova rose high over Tourtoufa, hurling glistening rays down upon the Ratna. Sammy looked overboard at the sparkling river. It splashed and rippled, reflected and shined. "We're close," she chirped, noticing gross clusters of trash floating by.

"Aye." Drake palmed at his head, nursing another headache from behind the ship's wheel. It was triangular, the wheel, and crafted from smooth teakwood. "Everyone gather round."

The Family obliged. Aypax leaned against a wet railing as Ava and Hendrix plopped into the cockpit beside Sammy.

"Listen closely." Drake unraveled a damp map. "Once we're in Starsgard, the damned Bintonns is everywhere. This map shows a line of tunnels beneath the city. Tunnels dug by pirateers and Tourtoufian shop owners as a way of smugglin' booze underground. 'Tis how we avoid the Bintonns taxes. They've been puttin' down hard levies on anything we pirateers try an' sell, so we struck a bargain with the local establishments." Drake ran his finger along a few lines of the map. "We've been smugglin' all kinds'a goods underground, gettin' richer than ever! Eh, sorry. Point is, the tunnels run beneath Stadium Starsgard, and we know some folk who've been breakin' slaves free."

A smile crept over Ava's face.

"Don't get mushy," said Sammy. "Yea, they free the slaves, but then they sell 'em right back with a wanted bonus."

"Nevertheless!" shouted Drake. "Their system works, and they could break yur sister out, so long as you lot listen ta'me." The Family nodded. "Good." Drake pointed to Hendrix and Aypax. "I saw a few bags of clothes below deck. We'll change you twos into new garb, make ya look like proper slave traders. That'll help us walk the streets unnoticed with Ava. No one'll turn an eye at the sight of slave traders. They're common as this damned rain."

"Finally," said Sammy. "There she is."

Everyone glimpsed the overwhelming city; its rooftops and chimneys, birds and flags; its rancid fumes polluting smoggy air. Starsgard.

* * *

Sir Edmund Drake inspected his Alyonian partners, both dressed in green Tourtoufian overalls. "You twos look the part. Hendrix, flatten yur hair. The rich don't ever look haggard. 'Tis a nightmare for 'em."

Jakko yelped, wincing from lingering pain. Drake knelt beside his treasured pup. "When we arrive, we'll need to secure two jars of Rememmine, and one case'a Ashboiler from the local witch doctor. Jakko needs the Rememmine fast, and we need the Ashboiler if we're gonna break Adora free."

"Witch doctor?" said Aypax. "Jakko should seek real aid from a proper apothecary."

Drake ignored him. "Everyone clear on the plan? It ain't catapult math here. You three get the potions whilst me an' Sammy find our tunnelers. We all meet on the Stars-bridge at second novafall."

Hendrix walked to the ship's bow. "Wow."

They'd arrived at the infamous docks of Starsgard, which exceeded all expectations. The Ratna ended here, funneling into an immense bay wearing trash and dead fish, perhaps wide enough for a thousand ships. Starsgard sat on the bay's opposite side with hundreds of piers stretching from its dirty port.

Aypax noted no less than fifty pirateer vessels, each more than capable of making the voyage to Taaivetti. This was it, the opportunity he'd been seeking. In truth, Aypax didn't *need* anyone in this "family," not even Hendrix. He could pay a different pirateer and be off for Hann within the hour.

But what if Hendrix was right? What if Katrin is alive?

"Aye, big man!" Drake held a rotting rope in hand. "Tie us off."

As their cog slid into a boat slip, Aypax obliged, securing a few ropes to various cleats.

Ava began to help tie the knots 'til she noticed… "Oh my." She averted her gaze from the ship nearest them. There were four pirateers on its deck, dressed in loose shirts, baggy pants, and tight bandanas. Their vests held daggers, cigars, and empty bottles. Dirty beards and rugged swords were abundant. These pirateers were busy. With a woman.

"Do something!" Hendrix hoped Aypax or Drake would somehow intervene.

The woman was bent over a grimy railing of an even grimier vessel docked in the adjacent slip. The drunken pirateers laughed while taking turns.

"Are you mad?" chirped Sammy, back on all fours. "You're supposed ta'be a slave trader; look away!"

Hendrix obeyed, though he wasn't blind to Aypax's rage. The big Alyonian finished tying off, then stepped down onto the docks. Countless piers connected like a surrounding maze, an intertwining web of wood.

There were Tourtoufians, pirateers, gamblers, traders, even a few Alyonians. Sailors carried chests and bags and booze. Birds ascended and descended all around as the smell of salty sea mixed with hostile body odors.

Aypax led everyone to the widest pier. Ships of all kinds were docked on both sides. Hendrix stared at a few in particular, reading their sides as he passed.

The Ada Mae. Greta's Grievance. Joanne of Tides.

Hendrix stopped and gawked at an impressive vessel. "I've never seen a boat so large."

"That's a four-deck high mast." Sammy kept her face to the wood. "More importantly—"

"'Tis mine!" Sir Edmund Drake said. "*The Wooden Lie* be her name. She's a beaut, eh?"

Hendrix and Ava admired the ship's many decks and sails, its decor and weaponry.

Drake's crew spat off the top. "How much for the bronzed beauty?" shouted one of them.

"More than you can afford!" Ava regretted her retort.

"Easy," whispered Sammy, as the insulted pirateer readied himself to come down.

"Cool yurself, Tynndale! This bunch is with me!" Drake's voice sounded different, commanding. "Bring us down a bit of water and bread!"

Tynndale pounded his vest, then spun out of sight. It wasn't long before he arrived with a basket of bread, biscuits, and salted meat. "Morgan Three Teeth Tynndale, they call him. Me first mate!" said Drake, as Tynndale paced the boat slip, his bald head shining.

Tynndale smiled upon arrival, proving why he'd been nicknamed Three Teeth. "Have at it, then." He tossed the basket down to the slippery dock.

Hendrix and Ava took to the food as Drake embraced his first mate. "Come here, ya ugly bastard!"

Aypax kept an eye on the pirateers, both of whom seemed to

whisper. When they finally stepped apart, Tynndale stole a quick glance in Ava's direction. "Enjoy the meal," he said, taking leave.

Drake waved him off, then looked Aypax in the eye. "Alright. You owe me thrice payment for savin' Ava. Though given I've agreed to rescue her sister, I'll delay 'til we return safely with her. But I'd like ya to look at me crew, and take a long thought about dodgin' me on what's owed."

Aypax did not look up. He knew they'd be leaning over the forecastle, sporting their most intimidating expressions. "I'm the last of the Honorable-Six. I shall pay what's owed."

Drake smiled. "That's very good to hear."

* * *

Having filled themselves with water and a speedy meal, The Family returned to their walk. Reaching the pier's end, they stepped off and put feet to dirt.

Starsgard.

A gargantuan balloon floated overhead, the town's greeting. Secured by soggy ropes attached to slick beams, the balloon had been painted green, albeit poorly. It took the shape of a naked Tourtoufian lady, or at least some artist's idea of what a lady should look like. After a moment of goggling, they set off down Carpet Street, according to the many signs, the central lane of Starsgard.

"This is…" Hendrix had no words.

Carpet Street was long and broad and filled with diverse kin from all over. The road itself had been stained in the distinct green and black of dried algae and charcoal. To Aypax's delight, the first buildings on both sides were brothels, and they appeared unsurprisingly fancy. *Perhaps it is possible to find her.*

A few gambling establishments neighbored. Tattered banners proclaiming free drinks were conveniently placed about, as were paid employees hoping to entice pedestrians. "Welcome, handsome," said one in particular. She ran a hand over Aypax's chest, scattering a few gulls nearby as her skirt fluttered in the breeze. Her green skin hinted at Tourtoufian blood, though she appeared to carry human genes as well.

"Hybrids all over," chirped Sammy.

The employee stumbled, drunk. She barely noticed a talking animal.

"Thank you." Aypax held her back by her shoulders. "What's your name?"

"Jesslicka."

"I'll remember."

Turning, Aypax followed Drake down Carpet Street.

31

TARYN

Fine Dining

"A fine establishment!" High Council-Lord Preem's dark eyes scanned the upscale dining hall, ignoring a foamy desert before him. "Wonderful choice, Taryn."

Taryn had grown quite close with Preem ever since he'd elected her interim queen. Preem's dashing green robe set him apart from everyone at the table, even his fellow members of the High Council. "My thanks." Taryn discreetly kicked Kornilious beneath the table. Her foot failed to steal his attention, however. Not much could.

Kornilious sat beside her, mind adrift whilst gawking out of a round window. Its smooth glass overlooked the Ryyan Canal flowing below, making this bridge-like dining hall an overwater attraction. Wide windows allowed customers to stare out afar, and in this moment, witness a beautiful nova-rise. Powerful rays painted Alyonia pink and orange.

"Please, High Council-Lord, finish your thoughts regarding the west farm region," said Taryn.

Preem forked a bit of fish skin from a shiny plate, inspected it. "I was merely suggesting that their ballots go astray on the way to Alyonia."

"Astray?" Kornilious snapped back to reality. He suddenly

heard the soft drumming of rain upon the restaurant's roof, the excited laughter of newcomers arriving from the canal's boat entrance below.

"Simply my word of choice, Kornilious. You may label the act however you please." Preem chuckled, prompting a few High Council members to join as they picked at Alyonia's finest foods.

Kornilious looked down at their plates, their portions of untouched corn and meat. *During a famine,* he thought. "Why are we so sure that the west farm region shall vote in favor of the Vetusians?" Kornilious had overstepped his place at the table, but Preem let this slide, for he appeared far too busy removing a tiny bone from his mouth.

"The west farms have always voted Vetusian." Preem flicked his bone to the floor carelessly. "It's nothing against you, Kornilious. Their very jobs are on the land itself. Naturally, they believe the more opportunities Novellusians create in the cities, the less valuable they and their farms become. I do not fault them for such beliefs, but the issue lies in their leadership over the other farmlands. Farmers and herders have always looked to the west for guidance. You lose the west farms, you lose them all."

"Not to mention the city of Paxtonia," added Orani. "They've sat on the border of Pallala for seasons, living in constant fear of war with the Rhi Empire. This peace treaty shall help, but the Paxtonians tend to lean toward whichever candidate or party promises them the most military aid. That promise currently belongs to the Vetusians."

"We shall send them what they need." Kornilious sounded sure, though his mind was clearly elsewhere. *A one-world function... king,* he thought, torn to his core.

"How shall you do that, if your campaign is centered around allocating seasonal tributes to fight against the many problems here at home?" questioned Preem. "Do not promise something you cannot deliver, Kornilious. Instead, promise something you can, and make the masses believe they need it. That is the key to a successful, and lasting, life in parliament."

"Brilliant." Taryn meant it. "What angers me is the Vetusians' audacity to pretend they care about atrocities overseas. They do not wish to aid any foreign lands, nor end the Moronian slave trade. They only care to expand our military conquests. Their hypocrisy knows no end."

"They're a party rooted in hypocrisy." Preem finally touched his dessert. "Forget about anything related to foreign aid, folks tend to grow hot while discussing such matters. Remember this: When the common folk cast their ballots, they care only about what's being done locally. What they can see."

Orani unfolded a hefty piece of parchment before sharing its many maps and numbers with the table. "If these early assessments are accurate, Kornilious is ahead in nearly every other region. I foresee a clear victory."

Preem smiled and leaned in close; his breath smelled rancid. "If that is indeed the outcome, we'll move on with our end of the bargain. We've always felt the Pallala-Accord has taken advantage of Alyonia for far too long. It's time to split ties." Preem looked Kornilious in the eye, probing. "Are you ill, Kornilious?"

"Yes," he retorted, wisely. "The damned rain. Never-ending. Cold lungs, I believe."

"Get better." Preem wasn't necessarily referring to the fictitious sickness. "It isn't kingly." He rose and wiped his mouth, then led the others down a set of spiraling stairs toward their boat docked below.

Kornilious watched them pass a few families, waving and pretending to care for their existence. Taryn didn't see these families, however, nor the theatrical High Council. She focused only on a crackling of flames from a fireplace in the corner.

"Taryn?" asked Kornilious.

But Taryn pointed toward a doorway. "Look who's here."

"I told you I did not wish to speak with him ever again, Taryn."
Nevertheless, she waved Trakkonious in.

He cut a rather handsome image in his favorite lavish tunic.
"My queen," he whispered, stopping before their table. "The reports
from below have been confirmed. We've captured the Alyonian
female who has been meddling. She's held in the Forest of Balo."

"Wonderful." Taryn reached into her pocket and pulled out
a sealed letter, then stood and walked Trakkonious away from the
table. "Have someone deliver this to Bandano-Rhi. Use his residence
at the city of Lachlan."

"Understood. Is everything in place for the next phase? Bow
and arrows have never been more dangerous…"

Taryn smiled. "In place. Release the story papers and schedule
me a speech to address the coming tragedies."

Trakkonious bowed and exited, leaving Taryn alone beside
a number of blushing families. She nodded toward them, even
shook forearms with one mother, before sitting back down beside
Kornilious.

"Taryn," he began sadly, "I think it is obvious how I feel of you,
beyond our arrangement. After the election, I shall keep my promise.
I shall sign off on Alyonia's withdrawal from the Pallala-Accord and
do all that I can to maintain our alliance with the Rhi Empire. For
the betterment of Alyonia."

Taryn touched his leg, awaiting what came next.

"But a one-world function… The things I saw in the forest.
Knowing what I do now, I shall serve the remainder of my term as
Master of Defense, then resign before I have the chance to become
king." Kornilious stood. "I know your heart, Taryn Kaldor. It does
not rest with them."

House Kaldor

From: Taryn Kaldor
To: Bandano-Rhi
343 A.B, Windy Season, 96th Moon, Double Novas

UPDATE
My dearest, our time draws near. Kornilious' time, however, has come to an end. I will find a replacement in time.

THE NEXT PHASE
Please send another wave of bowmen to the El-Road just outside of Nadoria. Have them intercept no less than four of my caravans heading to the Crossing. Make it messier than before; leave the bodies. I'll see to the Alyonian dance hall.

RECENT ACTIVITY
The High Council has received letters from various realms of the Pallala-Accord. The Ashland-Empire, the northern tribes (though those barbarians could barely scribble), and the free river cities of Kios, Oblia, and Myre. Each realm is more worried than the last. Their leaders have expressed grave concern over our peace treaty. The fear grows.

NEWS
I have wonderful news. Meet me tonight, late. Our favorite hour. Where we first met.

All my love,

Taryn

32

HENDRIX

Starsgard

"Welcomes to Starsgard!" shouted no less than ten beggars loitering on Carpet Street.

"Coins! Silvers! Trades them in heres!" said a high-class shop owner jingling a bronze bell.

"Witness the greatest magics of all the times!" This Tourtoufian looked like he might actually be capable of magic. As did his one-eyed feline.

"Sales on love! Passionate love! Our gals do it rights, the males too!" Another green-skinned brothel owner.

The sounds never ceased, presumably ever. Aypax's head pounded. "We should've brought cotton fibers or wax for our ears." He sighed, fearing his lingering fever meant something worse.

Carpet Street's aggressive cluster of bodies reminded Hendrix of Baa's town square. Folks ran amuck, each with seemingly urgent agendas. *This is a death trap.* He pulled Aypax aside. "Must we walk this road?"

"Matters not," said the big Alyonian. "It spread long ago. You can spot it everywhere."

Hendrix began to notice the minutiae, the things he'd have passed over had he not been instructed to look. The horrid coughs of homeless, the swapping of spit outside brothels, the colored slime piled atop wooden railings.

"Sickness ain't a worry here in Starsgard," said Drake. "We thrive off a' filth."

"This place…I like it not," said Ava. Hendrix nodded, sharing a mixture of disgust and homesickness.

"Ahhh feels great ta be back!" exclaimed Sammy. "Can't ya feel the air? The love and the spirit?"

Hendrix examined Starsgard's citizens, shouted over the chaos. "Half seem so cheerful! The other half seem…"

"The cheerful folks are visitin'!" Sammy now sat on Aypax's shoulder. In Starsgard, she was hardly a talking point. "The miserable ones live here."

"Or work here." Drake bent over to pet Jakko. The pup trotted alongside, struggling to keep pace. A makeshift leash, weaved with kelp from the Ratna, wrapped around Jakko's neck.

"Right here, folks! Purple is pure! Purest we've gots!" A saloon owner stood outside two double doors, offering purple drinks to sweaty travelers.

"Purple sand tornados," scoffed Aypax, seeing the colored liquid. Though he'd been deceived by the barkeep, that drink had helped heal his gash, even stopped his fear of infection.

"'Tis time." Drake paused at an intersection. "Me an' Sammy will find our tunnelers, then meet you lot on the Stars-bridge at second novafall. Yous get the Ashboiler and wait for us. The witch doctor's shop is just ahead on the corner of DoomRock. Good luck."

The disguised Alyonians nodded, then led Ava down a crowded road.

33

AYPAX

Brothels

Hendrix and Ava followed Aypax off Carpet Street and onto a side alley. The commotion died slightly, though numerous shops and huts still surrounded. Aypax peered about for the nearest brothel. It didn't take long.

HERES AND NOWS

"Aypax," said Hendrix, "Drake pointed us in the opposite direction. DoomRock?"

The big Alyonian paced forward without retort, forcing the youngsters to follow. The brothel's front wall displayed a plethora of windows. Some curtains had been shut, others open for public pleasure. *Say what you will of Starsgard*, thought Aypax, *but say they know how to sell.*

He pushed through a front door of splintery Tourtoufian Yellowstraw. Ava and Hendrix stared through the windows, watching. Sharing a quick glance, they entered to find a waiting room reeking of sweat and wine. Smoke and incense lingered as if seeping from the walls.

Disgusting. Hendrix saw no desk nor workers, merely a row of pink and purple couches. A few children sat upon them, hands on their hips, eyes glued to the floor. *They're young.*

"Wait here." Aypax forced Ava to the colorful couch, keeping character. Hendrix stood beside her, feigning guard.

Strangely, none of the children so much as peeked in their direction. It was only the brothel's matriarch who seemed intrigued. "What's can I dos for you?" she asked, stepping in from a connecting hall. The matriarch studied Ava. "She's beautifuls. You aims to sell her forevermore?"

Aypax shook his head. "No. I'm here of my own accord. I've laid with Jesslicka and wish to see her again."

The matriarch grinned. "Ahhh, Jess. She's not heres. I have her toward the docks. May I interests you in a similars lady? She'll go by Jesslicka, if it pleases you."

"It does," he replied. "Take me."

Ava watched them depart down a dark hall. She hadn't pegged Aypax to frequent such establishments, nevertheless lust for it.

"It's not as it seems," whispered Hendrix.

"No?"

"He seeks someone."

Ava laid her head against the nasty couch. "Who?"

"An old friend, I suppose."

She grinned. "No. Not a friend. You are an easy face to read, Sir Hendrix."

Hendrix turned away, if only to conceal his grin from the children. "Sir? I'm no Sir, believe me. Far from it."

"What does this mean?"

Hendrix knelt a bit closer to her, foregoing his cover. "*Sir* is a title bestowed upon those who've earned it through combat. Traditionally, only the bravest can obtain."

Ava reflected for a moment, seemingly at home in the repulsive room. "The pirateer? How has he earned this?"

"He hasn't. I believe it's a joke in his mind. Something to mock, perhaps."

A Tourtoufian, relieved yet dissatisfied, exited a hall lit by pink-colored torches. Scratching his scrotum, he walked quickly toward the waiting room and grabbed his son from a pink cushion. Hiding beneath a circular top hat, he led the child outside.

Hendrix stared down this new hall, wondering what other madness took place behind the many closed doors.

"Hendrix," said Ava, "have you ever made the love?"

He stayed quiet for a long moment. "I..."

"It is a simple question." She peeked up at him. "You have or you have not?"

"I have not." Hendrix wished to say more, to say that his betrothed was so wholesome and pure that she'd made him wait countless seasons until their marriage was true. He stayed silent until Ava glanced away, grinning.

"Do you judge me by this?" he asked.

"Yes. Though not in the bad of ways."

Hendrix shifted closer, gazed round the waiting room. "Then what sort of way?"

She merely shrugged.

"Well, what of you then?" he asked. "You speak of the subject with confidence—"

Three men suddenly pushed through the straw door. They were easterners, men of the Rhi-Empire. A bit of smoke left the room as they shut the door back in place.

"Matriarch!" yelled one of them. His green and grey surcoat appeared rather worn and dirtied, but then, so did everyone's, given Tourtoufa's rain.

"Happy mornings," said the matriarch, walking out and swaying her hips just enough. "Whats can I do for yous?"

Does she just wait in the shadows? wondered Ava.

"No beds nor broads," said one the men, looking down the hall. "We're searching for a couple of Alyonians. One strong and bearded, one young with long hair. Has such a duo come through?"

Ava's eyes met the matriarch's, pleading. She began to rise, muscles ready to spring for the doorway.

"Yes," said the matriarch. "They came in some times ago, left in a rush towards the docks."

The men sprinted for the doorway, darting right past Hendrix and Ava.

* * *

Aypax entered a tiny room to the sight of a slender Tourtoufian. Her skin was a lovely combination of light green and a tanned, yellowish pink quite similar to his own. Like other Tourtoufian natives, she appeared somewhat amphibious whilst maintaining everything he loved about an Alyonian or human lady. "They call me Jesslicka." She sat upon a pile of pillows, fully nude, pleasuring herself. "Are you readys?"

If Balo does exist, Starsgard shall be the first to burn.

Aypax walked toward her, taking in the small room. Ripped pillows lined every side. A ruffled bed rested in the corner. Faint light emitted from dusty lanterns overhead.

"No."

The lady eyed him suspiciously. Licked her lips. "I sees." She slid down to the floor and crawled. "You wants me to begs you?"

"No."

She huffed, irritated. "Then tells me what's you want——"

"Katrin." Aypax studied her eyes, desperate to read her.

"Is this an Alyonian words?" She stopped crawling, stood. "I do not knows the meaning."

"Not the meaning. The lady. You know of her, I can see. Tell me." Aypax nearly choked from the room's incessant perfume. Still, he held his stare.

She shrugged. "If I wanteds, I could scream and our guards would throws you onto the streets. Maybe kills you even."

"They would. But I'd reach you first, and you would not see tomorrow."

"Do you thinks this frightens me? Some nights, I thinks of doing this myself." She was far too serious. "Spare me the decision."

Aypax dug into his pocket, flipped her a small coin. "More than you'll collect all eve. Please?"

She lingered a moment, unsure. "I do know of Katrin. She cames to us long ago. Talented. But woundeds."

"Wounded?"

"Woundeds in the heart. Katrin looked of depression and despair. Her matriarch's cabin had been burned, and her ladies had nowheres to go. Thankfully, we tooks them all in, gaves them work."

She's alive. "Where can I find her?"

"A grand questions." She swirled round seductively, if only out of habit; even Aypax had trouble not gawking at her curves. "The Bintonns own our shop. They came lookings for her many nights 'til finallys, Katrin fled. I have not seen her since."

Deeming her truthful, Aypax made for the door.

"Wait…I do haves this." She walked behind her bed and picked up an old, crusty shirt. "Katrin wores this many times. If you do find her, tells her I never gave it to them. Tells her we tricked the Bintonns."

Aypax grabbed the shirt, his hands trembling at the closest thing to truly feeling Katrin. "You have my thanks."

She flashed her new coin. "You've mine."

Aypax exited through the door, casting his imposing silhouette upon the hall's shadowy pink walls. "My gratitude." Aypax handed the matriarch another coin, sweating at how few remained. The matriarch bowed and pulled Aypax into a whisper.

Hendrix and Ava watched, curious. The conversation went on for some time, but eventually, Aypax nodded rather seriously, then strode toward the young ones.

"Let's find this witch," he said, passing right by.

34

HENDRIX

The Witch of DoomRock

Aypax passed shop after shop, searching for the witch doctor. Peeling back a hairy, sticky bandage, he assessed his forearm wound. Nasty, foaming, though the alcohol had helped to clean it. Relieving his mind from the soreness, he studied Starsgard's scenery. It hadn't changed much, excluding the style of buildings and increasing number of Bintonns.

He looked at Hendrix. "Keep a firm hold of Ava. Rough her if need be. I can feel their eyes." Hendrix nodded, though he couldn't lay a finger on her if he tried. They passed a three-story shop composed of brick and more Tourtoufian Yellowstraw. Five Bintonns stood on a wooden porch outside, smoking some kind of rolled paper. "There it is." Hendrix pointed to a remarkably small market on the corner of Carpet and DoomRock. *DoomRock...*

He'd heard such a name before, somewhere other than Drake. The compact market seemed a curious place. Looking more like an outhouse, it could surely host no more than five or six bodies. Painted all black, it stood no taller than Aypax. Cobwebs consumed its exterior whilst old bones and feathers covered an even smaller front porch.

"I'm no expert on the witchcraft, but agree I must," said Ava. "This is likely the place."

They stepped onto the eerie porch and pushed through a door of Yellowstraw, a common local decor. The straw had been covered in long strands of beads and necklaces. Entering, they saw naught but a stairwell leading down into darkness. "Of course," muttered Hendrix.

They descended each stair cautiously, yet to their surprise, these stairs simply led to another door.

Aypax forced the feeble door open, bringing them inside the witch doctor's market.

"Cawwwww!" A sparrow crowed from a ceiling beam.

Hendrix eyed the bird, a bit shaken. *DoomRock?* He repeated. He'd heard it before. *Where?*

Ava glanced about. Lengthy rows of black shelves formed aisles. Jars, herbs, and dolls lined them. Books were abundant, as were crystals and thin chains made of seashells. Various animal limbs had been preserved, each with a price tag atop.

"A golden bracelet," announced an elderly Tourtoufian standing behind a counter. "With red and blue at heart…" She wore a dress of bright colored feathers, with heeled orange and red boots that added a full foot to her height.

The witch doctor.

Aypax studied her wrinkly green skin. "What did you say?"

The witch doctor gazed at her sparrow with narrowed brown eyes. "I don't remembers. That's part of mys gift."

Aypax looked stunned, a bit frightened even, but perhaps her comment was mere coincidence. He walked toward her counter, staring at a row of daunting dolls. "Do you carry Ashboiler or Rememmine?"

Ava searched the aisles with Hendrix, finding fewer potions than expected. There were scissors, chalk, gloves, but a lack of what they needed. Hundreds of decapitated goose heads hung from the ceiling.

"Both," stated the witch doctor. "I makes the Rememmine myself. It is powerfuls, though. Be warned. More powerfuls than... lost love."

Aypax sharpened his stare. "Keep doing what you're doing."

Once again she appeared lost in her own mind, never so much as glancing at Aypax. "Cant's say what I was doings. Part of the gift."

Aypax approached. "We'll take one case of Ashboiler. And two jars of your personal Rememmine. No, four jars."

The witch doctor finally met his stare, and now, she never blinked. "A warrior, no, an executioner...tormented by the screams of those he's taken. I see the number six—"

"Enough!" Aypax grabbed her by the throat and pulled the colorful witch over her counter. The sparrow crowed twice as loud.

"Aypax! Aypax!" Hendrix rushed forward, but the big one shoved him hard with one hand, easily controlling the witch with his other. "You shall tell me how you know these things! Where is my Katrin?"

Now flat on his back and bleeding from the nose, Hendrix put it all together.

Prophetics 11— The Witch and the Crow

1. It crows at first glance of the Doc, the Witch of DoomRock
2. From high above, amongst the heads of birds,
3. Long dead and hung, long dead and strung,
4. It crows twice to take flight, into the island's night
5. Black and frightening, polluted fog and sin,
6. Scared to leave, the honorable must believe,
7. A third and final time, the crow marks the truth of her binds,
8. Fake spells, a hoax with no truth,
9. Drill Bintonn betrayed, his destiny swayed.

"Where is she?" roared Aypax. "Where? How do you know of me and my bracelet?"

"I don't know anything!" spat the witch doctor, struggling. "My words are just a parts of the gift!"

He dragged her across the counter, knocking over various items, and released her. She dropped to the floor like a doll, like one of the many dolls nearby... Aypax eyed them, slowly realizing their shapes. "This doll. This one here." He lifted a small doll from its display. It appeared to be a youthful Tourtoufian lady. "Why is this doll positioned away from the rest?"

The doll did seem rather specific, and sat rows above the others, begging to be purchased.

"I put my best dolls on displays." She coughed, nursing her throat. "That is all."

"This is her..." said Aypax. "This doll is Katrin! The blue eyes and red hair, the cut pants and golden bracelet. I shall not ask you once more. *Where. Is. She?*"

The witch doctor stood and gathered herself. "You are nots who I thought you to be."

"You shall speak now," said Aypax. "Or I shall seem far worse than what you thought I might be."

"The gift cannot be pressed, it is nots in my controls. I am sorrys, but you must go—"

Aypax drew his dagger and pressed it to her throat.

"Buts perhaps!" she exclaimed, frightened. "Perhaps I could trys...just this once."

Aypax stowed the blade. "Seems the gift is in your control after all."

The witch doctor shook, her very limbs fearful. She walked toward her doll and frowned. "The truth is...I have no gift. I am simply a spice maker. And I simply knows the one you yearn for."

"Please...just tell me what I ask."

The witch doctor considered Aypax for a long moment. "Once upon a times, your Katrin was takens by those damned Bintonns. They saw something in her, so they broughts her here to me. Asked me to looks into her soul, to see if she was the one Drill Bintonn seeks."

Ava spun away at the name. Hendrix noticed. "Drill Bintonn?" he asked.

"Drill is the leader of the Bintonns. He has taken over Tourtoufa after defeating and executing the island's parliament, but ruling our island is not his goal." The witch doctor peered at Ava, her filthy clothes and ugly brand hiding on her wrist. "You see, Drill Bintonn seeks only one thing…"

Aypax grew frustrated. "Speak!"

"A woman!" continued the witch. "Young, beautifuls, said to possess a rare ability. Drill claims he saw hers in a dream. He thinks she's a Tourtoufian, but I'm nots so sure."

Aypax stepped forward. "How do you know the one I yearn for?"

"When they broughts Katrin to me, Drill Bintonn himself came too. Katrin was to be killed for her husband's death… But Drill tolds me I had 'til moonfall to unlock her power. Said he knew she was the one. She wasn't."

Katrin. Aypax felt the heavy burden of shame and the ever-returning voices he'd fought so long to silence.

"Drill Bintonn tried to make her perform powers. He did many harsh tortures to Katrin, but she was unables to do the magic he thought she possessed. So he brought her heres, thinking I might extract her gifts. I helped Katrin escape that eve. That's when she tolds me of you, Aypax. The biggest Alyonian, she says, with a heart that is sour but true. She tolds me you would come for her and that you would be known by your size, your honor, and your kindness."

The witch doctor walked back behind her messy counter. "But

things change. I've left the doll there evers since, waiting for the big Alyonian to see it. You saws it the moment you ducked into my shop. And I knew it was you."

"Caaaaaccaaawwww." The sparrow cried a third time.

Hendrix felt another pull. They were growing more consistent of late. *A third and final time, the crow marks the truth behind her binds.*

"I cloaked Katrin and sent her to the docks for escape," continued the witch doctor. "But she was captured that sames eve by Drill. I haves not seen her since."

Aypax swallowed. "If what you say is true, why did the Bintonns spare you?"

"Simple." The witch doctor pointed toward ten dolls wearing orange vests, all laying inside a bucket. The dolls inside had been covered in a variety of spices and flakes akin to a stew. "Drill Bintonn is a very superstitious gangster...just like the local pirateers. I tells the Bintonns that this is my Dream-stealer. Tells them if I perish, the stealer steals their dreams, taking away Drill's memory, and his destiny."

Hendrix rose a brow. "What is it truly?"

"Truly?" She smiled. "A bucket with pepper flakes and hair dust. The dolls I simply painted orange."

They chuckled. Even the sparrow seemed to join.

"A moment." The witch doctor bent down and rummaged behind her counter, then placed four jars in front of Aypax. "Takes the Rememmine for free. But be warned. Powerfuls."

Aypax grasped the items. "You've our thanks."

Ava turned around suddenly, glancing out of a skylight. Had she just seen Sir Edmund Drake?

"What troubles you, young one?" The witch doctor approached her window and gazed up into the rainy streets. "Ah, I see...the fear follows you wherevers you go. I suggest you all runs toward Katrin, fast."

House Rynn

Letter type: Urgent, Informative

To: Taaivetti Kaldor
From: Sir Rynn of Kaldoria
343 A.B, Windy Season, 96th Moon, Double Novas

My prince, I write from Naomiback. Our army rides to your aid. Bolden was easily convinced (dare I say, I told you he would be).

He appears eager to "kill the brainless beasts." Our numbers are incredible: ten thousand.

We are perhaps one moon away and should arrive during the peak of tomorrow's heat. Bolden has commanded we rest and have our fill of water before engaging. But you'll see us, Taaivetti. You'll hear us.

Stay true, stay in worship (preferably ours). Tomorrow we find out why you're at Hann.

Sir Rynn of Kaldoria

35

TAAIVETTI

A Red Tide

Prince Taaivetti held Sir Rynn's letter tightly, angrily. *Too late,* he thought, crumbling it.

The prince stood shoulder to shoulder with nearly one hundred Alyonians, all cluttered upon Hann's wall walk. Clad in green and gold, these warriors stared down into the desert below, all ready for war, yet all wondering one thing.

Whyever did we stay?

Positioned over Hann's center gatehouse, Taaivetti's unit stood in the midst of it all. He saw fear in his troop's eyes as their enemy approached. He saw regret. The Gorsh were still a distance away, too far to make out, too far to truly fear, but the feeling was creeping…

Taaivetti pulled out his longscope. With its tight and narrow view, he could see most of the horde. Red sand rose into warm air as the Gorsh marched forward in surprisingly efficient ranks. Olivorio had been correct. *It is truly endless.*

"Make way! Make way!" A few Alyonians struggled up a wooden stairwell behind, carrying boxes of arrows and stones to the wall walk. There was little room to maneuver, however, for tight rows of archers and barrels of boiling sand blocked their path. This terrible cluster only added to the heat, stench, and restlessness.

Another three hundred Alyonians formed perfect lines in front of the wall, each warrior ready to give their all, or perhaps just ready to accept the inevitable. Taaivetti scanned his makeshift defenses.

"Eight rows of struggle," said Zo, also examining their sandy fortifications. A series of deep trenches had been dug one after another, with spiked wire separating each. "They shall cost the Gorsh valuable time to cross before meeting our front line."

Taaivetti scratched his blistered lip. "The brethren dug well."

Zo agreed. "Six moons of digging. Thorns, spikes, and shredded glass await our enemy at the bottom of each."

Taaivetti knew that. He also knew such defenses would only serve as a minor annoyance, a clumsy death or two at best.

"We'll rain arrows upon them as they ascend and descend each," continued Zo. "They'll likely lay down ladders to cross, but that narrows them. Easier shots. If they leave the alley and venture round us into the volcanoes, that adds time for Rynn and Bolden. Valuable time."

"Agreed," added Sir Arrevon. "All we need to do is hold them off 'til Bolden arrives." He referenced the courtyard behind them. "We've three catapults; they've none."

These catapults were loaded and ready. Another hundred warriors surrounded them—reserves.

"Our bows have distance to their slings," continued Sir Arrevon. "We may be able to frustrate them as they trample over one another. They could withdraw and replan."

"We're giving their warlord a good deal of compliment." Taaivetti wiped sweat from his brow. "Olivorio claims he's the wisest of the beasts. But withdrawing, replanning? That requires wisdom."

"To the north!"

A lookout's voice traveled from a small bartizan above. Five hundred heads turned at once, each hoping to see what they'd desperately been waiting for.

"They're here! Bloody Perdition, they're here!"

Hann's defenders cheered and waved flags as more sand swirled over a dormant volcano to the north. A second force.

Taaivetti smiled. *Just in time.*

"My prince..." Zo's words trailed off.

Then Taaivetti saw it too, as did everyone. A hefty red banner rose over the summit, followed by another hundred banners, each red and torn, each sharing the same emblem: a black skull with vile horns twisting upward. Two rusty blades pierced both eye sockets.

Zo stared, confused yet impressed. "They've crafted banners?"

Taaivetti said nothing. Thunderous drums began to beat, adding to the deafening footsteps of the Gorsh. *A second force. A tactical flank? That requires thought...wisdom.*

"They've catapults." Sir Arrevon swallowed. "Fifteen."

Taaivetti counted. "Twenty. And with high ground."

The first horde had now closed in, though these Gorsh looked more like an army than a horde.

"They've formed ranks." Zo rubbed his weary eyes and squinted. "They're even wearing armor. Heavy plates too." He grabbed Taaivetti's longscope and considered the approaching beasts.

The Gorsh were heinous things. Red creatures. Taller than the largest of Alyonians and with far greater muscle. Two curved horns protruded their rough, scaly heads.

"They've never deployed tactic," Zo said. "Yet here they are, appearing as if you were leading them."

"It's not possible," said Taaivetti. "Even with time, these creatures could never build such devices. They could never craft such fine armor."

Zo thought about the passing Askari and secret fliers of the night. "You mean to imply they were aided?"

"It matters not." Taaivetti's legs shook. "My honest count is more than one hundred thousand. We've no chance here. Not even with Bolden. This is a night terror."

The Gorsh drums stopped abruptly, as did both hordes. They halted a safe distance upon command as their leader rode forward on the back of a slimy beast.

Zo twisted the longscope, zooming in. "What is that?"

"Far too big to be a serpent." Taaivetti evaluated the creature as well, squinting. "Seems broken in. Tamed."

The slithering beast torqued its black body, knocking hefty Gorsh around with ease. The rider on top could not be mistaken. His colossal horns said it all.

"Their warlord," whispered Sir Arrevon.

"Arknah-Forticah!!!" shouted the warlord. He leapt from his slithering creature, then stood in front of his armies and inspected the battlefield's trenches and traps.

Zo focused. "He's far larger than the rest."

"And thinking," added the prince. "He won't think for long."

A silence crept over the trio as they began to smell their comrades. Literally.

Taaivetti turned to a nearby commander. "Prepare as many Naomi as possible. Draw them to the back of Hann. Dispatch our birds and send word to Alyonia immediately—"

"My prince!"

As if on cue, a group of soldiers yelled from the courtyard behind. "The ravens are gone! Unleashed! And there's no sign of Patriclous or Zander."

"Planned from within," said Zo. "This entire thing—"

"Arknah-Forticah!!!" The warlord raised his hand high, then did precisely what Taaivetti hoped he wouldn't.

He pointed toward his catapults.

"Take cover!" Alyonian commanders shouted as countless boulders hurled toward Hann with frightening speed.

"Fire!" screamed Sir Arrevon, returning three of his own. A pointless endeavor.

Taaivetti looked up. An array of stones blocked out any novalight, then descended upon his walls like a tidal wave to a sandcastle. Flimsy wood exploded upon impact, slinging deadly shards in every direction.

Blood splashed about. Bodies took flight. The ground itself fell beneath feet, dragging Alyonians four stories to their demise. Naomi cried and ran wild amongst the courtyard.

Panic took control whilst the enemy reloaded. Taaivetti's units shuffled and looked for guidance.

"Arknah-Forticah!!!" The warlord's words roared through The Red Sand Desert like a weapon. More stones took flight. Taaivetti glanced to the skies, then clutched his pendant.

Everything went black.

36

CRIMSON
A Cup of Ale

Captain Crimson snickered up at the Rommani manors from the center of a dirt road. King Street. Still mounted upon his Naomi, he trotted forward for a better look. Sporting decrepit blue shutters, the old manors weren't much on beauty. *But they'll do*, he thought.

Sat perched atop a slanted hill, the Rommani rose three stories high, with withering gardens and decaying fence lines. The dying gardens were split by a thin walkway of dirt leading down to King Street. Snow covered everything, working tirelessly to add an element of charm, but failing. Crimson ignored it all, lost in his own mind, ever fighting the pounding headaches. *Burnt necks here at the Crossing? Why humans? Tiannu's letter warned only of Alyonians.*

Nario pulled beside Crimson, then waved up at his beloved Rommani. "Our finest manors."

His smile was endearing, at least. Crimson scanned the run-down city surrounding King Street, its rickety buildings and unkept sewers. The Rommani really were its finest.

"A roof is a roof." Gable pulled beside them both.

"Aye." Lukon followed suit. "Our recruits are lucky to have

anything overhead. The snow piles only to our ankles. They should cherish such conditions while they can."

Crimson's shivering recruits entered the manors in a line, his Green Capes steering them like cattle.

"You know where to find me." Nario bowed before taking leave.

Gable rubbed his gloves together, shaking off the cold. "Shall we? Maybe the alehouse'll have a damned fire pit."

Crimson dismounted. "I could drink. So long as I don't hear your moaning in the early morn—" He stopped, suddenly noticing a tiny bird plummet to the ground beside him. Crimson stared at the dying bird, writhing and wiggling amongst a thornbush, a dance of death.

Lukon stepped forward. "She freezing to death?"

Crimson evaluated the strange bird. It seemed healthy enough, yet spasmed uncontrollably. Aggressively. "Tie off our Naomi in the stables. I'll await your return."

* * *

The trio hustled through backstreets of the Crossing. Crimson had dug a paltry grave for the tiny bird a few hours prior, dampening the mood and putting their night of drinking a bit behind. Odd shadows had plagued his peripheral ever since, though they'd stopped right around nova-set.

"Gettin' dark fast," said Lukon, sipping from his flask.

Darkness had indeed engulfed the Crossing before they'd even passed into mankind's section.

"There's the El-Road." Crimson referenced its perfect pavement, lit only by street torches fighting for life against the light snow. "She's always empty here."

"Aye, an unspoken barrier," said Gable. "May as well be a wall."

Crimson nodded. "Be on guard once we've crossed into man's territory, and see to behaving yourselves."

Gable shrugged. "Aye."

"Fine...aye," followed Lukon.

They stepped onto the vacant El-Road. Gable spat on its pristine gravel, then took in man's section ahead. Their manors were larger, better kept too. Impressive statues of bears and ancient Rhi family members lined the polished sidewalks. Even the streets and alleys appeared clean, perhaps swept daily. Snow had been shoveled aside. Shops and saloons of half-timber and half-stone stretched afar.

"Waste of coin, it is," snapped Lukon jealously. He watched a group of men pass by nursing smokes. "And too many men, too few women."

The Alyonians came to an intersection. Wooden manors covered in ivy rested on all four corners. Crimson glanced up at a particular window. A troubling amount of messenger birds came and went. No less than ten by his count. A few Askari, even. Crimson stood eerily still, as if listening to the wind or the flapping of wings. A faint whisper seemed to echo here...

"Ignore 'em," said Gable, as more humans walked by, staring. The Alyonians dark skin and thick furs were hard to spot in tonight's snowy shadows. Still, each passing man appeared to be watching.

"I need ale, mates." Lukon grew angry with the constant glares and belittlement.

"Seek and find." Gable pointed down an alley to a sign swinging through light winds. "The Yellowfish Inn. Now that looks like a proper place. What say you?"

Making their way toward the establishment, Crimson observed the wooden sign: a Yellowfish made of bone, resting over an empty plate. Mugs of ale surrounded. Arriving, he breathed on the inn's foggy window and peeked inside. Its interior buzzed with life.

Gable pointed through the new hole of breath. "Well, I'll be damned!"

Lukon laughed. "A fire pit."

Gable rushed for the door like a toddler. "Let's go. That's a sign if I've ever seen one."

"Wait." Crimson lingered. Something felt off. "Too many men inside. Too close quarters. We may as well bathe in the sickness."

"Ah, Captain, come now!" Disease may have been rampant, but Lukon was dying of thirst, Gable of cold.

Crimson furthered his examination. This inn was merely the first floor of a far bigger structure. More stories covered in ivy stretched high above, casting an eerie presence on everything below. Flags and wind chimes dangled from wooden beams. Crimson recognized the shapes of these chimes, though he couldn't recall why.

Keys. Red and green in color.

He peeked through his evaporating window hole and noticed five men by the fire pit, one of them with a clear burn on his neck. "This'll do."

"Yes!" Gable swung the door open mightily, ensuring a grand entrance. Forty men turned their heads. The inn's noise and buzzing of life came to a screeching halt. Its violinist stopped. Mugs dropped. Conversation died. All eyes shot toward the three Alyonians.

"I know I'm a looker, but let's try and keep it together mates," joked Gable in that deep voice of his. Not a soul so much as chuckled. "Just looking for a proper cup of ale." He gestured to a sign over the bar.

Cup of ale - 3 Terrats

A painful silence ensued, followed by grunts and a few racial slurs. Crimson scanned the room for threats, exits, and allies. Nothing seemed unordinary, excluding those five men seated by the fire pit.

"Damn, and I thought it was cold *outside*." Gable smacked Crimson's shoulder, then sauntered toward the bar. "Evenin'. We're lookin' for your finest cup."

The bearded innkeeper ignored Gable's eyes.

Lukon leaned over his countertop. "He said evenin'."

The innkeeper glared at their long forearm hair tickling his bar top. "I heard him." He reached below and pulled out another sign.

If I don't like ya, I won't serve ya.

Gable could only laugh. "How do ya know ya won't like me? I could be the funniest chap in this shithole."

The innkeeper rolled up his sleeves and nodded to a group of men. A few drunkards rose from their seats, but Crimson never shifted his stare from the five by the flames.

"Whoa, whoa, hold on now…" A mountainous man with fiery red hair slid down the bar and intervened. Extending his arm in front of Gable, he calmed the innkeeper. "The Alyonians' ale is on my coin. Plus a bit extra for your hospitality."

Crimson knew the voice, knew it well. "Delphious-Shri!"

The red-haired man met Crimson's eyes. "We live in a small realm, old friend."

Crimson smiled wide before gripping Delphious-Shri's forearm. "It grows smaller with every moon."

Accepting reluctantly, the innkeeper poured three mugs of ale. Lukon winked. "You've my complete trust. I'm just watchin' your pourin' technique."

Gable laughed and sized up this Delphious-Shri, seemingly unsure how he felt of the man. Delphious wore a long coat of yellow and purple wool, but too few layers for this time of season. Gable watched him walk back to a sturdy table. His boots elevated him higher than everyone around, or maybe he was just that *big*?

"Come, join me," said Delphious.

Lukon gathered all three wooden mugs and followed. They sat, ever aware of the many eyes over their shoulders. Crimson let his green hood fall, a rare thing. With nothing hiding, he cut a handsome yet exhausted figure. Disheveled white hair fell to his bronzed forehead, just above two dark green eyes. Fleshy pouches of purple bags sat beneath, swollen from freezing weather and a lack of sleep. "Delphious, this is Gable and Lukon. Both Green Capes, both honored members of Emerald Company. More importantly, grand friends."

Delphious-Shri locked forearms with them as well, each competing for the firmest grip. "A raising of ale!" Delphious lifted his own mug. "To good friends in shit places."

The four smashed their mugs and drank. Even Crimson yielded his guard. "How long has it been?"

"No less than ten years, mate. I last saw you with your screaming babe and the beautiful Tiannu Preters. How do they do?"

The reminder hit Crimson like a brick. *If only I knew.* "They do well. Tiannu has turned our library into a proper pillar of Alyonia. And Madison stands to my shoulders."

"Gods!" Delphious-Shri smacked his mug against the table. "I'm old."

"You are," said Crimson. "Though with age comes wisdom."

"And with wisdom comes cunning," added Gable, still reading the red-haired giant, curious of his allegiance.

Delphious-Shri nodded as more human patrons pointed in their direction. "Some of them are good men," he assured, dodging Gable. "Many others, well, I needn't say."

Crimson leaned in close, motioning everyone to a whisper. "Let me ask you, Delphious. The men in the corner by the fire pit. What do you know of them?"

Delphious-Shri turned covertly. He saw the five men, each smoking and drinking. They held notebooks and fine ink pens. "Not enough. They arrived some sixty moons ago. There seem to be a few more, if you're referring to what I think you are. Maybe nine or so, far as I've counted."

"Would you lend me a favor whilst we're here?"

"I will," replied Delphious-Shri. "Though I cannot guarantee I find anything. You're not the first to be curious of them. Though you would be the first to uncover anything."

Crimson sipped. "That's perhaps all I needed to know."

"Another question," began Lukon. "What do you make of those large tracks in the fields just south'a here? We passed 'em comin' in through the Eagle Tail Mountains. Headin' west, they were."

Delphious-Shri sunk his voice even lower. "I've a theory." He paused a long moment, unsure how much to reveal. "Bandano-Rhi deployed my cohort north last rainy season. Said we were to dispose of Huskon raiders coming inland toward a popular intersection of the El-Road." He chugged his ale with one aggressive sip, then motioned the innkeeper for another. "When we arrived, there were no Huskon raiders, no signs of conflict at all. But upon our return to the Crossing, we saw many new faces. Or new necks, I should say."

"Interesting," interjected Crimson.

"Indeed. More importantly, there was another cohort that had arrived here during our absence. And as I'm sure you saw, there are more appearing as we speak. They're due for a season's stay. That's a lot of soldiers."

The innkeeper approached with Delphious-Shri's ale. "Here."

"Many thanks." His red hair fell beside his eyes. "I believe Bandano-Rhi is preparing the Crossing for something. I just don't know what nor why. Far as the tracks, I believe he's trading large weapons of war to the free river cities of Kios and Oblia. Siege equipment, war beasts, armor, and catapults. That's the only reason such large tracks would be moving westward to the desert. It's the only reason such a force would travel here."

Crimson started sweating through the crippling cold. "Let's take a walk."

37

TIANNU

The Kaldorian Guard

For a full moon Tiannu Preters had yet to sleep. After finding Priest Yalino's body and returning home to the news of her daughter's encounter with Taryn, she simply couldn't. But today was anew, and she'd spent its hours working tirelessly to uncover more on the red robes. For half the morn, she'd studied Yalino's journal in the safety of her library, but now, even that felt dangerous.

As the day passed, a red moon rose slowly over Alyonia, beckoning Tiannu for slumber. Her studies had yielded no gain, and her brain struggled against the arduous effects of relentless stress. *I must start over.* She fought to stay awake. *I must begin where Hendrix suggested. Blacksmith Justillian.*

* * *

Nightfall arrived as Tiannu walked through another series of dark alleys. She'd seen many alleys of late. *I've shared my findings with fellow scribes, and not a single soul knows anything of these mysterious red robes, nor why they'd murder Priest Yalino,* she wrote.

Folding her journal, Tiannu stopped mid-alley. Something always seemed to follow her: a feeling of unease, of being watched.

Even now she couldn't shake it. The manors on both sides extended far overhead, three to six stories each. Ignoring the fear and constant rain splattering atop her hood, Tiannu continued her chilly walk. It wasn't long before she reached her destination:

JUSTILLIAN'S: BETTER BLADES

A sign for Justillian's smithy had been nailed to its back door. The smithy rested at the end of this alley, marking the corner of a busy intersection. A prime location during day, but now there was only silence. Tiannu made for the back door, revealing a handheld lantern from inside her cloak. Raising it to eye level, she peeked inside a glass window. *Damn.* Still too dark to see.

She knocked. Nothing. She knocked once more. A new fear crept into her mind. *Is Hendrix right? Is Taryn truly killing off witnesses? No...* Leaving wasn't an option.

Tiannu reached back into her cloak and pulled forth a small dirk with a thin wire attached to its handle. Sliding her contraption into the doorknob, she twisted with precision.

Click.

She turned the knob and entered Justillian's smithy.

"Hello! Justillian?"

The small lantern lit her freckles and white hair, though not much else. Darkness limited vision to an arm's reach, forcing her to walk carefully, for bumping into anything in a smithy could prove perilous. She halted at the feeling of water. *No...much thicker.*

Drawing a deep breath, she knelt and shined her lantern upon the source.

Oh no...

Tiannu crawled, light in hand. A few more feet revealed Justillian's entire body, lifeless in a pool of blood. *Déjà vu.* Here she knelt again. Two witnesses, two deaths. Only now, Justillian's head was half severed, the beginnings of decapitation. Tiannu vomited, adding to the foulness.

Then Tiannu felt the cold and dreadful pain of steel sliding through her shoulder. It pierced one side before puncturing out the other. Rivers of red left her body, forcing her eyes closed. The air slowed as the steel blade retracted and came back for more.

"Jari, now! Help her!"

Tiannu's ears rang as metallic sounds clinked loudly all around. She fell flat upon the floor of blood, eyes closed and welcoming death.

"Jari, negate! Save the lady!"

Tiannu's eyes suddenly shot open, so open she couldn't close them. She gazed at barely lit feet shuffling throughout the smithy, at blades clashing. Tools fell from walls, blurry horseshoes hurled through warm air.

"Jari, to your left!"

Jari, she thought and almost smiled.

* * *

Tiannu awoke on an extremely old and rather smelly couch. Lifting herself, she quickly fell back as her shoulder screamed in agony. A brittle pine table rested beside her, marking the center of whatever common chamber she was in. She heard voices from behind.

If only the damn couch weren't blocking her view.

"Hello?"

She winced as the screeching of chairs being pulled across hardwood assaulted her ears. Footsteps came next as a few bodies approached.

"Glad to see you're awake and alive," said one of them. "We were worried the blade had struck your torso. Lucky."

He was an odd-looking Alyonian—heavyset with a strong yet overweight frame. His green suede vest could've been two-thousand-seasons old. The vest had been somewhat hidden by an equally ancient surcoat with an emblem of *K.G.* over its chest. The surcoat had once been gold, perhaps, but was long-stained to grey and black. *The oddest thing of all, however, is undoubtedly his face,* thought Tiannu. *It's as if he's both young and old. As if he's fifty-seasons young, and yet one-thousand-seasons of age.*

The heavyset Alyonian knelt beside Tiannu to assess her wound. Only now did she notice that it had been bandaged expertly.

"My name is Jari," he said as he gave her a peculiar smile. Jari had wrinkles beyond that of any Alyonian elder, yet his face and body posture were unquestionably youthful, as if he were no older than Tiannu herself. His large muscles were somehow covered in flabby, deteriorating skin.

"Get on with it, Jari!" said another of the voices. He, too, became clear as he and two additional Alyonians entered the room, each sharing Jari's bizarre skin traits. They sat in various chairs of wood. "Name's Cicero," he continued. "Cicero the Bald. You're welcome for the bandages."

"Cicero." Tiannu felt a little strength returning. "Jari... You've my thanks."

Thick black curtains hung down the windows behind them, ensuring no one could see in. These Alyonians matched Jari's attire. Green vests, gold surcoats, each dirty and ancient. They, too, shared the *K.G.* emblem; they, too, appeared both young and old.

Then Tiannu remembered. "Taryn."

"Yes." Jari frowned. "Taryn."

"Cold bitch," added Cicero, his bald scalp reflecting the overhead lights.

Tiannu managed to lift herself slightly. "It's true, then. She's killing witnesses."

Jari nodded. "Rumors claim she killed Queen Lizabeth herself. Perhaps even King Kaldor. We believe Yalino and Justillian were the only eyes to witness either murder. Makes sense she'd start things off by getting rid of them."

Tiannu tried to wiggle her shoulder. "Start things off?"

"You've got that bloody correct." Cicero grabbed his mug from the pine table and sipped aggressively. "Taryn is planning something. Something big."

The other two nodded, demoralized. Jari walked toward the black curtains, though he dared not pull them back. "We believe Taryn is preparing for a second Great War. If she succeeds, it'll be the last."

"A second Great War," echoed Tiannu. "Why?"

Cicero downed his drink. "*Why* is the grand question. Why Taryn wants war is anyone's guess. But we do know she wants it. Alyonia has damn near struck an alliance with the Rhi Empire, for bloody sake. We're aiding our realm's greatest threat. The Rhi Empire has never once had an ally, not since the first Great War. The Pallala-Accord killed that notion long ago, mandating that the Rhi Empire could not strike any official alliances without its written permission. So we must ask ourselves, Why abandon the Accord? Why join Rhi now?"

Tiannu remained still, unsure how best to respond.

"Because Taryn and Rhi are bracing for war, damn it!" continued Cicero the Bald. "It ain't a riddle! The Rhi Empire has a mind to take back what they feel rightfully belongs to 'em. Bandano-Rhi and his ancestors have always hated the Pallala-Accord. They believe our lands should be theirs. They believe their god Elo to be the only way of lasting peace. They're preparing to attack the Accord, I can feel it. Why Taryn wishes to leave the Accord and help them is the question, and the reason we're all gathered here tonight. We must stop her."

Tiannu stared. "And who exactly are *we*?"

"We are the last of the Kaldorian Guard," said Jari.

No.

Tiannu couldn't believe that. The Kaldorian Guard were legend, a myth found in books and folktales. The Kaldorian Guard had been created by Alyonia's prehistoric founder, its very first king: King Kaldoria. Or at least that's what the stories claimed. But Kaldoria was three-thousand-seasons dead. His guard couldn't possibly be alive.

And yet.

Those faces. Those wrinkles and scars.

"You do not believe." Jari nodded in understanding. "I blame you not. Your disbelief is why Taryn shall win. If the truths of old turn to legend, Alyonia can never learn from its past. She wishes to control the history books. To erase what once made us great and replace it with new ideals."

"None of that shit!" Cicero smacked his own cheek, readying himself. "Cut to the point, we've little time."

Jari took Tiannu's hand. His skin even *felt* ancient.

"Tiannu Preters, I speak truly. The Kaldorian Guard are real. The legends are true. The comets, the magic. Perhaps even the altar. Taryn means to find it, and if she does, she and Bandano-Rhi will be unstoppable. They could conquer the known world with ease. Now brace yourself. We need your husband's help to stop her."

Tiannu managed to sit up. "My husband? Why? And if what you say is true, why is this history not recorded? Why are there no academic books nor recounts of your Kaldorian Guard actions other than fireside stories?"

"Silence. 'Tis happening..." Cicero put both hands to his temple and pushed. "Ehhh! Give me the damned dust!"

One of the Kaldorian Guard handed him a fragile wooden box. Opening it, he pulled back a layer of fake foam, revealing a small pouch of grey dust beneath.

Tiannu's eyes lit up.

Jari grabbed the pouch and held it below Cicero's nose. "Snort, Cicero! Now!"

He did just that, inhaling the dust in one aggressive sniff. Cicero thrashed his head as his eyes turned grey. Then dark grey. "More!"

"No!" Jari grabbed his wrists sternly. "See what you must and leave."

Cicero stopped. Every muscle. Every vein. It all simply halted. The entire home fell quiet.

"Calm your mind, Tiannu Preters," said Cicero, his eyes fully glazed over in grey. "Your daughter shall be fine…"

Tiannu rose. "Jari, make him stop. You are mad!"

Cicero's eyes never opened, yet he smiled at Tiannu. "Your husband, Crimson, is the one you must worry for."

Tiannu moved toward Cicero.

Cicero focused, his cheekbones tightening visibly. "A good Alyonian, but without much time. A shadow god hovers over your husband. A shadow god of Stralli's. It aims to enter Crimson, to strangle the life from him."

Tiannu Preters froze, stunned. Balonity had long preached the dangers of Stralli and his many shadow gods. As a believer herself, she'd done all she could to keep her house safe from such evils, though Crimson and Madison had merely laughed at the notion. But after countless seasons without so much as a passing shadow, even Tiannu, admittedly, had begun to wonder if they truly existed.

"You must write him," continued Cicero. "Tell him to fall on his knees in worship. Your husband needs Balo himself. He needs intervention. Light gods are our only protection from shadow gods. Without them, we are susceptible. The spiritual realm is far more grim than even our own."

"Please," she beseeched Jari. "Please stop this. I, I believe in Balo, but this I cannot—"

Jari placed a loving hand over her good shoulder. "Cicero has 'Sight of the Spirits,' one of the seven gifts brought by the comets. He can see shadow gods and light gods alike. What he speaks is truth. Do not interrupt."

The others gestured an affirmation as Cicero began to bleed in his chair. "This shadow god has a hold on your husband." A bit of blood trickled from his nose and eyes, even the pores on his cheeks. "He'll be having night terrors…brain-aches, and worse. Even the days are not safe with this shadow hovering over Crimson."

"Prove this." Tiannu felt another wave of vomit roiling through her belly, yet somewhere deep down, she knew it was true. "Prove this!"

Jari scowled, then clutched the pouch of grey dust. "How do you think your shoulder healed?"

Tiannu pulled up her sleeves and gazed at her aching shoulder. The wound was nasty, sure, and still a dull-red streak. But the gash had nearly closed entirely.

Jari pointed to a long-haired Alyonian behind Tiannu. "Healing. Another of the seven gifts." Jari dumped a bit of the dust into his hands before rubbing it together, then put his nose to both palms.

"Careful, Jari…" said the long-haired Alyonian.

Jari stood idle for a few seconds, then his eyes began to change. Grey. Dark grey. He placed his hand on Cicero's chest, and with a powerful shock, Cicero returned to normal.

He slowly came to, weary and disoriented. "Bloody Perdition, Jari! I wasn't finished. That husband of hers has a part to play, a big one!"

Jari turned to Tiannu, breathing slowly. "Negate. That's my gift. Negation. The ability to stop other gifts. Proof enough?"

Negate, she thought. "I heard one of you scream that back at the smithy. Why would you negate your own abilities?"

Jari shook off his fatigue. "I didn't. I negated the gifts of another. The assassins responsible for your shoulder and for the death of blacksmith Justillian, the twins… They are Taryn's, and they are dangerous. Come, let us show you."

38

TARYN

Where We First Met

Taryn had ridden nearly all day and night. Her legs were bruised, her stomach cramped. Both feet had gone numb, as if becoming a very part of the stirrups. Her red rain-soaked cloak draped heavy and damp, allowing water to drench her skintight vest and tunic. It was the longest she'd ever traveled alone, the most challenging too. Though she was sure the journey would be worth it.

Taryn had reached the end of a ridge positioned just off the El-Road. This ridge overlooked a vast graveyard filled with thousands of memory stones, oak trees, and ancient monuments. Taryn's Naomi gave an exhausted whimper as it came to a stop. She dismounted before the Naomi fell flat upon the ridge. Taryn knelt on the cold ground. "A wonderful job," she whispered, stroking the beast's soaking mane. "Rest. I shall return."

Taryn detached two saddlebags and stood. Leaving her Naomi, she made toward a cluster of high rocks. Climbing the wet, smooth stones was a pain, but once peaked, she gained a better view of the moonlit graves below.

There you are.

Her face went smitten beneath her ruby-red hood. She gazed down at Bandano-Rhi, standing just where she knew he'd be.

DUST

Her grave.

* * *

Taryn descended the ridge and navigated the rainy graveyard. She passed a few statues she'd deemed landmarks from above.

He is near.

Fog lifted all around, as if the clouds themselves were resting here, dancing and twirling with the moon's powerful light. Constant rain turned the ground into a slippery trap of mud, forcing her to step carefully.

Where are you?

She continued onward, passing archaic cairns, tombs, and obelisks of great men and Alyonians alike. Finally she saw him, far off through thick blankets of white. He knelt before a tiny head-stone. Tired of the rain, Taryn trudged beneath an old oak tree and watched Bandano-Rhi, moved by his devotion and pain. Light drizzle drenched his hair and slid down the back of his yellow and purple leather jacket. Bandano-Rhi held a bundle of soggy flowers in one hand, a smooth wineskin in the other. His forehead rested upon the chilly headstone, allowing his tears to trickle down its side.

A long moment passed and still he said naught. Taryn laid her saddlebags against the oak tree's stump, then paced toward him. "She would've loved those flowers. And she'd be so proud of her brother."

Bandano-Rhi remained silent, tightening his grip around the dead blossoms. A few thorns nicked his fingers, causing blood to seep. "I watched the life drain from her. I watched the welts and sores take her. When the sickness became apparent, I couldn't even stand by her side."

"You had no choice," said Taryn. "You're the emperor. Your people couldn't risk you being around her—"

"She died alone." Bandano-Rhi rose, never taking his eyes from the grave. "Afraid in a dark cell…preparing for execution." He

271

took a long swig from the wineskin before facing Taryn. "They filled her heart with arrows from a slit. Just to stop the pain. Just to end her misery."

Taryn stepped forward, struck by his tone and the swelling beneath both eyes. "Those are your laws, my love. You protected your empire by stopping the spread. You did what was right. In time, even the sickness shall pass."

"It will not." Bandano-Rhi collected himself. "I am sure of it, for I, too, have news."

Surprised, Taryn said, "Speak."

He gazed up into the foggy sky. "A shadow god has been spotted in the city of Coyo. A real shadow god…seen by the masses. A creature of shadow, bone, and flesh. It is just as Elo warned us. Our god said this would happen if we forsook him. The birth of these shadows through man's fall. The shadow god Stralli's creation of plagues. It's all foretold. It's all so very real. We're being punished."

Taryn nodded, fascinated, her mind racing.

"We've reached a dark place," continued Bandano-Rhi. "A new low in civilization. These heathens drench themselves in lust and murder. Their iniquities have allowed such shadows to surface, such darkness to take root. This sickness, this famine, these times of rain and war. Doubtless the work of our world's most heinous shadow gods. Shadows that only grow stronger as we fall further from Elo's holy edicts!"

"Agreed. Our world has gone dark. Far too dark." Taryn's fingers twitched with excitement. "They must be killed. The shadow gods, the fallen men, all of them. We cannot have peace whilst they exist. Elo will guide us."

"You speak truly, my love. I will no longer tolerate heresy." Bandano-Rhi glared at his sister's grave. "Its effects are clear. These heathens of Coyo birthed the very illness that took her. I will bring fire to their disgusting city!" Bandano-Rhi squeezed the wineskin so powerfully it burst, though nothing came out. "The sight of this shadow god has changed everything for me. Its existence is proof of what we have always believed, proof of the spiritual realm…of Elo and his fellow light gods. Elo's holy edicts are clear. 'When the shadows show themselves, the end times are near.' I must declare for war on any nonbelievers immediately if we are to have any chance of appeasing Elo, of returning to his good grace. I've waited for Alyonia's support long enough, I can wait no longer—"

"Good," she interjected, "for you do not have to."

He froze. "You've done it?"

Taryn grinned. "I have. Messenger birds have been sent forth to every realm that currently holds a seat in the Pallala-Accord. By morn, they'll all know the news. Alyonia has officially withdrawn."

Bandano-Rhi took a knee in the mud and kissed his forearm tattoo. "Praise be to Elo."

Taryn moved closer and pulled his head into her stomach. "Praise him. Without Alyonia's protection, Coyo is weak. The sickly city is already at death's door. Go and finish it. Once they fall, wage war on the east. One by one, we will cleanse all of Adria."

Bandano-Rhi stood, looked into Taryn's eyes. "Well said. But without Alyonia, the *entire* Accord is weak. Coyo will be a clear message to the other realms. Let us pray they see the folly of their ways and repent. If they do not, well, I've amassed my armies in every city throughout Pallala. From the Crossing to Selma, from the Outpost to Dresden, there isn't a city nor province without a cohort awaiting orders. When I give signal, a new great war will wage across Adria without warning. The east is just the beginning. It will all happen too fast. And with your aid, a new world is inevitable."

Taryn's damp tail wrapped around Bandano-Rhi's calf and slowly caressed him. "And your people? You believe them ready to support such a harsh war?"

He nodded. "My citizens want real peace. Lasting peace. They want a world that supports and loves one another. They want to share borders with peaceful empires, not heathens who might attack at any moment. By killing now, we face hard times, but in the end, the Rhi Empire will be remembered for saving Adria from these plagues and shadow gods. My people yearn for good, they yearn for a harmonious world that their children can grow old in. A two-realm function between Alyonia and Rhi will achieve just that."

"That it will." Taryn paused and reflected. "This shadow god spotted in Coyo, did it have a fiery aura? Perhaps with strong, yet thin and bony limbs?"

Bandano-Rhi's arms fell to his sides. "Yes…that's precisely how it was described. How did you know?"

Her eyes flickered, preparing to lie. "A dream."

Bandano-Rhi was no stranger to prophetic visions. "This dream, tell me of it."

"Elo stood in the corner of my bed chambers, watching me sleep. Upon first glance he appeared a dark and shadowy figure. But I simply blinked and realized his true form. Elo was a beautiful man, strong. He was you."

"Me?"

"He was you, Bandano. He said, 'Find me, draw me to the graveyards where we first met.' Elo had taken your physical form, but I knew it to be our god. He whispered into my ears lovingly. He said, 'Warn me of the shadow god. The shadow of fire and flesh and bone. Tell me I must kill it before it's too late. Tell me it dies by my sword only. Tell me that Elo shall carry me to victory.'"

Bandano-Rhi shook, his limbs going cold from the night and the story. "Praise him," he mumbled. Taryn's chest and tail warmed him a bit, but still he shivered inside and out. "I've no doubt of your vision. Though I must admit, a shadow god is a frightening foe."

"I've had many dreams such as this," said Taryn, lying. "But none clearer. Elo needs you to go and face this shadow. To go and burn Coyo. Do not be afraid. Our god is with you."

Inspired, the emperor embraced Taryn, then left his sister's grave. He moved toward his horse a few paces off. Taryn followed. "I've done what I can to force Alyonia's love for you, but half will never change. Once you've conquered Coyo, many Alyonians shall grow restless. Civil conflict could come quicker than we think."

Bandano-Rhi saddled up, then put both feet into matching yellow stirrups. "Just be ready when it comes."

Taryn gave a quick nod. "I shall."

"Then I will see you soon."

Bandano-Rhi whistled loudly. The sound of hooves pounding far off punched through the haze.

Taryn raised a brow. "Have they been here all along?"

"You'd never see them coming." Bandano-Rhi smirked as his honor guard descended a boggy hill.

"Oh, and Bandano...the key is nearly at the Crossing. It will make its way north to the Lookout within a few moons. My finest Alyonians are on the job."

Bandano-Rhi leaned down and kissed her lips. "Well done, my love."

39

HENDRIX

Stadium Starsgard

The Family stood together atop a great stone bridge, each drenched and panting from a long ascent. Hendrix and Aypax leaned upon a slick balustrade, gazing out over Starsgard. The once untainted Ratna River flowed below, but here, it ferried dingy ships and wooden rafts through piles of drifting garbage.

"Place looks to have seen better days," said Hendrix.

"Raft ferries." Sammy scratched herself. "The Bintonns use 'em to sail rich folk round the island, feedin' 'em lies about landmarks and magical coral."

"Aye." Drake rubbed his forehead, nursing yet another brain ache. "When is this bird of yurs gonna show—"

"He's there." Aypax removed a soggy combat boot and lifted it high. Waving his boot back and forth, he whistled toward distant clouds. "Pattar, *Ramos*!"

Hendrix could barely see the boats below, never mind Pattar, through such persistent rain. "If our first attempt was a failure, how will Pattar know to set a different course for Hann?"

Aypax grinned as his beloved Askari pierced into visibility. The creature soared slowly, yet seemed to have healed decently. "Don't trouble yourself with such things, Hendrix. Stay focused on Edmund

Drake's plan."

Sir Edmund Drake exhaled, ignoring the striking brain ache. "I noticed ya don't refer to me by me full title. Dare I assume ya think I never earned it?"

Aypax had known this would arise at some point, but no, he certainly did not think the pirateer had earned the title of "sir." Still clutching his smelly boot, Aypax smiled at Drake. "The title is—"

"Sweet-honey-breasted wench! That boot stinks." Sammy covered her nostrils and ended the argument. "I'm far less impressed by your bird's nose at this point."

"Paaaaattttttaaaa!" The Askari landed upon Aypax's shoulder, forcing Sammy from her new favorite position.

"Hey!" Sammy dropped to the slick bridge angrily. "You oughta train that thing, pal."

Aypax removed Katrin's dirty shirt from his travel sack and let Pattar get a long whiff, then pulled forth their letter for Taaivetti. The Askari clutched it and took flight.

Hendrix could not help but notice that their letter looked fresh, almost unscathed. *A second penning, perhaps? And what was the need of this shirt?*

"Is Jakko feeling healthy?" Ava ran her fingers through his thick fur, concerned. The pup lay by her feet, curled. "He looks a bit...sleepy."

Jakko stood upon hearing his name. His ears pinned back. The dog wished to bark, though he couldn't. He'd guzzled down a full portion of the witch doctor's Rememmine and lost dexterity by the minute. A long sleep would follow.

Drake joined Ava, now stroking Jakko's neck. He laughed as the dog's tongue lolled out of his mouth more than usual. "He'll live."

"Look." Sammy pointed. "Just beyond the grain and water mills. Stadium Starsgard. Rumor has it, she took ten seasons to build and cost twice the island of Bora."

Hendrix could barely fathom such a stadium's existence. More of a coliseum than anything, the structure was magnificent, a clear work of Drill Bintonn's coin. Its tallest pillars loomed over the city, hoisting orange flags for all to see. Glorious windows and spectacular aqueducts were visible, even from the outside. Its unscathed stone exterior had been covered only by more orange banners dangling from above.

"Ten Bintonns ahead," stated Drake.

Ava averted her eyes, doing her best to hide.

Aypax surveyed them. "Shit, what are they doing up here?"

The group of thugs stood beside a poorly built booth nestled against the bridge's balustrade. A long line of customers surrounded.

"The High-Plunge booth!" chirped Sammy. "Loony bastards, divin' from this height. That ain't a rush, just a death wish."

Aypax surveyed these Bintonns, waiting for them to see through his disguise, but they didn't. *Interesting.* The thugs concentrated on their long line of patrons, though Aypax remembered Drake's warning... The Bintonns were proficient in observing their surroundings, masters of false busyness. *They could spring for us at any moment.*

He was correct. The Bintonns suddenly locked eyes on Ava. They stared quizzically as The Family crept closer, passing diverse travelers and boozers. Feeling pressured, Aypax grabbed her roughly. "Sorry." He shoved Ava and pulled her hair forcefully.

Understanding his ploy, Ava used the moment to spit in Aypax's face. Aypax knew he needed to hit her, as did she. To let such an action go unpunished would surely break character. Aypax could feel Ava's limbs bracing. All eyes shot to him and that unpredictable rage.

But Aypax did not hit Ava. No. He simply wiped his face, then looked to the Bintonn in charge. She was tall and lean, like most of them. Dark green skin and loose orange clothing matched her followers. She differed from the others by wearing an even bigger hat with classic stripes of honor woven into the felt.

Aypax could not fathom what possibly earned stripes in such an organization. *Is slavery considered heroism? Robbery a form of esteemed handwork?*

The Bintonn leader smirked, insulting this stranger's lack of spine. Aypax's anger swelled. He recalled the witch doctor's words of Katrin, the way these Bintonns had treated her.

Two movements, he thought. *That's all it would take.* A blade to her trachea, a hip toss over the railing. Simple plays, and yet, none were the answer. He calmed himself, even managed a smirk of his own. The Family walked right by.

* * *

Twenty minutes passed as they'd crossed the bridge and descended a grassy knoll to its east. This knoll stretched down to the Ratna, where hundreds of tents covered a polluted waterline. Tourtoufians and unknown islanders casted nets and fishing rods into the river, their lines constantly caught by heaps of trash. A few homeless milled, trading and drinking with sunburnt locals.

"Where are your comrades?" asked Aypax. "I see no pirateers—"

"Aaaaaah!"

Everyone looked back toward the bridge, the Bintonns, and their booth. A body suddenly plummeted, yelling with excitement the entire way down.

Splash!

Aypax held his gaze on the rippling river. The body never resurfaced.

"They're all around us," said Drake. "A good deal a'the beggars ya see ain't actually beggars. We've got a'system here."

A system. Aypax tried to forget the fool who'd just dived to his doom. *Let's hope your system fares better.*

Sammy scurried forward. "The tunnel's drop point is in'a tent just ahead. It'll take us right under the stadium."

"Sir Edmund Drake and Sammy the squirrel!" A short human emerged from inside the aforementioned tent. "Mys two favorite friends!"

Sammy hopped onto the man and burrowed into his weathered tan hands. "Dorian!"

Dorian wore brown cattleboy clothing with the same heart and fist emblem as Drake. He tipped his circular hat to the rest of The Family. "Jakko don't looks so good."

Drake ruffled the dog's ears. "Rememmine."

"Ah, I sees," said Dorian.

Drake waved him off. "You can drop the accent. These folks are with me."

"Cheery," replied Dorian. "That accent angers me like nothin' else. Please, come in."

Everyone entered his shabby tent, gaping at its complexity within. Fine silver rested atop masterfully crafted shelves. Weapons and stolen jewels covered the blanketed floor. Bags of tools piled over a sanded-down tree stump.

In the corner, Hendrix spotted an impressive hole, no less than six forearms wide. A thick rug and two wooden cots, which apparently hid the hole, had been pushed aside. Three lanterns sat around the edge, fully lit and ready to descend with anyone brave enough to carry them.

"I received your gull," said Dorian. "I've already alerted the others. Jones and Yenna will stand watch by the bridge. The others will fish nearby, secretly guardin' our tent. Sir Drake, as usual, you'll stay in here and cover up the hole. Just in case." Dorian looked around. "Shall we?"

40

TARYN

Funeral Games

Tears filled the eyes of Madison Preters as she stared at a long row of caskets. Wooden, sealed. All lined beside their awaiting graves. All sized for children.

"And having just lost my own family..." Taryn choked up, using her written speech to wipe the coming tears. "My apologies." She set the speech back down upon a podium positioned in front of the caskets. Nearly one hundred Alyonians surrounded, each dressed in black, each hysterical. Preem, Orani, and a few others from the High Council were present, as were Taryn's house protectorates; though strangely, these warriors were unarmed. "Having just lost my own family, I can tell each mother and father here one thing: Though our loved ones shall become memories, it is up to us to decide what kind. Our memories can grow into pain or into riches. We may focus on the sting of death or on the gift of ever knowing those we cherished so dearly."

The speech uplifted crying parents, even if only a little. But this was all Trakkonious needed. Taryn's High Public Heed stood behind the crowd, surrounded by a committee of scribes and artists. Trakkonious had long prepared to render today's funeral on parchment, having selected three scribes to carefully pen each of Taryn's words several moons before the first child was ever struck down.

Trakkonious' painters were hard at work too, graciously depicting Taryn's pained face to the front page of tomorrow's story papers. By tonight, he would need only to hire enough pens and brushes for mass production.

"We've gone not four moons since Bandano-Rhi wisely pointed out Alyonia's senseless violence," continued Taryn. "And yet here we are, mourning thirty-three little ones and their beloved dance teacher, Bree of House Dashinggton."

Bree's parents let out a guttural noise in the audience, both positioned next to the last and largest casket in line.

"Though this is of little comfort, her murderer shall be held accountable," said Taryn. "The bowman was obviously skilled and somehow knew the unsecured entry points of our Alyonian dance hall. But we shall find him. Until then, I can merely be an example of change. As you see, my protectorates do not carry bows, nor shall they ever again. I cannot possibly share your sorrows, but I can share your tears and share the Kaldorian manor with each of you tomorrow. Our little ones deserve a proper celebration of life, and I tell you they shall have it."

Taryn bowed as pained claps erupted, none louder than Trakkonious and his followers. She exited the stage and made for their side when she suddenly grew wide-eyed. *Kornilious?*

A rather sorrowful Kornilious conversed with a few emotional members of House Dashinggton a short distance from the stage. She trekked toward him, easily reading the Master of Defense. *Pain. Change.*

"Kornilious?" Taryn stopped beside the group and extended her hand for a kiss.

He obliged, then bowed his way free of Dashinggton. "When I heard this news, I wept. I broke." He watched the crowd disperse, leaned closer to Taryn. "I went from house to house, paying condolences and slowly understanding the act's severity. Each mother, each family, changed forever by the loss of their child…and yet perhaps worse is the impact upon our realm. The fear that such a thing could ever happen again. Our hearts are corrupt." Kornilious paused, his hair blowing through rainy winds. "We are a wicked and vile heart, the all of us. Alyonian. Man. You. Me. As Master of Defense I can only oversee our military's actions. To stop such atrocities here at home would require a much greater title. Show me what needs seeing. A king must know everything happening in his realm."

* * *

Jari adjusted his longscope to Tiannu's eye, helping her watch the funeral adjourn from afar. "The one wearing a beige tunic," said Jari, "he's the worst of 'em."

"The twins are far worse," said Cicero, his bald head covered by a black hood. Standing beside Jari and Tiannu, Cicero kept watch of a wooden door behind them. They'd trekked to the tallest floor of the High Hope Inn and arranged for sleep in a room with a window view of the funeral taking place outside the city limits.

"Fair," said Jari, grabbing the longscope for himself and studying Taryn's movements. "She's limping."

Cicero walked back to the bed and sat. "A ruse for the public. Likely brought on by the beige bastard himself."

"Who are the twins?" asked Tiannu.

"A hard question." Cicero rested his weary head. "Once our brethren, they were. Sworn members of the Kaldorian Guard. But one dark moon, they changed."

"Aye, we've hunted them for seasons," added Jari, now patting his hungry belly. "Never able to find them, and upon our return to Alyonia, we were disbanded the moment Taryn took power. Once she was made interim queen, the twins also returned, and she sent them for our heads."

"Her first mistake," said Cicero. "The Kaldorian Guard are the realm's greatest secret, known only by the king himself, and each king before. Taryn should have never known we even existed. In this, she revealed prior knowledge. Forbidden knowledge."

"Brought on by the twins?" questioned Tiannu.

Jari nodded. "We believe they were working for her, or for someone else, all along. The Kaldorian Guard were ten strong under King Kaldor, ever protecting him in the shadows, ever ensuring his family secrets remained secrets. Once Taryn took over, the twins and her red robes killed four of us in the eve. Cicero, myself, and our two brethren you met back at home are all that remain."

Tiannu sat upon a hardwood chair in the corner. "And all of this to start a new war, to find the altar and dust?"

"Only time shall tell." Jari moved for the door. "Come, we've much more to show you."

41

HENDRIX

Pitch Black

Dorian guided The Family through the lengthy, pitch-black tunnel. It had been a silent trek, slowed by fear and low visibility.

Dorian dangled a metal lantern an arm's length ahead, then stood on his toes and pressed an ear to the worm-infested dirt above. "Quiet," he whispered. "We're gettin' close. The passage'll narrow soon. Lock arms and move slowly. When we get deeper, cover your nose from the dust. *No* coughing. The Bintonns'll be right above us."

Sammy rushed forward. "Gonna go find the mound. Everyone stay true. Hendrix, don't be a Skelpie-baby."

"A what— ?"

Ava put her hand over Hendrix's mouth, chuckling silently at the familiar Moronian insult. The air grew more humid. Dust lingered.

"What is a Skelpie-baby?"

Ava squeezed Hendrix's hand. "Did you hear not? Quiet."

Damn. Hendrix cursed his own stupidity, but at least she couldn't see his self-loathing. He pressed on, his back sliding against a wall of dirt. With the narrowing path, Hendrix felt twice as contained, twice as anxious. Worse, Dorian's lantern gave off enough light to illuminate the many bugs on either side, leaving no room for imagination.

"Four span ahead," whispered Dorian. "We're close."

Sammy reappeared without warning, her furry face made clear by the lantern's glow. "Found the mound. We're here." Sammy led the way to a heap of sand and dirt some twenty paces ahead: a blockade midway through the tunnel.

"The sand pile acts as a false end," said Dorian. "Just in case the Bintonns ever make it this far. Help me clear it. Spread the access dirt on the ground and we'll rebuild on our way back."

Aypax dropped to his knees and dug furiously at its bottom.

"Alright, we get it, you're strong," chirped Sammy.

The mound quickly collapsed as everyone stepped back, each covering their face and fighting urges to cough.

"Once we move past," said Dorian, "things can get a bit unnervin'." Echoes of screams funneled through the tunnel, no longer blocked by the sandy wall. "Like I said."

* * *

"How long have we been down here?" asked Hendrix.

Even Dorian had no way of knowing. "Time moves quickly when tunneling—"

More screams cut him off. They'd bellowed through the passageway every few moments, each paining Aypax in multiple ways. If that weren't enough, the tunnel had tightened further. Its edges became sharp, and the ground above felt as if it would crumble under the weight of heavy footsteps. More dust fell from overhead, as did a new stench.

Hendrix inhaled a rancid whiff. "What is it?"

"Slaves aren't gifted bathin' times," said Dorian.

Sammy stopped and sniffed their surroundings. "We're under

the stadium, just beneath the cells."

Dorian pointed. "There." A small glimmer of light protruded from the top of this dirty tunnel. "Let's begin." He knelt and unzipped a velvet bag, then pulled out the two glass jars of Ashboiler, both small but dangerous.

The Ashboiler, a pink liquid, bubbled and popped inside each jar. Dorian handed one to Sammy.

"See ya soon." Sammy pawed the tiny jar, then darted toward the angelic light. Scaling the tunnel's roof, she dug away a thin layer of dirt, creating a hole for herself. In a flash, she was up and out of sight.

* * *

Sammy had been here before, though such knowledge never eased her nerves. She found herself above her own hidden passage, in a tunnel much the same. The smell, the screams, the dirt walls and dust, a mirror image. One thing was always different however. *The bats.*

This tunnel was much brighter than below, thanks to the blinking eyes of chained critters. Hundreds. Blood bats, as they were known, all nailed or chained to mucky walls. Due to incredible lifespans, they were tasked with two things: to blink and to die. In that order.

Sammy shielded her pupils from the relentless flickering of light. "Gonna get the freakin' spasms in here." She continued down the long passage. Small cells became abundant on either side, marked by numbers painted onto hard soil. *11,* she thought, reading a cell. *13, 10.*

She came to number fourteen, the real test. Sammy looked inside, no one. *Sweet maiden of large nuts. Never been this easy.* Sammy hurried onward, reading along the way. *21, 25, 30.* She was getting closer. *31. Perfect. They'll write ballads of me.*

Sammy looked through the rusty bars. What she saw struck her.

A young girl she presumed to be Adora lay inside. Her clothes were ripped and torn, more bloody rags than clothes. Bruises covered her swollen, sweat-drenched body. Clumpy knots tangled in her brown hair.

Get it together. Seen much worse.

Sammy slid into Adora's cell, then removed her little jar of Ashboiler. Pawing it tightly, she poured the entire jar onto the dirt floor and watched the pink liquid melt its way down.

* * *

Directly below, Dorian stayed perfectly still, waiting. "There."

Seeing a pink glow above, he moved toward it. Revealing his own jar of Ashboiler and a sharp knife, Dorian dug a tiny wedge in the grime overhead. Then, lining his open jar directly beneath the pink glow, he shoved it upward and hurried back to the others. "When Sammy's Ashboiler melts through the ground, it'll collide with our own, causin' the grain powders and Tourtoufian acids to explode. A small hole's gonna open up; that's when we grab your sister. We'll want her to see Ava first so she don't scream. But listen, the Ashboiler's acid is *very* bitter. If you inhale any dust after the explosion…well, it ain't good—"

The *bang* wasn't as loud as they feared. A pink explosion lit the dark tunnel momentarily. Dorian covered his mouth before charging. "Go!"

Ava sprinted for the hole and poked her head through. "Adora!"

Adora coughed, stopping at the sight of her sister. "A-Ava?"

"No time." Ava saw her sister's torn clothes, her bruises and broken soul. She saw the state of the cell and her sister. "Come!"

Sammy gestured toward the hole. "Plenty a'time for hugs later. Let's move."

Wrapping her face with filthy rags, Adora shimmied her way down the hole.

"Get the wood set," muttered Sammy.

Dorian was already lifting a few sheets of thinned timber from his velvet bag, just big enough to slide up through the hole. "Put more dirt over the wood than usual. Our fourth escape this season. Bintonns might start diggin' around."

"See ya back on top." Sammy maneuvered the wood over the hole and began spreading dirt upon it all. It took far longer than she'd wished, but the job required perfect execution. *Looks better than when I got here.* Once finished, Sammy used the stolen key to unlock Adora's cell. After leaving its gate wide open as a ruse, she raced away into the black.

* * *

Back through the eerie tunnel and through their crafty blockade of dirt they went. Dorian and Aypax rebuilt the mound quickly, excluding a small hole for Sammy. Once finished, their group hurried for Dorian's tent. Adora slowed pace, exhausted and painfully tight from countless moons of stillness.

After a long trek, they finally came to a slope in the passage. "Straight up to my tent from here." Dorian shouted upward. "Sir Drake! Toss the rope!" A few seconds passed. "Drake!" A sound ruffled overhead. An uncoiling. "Clear yourselves," continued Dorian.

The rope descended.

One by one, they climbed up and out of sight. Dorian first, Hendrix second, Ava third. Aypax prepared to ascend last. The only member strong enough to carry Adora over his shoulders, he needed a moment of rest.

"No!" A shout reverberated from Dorian's tent as the clinging of steel sounded loudly above, followed by a body's dull thud to the blanketed ground.

"Ascends now!" bellowed an unknown voice. "Ascends now, and we wills not harm you furthers. We's only want the girl!"

Aypax grunted. "Bintonns."

The voice boomed again. "We've slain one up heres. But we lets the other live. We'll shows you the same mercy, if you works with us."

"Your choice?" asked Aypax, glancing back down the tunnel, the pitch-black taunting.

42

TAAIVETTI

Hann

Prince Taaivetti opened his eyes. *Balo, save us.*

His vision had been split, one eye not functioning. He could hear only the sound of ringing, constant ringing, as if bugs were shrieking from the depths of his ear canal. Taaivetti reached for his helmet. *Gone.* Perhaps displaced during his fall from the wall. *Catapults...*

He shuffled on the hot sand of Hann's courtyard, surrounded by hundreds of screaming Alyonians. He couldn't hear their cries of agony, yet he could see them, he could imagine them. Taaivetti placed a hand to his left eye. Blood seeped from his swollen socket down into his palm, but the eye was still there, for now. A mixture of severed limbs, blood, dented armor, and rubble littered the ground.

And then there was Sir Arrevon, sprawled across the sand in two pieces, his guts hanging from both ends, his green tunic fluttering in the wind.

"Help!"

The ringing in Taaivetti's ears suddenly eased as his hearing returned. The prince tried standing but soon realized the true issue. His leg was broken, fractured at the kneecap. Taaivetti began to dry heave, far too dehydrated to vomit.

"Arknah-Forticah!!!"

The prince recognized that noise. Adrenaline drowning any pain, he refocused on his surroundings.

Hann's walls and many buildings were shattered and aflame. His warriors filled the inner bailey, scrambling for the main gate, but hundreds of Gorsh had already fought their way in. The beasts funneled through the gate and over crumbled walls like a tsunami of red.

Swords and axes collided in all directions. Flocks of black birds flew speedily overhead, dropping rocks and clumps of debris. The prince could do not but watch his dear soldiers die. All around him, one by one, each kill more gruesome than the last.

Does it end here? he wondered, thinking back to the Arch Sibyl's vision.

"Form at the gate! Shield wall! Archers focus on our flanks."

Taaivetti knew that voice too: Commander Zo, doing what he did best. The prince watched Zo and twenty others form a defensive line, shields and spears pushing forward into the desert savages. Hope.

Gritting his teeth and screaming, the prince pulled himself up upon a passing warrior. The warrior stopped in place, honored that Taaivetti had chosen him as a crutch.

"To the prince!" shouted the solider, waving at anyone nearby. Few remaining Alyonians had any wits about them; still, they made for their wounded leader.

A small group formed around Taaivetti and fought valiantly, holding off sporadic attacks from the veiny creatures of red. Still leaning on his comrade's shoulder, Taaivetti felt for his sword. *Still there.* He unsheathed it and swung pathetically, keeping a few Gorsh at bay. Seeing them up close and armored, they appeared more frightening than ever. The creatures' red skin bubbled in the novalight. Their muscles twitched. Twisted horns shot through the tops of their spiked, black helmets. "Arrccnahhh!" they howled, spitting through crooked teeth.

"Fall back!" screamed Zo.

Taaivetti looked toward his struggling friend. Zo's shield wall had already broken, and his unit was being swept by an unrelenting horde. Gazing up, more Gorsh encircled the bailey as they sprinted around the remaining wall walks.

This would be over soon.

The prince's stabilization ended abruptly. His comrade had taken an arrow to the neck, splattering blood upon Taaivetti's face. The prince toppled over and fell down upon him. Now floored, he saw hooves. Naomi hooves. They thundered out of burning stables and made for Taaivetti's position. Their riders were clad in dirty green armor, their golden stripes doused with red blood. "To the prince!" they bellowed.

Feeling another glimmer of hope, Taaivetti forced himself onto both elbows. "No!" he yelled, as Commander Zo took a spear through his lower back. He collapsed upon sandy ground a few feet from Taaivetti. The prince crawled toward him. "Zo, Zo!" Taaivetti grasped his commander's arm. "Eyes on me, brother, don't close them now."

More cries of pain sounded all around as Alyonians fell by the dozens, desperately circling their prince. The Naomi riders closed in, falling a few enemies upon arrival.

Taaivetti tried once more. "Zo!"

His commander couldn't speak. Zo rolled onto his side, blood pouring from his mouth to the red sand below.

"Zo..." Tears flooded Taaivetti's one good eye. The other merely pulsed in pain.

Commander Zo nodded toward his forearm, toward his wife's ring and bracelet glimmering in the bright light. Taaivetti knew what had been asked.

"She'll have them," he said, whilst sliding off the items. For a brief moment, everything seemed to stop. The chaos, the noise, the slaughter. It all halted as the two Alyonians saw only one another. "It's been an honor," said Taaivetti.

Zo lifted a broken hand over his own heart. "An honor," he spat, before closing his eyes.

"Leap down and grab him, damn it!"

The three riders landed beside Taaivetti. Surrounded by sacrificial Alyonians, they had just enough time to heave Taaivetti up into a saddle. They tied him down and secured him to the back of Sindria. Knowing they'd never see any of these faces again, his riders bowed to their brethren quickly, then galloped toward the back gates of Hann.

It was a tough ride. Arrows and spears zipped by from behind, rocks hurled through hot air. The riders stabbed downward into a growing crowd of Gorsh, killing and stalling just enough to escape. Carrying the prince of Alyonia and three precious riders, the brave Naomi sprinted under a rear gatehouse and exited the burning fortress of Hann.

43

CRIMSON

Delphious-Shri

For twenty-six moons the rain had yet to cease. Shielding his eyes from drops, Delphious-Shri gazed despairingly at a thick bundle of story papers in hand. "Children...I just, I cannot understand—"

"And no use tryin'," said Gable, looking up at the slanted rooftops of surrounding taverns and barns, granaries and bakehouses. They lined the dark streets around him, lit only by stars and moonlight. Desperate to ignore the tragic news, Gable lost himself in the rainfall blowing sideways with brisk winds. Sliding down building gutters, rain pulled clumps of snow to the cold streets below.

"Aye," Lukon said as he nodded in agreement. "Not surprised these days, whole world's goin' to shit if ya ask me. But bowing down youngsters at a dance hall? There's a special place in the realm of torment for the archer."

Crimson remained silent, as he had since stumbling out of the Yellowfish Inn. Delphious-Shri had grabbed the story papers from a late-night street salesman not five minutes after their departure, and he'd regretted the very moment he saw Taryn weeping on its cover.

"I suppose there's no better time." Delphious-Shri made sure he had everyone's attention. "My words remain with us?"

Crimson nodded and stepped over a deep puddle. Even here

the water had flooded once perfect human roads.

"Good." Delphious tossed the story papers to the mud. "Then I will tell you more of what I truly believe to be happening. Bandano-Rhi's traders have been spotted moving weapons of destruction to the southwest. Catapults, ladders, siege equipment. My first hunch was a simple trade with the free river cities of Kios and Oblia. But then I thought to myself, I've seen no goods coming back in exchange, and believe me, if something were going through this town, I'd know."

Delphious-Shri led them past manors of limestone, subtly searching for any tails or ears following. "My next thought was that Bandano-Rhi has been sending Kios and Oblia free weaponry to help them hold off the rumored Gorsh hordes growing in The Red Sand Desert. After all, the Gorsh are a common enemy, and our empire has weapons to spare. But then I thought with the Pallala-Accord all but dead, why would Bandano-Rhi wish to strengthen his enemies of Oblia and Kios?"

"He wouldn't," said Gable, still trying to decide if he trusted Delphious-Shri.

The red-haired giant smiled. "You are correct, Gable. This leads to my conclusion. I believe Bandano-Rhi is sending weapons to a secret force in the southwest. A force I believe will soon attack Kios and Oblia. If this were to happen, the remaining realms of the Accord would be forced to respond, putting another great war on the horizon."

The drunken group stopped in place, processing as fast as the ale would allow.

"Bloody Perdition..." said Lukon. "That's too much for tonight—"

"Ahh!" Crimson palmed his forehead and bellowed out in pain.

Gable sprinted to his side. "Captain!"

Crimson pushed him aside and buried his anguish as the air grew oddly warm around them. "I'm fine."

Gable raised a brow. "Ya don't look fine, Captain."

Crimson inhaled a few breaths, then turned back to Delphious-Shri. "Alright, another great war. I value your words, but I've heard this before, and it never comes to pass. Get on with the burnt-neck men."

Knowing Crimson would speak of his brain aches no further, Delphious-Shri pressed forward. "On my return from the north, I witnessed carnage like I'd never seen. My regiment was riding through the northern tribal lands when we passed a few of their villages. Ponca, Karok, and Haana. They'd all been burned to the ground, their straw huts, their wooden shacks, all aflame. The women and children had been abused and left for dead, the men butchered. But the boys, the boys had been taken."

"Taken?" asked Crimson, still fighting a migraine.

"We began to notice a commonality. Each settlement we passed, the young boys were always gone. I sent word to other trusted commanders. Over time, they confirmed my suspicions. The empire is stealing children."

Gable spat ale from his mouth. "Come again?"

"They're stealing children, and not just from the north," continued Delphious-Shri. "Whispers spread across Adria. Whispers I never thought true. But now…they say Alyonia has a secret society, and Elo's truth, they say men from all over have joined. The common folk call them 'Night Raiders.' They've been raiding villages in the north and in the Pallala countryside, stealing any male children."

"Bloody Perdition," said Lukon for the second time this eve.

"Aye, and these Night Raiders, they're rumored to share one thing in common," continued Delphious.

"Burnt necks," muttered Crimson.

"Aye," nodded Delphious. "Burnt necks."

Lukon sat his flask down upon a short fence. "But why? Slavery?"

"That's the grand question," said Delphious-Shri. "We know someone is taking the children. We just don't know why."

"Ahh!" Crimson collapsed.

"Captain!" Gable rushed to his side. "Lukon, run to our apothecary. Bring him!"

"Leave me be!" Crimson struggled on all fours, then rose to both knees and squeezed his temple, fingering his eardrums.

"You're not fine," said Delphious-Shri, sobering quickly. "This much is clear, old friend."

Lukon stepped forward. "Captain, you need to speak to us. Now. What's happenin'?"

Crimson looked to Gable, but even his oldest friend demanded truth. "I've been plagued by brain aches and night terrors of late. The aches grow worse with each moon. The terrors too. They've stolen my sleep, which leads to the pain of each day. Simple."

"Night terrors?" questioned Delphious-Shri.

"Yes. Though they aren't merely harsh dreams. Each night they come, it's as if I'm alive. And each night, it's the same terror." Crimson watched the rain slam against puddles all around him. "I'm sleeping in my bed, and when I open my eyes, I see something standing in the corner of my chamber. A dark and shadowy figure, staring right at me. I wish to move for my sword, but I cannot. I'm completely frozen. And when I wake to reality, I remain ice cold…"

The Green Capes stared at their captain. Crimson had always been a pillar of strength, an immovable object. He worried that showing his true hand might diminish that. "How does it end?" asked Lukon.

"The same way each time. I try to move, but I cannot. And as the shadow approaches, it takes the form of my Tiannu. She speaks lovingly, tells me the same thing each night. 'Return home. I need you.' And then she kisses me. But I know the taste of my Tiannu, and this is not her…"

"Aye," mumbled Gable. "You're givin' *me* a brain ache."

Delphious-Shri chuckled. "He jokes, but this is no laughing matter. You should seek aid, Crimson. From someone who knows the meaning of dreams."

The Green Capes agreed. "Aye."

"My friends." Delphious looked guilty. "There is another reason I've shared my information with you."

Ah, here it comes, thought Gable. *The truth.*

"As I rode through the village of Haana, I ordered my men to stop. We made camp for the eve and spread our provisions throughout the remaining hungry and beaten tribe."

Gable narrowed his gaze. *Hmm.*

"I met a woman. Brown of skin, a true northern tribeswoman. She lived with her daughter by the name of Nit'a. This girl was no older than six years by the Rhi calendar. Nit'a was starving, her mother ill. The mother wept and wept. She asked if I could take Nit'a away to a better life. But I knew I could not. My regiment couldn't risk any type of sickness. Besides, word would've eventually spread."

"I do not love where this is headed," said Crimson.

"Old friend." Delphious-Shri's eyes pleaded. "There aren't many hearts like yours. Not these days. There was something about this girl. And when you spoke of your daughter, Madison, back at the inn, I knew that Elo put you in front of me for a reason. You've got to help this Nit'a and bring her back here to the Crossing. She's on your way to Frost Bight. It won't even take you off course. Send her back with a few Green Capes, and I'll make it worth your while."

Gable applauded his own instincts. *He's finally shown his true hand. Though I suppose it could've been worse.*

Crimson thought long and hard. He was already leaving the Crossing at first nova-rise, less than a few hours away. The idea of extra work seemed daunting.

"I gave her mother my word," admitted Delphious-Shri. "I promised I'd bring her daughter to the Crossing and give her a better life. I'd go back myself, but I'm stationed here to report nightly. I fear she'll be long dead before I can return."

Gable studied him further. *The truth? Or an excuse to send us off course?*

Crimson tucked away his flask and killed the night's spirit of fun. He turned to his Green Capes. "Wake the company. If we're to make a stop, we must leave now."

44

HENDRIX

Drill Bintonn

Hendrix awoke to immense pain. Head pounding, his muscles ached with small cuts and bruises, his flesh stung with every fidget. Unable to move, he could provide no comfort to either wrist. They were purple and pulsating with agony. Tight chains bound him to a brown dawn-wood chair, cutting circulation. *Where am I?* He torqued his head and saw Aypax. The brute, looking worse than ever, had been tied to another dawn-wood beside him.

"Hendrix—"

A colossal fist struck Aypax's cheek, splattering blood upon his stolen overalls. "No talkings," said a massive Tourtoufian. He shook his green fist, signaling it might've taken the worst of their exchange. "Stays still 'til Drill arrives." This Tourtoufian stood nearly the size of Aypax, the biggest local Hendrix had seen. Undoubtedly a Bintonn, his orange hat matched a tight vest of the same color.

Looking left, Hendrix noticed Sir Edmund Drake. He, too, was shackled and covered in bruises, though something else seemed to be affecting him. *The brain aches perhaps?* Hendrix's eyes left the pirateer and continued their dance, hoping to discern his location. The last moment he recalled was being knocked unconscious in Dorian's tent. *How did we arrive here?* The sizable room was adorned with one gargantuan circular window overlooking the entire city of Starsgard. *I suppose we're rather high.*

A pristine table of gold and copper sat a forearm's length in front of him. The glamorous table could've cost as much as any ship he'd seen back at the docks. In fact, this may've been the wealthiest room he'd ever seen.

A soaring bookshelf, filled with books, plaques, and cigars, butted against marble walls to his right. A fire pit rested in the corner, boasting a smooth mantel above. Countless medals and trophies for animal wrangling displayed themselves over the mantel. Three buffalo heads mounted a wall near the enormous window. A few paintings depicting famous cattleboys riding bulls and other beasts hung beside them. A rug of cowskin blanketed most of the marble floor, presumably swept hourly.

"Keep your eyes down!" bellowed another voice from behind.

Hendrix couldn't see the speaker, courtesy of tight chains. *How many are behind me?*

A door swung open and bodies shuffled, informing Hendrix there were quite a few.

"Welcomes, ma'lord," said one of the voices.

"Greetings, ma'lord —"

"Quiet." Drill Bintonn rounded the three fugitives' chairs and came into view. He appeared an impressive Tourtoufian, no denying. His slender green build resembled some mixture of man and lizard, akin to the other natives. But Drill Bintonn looked stronger, with muscles bred to swim or sprint. He stood tall like his punch-hungry lackey, though far less bulky. Drill also wore a tight orange vest with expensive linings and pocket trims. His orange pants were rather loose, however, and tucked into a pair of fine black boots. A fancy felt hat, with jewels woven into its brim, snuggled his bald green scalp.

"Seems I finally got one of yas, huh?" Drill sank into a cushioned seat behind his desk and pulled out a cigar from a drawer.

Lighting its tip, he placed both feet upon a side stool. "Nothings to say? Every moment of silence is anothers moment your little gals spend with my friends."

Still the trio said naught, though Hendrix knew that wouldn't last. Sir Edmund Drake appeared livid, more so than ever. *He must have a past with Drill Bintonn.*

"Somethin' on yours mind, pirateer?" Drill blew a ring of smoke in Drake's direction. "Ya looks angry."

Yes, thought Hendrix. *A past.*

Drill gazed out of his magnificent window, staring down at hundreds of docks in the distance. "Now imagine how I feels? Imagine hearin' the same thing every moon. More pirateers, more smugglin'. More dirty businesses, more smugglin'. Eight realms of torment, it's rider's luck I makes any coin at all." Drill stood. "We found your tunnels, and others. I should kill you all right here and nows, but I ain't after your heads—"

"Then what are you after?" asked Aypax, getting to it.

Drill leaned over the desk, his webbed fingers spreading across its copper surface. "I like yous. Wise. What I wants is simple. Names, locations, and ships. Tell me which ships belongs to which smugglers, and which of my own Tourtoufians is runnin' the underground booze. Ya tells me this, and I'll not only let ya's live"—he nodded toward a large chest by the fireplace—"I'll rewards ya's. 'Nough silva, in that chest to sends you three off for life."

Aypax knew Drill wouldn't let them leave this place alive, let alone coin them, but young Hendrix saw life differently. "And you'll free the girls?"

Drill's dark snakelike eyes shot to him. "Well, I didn't say that nows, did I?"

Sir Edmund Drake spat over the desk, dampening Drill's spotless vest. "Spare me. Talkin' of smugglin'. Yur the most corrupt sack'a shit on this bloody island."

Drill didn't retaliate; his heavy-handed Tourtoufian took care of that. "Corrupt? I'm as straight as they comes. I'm what keeps this island runnings. Before me, there was real corruption. There was fake levies, lust, theft, ands violence."

Drake gave a pained smile as blood trickled down his chapped lips. "And now 'tis a land of rainbows and rabbits?"

"Now 'tis a free land of wealth ands power." Drill sat and motioned to one of his guards, who quickly made for a flashy bar top. Grabbing a glass of purple liquid, he handed Drill the drink. "Wealth." Drill lifted his fancy glass and sipped. Sucking it down, he pointed toward the brawny guard who delivered it. "Power."

Sir Edmund Drake nodded to Drill. "Twat."

"Say what ya wills, pirateer. But befores me, befores the Bintonns, this island was dead. She was for the few. Now she's alive and fors the many! Now we've a future. Eight realms of torment, give me six more seasons and we'll haves an army."

Hendrix shimmied in his chair. "The girls, let us bargain. What would it take?"

"It would takes a flying ship full of twenty thousand virgins who piss ale and shit silva'."

Drill's followers broke into laughter, though they were fast interrupted by Aypax releasing a series of nasty coughs. His phlegm and saliva splattered across Drill's desk. Then Drake burst into laughter.

"Tells ya what"—Drill glared at the slimy stains, angered by such imperfections—"one of you gives me the names of whoever's runnin' the underground smugglin', and I won't cuts your balls off in the next ten seconds. How's that for a bargain?" The captives glanced at one another, none wishing to give way. Drill took a seat, yielding a moment or two of patience. "No?" He swirled his purple whiskey. "I see."

One of Drill's guards paced forward and lifted Aypax's chin, then placed a sharp blade across his windpipe. Eyes to the ceiling, Aypax saw an array of buckets hanging from the ceiling. *Dream stealers.* His neck began to bleed from sharp pressure. *These could be used.*

"A final chance," hissed Drill. "Truly easy it is, to merely tells me a few names."

"You kill us, you're back to nothing," said Aypax, his throat bloodying the blade with each word.

"As I said...wise." Drill lifted his purple drink and nodded to his lackey. "Let's try it this ways."

Thump.

The blade fell fast, severing half of Aypax's middle finger from his hand.

"Aghhhh!"

The big Alyonian's head fell limp with shock as his remaining four fingers convulsed. Tied and unable to slow the blood, they played an invisible piano.

Drill looked at Hendrix. "Hims next."

Hendrix stared at half of Aypax's detached bone and ligaments hanging by the knuckle. The youngster felt a shiver of ice spread through his veins as the large Tourtoufian wiped his blade with a sliver of cloth.

"Wait!" bellowed Aypax, fueled by rage and adrenaline, fueled by the loudening voices. "I know the damned names."

"Like I said." Drill shrugged. "Smarts."

Aypax lifted his eyes and burned a hole through Drill's, perhaps frightening even him. "Tell me where Katrin of Goderdale resides, the Tourtoufian of red hair. You tell me this, and I'll give you the bloody names." Aypax nodded up toward the dream stealers, having recalled the witch doctor's words of Drill's superstitious nature. "But lie, and I curse your firstborn."

"A fair deal." Drill stood and extended his hand comedically toward Aypax, birthing a few laughs from his followers. "But yous first."

"*The Ada Mae*," grunted Aypax, truthful, yet covering for Drake. "*Greta's Grievance*, agh, *Joanne of*, of something, *Joanne of Tides*. All ships I saw at harbor, all part of the smuggling."

"Excellent." Drill waved off his knife-wielding servant. "Katrin is buried in the woods out backs. I killed hers myself." He stood and made for an exit, stopping beside a guard. "Throws 'em down below. Keep 'em in holding 'til we finds these ships he speaks of."

House Kaldor

Letter type: Urgent, Informative
To: Madison Preters
From: Hendrix Kaldor
343 A.B, Windy Season, 103rd Moon, Double Novas

Madison,

Since my last letter, I've befriended a pirateer. Together, we managed to rescue the elderly Moronian women. But now, now I fear for my life.

I've wasted away the last six moons in a Tourtoufian jail cell with Aypax and the mentioned pirateer. Starved and beaten, only water has kept us alive. I've never faced such hardship. Still, I must write. You _must_ spread the truth. The conclusion of my arrest and Taryn's lie.

As stated, your father had just shown up to the Peace Parade with members of his Emerald Company. He calmed the audience and beckoned Taryn's guards to give Aypax and I a just trial.

But then Bandano-Rhi came thundering in. With Taryn and Kornilious already together, the emperor's presence empowered the trio. Bandano-Rhi's honor guard encircled us and ordered we lay down our weapons on behalf of Taryn. Aypax refused, as did his famous Honorable-Six.

Sensing things could get dangerous, your father shouted for peace once again, but tensions were high, and Taryn is tricky. Even safe in the plaza, she managed to portray us as an immediate threat. No order was given publicly, but I watched her motion to Kornilious some kind of signal. Then it happened.

Arrows flew and Bandano-Rhi's honor guard slaughtered the few Honorables. The crowd screamed with horror and dispersed as blood filled the plaza. Your father could not help us, for it all happened too quickly. Aypax and I were apprehended and taken away in shackles. That night, we were thrown into Alyonian cells. You know the rest.

What Now?

I've revisited the story hundreds of times. The sights, the smells, the emotions and speed, but these past six moons in captivity, I've begun to see it a bit differently. I've begun to see plenty of things differently.

I'm unsure if you've received any of my letters, but I must leave you with this: These past moons, writing to you has been the only thing keeping me alive. If we never see one another again, just know how much I love you. Know that I do not deserve you. And if I don't return home... well, know that I simply want you to be happy. Whatever that looks like.

All of my love,

Hendrix

45

HENDRIX

A Dark Cell

Aypax clutched his nub finger, gritting cracked teeth to ease the suffering. After six painful eves, his adrenaline had long subsided, leaving extreme throbbing and a broken heart. He sat dreadfully still, shattered, silent.

"Do you plan on writin' the entire time we're down here?" spat Drake. "That damned pen scratchin' might drive me mad."

Hendrix lifted tired eyes from a piece of parchment he'd been struggling to write upon with such limited light. "I might."

Drake coughed. "You think the Bintonns are really gonna send yur letter, kid? You think they're gonna mark it, then spend the coin to send a bird halfway across Adria? Just so yur little lover can sport a quick smile?"

Hendrix hadn't thought so deeply. So far as he was concerned, he truly believed the Bintonns would. "They said we each get one prison letter." He referenced the parchment in hand. "They gave us the ink and all. They were true in this. Why waste their time otherwise?"

"To see who we're communicatin' with. They won't be sendin' yur letter. They give them to everyone down here, just hopin' to catch someone else by association." Drake grunted, leaning against the warm steel of their cell bars. Like Aypax, he appeared weaker than ever, meaner too. Sweaty, bloody, and sick. Sitting with his back away from the Alyonians, one would've presumed Drake furious, though he'd removed himself from their company for a different reason.

"Sir Drake?" Hendrix said on an exhale. "What truly ails?"

Drake writhed in pain, his body rocking back and forth. "Leave me be."

Their cell was a tight square with metal bars on all sides. Hundreds of others surrounded, each filled with crazed prisoners adding to the noise in the nearly pitch-black atmosphere. A few walled lanterns offered light, though even this felt a cruel means of showing newer captives their future. A rotten corpse graced the farthest corner of their cell, producing smells foul enough to induce vomiting, but the trio was long past such a point. Their puke had dried three moons ago, inviting droves of maggots to the stone floor. Aypax stared at these insects, thinking.

"Aypax?"

"What?"

"I'm sorry about Katri—"

"Don't."

Hendrix nodded, folding his letter. A long silence befell, forcing the youngster's hand. "Did Taaivetti ever tell you of his hound Starry?"

Aypax said naught, though his angry shrug inferred enough.

"Figured not, he never told anyone really." Hendrix slid closer, avoiding a few bugs. "I was quite young, just old enough to recall, but I do remember the morn. Father returned home with two pups, brother and sister, one for Taryn and one for Taaivetti. Beautiful hounds, they were. Taryn named hers Ruby. Taaivetti of course named his Starry. The pups were inseparable, even brought Taaivetti and Taryn together for long walks and a rekindled love between them."

Aypax turned to him, allowing the story to combat his throbbing.

"One moon, Ruby never returned home. Taryn was sad for a time but eventually got over it, but Starry...Starry was never the same. The hound refused to eat and would not so much as accompany Taaivetti on a walk ever again. He tried bringing in new hounds, yet still Starry tucked his tail and hid. He grew thin and refused to go near any female hounds. Eventually, Starry died."

"Is this revenge for my bug parable?"

"No. It's merely an observation. All Starry needed do was eat... perhaps play. The hound did not try to take his own life, but eventually, he did."

* * *

Their weary bodies forced them to sleep, but laying on painfully hard ground, even severe exhaustion wasn't enough to keep young Hendrix down long. He awoke to a growl.

"Agghh."

Hendrix remained still, unsure how close the frightening noise truly was.

"Aggrrhh."

It came again, this time showing itself.

"Drake?" whispered Hendrix, slowly lifting his eyes in the pirateer's direction.

"Agggggrhhhhh." Drake's grunt grew harsher, pained and yet quiet. He rolled aggressively, wrestling himself.

"Drake?"

The pirateer's head shook as a guttural noise bellowed from within.

"Are you—are you ill?"

"Ahhhh!" Drake stopped, shaking his head and sounding

himself once again. "Bloody maiden! The damn brain aches—"

"Down below!" A new voice came from the prison entrance. "Stops! Stops where you's are!"

Metal clanked from afar as footsteps thundered down a spiraling stairwell of stone.

"Hendrix, hide beneath the corpse," said Drake. "When they bind me hands, make yur play, and we'll do what we can to disarm 'em." Drake motioned to Aypax, but he remained seated and silent.

"Hurry!"

More voices rang from above as torsos toppled down the dark stone stairs, each bloodied or dead.

Hendrix squinted in the commotion's direction. *I've seen them.* Three men wearing green and grey chainmail fought their way into the now-silent prison, stepping over the deceased torsos. "Hendrix Kaldor!" shouted the closest of them, a towering man with black hair. "Hendrix Kaldor!"

"Here! I'm here!"

That voice. Hendrix knew it well. *Ava...* Remaining hidden, he watched the soldiers sprint to Ava's prison cell, furious that he'd never known she was a mere hundred forearms away. He imagined the state of her sister.

It was difficult to see, so the black-haired soldier wasted no time. Brandishing a grey battle hammer, he lifted the weapon before dropping it upon Ava's cell lock.

Clank.

She was free.

"Hold!"

He stopped Ava in place.

"I see no Hendrix Kaldor. We cannot risk your escape, get back."

"Please, please, I know him! We can find him together—"

"Here!" shouted Drake, drawing the soldiers' attention. They sprinted in his direction as nearly every prisoner began to claim the name of Hendrix.

"Here!"

"Over here!"

"I'm he!"

The black-haired soldier rushed to Sir Edmund Drake, quickly seeing Hendrix just beside.

"He's here." He smiled, and down came the hammer.

46

TIANNU

A Night to Remember

Jari moved like a fox through the pitch-black Forest of Balo. Following muddy boot prints and broken twigs, the rain had made for easy tracking. Tiannu trailed him, careful to keep concealed. Thick trees and tall shrubs allowed for effortless hiding, but open woods lay ahead.

"Hold here." Jari lifted his fist, a signal for Tiannu and Cicero some ten paces behind. "I see their camp. Past the open plains. More huts than ever…" Jari looked down, contemplating. "The mud has made simple tracking, perhaps too simple."

Understanding his meaning, Cicero searched for potential traps. *Seems clear.* Satisfied, he darted through the clearing and made for a muddy bluff. This bluff slanted upward and housed small rocks and briars. Peeking over, Cicero saw the camp more clearly. It looked vast, yet poorly built. Tiny clothes and toys lay everywhere. The camp's blanketed huts were withered from persistent rain. Oddly, everything appeared to be built by children.

Bloody Perdition… Cicero glimpsed a sight he'd seen one too many times.

"More children?" Jari breathed heavily, having made his way to Cicero's side.

"Aye." Cicero winced. "Ten, maybe fifteen this time round. Most face down—" He stopped, silenced by a rumbling of the ground itself. Bushes swayed fifty paces south. *Red robes.*

"There must be two hundred," murmured Jari.

The red robes marched into open plains in a line with seemingly no end. Each member held a tiny lantern in hand, a green bag in the other, their faces masked by hoods and the forest's darkness.

"This is beyond us," said Cicero, as their line marched into the dismantled camp.

Strangely, the camp's children didn't scatter, though Tiannu soon realized why. "Look just beyond the tents. Guards on every side."

She was right. As the red robes strode by, a few guards dressed in all black joined their line.

"Tiannu," whispered Jari, "I hope you're not easily nauseated."

* * *

Half an hour passed as the red robes vanished to the camp's opposite side, dragging nearly every child with them. "The ones they left behind," Jari noted, "I fear their fates have been decided."

"We'll soon see." Tiannu stood and hurried toward them. Closing in, she flipped the nearest child. "Hello."

The boy's face was wet and muddy. It had been tough to tell from afar, but he was surely human. His eyes were closed, cheeks bruised, and he lay shirtless and shivering. The boy inhaled, regaining consciousness, though Tiannu wished he hadn't, for his eyes relayed a fear like she'd never seen.

"I shall not hurt you," she muttered. Her words eased him, or perhaps his energy simply fled.

Jari stepped forward. "Cicero, take the boy and make for Alyonia. I'll show Tiannu what needs seeing."

"Don't linger." Cicero heaved the woozy boy over his shoulder and jogged into the night.

Tiannu stood stagnant in the rain, cold and quivering. "We must alert the High Council. There are still honest leaders in parliament."

A flock of birds flapped in the trees above, alarming the duo. "No." Jari watched them take flight. "Trust no one, not even the High Council." That seemed a terrible notion, though a very possible reality to Tiannu. "Follow me."

There was no choice but to abide. She trailed him away from the campsite, adding footprints to the thousands of tracks in every direction.

"Hold here." Jari paced toward a decaying tree. An odd finger painting had been splattered across its slimy bark, kept somewhat dry by thick foliage above. The painting depicted a key, red and green in coloring.

"We're close." Jari noticed smeared red dots on a line of wet trees nearby, leading deeper into the woods. Following these dots, they emerged into a muddy clearing that gave way to a drop-off. "We crawl from here." Jari dropped to both knees. "Your answer is just over the edge."

Crawl they did. The muck stained their cloaks, though it only camouflaged them further. Traveling on all fours, Tiannu unexpectedly felt the ground begin to heat, as if a dormant volcano rested below. *Odd,* she thought, given the cold rain. They reached the drop-off, then peered out over a meadow of tall shrubbery below.

A path had been cut through the shrubs, leading straight down the eerie hill. A wooden archway rested at its bottom, some great distance below. That wasn't what scared Tiannu, however. The shrubs themselves shielded countless bodies in red robes, all kneeled and bowing toward the wooden archway. There were hundreds, all in red, all engulfed by the forest's dark green. Their lanterns lit the meadow, showing how numerous their group truly was. *What is happening here?* she wondered.

Ancient trees of black bark, each worn and withered, filled the bordering woods. These trees appeared far older than any she'd ever seen. Squinting, she caught sight of shadows within them. *Strangely, the shadows themselves seem to move.* Though hidden, Tiannu's feeling of being followed suddenly returned.

A shout gave way from behind the wooden archway. She and Jari looked to the noise, where they saw a long rope hanging from a tree, slightly concealed by shrubbery.

"Is the rope moving?" she asked.

Jari watched this rope slide up and down an abnormally large branch of the tree. "It is."

It soon became clear that someone was pulling the rope from below, hoisting a lifeless body for all to see. At first Jari was too far away to be sure, but eventually he recognized his dear friend. "Galia," he said, fighting a tear. Jari struggled through the sight of his own Kaldorian Guard being lifted high into the air, the rope firm around her neck. *Why?* he wondered. *She's clearly gone. Why hoist her body?*

When Jari and Tiannu saw the answer, their lives changed forever.

47

CRIMSON

Frost Bight

"I've a mind to sleep endlessly when we reach the Bight." Gable spat into frigid winds. The fat Alyonian rode beside Crimson and Lukon down a winding, snow-covered path. Emerald Company lagged slowly behind, for they'd been woken early back at the Crossing and hadn't stopped since. The snow grew thicker with each mile, and the ground mocked as it rose higher and higher.

"Aye," said Lukon, shivering. "For once, I must agree with the lard. Been nothin' but alps and steep hills since the Crossing. A warm bed at Frost Bight sounds damn good."

Too busy surveying his surroundings, Crimson did not chime in. Frozen alps encircled, white and bare of trees per usual, yet something felt different. His wagons were having a hard trek toward the company's rear, though he knew that would be so. His recruits whimpered and whined, yet that he expected too. Something else seemed awry. The near silent buzzing of a bee or wasp perhaps, though such critters did not exist in these parts. "We're being trailed."

Lukon and Gable noticed their captain's tail had slipped from the safety of his belt, its hair slightly raising. "Shall we send scouts to search?" asked Lukon.

"No." Crimson kept scanning the horizon. "I cannot task them with anything further. Morale."

"How far 'til the village of Haana?" asked Gable. "We must be close. Perhaps we make camp near the brown-skins, and trade for goods or drink that might lift our company's spirits? Maybe even a soft ass or two…"

Lukon pointed. "Not far, it seems." He held a map in hand, though it wasn't needed. Clusters of smoke danced high into the air over a collection of snowy peaks some five hundred span north. The smoke seemed far off their current path, however, and would be impossible to reach with wagons. "Map shows Haana to be in a valley behind those peaks. But, Captain, that smoke appears fresh."

"Give me the seeing glass," said Crimson.

Lukon dug inside a rawhide bag and revealed a warped shard of glass. Crimson held it inches before his eyes and squinted. "I see men. Riders headed east, leaving the village. They appear shaken, perhaps bloodied."

"Pass it here!" Gable was unable to see far without the glass. "Aye. The snow makes a bitch of things, but I reckon them at no less than twenty men. Black and white armor. Perhaps just black, damn snow. No banners nor sigils." Gable trotted forward off the path to get a better view, refocused the seeing glass. "Captain, this is a bit strange. I'm seein' two or three riders wearing red. Not armor though. Maybe cloaks?"

Crimson whistled for the rest of his Green Capes, then turned to his oldest friend. "Gable, stay here and guard the wagons. Keep everyone ready for a trap or counter."

Three additional Green Capes arrived. "Orders?"

"Gather five veterans." Crimson stretched his freezing limbs. "We ride quickly for Haana."

"Captain." Gable swallowed. "I do not like this. Delphious-Shri tells you to make for this village, and without warning, we spot armed riders hiding behind it. What if it's an ambush? What if the man set you up?"

Crimson stroked his Naomi's wet mane as a few veterans formed around him. "They aren't hiding. They're too easily spotted. If it is a trap, maybe one of 'em will be skilled enough to finally end this bloody brain ache. Whoever they are, they're bold. Let's find out why."

* * *

Crimson's veterans galloped swiftly through dangerous alps. Now void of a path, his riders steered clear of slippery rocks, drop-offs, and hidden traps of the Haana. Even their Naomi fought harder than usual, for such constant downpour had piled white to their calves. Stopping near a group of boulders, everyone arrived at the edge of a peak.

"Orders, Captain?" Lukon appeared truly frightened, a first.

The village of Haana sat below, amidst a secluded valley. It had been burned, ransacked, and desecrated. Wooden carvings of Haana's gods and goddesses had been chopped down and urinated upon, but even this seemed tame compared to what rested nearby. An array of dead bodies had been positioned in the snow to form a particular shape.

The shape of a key.

"Dead tribesmen," said a veteran.

"And tribeswomen," added Lukon. "Have they been... painted?"

Each body appeared covered in some sort of paint or pigment, always the same color: green. *Their spilled blood surrounds them,* thought Crimson. *They've formed a red and green key.* He thought back to the Yellowfish Inn, to the chimes dangling above.

"Wait." Lukon revealed his precious seeing glass. "I see more bodies. Easterners, and from the Rhi-Empire by the looks of it. Though I don't recognize their garb or colors. Grey and green armor?"

"I'm unfamiliar," said Crimson. "Where?"

Lukon pointed. "Piled beside those tents to the west."

Crimson didn't need the seeing glass; one look at this place was enough. "Any signs of the riders we spotted?"

Lukon put his eye even closer to the glass. "None."

"Then we've no need to descend. This type of evil does not leave survivors. Tell no one what you've seen 'til we reach Frost Bight. I'll handle it then."

Reserving his emotions, Crimson swung his Naomi round and sped back to the company.

* * *

The ride grew harder with every hour, more quiet too. A grueling silence, the kind one could feel in their bones. Crimson found himself back in his favorite position, the point. Not even his trusted Green Capes flanked. *I'll speak with Commander Harold at the Bight. He's likely had some experience, some interaction or scouting report with Haana.*

Emerald Company hugged their own chests as freezing winds assaulted. Two recruits had succumbed to intense frostbite whilst another fell too ill to move. They'd been blanketed and placed into a grain wagon, though even the wagon had repeatedly broken down, slowing everyone's pace and making cold hands attempt laborious woodwork.

Forgoing Crimson's demands, Gable galloped ahead and caught him. "The second nova has begun her descent. She'll set within hours." Gable nodded out at a nova setting over the cruel northern landscape. Its rays reflected off seemingly endless mountains, painting the sky's dark clouds in a wondrous pink and orange.

"Red skies at night, travelers delight. Red skies at morning, travelers take warning. The clouds give hope, Captain. Tomorrow shall be a fine day. We should make camp now and arrive at the Bight by morn with fresh legs."

"No." Crimson gazed out at rivers of pure ice in the valleys below. "The second nova shall set soon indeed. But by the time she does, we'll be at the Bight."

"At our current pace? I wouldn't count on that, Captain. Lands, I wouldn't count on another hundred span. We should make camp now. You spoke of the company's morale yourself."

"We press on." Crimson waved him back to his prior position.

Gable gripped his Naomi's reins and prepared to fall back. "Ya know, I've never questioned ya, and I never shall. But ya chose me as your second for a reason, and if ya don't plan on takin' my advice, do me a favor and send me outta the north. Maybe Lukon'll do a better job."

Crimson knew Gable had been angry of late, even questioned a few decisions, but he'd always hid it well. He wondered if his Green Cape was out of line, or if *he* was. But as several hours inched by, the quarrel left Crimson and was replaced by intense hunger and shivers. It was also replaced by the ever-present image of Tiannu approaching his bedside from the corner of his chambers. Every night, every time, the same damned night terror. *And that kiss, the kiss of death.* He snapped out of the reverie, then peeked up toward the stars.

Adria's second nova had finally set, giving way to the dangers of a dark night in the north. But Crimson knew this land well. "Thirty span ahead! Form up." Crimson's teeth chattered uncontrollably, yet he smiled. They'd finally reached the alp's summit, the steepest point of their expedition, and there was only one way forward. Down.

Now in the open, a salty breeze lashed his thick furs. Dismounting, Crimson felt the ground beginning to slant downward.

Frost Bight was below. "The Bight is upon us! Dismount, and guide your Naomi with caution!"

There were no celebrations; his recruits were far past such a point. But reaching the summit, they, too, marveled. The alp's hills sloped into the unmistakable cliffs of Frost Bight. These cliffs created a coastline, the final piece of occupied land. A drop-off. Frost Bight looked out over an endless sea, vast and treacherous. *The Frozen Sea,* thought Crimson. A welcomed sight.

Emerald Company gazed through moonlight. From this altitude, they could see it all. Monstrous icebergs pushed out of the deep and loomed over stormy waves. Sleet and snow thrashed against jagged cliffsides, dragging wet algae down to the Frozen Sea beneath. A web of eroding docks stretched over the icy water, connecting where the ocean met the bight's bottom far below.

"To the cabins!" roared Crimson. "Prepare for inspection!"

Rows of white cabins were built near the edge of this clifftop, as if daring the land to shift an inch. True to Alyonian architecture, such cabins connected with one another by rear balconies dangling high above the sea, another dare for nature.

Treading carefully, the hill was easily descended as Emerald Company followed Frost Bight's only lane into town. Snow had been shoved aside, clearing a way for wagons and Naomi.

"Captain Crimson!" shouted Commander Harold. "As I live and breathe…"

Harold marched forward through the black night with a number of hard-looking Alyonians close behind. Dressed in furs thicker than Emerald's Green Capes, these folk clearly never left the Bight.

"Commander Harold, looking cold as ever!" Crimson approached.

"Feeling cold as ever. Old as ever too. I'm gonna die in this damned place." Harold took Crimson's forearm and embraced, then motioned to his followers. "Well, go on! Help this lot into their overnights!"

Harold's Alyonians wasted no time. Accustomed to aiding weary travelers, they relieved Emerald Company as Harold led Crimson toward his own cabin. "Come, Crimson, I've got somethin' to show ya."

* * *

Emerald Company had been shown to their cabins, where they gladly slept for the eve. Crimson, however, had begun to fear the idea of a decent night's sleep.

"What'd ya think of what I've done to the ole' Bight?" Commander Harold lit a long cigar and passed another to Crimson. "She's far better than your last visit, aye?"

Crimson took in the newly painted cabins and cottages on both sides as he followed Harold through the Bight. There was even an alehouse now. "Aye," admitted Crimson. "Far better."

It wasn't long before they reached Harold's personal quarters, two stories, painted green and white. The inside had been decorated with pelts and prized animal heads. Lanterns hung from stout chains overhead. Impressive jugs of whiskey lined a few countertops. "And I see you've developed a new hobby."

"Drinkin' ain't a hobby." Harold poured himself a glass, his large hands easily palming the jar. "It's a way of life." Utilizing a wheeled system, Harold slid a hefty sheet of glass to the side, revealing his outdoor balcony. More salty winds whistled into the room, shifting the flames of Harold's fire pit.

"You don't fear the flames spreading? Your entire chamber is made of wood."

"I fear nothin'!" said Harold, raising his glass. "Save another way of life."

They both laughed before walking out onto the balcony. Fighting shivers, Crimson leaned over a railing and took in the unforgettable waterscape.

"Ironic, ain't it?" Harold followed a swig with a puff, nearly lighting his beard aflame. "Pitch black out there, and yet, she's the prettiest sight you'll ever see."

"Perhaps there's beauty in all darkness, and it's simply our task to find it." Feeling a bit better, Crimson had caught something of a third wind.

"Save your poetics for another eve." Harold flicked his cigar ashes over the rail, then watched them disappear into nothingness. "I've ill news."

"I expected as much."

"A few of my own got caught up in a nasty skirmish a couple of leagues south'a here. I lost three good Alyonians."

Crimson had a feeling he might know where. "What happened?"

"They were ridin' for the village of Haana. When they arrived, the place was burnin', and men were fightin' in the snow. Hard fightin'. My lads said they didn't recognize either side. Rare, given we run the only damn ferry to the Quiet Lands." Harold kept his eyes over the sea. "When my riders returned, they weren't alone."

"Who else?"

"About five men, most wounded. Each was outfitted in a flimsy chainmail of grey and green. Another ten or so tribeswomen, natives."

That lifted Crimson's brows. "They're here?"

"Aye." Harold scratched his beard. "I've got 'em all down below, hidin' in the cliffs. Just in case."

"In case what?"

"They claim to be involved in somethin'…well, I'll let you speak to 'em yourself."

"What was the fight over?" asked Crimson.

Harold set his whiskey on the rail and whistled back into his cabin. It took a moment, but soon enough, a young girl approached from a back room. She was small, brown of skin, and clearly starving. Young too. She appeared sickly, yet full of spirit. "They say it was over her."

Crimson studied the girl. A short buckskin dress hung just below her knees. It had been muddied and ripped, bloodied even. Her moccasins were missing chunks, exposing a few black and purple toes. The girl's braided hair hung past her shoulders.

"Do you speak the common tongue?" asked Crimson.

She nodded. "Yes."

"What is your name?"

The young girl acted skittish, as if she'd been raised to keep this a secret. "Nit'a."

48

BANDANO-RHI

Coyo

Bandano-Rhi maintained a steady trot, never forcing his horse to gallop. He'd always adored animals, even hated pushing them, but here he rode slowly for a different reason. "You've captured her likeness wonderfully." Bandano-Rhi stared down at a chalk painting, a lovely illustration of him and his sister.

"My honor, Lord," said Cassius-Thrimm. Cassius smiled, for today he found himself riding beside his emperor at the front of their battalion.

Unable to move his eyes from the painting, Bandano-Rhi did all he could to kill the painful memories, though the wine made it difficult. Hoping to distract, he surveyed his impressive force. Three vast lines of soldiers spanned down a dirt road behind him, each man wearing yellow and purple armor, each man ready to bring justice to the heathen city of Coyo. *You'll be avenged, sister.*

Bandano-Rhi handed the painting back to Cassius and chugged what remained of his newest wineskin. "Take the painting to my wisemen, and give it to them for safekeeping."

Cassius bowed and led his horse toward the rear.

Watching him go, Bandano-Rhi took a more serious tone. "Felix."

"Yes, Lord?"

Felix-Donro also rode beside the emperor, though in fairness, he never left Bandano-Rhi's side. Felix-Donro's golden armor inferred he was a member of Rhi's Honor Guard, and his position in line suggested an important one.

"There's a split in the road ahead," continued Bandano. "Upon arrival, escort our catapults to the hill northwest. The wisemen have foreseen our victory; we will not bloody a single sword."

The wisemen... Felix raised an eyebrow, though he knew better than to question. He bowed from horseback and scanned the horizon. Small, half-deserted villages lay ahead on both sides of the dirt road. "I can smell their wickedness from here."

Bandano-Rhi's repugnance had been long painted across his face. "Indeed. Prepare Captain Alacus' cavalry. Ride forward and burn it all, then let flames cleanse the air. I don't want our infantry catching whatever lingers."

"Yes, Lord."

Felix gripped his reins and circled off the dirt road. Bright-green grass filled a field beneath him as he rode by the battalion. "Captain Alacus-Yuri!"

As Felix rode farther away, Bandano-Rhi refocused on the road ahead, on the villages and their many potential traps. One thought never escaped him. *The shadow god of Coyo... Where are you?* Bandano-Rhi burped drunkenly, then recalled Taryn's words: *Elo needs you to go and face this shadow god. To burn Coyo. Do not be afraid. He's with you.*

"He's with me," muttered Bandano, stroking his sheathed sword's golden pommel.

"For the empire!"

Captain Alacus-Yuri's voice thundered through the green field to Bandano's right. The emperor smiled at the sight of fifty horsemen striding through open grass, weapons drawn, cloths over bloodthirsty faces. The riders covered impressive ground and reached each village quickly. Then Bandano could hear only screams.

* * *

Bandano-Rhi's infantry eventually reached the carnage. Captain Alacus' cavalry had made swift work of any remaining citizens, though most had fled for Coyo's walls long ago. The villages now burned as Rhi's foot soldiers marched past.

Foul-smelling smoke swirled about. Statues of various gods had been decapitated, with sacrificial animals strewn headless beside their wooden altars. Bandano-Rhi judged such wretchedness with tired eyes.

Leaving the poor animals, he focused on the city of Coyo a mere three hundred span ahead, perched atop a small bank. Another few minutes' march and his ranks would find themselves within range of long-distance fire—if Coyo's defenses had any to provide.

"You." Bandano-Rhi extended his hand toward a tool bearer trotting slowly behind. "Longscope."

The bearer dug into a yellow sack tied to his horse's saddle, then pulled forth the item. Grasping it, Bandano-Rhi observed his soon-to-be prey. Coyo looked *weak*. "The time is upon us."

Exiting the smelly villages, Bandano-Rhi's battalion reached a split in the road. Prepared, Felix-Donro led his catapults to position as the rest of their army marched forward. Leading the soldiers, Bandano-Rhi found his nerves entirely missing, drowned by wine and anger. Still, one fear remained unshakable. *You are here, but when will I see you?*

A trio of scouts galloped down the road toward Rhi and his Honor Guard. Their fastest rider pulled short. "My Lord, the city is weaker than expected. Perhaps two hundred men outside the walls, another fifty atop with bows. By the looks of it, they aren't even longbows…Most of the women and children have fled into the woods behind. They're abandoning Coyo." The rider appeared sad, knowing precisely how the next events would play out.

Bandano-Rhi nodded. "The wisemen have seen clearly. Elo has already broken our enemy. Keep everyone at distance. I won't risk a single man catching their sickness. Have our longbows and ballistae brought to the front, and tell Felix to unleash his catapults at will. We'll watch Coyo burn from afar."

A few of Rhi's Honor Guard passed glances of judgment, though it was hard to see beneath their helmets. "My Lord," began Maccius-Lin, the bravest of them. "Should we not at least meet their infantry in the field? Warrior's code?"

Bandano-Rhi did not dismiss him. "Worry not, Maccius, for these men aren't warriors. By Elo, I tell you, they're barely even men. It would surprise me not if half lacked souls entirely. Do not question your own honor, my brother. I will need you for something much greater."

Bandano-Rhi's Honor Guard questioned him no further. Instead, one guard opened a box of exquisitely curved horns.

"Yes, Lord."

Maccius-Lin picked up the largest and blew loudly. The cue of battle.

At the sound, Bandano-Rhi's infantry left the dirt road and formed tactical lines on a meadow some distance before Coyo's walls. The Rhi archers followed whilst their engineers wheeled ballistae.

Coyo's defenders were close enough to see their enemy gathering before them. The two hundred courageous protectors standing outside their tiny wooden walls began praying to any gods they knew.

"Fire at will!" yelled Bandano-Rhi.

His archers anchored and took aim as the ballistae were tightened and loaded. Before letting loose, a barrage of seven stones whirled overhead from the west. Bandano-Rhi's inebriated eyes followed the enormous stones as they pummeled Coyo's walls, turrets, and gate-house, smashing wood every which way.

The city's defenders scattered as debris crashed down upon them. Many ran forward, making easy targets for Rhi's bowmen. Arrows darted through crisp yet acrid air, falling the unorganized men of Coyo. In disarray, they could only charge forward. Their force was already cut in half, now a mere brigade of martyrs. Ballistae added to the bloodshed, forcing many of Bandano-Rhi's men to look away.

As was said, thought Bandano, *not a single Rhi sword needed bloodying.* Guzzling from a third wineskin, he gazed over Coyo's lookout towers. This shadow god would surely be here somewhere.

"My Lord?" Cassius-Thrimm had reappeared, and now pointed toward a particularly decimated area of Coyo's walls. "How would you prefer I paint this great victory in the story-papers? The image of a falling city, or the depiction of your forces watching it collapse?"

Bandano sipped slowly, pondering. "There was no great victory. Merely justice."

The emperor continued his search for Taryn's foreseen shadow god, but it never showed.

49

KORNILIOUS
Lampade

Her body swayed in the cold night's breeze, the rope still firm around her neck.

The Kaldorian Guard, thought Taryn, staring up at the lifeless Alyonian. *At least now there's one less.* Taryn whispered into Kornilious' ear, "Any moment."

The Master of Defense stood by her side, defenseless. *This can't be real,* he thought. *This isn't Taryn. You've known her since birth.*

A harsh *screech* sounded above, forcing Kornilious to cover both ears as he closed his eyes in hot anguish. *What have I done?*

"Look there." Taryn focused upon the treetops shaking from afar, their very leaves and limbs shoved aside as something forced its way through.

But the interim queen wasn't the only one watching. Tiannu and Jari remained silent from the muddy drop-off, bellies to its warm dirt, eyes toward the shaky canopy.

"Lampade! Feast!" Kantis' voice boomed through the forest, followed by a chorus of chants.

"Scythini, Stralli! One union! Scythini, Stralli! One union!" chanted hundreds of red robes.

Ignoring the daunting shouts, Kornilious kept his eyes on the trees, which shook more aggressively with every second. Something, some *being*, was drawing closer. *What are you?* His answer came as the canopy suddenly split in two, paving a path for a heinous beast. A red beast. A horrific monster.

Sending leaves in every direction, this creature flew at speeds Kornilious thought impossible. Its large wings expanded as it descended upon the dangling Alyonian. Bony limbs and sharp teeth tore into her body, slashing through flesh and bone as if mere parchment. Its talons alone were the size of Kornilious' arm, its wings as tall as he.

Balo, intervene, thought Tiannu.

But no help came.

The beast finished its meal in seconds before tossing bloody remains to the damp ground below. The creature let out another screech, then took back to the dark sky.

"Magnificent," Taryn whispered as she watched in admiration. She turned to Kornilious, who was frozen in disbelief. "The last time I brought you here, I merely showed you the comet dust. Now you see one of its true powers: the power to conjure."

"This creature…" Kornilious paused, trembling. "This is why our realm believes they've seen a real shadow god. This is what they've been seeing in the eve?"

"I don't know," said Taryn. "Perhaps they've seen real shadow gods. Perhaps they've seen my Lampade. I for one believe in the Realm of Torment, so it seems quite possible that its shadow gods could escape into our world."

Kornilious' quivers did not depart. Whether due to the creature, or Taryn's measured response to it, he couldn't say. "That beast…we must—"

"That beast is our answer, my love." She turned to him. "That beast is how we stop the Gorsh, how we save Alyonia and all of Adria. How we create a one-world function."

Kornilious barely heard her. His attention lay solely on the victim's lower torso. Her mangled remains rested next to a group of young boys, each tied to various tree stumps, each red with fear. A lengthy row of torches encircled them and the entire hidden clearing, converging only at Trakkonious' dreadful archway. Kornilious looked down. A lone path of green limestone stretched from the arch toward his position.

"Are you ready?"

Taryn's eyes dug into Kornilious, and for a moment, he could no longer see his childhood love.

"I want you to see why I've brought you," she said. "A king must know everything." Taryn swirled round and paced the limestone path, each step bringing her closer to a wide dirt hole in the center of this clearing.

Leave, Kornilious. Simply leave... He glanced about. *Far too many of them. But would Taryn order me detained?*

"My love?"

Taryn had made it halfway down the hole, her body now sticking out of it. Kornilious couldn't look away. Her neck, her smile, her gorgeous white hair, all accentuated by surrounding torches. His mind raced back to better times: swinging with Taryn at the youth academy, sneaking into Preem's ball. He thought of their romantic eves on the Lukonite Lake, of his promise to never leave young Taryn alone...

Down the green path he went.

* * *

Kornilious' legs grew weary, though in truth, they hadn't walked long at all. The dirt hole had taken them deep underground, where a broad and even muddier tunnel awaited. Unlike the forest above, this tunnel blazed with heat and led in a single direction. Distant cries and shrieks travelled from its opposite end, shrill in Kornilious' ears.

Yet he walked on…the shrieks growing louder and more frightening. Worse, Kornilious' feet began to sizzle from the ground's warmth. Sweat beaded his forehead. The cries became louder still, so loud that Kornilious felt he knew precisely what caused them.

"We're here." Taryn placed her arm before him and gave an innocent smile. "Their den."

Kornilious halted as the tunnel ended abruptly and gave way to a well-kept wooden balcony. Looking down, they now stood at the top of a deep pit, with only a railing to stop them from plummeting in. Gazing side to side, Kornilious noted that the balcony extended from their position and surrounded the entire pit from above. Ten stone tables had been erected upon the balcony, each separated by equal distance.

What is this place? Kornilious couldn't understand it. Steam rose from the bottom of the pit and spiraled all around, blurring his sight. Still he stared; he stared at ten young boys, each dead or unconscious. Their bruised bodies laid over the tables. *No…*

Groups of sweaty Alyonians gathered round each altar, holding candles and weathered green books. Kornilious recognized many of them. *Patrons.*

Wealthy members of House Bartellus were present, House Dree as well, even the once savage member of the Honorable-Three, High Lord Mekall of House Merab.

"Scythini, Stralli! One union! Scythini, Stralli! One union!" The Alyonians chanted in unison whilst lifting lifeless children from their tables, then heaving them into the pit.

Taryn placed both hands over her ears. "Cover, dear."

Kornilious obeyed just in time. Even muffled he heard the horrendous screeches from below. The cries and high-pitched screams of children as hungry beasts tore into them. Bones and even a few of the beasts themselves collided with dirt walls below, fighting one another over their prey. Such awful sounds ended quickly, however, then the air doubled in heat. Kornilious' throat went painfully dry, his fur soaked in perspiration.

"Beautiful, aren't they?" Taryn dragged him toward the ledge where Kornilious gripped a sweltering balcony railing, then peered down into the hole. Thirty beasts resembled the nightmare he'd just seen in the forest.

"My Lampades. They're only babies." Taryn watched the infant creatures swarm one another and continue ripping the dead boys apart. "But they'll grow." She pointed toward the many weathered green books, all sharing one title: *Lampade: Beasts of the Flame*. "Surely this seems barbarous, ancient, cruel. For you and your beautiful heart, this likely seems mad."

Kornilious did not move nor answer.

"But here's the predicament, my love. Dark times are upon us. This seems fact. The Gorsh hordes will not be stopped by our armies, nor Bandano-Rhi's. So these Lampades, we need them for a great many reasons. And they're only bred one way."

He deemed it best to nod.

"We only take children convicted of heinous crimes," explained Taryn. "Each boy has stolen, raped, or worse."

"I see…"

Taryn read him quickly, his disapproval apparent. "Once these Lampades have grown, we'll use them for good. This allows us power over the future. A future I want you to lead."

Kornilious heard her loud and clear.

50

HENDRIX

The King's Son

The carriage jolted, thrashing Hendrix against Aypax and Drake. Clumps of Yellowstraw engulfed them, still their colliding seemed inevitable. It had been a smooth ride since they'd escaped Drill's holdings and entered the carriage in secret, but suddenly turned bumpy as could be.

"Wood," whispered Ava from a row behind. She and Adora poked their heads from beneath more Yellowstraw.

"Wood," echoed Hendrix. "We're near the docks? Should we make for our cog?"

Aypax's silence paved the way for Ava. "We should not abandon whoever saved us." She huffed and swatted a group of pestering flies. "They have perhaps conjured a bigger plan. We should see to it."

"Could be a trap," said Hendrix, gazing out of a small slit. He saw two bulls attached to reins, pulling their carriage quickly. Next he saw bar signs and the unmistakable nude float marking the transition between docks and land. Their carriage passed more brothels and groups of excited seamen rushing toward Starsgard.

Aypax finally whispered, "Whoever came to our aid, they knew precisely where we'd be. It would be wise to find out how. If it were a trap, if it were Taryn's bunch, they'd have gutted us in the cells."

"Quiet back there!" snapped a female voice, presumably the carriage captain. Halting her bulls, she leapt to the wet ground below, then walked around to a sliding wooden door. She opened the door and lifted a brow at the foolishly contorted group. "You two, put these on," she said, tossing Ava and Adora two grey tunics.

The sisters complied. Stepping out, the group saw the woman more clearly.

The one with a deep voice looked strong. Dark of skin and large in muscle. Long strands of braided hair fell from her head. Her jaw was tight, not an inch of fat. She wore a well-fitted grey corset, though it was lined with shades of green.

"Follow me," continued the woman. "Don't linger, don't stop, don't run. Move like you belong." She took off down a worn and slippery dock, forcing the group to trail her. Ships bobbed to the right and left as Hendrix breathed in the docks' nasty combination of odors once again. "Three slots ahead," continued the woman, making her way toward a boat slip. "Follow me aboard and get below deck. Fast."

The group obeyed, but as they reached the vessel, Aypax noticed its sails. *All grey. Perhaps painted over a prior symbol.* He'd seen this same ship on the Ratna some eight or nine moons ago, hard to recall after his time in Drill's cell.

"Welcome aboard *The Thorn of Pallala!*" A bulky human stepped to the bow, watching them with crystal green eyes and thick black hair.

He was the same man who'd broken them free not long ago.

"Come below deck. We need to set sail."

* * *

The Alyonians sipped on hard booze and much needed canteens of water. Exhausted, Hendrix thought them at death's door, but Aypax knew better than that. He'd been there before.

Drake sat on the cabin's cushioned bench a few forearms afar, keeping to himself and refusing drinks entirely. Ava and Adora had gone farther below deck, each in desperate need of the ship's apothecary.

"I am called Maxoff," stated the black-haired human. "Maxoff-Rhi."

Aypax lowered his potent drink, nearly choking. The pale face and green eyes, the dark hair. It made sense now. Maxoff-Rhi had done his father's bidding.

"Yes." Maxoff-Rhi gestured. "Bandano-Rhi is my father. But lower your guard, I mean no ill will."

True or not, Aypax scoured the cabin, calculating his odds of victory. *Impossible. Even with Drake's aid.* There were eleven men, another six women, all armed, all dressed to fight or sail. Each the same grey and green. This group appeared trained, at least to some degree. The large hammer that had shattered their prison locks not long ago lay beside this Maxoff-Rhi. "Then what do you want?" Aypax asked, the pain of Katrin still ripe in his weary eyes.

Maxoff-Rhi sat. His clothes were dirtier than his comrades', which was odd, given his stature. Maxoff-Rhi was the unquestioned prince of the Rhi Empire, heir to the mightiest of thrones. "It isn't what I want," he said.

The woman from the carriage burst in through a connecting door, then sat beside Maxoff-Rhi. "Is it done?"

Aypax watched her kiss him tenderly, watched her fall into his arms and unwind in the way that only the truly weary can comprehend. He knew their exhaustion well, though what truly ailed him was their seemingly deep love. A dream he'd lost yet again at the hands of Drill Bintonn.

"Who are you all?" asked Hendrix, sipping his drink a bit slower than Aypax.

The woman sat up, feigning respect. "I'm called Julieta, and we're the Thorns of Pallala." She referenced everyone around. The wearied group looked relieved to be back in the safety of their vessel.

"I'm unfamiliar." Hendrix studied the cabin's details—its battered wood, boxes of grain, and stacks of old parchment.

"Then we've done our job," said Maxoff-Rhi, turning to a few members of his crew. "Help Chu'a and the others set sail. Half speed along the river, undetected, full speed upon open water." Maxoff's crew nodded and took to the deck above. "I created the Thorns of Pallala many moons ago." He poured himself a second glass of red wine. "We're small in number, but large in impact."

"How's that?" asked Hendrix.

"Pallala has seen strange times these past few years." Maxoff-Rhi locked eyes with Julieta, saddened. "Our young boys vanish at frightening rates. Many blame Stralli, others think the boys are simply hiding somewhere, playing a great trick on their loved ones. But we know better."

Julieta furrowed her brows. "We began to spot riders in black, aided by strange folk in red cloaks or dresses. They raid our countryside villages by night, stealing as many young males as possible."

Aypax leaned forward, curious.

"Over time," said Maxoff, "we banded angry parents with my own loyal soldiers and fought back in secret. We've tracked these riders from the Eagle Tail Mountains to the frozen north of Frost Bight. They pillage my empire, yours, and even the northern tribes. Seems they'll take young males of any kind." He dug into a small pouch. "But the point of our story is for later. We've a much more pressing matter." He pulled forth an ancient-looking key: large and heavy, barely fitting in his powerful, weathered hand. "I've been instructed to give this to you, Hendrix. You must die with it. Or for it." He extended the key, pulling Drake's darkening eyes.

"Me?" mumbled Hendrix.

"Yes." Maxoff-Rhi closed Hendrix's grimy fingers around it. "You."

51

KORNILIOUS

Election Day

Kornilious found himself back on the Kaldorian theater stage, silently reciting his preprepared victory speech. Both legs trembled as his conscience screamed, yet he managed to appear strong. He had to. The uneasy masses below were nearly as numerous as they'd been for Bandano-Rhi's speech, though undoubtedly more anxious. He also found himself flanked by countless members of parliament. In fact, the entire High Council stood behind him, forming their usual row of dreadful green robes and unanimated expressions.

To his left stood Jackkdon Religos, beloved candidate of the Vetusian party, and once-commander of the Honorable-Six. Jackkdon was short in stature but carried himself like a giant. He'd accumulated an impressive collection of war medals over his many seasons fighting in the slave crusades of Gondol, and to this day he wore them proudly upon his green and gold surcoat. He was well-spoken, royally educated, and always appeared unsatisfied with the state of Alyonia. A perfect candidate.

"My dearest Alyonians," shouted Taryn from just behind them both. She'd limped her way to center stage where the morning nova could highlight her black mourning gown. "Within mere moments, our ballot collectors shall present us with the official results. Very shortly, we shall welcome Jackkdon Religos, your new Master of Defense, or congratulate Kornilious Debower on reelection!"

The crowd shouted and cheered. "Upon announcing our winner," she continued, "we shall press on to the results of this Bright Season's voting cycle. Two primary issues have been decided: the famine, and Alyonia's standing within the Pallala-Accord." Taryn scanned her audience. Facial cloths, umbrellas, and rain hid their expressions, though she didn't exactly care how they felt. *Ah, look who it is.* Taryn spotted Madison Preters standing beside her mother. She smiled in their direction. "But before we move forward, let us close our eyes and commence a moment of reflection for our little ones lost at the Alyonian dance hall."

The crowd followed, gladly paying their respects.

"Thank you," said Taryn. "Truly, thank you all. Now let us commence!"

After a long moment of silence, a line of sleepy ballot collectors hustled up the stage's side, each carrying boxes of ballots and public surveys. These collectors placed one box before each member of the High Council. Taryn yelled in their direction. "Begin!"

The High Council tore open their boxes, then quickly pulled forth a slip of parchment from each. The farthest member raised his right arm, signaling the results of the first ballot box: Kornilious.

"Ahhhh!" Thunderous shouts filled the air from the Novellusian party.

The next member raised his left arm: Jackkdon.

This process repeated itself as one by one, the High Council announced new results from each box. A tight race ensued, perfectly even before arriving upon the final two members, each of whom raised their right arms high.

"Kornilious Debower!" Taryn shouted loud, doing her best to remain unbiased. "Please raise your arms for Alyonia's reelected Master of Defense! Let us unite, and show him your support!"

Half the crowd did just that. The other half moaned and groaned, ignoring Taryn and leaving the theater grounds entirely. Jackkdon Religos maintained his usual position of strength and honor, raising his right arm and cheering halfheartedly for his opponent. His team could not bear the same. Angry and defeated, they departed, leaving their candidate alone center stage.

Jackkdon swallowed his sorrows and walked toward Kornilious. "My respects." Jackkdon extended his forearm for a proper shake.

With his sleeves slightly rolled, Kornilious could see Jackkdon's brand upon his wrist:

Honesty. Heart. Honor. 6.

Pained by true respect for Jackkdon and true disdain for himself, Kornilious returned the gesture, and the two embraced. "Thank you. You've mine as well."

Jackkdon motioned out to the crowd, then back to the High Council. "Remember, Kornilious…honor is doing what's right, regardless of what you're told. Obedience is doing what you're told, regardless of what's right."

Kornilious held Jackkdon's eyes, careful not to signal his unease. "Wise words."

"Kornilious and his high-aid Sir Dyman Kelterbury shall be re-sworn into their positions come novafall!" Taryn's voice silenced the loud crowd, allowing Kornilious to step away from Jackkdon. "Now for the results of our Bright Season's voting cycle."

Taryn called forth an elderly Alyonian standing beside Kornilious. "It is my honor to reintroduce Sir Kelterbury, Kornilious' high-aid and renown orator! As is custom, he shall share this season's results." Taryn bowed and stepped back, yielding the floor to Sir Kelterbury.

"Many thanks!" announced Sir Kelterbury, hobbling toward Taryn. His voice remained undeniably powerful for one so old and feeble. "The famine!" He stayed quiet for a moment, letting a frustrating silence sink in. "Is over! No more rationing of foods!"

The crowd leapt, literally. They jumped and screamed. "There shall be no further restrictions upon markets nor households with regards to limiting consumption. Thanks to our treaty with the Rhi Empire, we now have enough supply to endure three seasons. This should give our farms time aplenty to restore themselves and come back stronger than ever!"

Sir Kelterbury drew a long breath, exhausted from all of this yelling. "Further, we've reached the point of agreement on Alyonia's long-standing position within the Pallala-Accord. You all have spoken, your votes have been heard. Alyonia shall announce its official withdrawal!"

Scattered applause roared once again, half the crowd elated, the other terrified.

"In times such as these, we must grow stronger than ever!" continued Sir Kelterbury. "May we not let our past cloud our judgments. May we look with clear eyes at the horrific challenges ravaging our lands today. If we're to survive hardships ahead, we must unite two great realms and stand together for a common good!"

"Wow." Taryn clapped beside Sir Kelterbury. "Historic!"

High Council Lord Preem paced slowly toward them both. He revealed his little blue box and slyly pulled forth the ancient ink pen.

Taryn smiled.

* * *

An hour passed. Rulings had been signed and more speeches delivered. The crowd emptied as Kornilious prepared to exit with his campaign team. The Master of Defense stuffed his rucksack with small tokens of written felicitations he'd received from various members of the High Council. An honor.

Kornilious followed his delighted team offstage when he felt a certain pull… an odd feeling, and one he'd noticed rather frequently of late. *What is this?*

Midway down a set of spiraling stairs, he sensed the need to turn toward the dissipating audience. To his surprise, an Alyonian lady had her sights directly upon him. Her stare felt strange, powerful. *I recognize her. But from where?*

The lady pulled down her facial cloth, then Kornilious quickly understood.

Tiannu Preters.

"Sir Kelterbury!" yelled Kornilious. "I shall meet you all at the Kaldorian hall, carry on."

Kelterbury nodded and moved on with the rest of his team, leaving Kornilious alone with a few guards. "Leave me, I need a moment alone."

The guards obeyed as Kornilious crept beneath the spiral stairs and waited.

Tiannu stepped to his side and wasted no time. "I saw you last night, in the forest. Before you react, know that I've made arrangements with my husband and many others. Should I turn up dead or missing, word shall spread across Alyonia faster than even you could kill it, though maybe not as fast as Taryn could. I have evidence of your murderous streak. All of you. The children, the Kaldorian Guard."

Kornilious' face tightened. *The who?*

"And yet even with all of my evidence, and with more than a handful of witnesses, my word would mean little in a trial with the High Council."

Kornilious hadn't expected that. "Likely not."

"But your word would," she said. "Your word would go a rather long way. A public announcement, perhaps something outdoors, where more than a few eyes can see."

"You've already admitted your current lack of power in trial." Kornilious stood firmly. "You're not very astute to bribery, my old friend."

"Agreed," said Tiannu. "I was never much good at it. But bribery isn't what this is."

"Then what is it?"

She locked eyes on his. "A chance to do what's right."

Kornilious wiggled his mouth. *Does the bitch know Jackkdon?*

"I remember the old Kornilious," she continued. "I knew him well. I may not be one for bribery, but I'm an expert on hearts. And yours does not reside with her."

Kornilious turned away from Tiannu as he caught a glimpse of Taryn through the corner of his eye. She'd made her way to the theater grounds and now handed out bread baskets to lines of hungry citizens.

"Your library has eyes on it," he said. "Meet me tonight. The splash bottle alehouse. Find the barkeep named Rexx. Darkest hour."

"'Til then."

Tiannu strode off.

52

AYPAX

Getting Past

Hendrix's eyes examined the key in his hand. It felt heavy, in more ways than one. He could feel its weight and history, its stories and allure.

Maxoff-Rhi sank into his softly cushioned bench, exhaling. "Never let another take this, no matter how much you trust them. It shall be this world's salvation, or this world's demise."

Tucked in the corner, Drake's eyes widened.

"No." Aypax slammed his fourth glass of booze upon a dirty wooden table. "Shut your lips. Hendrix, do not heed this. It's a tale for toddlers. We must go."

Maxoff-Rhi reached behind his bench and grasped a dusty scroll, then unraveled it upon the table. "Here lies a full map of Adria. From the Red Sand Desert to the Quiet Lands. From Alyonia to all of Pallala above." Maxoff-Rhi's finger tapped four dots on the map. "Four dots representing four keys. You now hold one of them."

Aypax scoffed. "So this is one of the four keys of old? You mean to tell us of the altar too? Why, I suspect Balo himself shall descend upon our ship any moment."

"Let him finish." Hendrix had a mind to know this. His prophetic studies had told the story a thousand times. He knew the classic tale of the original comets, their dust's power, and the altar that locked them away. His mother had told him time and time again that perhaps that altar still existed, and perhaps those four keys that opened it were out there. Somewhere.

Maxoff poured himself yet another glass of wine, having finished his first two nearly as quickly as Aypax. "That is precisely what I tell you, excluding the sarc bit about Balo. I say *tell*, because it is true. It is fact."

"Fact and legend are hard to distinguish of late," countered Aypax. "If legend lingers long enough, it tends to become history. History becomes fact."

"An example?"

"Legend says the sea is endless, and our realms have accepted this as fact." The big Alyonian burped drunkenly. "But I've sailed to the Five Falls. The ocean itself drops into a waterfall. It is, in fact, not endless."

"Have you traveled to the bottom of the Five Falls?"

"No one has. It is impossible to survive the drop."

Maxoff poured them both another hefty glass. "So you cannot say for certain that the sea ends at such a waterfall? Perhaps it curves beneath itself, and creates an ocean under the land we know and step on today."

Aypax sneered. "By such logic, anything is possible."

"Precisely." Maxoff-Rhi's eyes shifted to Hendrix. "One year ago, I had a dream. I was asleep in my bed when a heinous presence appeared in the corner of my chambers. It was dark and shadowy, and watching me."

The Alyonians leaned in, entranced by the story for different reasons.

"But it disappeared in an aggressive swirl and became something lighter...something that made my heart pound and then stop. Something beautiful. It was Balo."

Aypax shook his head whilst Julieta watched her husband reminisce. But she wasn't the only one watching. A pair of chocolate-brown eyes pierced through the cabin door, watching in secret.

"Balo began to speak," continued Maxoff. "Though I never saw his face nor mouth."

And yet you knew it was him, thought Aypax, squeezing his nub finger.

"He told me to 'go and find the Alyonian called Hendrix, for he is my vessel.' Then I saw you, Hendrix. I saw your face, right next to this one's." Maxoff nodded to Aypax. "You were both standing before the altar. Balo showed me the comets locked deep below. He showed me what must be done."

Aypax nodded deliriously, tired of the typical story. Balo, Elo, Indigon—these gods always seemed to come by dream. *Funny they never show in reality.* "A fine tale. Well-crafted, perhaps true, even. Hard to decipher what our mind does during sleep. But answer me this: If what you say is accurate and you felt compelled to follow Balo, why did your father, the most famous of all Balonian persecutors, allow you to take this 'valuable key'? Wouldn't he, too, need it to unlock the altar?"

"Father did now allow it." Maxoff-Rhi's demeanor went limp. "He knew not of my actions 'til it was too late. Bandano-Rhi has not been himself of late. He's changed since the loss of my beloved aunt. To lose her the way he did, it is hard to comprehend. He needed somewhere to place the blame, and Balonity seemed an easy option."

"Placing blame and waging genocide are quite different things," Aypax sneered.

Maxoff agreed. "Many books of Elonity preach violence as a means to ultimate peace. I believe losing my aunt helped father adopt such a radical outlook."

"One of the many problems with faith," said Aypax. "It starts wars that regular folk die for."

"Does faith swing the blade? Or the swordsman?"

Aypax burped again. "Fine. But folks tend to swing a lot harder for a cause they believe in."

"Good," said Maxoff-Rhi. "For evil shall always exist. And it will always be swinging hard. Without a force of good swinging back, I fear what this world would look like."

Aypax dug a finger into his glass of booze, then swigged the liquid with abandon. "What if our definitions of *good* are not the same?"

Again Maxoff grinned. "Therein lies the great dilemma... without a higher good to guide us, this world's justice is merely my view against yours. Your tribe's against mine. And that will always descend into violence. Faith allows us to strive toward the same good, a good we know to be—"

"Set sail!" announced a voice from above.

Maxoff ignored the command, and instead kept his eyes on the big Alyonian. Aypax bobbed up and down with each wave. His once-tanned face had gone a sickly pale, covered in welts and bruises.

"You place me in a predicament, Aypax the Honorable," Maxoff-Rhi said. "For without your belief, I have failed."

"Well, they say failure is the great teacher."

Maxoff chuckled, shifting tactics. "A pivotal night awaits. My men have prepared you a small cabin. Rest."

* * *

"Wake up!"

"Wake up!"

Murmurs. Shouts. Sweat.

"Wake up!"

Aypax's shoulders shook. "Easy, easy!" he roared, slowly coming to. "I'm awake..." He coughed and rubbed his red eyes, more sickly than ever.

"I almost shit my overalls." Hendrix slouched back against a wooden door, taking deep breaths. "Are you okay? Why weren't you answering?"

Aypax sat up upon a musty cot and stared ahead. A lack of windows had allowed for much needed sleep but brought forth merciless booze-induced brain aches. His sheet was soaked from night sweats, his clothes still damp and foul.

"We've been summoned." Hendrix grabbed a handful of scented olive oil and ran it across his armpits and neck, desperate to quell his smell before possibly seeing Ava. "Aypax?"

Aypax glared at the brown wooden walls, their cracks and crevices. Drool fell from his dried lips as his head swayed.

Hendrix studied him. "We need to go *now*."

"No."

They sat in silence for a long moment.

"I'm done, Hendrix. I'm done."

Hendrix inspected his savior, void of a proper response. "What do you mean?"

"I can't." Further silence and drool. "I can't...keep going. This life. It's drained me. Katrin was all I had left."

It was then Hendrix noticed an abundance of seed residue staining the wet sheets, realizing what Aypax had attempted last night.

"Every night," continued Aypax. "I used to hear their cries. Now I just hear Katrin's."

Hendrix eyed the seed residue, shocked by his savior's sudden weakness, by how fast even he could lose control of the pain he'd hidden so masterfully. "Such actions dishonor Katrin. They dishonor her son. I even forewarned you of this."

"At least he finished the job."

Hendrix moved closer, dusting residue from the cot. "You are an Honorable."

"An Honorable..." Aypax trailed off, the word seemingly hurting worse than any of his bodily wounds. "When you were young, I beheaded Priest Eros, as you know. But what you never knew, what I discovered so many seasons later... I killed an innocent man."

"What?"

"Eros did not defile your sister, nor anyone for that matter. Taryn set him up."

"How?" said Hendrix. "How do you know?"

"Ellara, Eros' bride to be. After his death and her many moons of mourning, Ellara showed face at another execution. And then another. For thirty seasons straight, she never missed a beheading... and never changed her spot in the crowd."

Hendrix listened, wide eyed.

"Your father and I felt her stares each time, her hatred... She made it so difficult to swing my blade that I eventually approached her. I could not comprehend how one could return to such a place after all she went through, all she witnessed. She said it was the only place she felt Eros' spirit, and if her presence could sway Kaldor from such a heinous public practice, then perhaps Eros' death would not be in vain."

"Bloody Perdition..."

"We spoke further, and she showed me that Eros had an alibi, a clear out on the eve of Taryn's suffering. Ellara proved it all rather easily. I approached King Kaldor on the matter...and let's merely say he shut me down. I have lived with the lie ever since, with the knowledge of my own involvement in such a deep injustice. Then came Katrin, and the fallout of my actions toward her... This world, Hendrix, this life. It's black and grim and pointless. It is unjust. My shoulder creed, it burns daily. I am a fraud. Katrin was my last hope at righting my many wrongs. And if they do exist, she was my last hope in ever finding a place in the warrior stars."

Hendrix breathed, stunned. "I don't know anything about taking life…so I won't pretend to. I don't know anything about the warrior stars. But I do know about covering up my father's wrongs. I know about guilt. About shame." Hendrix nodded toward the seed residue. "And I know quite a bit about that… So I also know, if anyone can defeat their own voices, it's *you*."

Aypax nodded. "How does one defeat themselves?"

Hendrix thought long and hard about his own journey. "One day at a time."

53

CRIMSON

Nit'a

"She speaks well," muttered Crimson, keeping his eyes upon a frozen slippery path beneath him. "Highly intelligent, this Nit'a."

Commander Harold nodded, though he paid no heed to the dangerous trail. He'd walked it one hundred times before. "Aye. Far too smart for her age."

"Or her upbringing." Crimson lifted his boot cautiously, avoiding a patch of black ice.

"Never seen you so unnerved." Harold smirked, then poked his head over the path's daunting cliffside no more than a forearm to his left.

Crimson ignored the comment, along with the constant snow battering his green hood. "Focus, Harold. How could she have garnered such education?"

Harold shrugged, desperately trying to stoke his cigar through harsh winds. "Damn it!" He tossed it over the cliffside, watched it fade into darkness. "I can't say. Though I can tell you this. I've seen her act strange, Crimson. Very strange."

"How so?"

"She sees things. Things others don't."

Crimson wasn't sure what to make of that. "Hallucinations are common amongst children who have gone through hardship and abuse."

"No, not hallucinations." Harold stopped, gazing far ahead. The path curved and descended farther down the cliffside. "We're nearly there."

"What of her mother?" asked Crimson.

"Why so keen on the girl?"

"Call me curious."

Harold's face suggested he didn't like that response. "I wasn't there, Crimson. But according to the reports, her mother was odd. Our scouts penned her as ancient looking, wrinkly, yet somehow no older than forty seasons."

"What does that mean?"

"I know not," said Harold, still leading the way. "Evidently, she died protecting Nit'a. But…"

"Spit it out, Harold."

"They say the mother had a small pouch of dust with her."

Crimson spat. "I see."

Harold stopped just shy of an extended rock face, examining a flickering of flames barely visible from behind it. "You will shortly."

* * *

Commander Harold had led Crimson another thirty paces before stopping and picking up a few wet stones. "Hold here." He tossed them one by one at the backlit rock face.

It wasn't long before the boulders began sliding backward, exposing torchlights and an open cave. A few of Harold's men waved, ushering him in.

Bloody Perdition, thought Crimson, seeing how these folks had been living.

"Aye," moaned Harold, sensing Crimson's sorrow. "Gave 'em what we could. Sadly, they're better off here than their home."

Ten humans eyed Crimson, their deep brown skins covered entirely by thick wools and blankets. Ice had taken root inside a few nostrils and frozen over many black and blue extremities. Dim fires were abundant, as were bags of grain and corn, both hard as the rocks hiding them.

Two of Harold's own Alyonians were here, keeping guard and ferrying supplies back and forth. "Captain," they said in unison, shivering, but Crimson's focus had fallen upon a group of young boys resting in the corner, bundled together beside the brightest of torches.

"Mums won't let us near 'em, and I wouldn't try," whispered Harold.

Crimson quickly felt the stares of death from a small clan of mothers huddled next to their children. They, too, had nearly frozen, saved only by the provisions of Frost Bight.

"You should meet the Thorns first," said Harold, heading toward a few men in the cave's rear.

First? thought Crimson, following him through this moonless cavern. He passed colder and weaker folk with each step, slowly reaching the "Thorns." There were four, each seated upon a frozen and ancient sea log, likely here from countless seasons of lowering tides. These men had lost one of their own, based on a damp blanket rolled away in the corner.

"Chaps," said Harold, obviously wary around these humans. "This is Captain Crimson, one of the finest Alyonians to ever do the damn thing."

The humans extended shaky hands, a far cry from the Crossing. "Decia-Pri," mumbled the shortest of them. "You our way outta here?"

Crimson wished he were, even thought about how he might be. These men looked virtuous, each clad in dirty green and grey.

They did all they could to smile, unaware of the crippling frostbite slowly overtaking them. Crimson opened his mouth to speak, but nothing came. He couldn't ferry such a party to the Lookout undetected, and he lacked means of doing much else.

"He's not," said Harold. "Not yet at least. Crimson, these are what remains of the Thorns of…of—"

"Pallala," said Decia-Pri.

"Aye, of course," said Harold. "Crimson, good men here. Weren't for them, none of these tribes folk would be alive." Harold motioned toward the cold humans of Haana.

"The burnt-neck men," said Crimson, rather abruptly. "Who are they?"

Decia-Pri looked to his comrades, but he eventually spoke. "The burnt necks? They ain't men, my friend." He gestured toward Crimson himself. The meaning washed over the captain at once.

"Alyonians?"

Decia-Pri shook his head, affirming. "Most, but not all. We were tipped to an ambush. Word said Haana was next."

"Next?" Knowing these men might not see tomorrow, Crimson wasted no time.

"Yes." Decia-Pri quivered through soft words. "There were a series of raids on the tribes folk, nasty business, and whispers said Haana was next, so we laid trap and waited."

"The raiders were after the tribe girl? Nit'a?"

"You know a good deal of this…" Decia-Pri's cold expression shifted to insinuation.

Crimson waved that off. "It's my job to know everything. Were they after the girl or not?"

"After her family." Decia motioned toward an elderly tribesman, twice, maybe three times the age of anyone nearby. His eyes were closed, his face thin yet flabby. The bags beneath both eyes had bags, and his bones nearly contorted through two ancient cheeks.

"Just like they reported the mum," said Harold.

Crimson walked slowly toward this elder, forcing a few protective tribeswomen to their feet.

"*Allectum collidorum*," said Crimson, having mastered the northern tongue long ago.

The tribeswomen appeared shocked, yet relieved. They sat slowly as Crimson knelt beside their elder and studied his every blemish. The man's skin conveyed a hard life, each scar telling its own story of pain. Mere inches away, Crimson wondered how he'd managed to live for so long.

"*Pallala-Rhi! Pallala-Rhi!*"

The old tribesman's eyes shot open quicker than Crimson could fall to his backside. They were grey and white with wide pupils. "*Pallala-Rhi!*"

"*Kinya, kinya!*" whispered the closest tribeswoman, comforting him, and lowering his voice.

The elder slumped, calming. His eyes moved round the dark cavern. "*Sustus!*" he demanded.

It wasn't long before a different tribeswoman arose and slyly maneuvered her way beside him. Clearly used to subterfuge, even Crimson could barely detect her motions.

"*Sustus!*" demanded the elder, as the tribeswoman opened a small pouch and fingered bits of dust. "*Sustus!*"

Decia-Pri took a step back and watched, his blade hand ready to draw if need be.

Harold motioned to him. "No need. *Sustus* means 'dust.'"

Crimson himself felt a need to draw, but remained seated as the tribeswoman lifted dust beneath her elder's nose. He took a deep inhale, the powdery dust disappearing into his body. Crimson marveled as the elder's eyes went greyer, his fat and wrinkles spasmed, yet only slightly, for he seemed used to such a feeling.

"Crimson," whispered Harold, "get ready."

54

HENDRIX

The Rain's End

Aypax trailed Hendrix to a long corridor filled with barrels, paddles, and rope. Wooden stairwells lived on both sides, leading up to the ship's main deck. A few bearded men nodded, discreetly eyeing their dirty furs and untucked tails. "Up top," spat one of them. "Quarter deck."

Hendrix gave thanks before ascending. Not a moment later he found himself in the open. Tourtoufa's warm breeze danced by as the ever-present rain splattered across the ship's old, splintery wood.

Maxoff-Rhi and Julieta leaned against a slick rail, drinking what must've been their twentieth glass of wine. Maxoff held her tight, caring not for the weather.

"The eve is turning over into the one hundred and third moon…" Maxoff hadn't taken his eyes from Julieta, yet he clearly spoke to both Alyonians. "The time will soon be upon us."

Hendrix noticed another man near them. He wasn't smiling like Maxoff-Rhi. This man looked depressed, teetering on tears. His brown skin was reminiscent of the northern tribesmen Hendrix had seen in one of Tiannu's library books. The man had a shaved head and a longbow slung across his back, barely sticking out of a leather case. Tonight's rain drenched the case and battered screaming sails above, yet the man stood strong.

"I trust you've slept well?" Maxoff-Rhi said to Hendrix as he rubbed Julieta's neck gently.

"Yes," said Hendrix, feeling energized by his own words to Aypax. "How long were we under?"

"A few hours." Maxoff-Rhi looked up and considered the stars through a few holes in the dark clouds above. "Very soon, something glorious must occur. Hendrix, I need you to understand the severity of what I've placed upon you."

Maxoff turned to Aypax. "And you, well, the only way I can convince you to believe is for me to prove the key to be true. But I cannot prove such a thing without the Altar. So I shall instead prove *The Prophetics* to be true."

Julieta walked toward the bowman, distraught. "The western stars have crossed," she cried. "It is officially the one hundred and fourth moon!"

Maxoff shouted over growing winds. "*The Prophetics* are your guide, young Hendrix! Without them, we are lost! Look deeply."

An odd gust of heat fought through stormy air, nearly pushing the rain away completely. Maxoff-Rhi felt the abrupt change in weather. "Hendrix, conserve water." He leapt onto a slippery railing as Julieta crumbled to both knees. "Don't cry, my love. It's all been foretold."

Julieta ignored him. Tucking into a ball, she screamed furiously into both arms. Gutteral.

"Do it!" shouted Maxoff-Rhi.

The bald man winced, then let an arrow fly. Its tip struck Maxoff-Rhi in the heart.

Julieta's cries grew louder as her lover spat blood, then tumbled over the rail. His body fell for an agonizing moment before splashing into the rushing Ratna below.

Hendrix and Aypax went wide-eyed, neither understanding.

"What've you done!?" cried Aypax. He strode toward the bald archer.

"No!" cried Julieta. "He is ours. Maxoff ordered this!"

Hendrix's heart began thumping wildly. *What...is happening?*

"He *had* to kill Maxoff," she furthered, still on her hands and knees. "It has been foretold."

"Incoming!"

Shouts screeched from the main deck as flaming arrows descended. Their red-hot tips pierced wet wood, some lighting miniature flames, others extinguishing upon impact. Hendrix watched as four Thorns of Pallala were struck by deadly arrowheads, each shrieking and falling. With the ship's scattered lanterns as his only source of light, Hendrix knew more men had likely died in the shadows.

This was an assault.

"Find Prince Rhi and the little simian!" bellowed a voice through the black. "No others alive!"

Aypax searched for the voice as a behemoth of a ship pulled beside their own. Its sails were twice as large, its ballistae double in size. Looking up, Aypax noticed a few more arrows whistling over-head. "Get down!"

"Ballistae, let loose!"

That same voice echoed from afar as Hendrix felt their ship begin to sway. The largest arrows he'd ever seen collided with its side, sending wood in every direction.

"Another round! Board!"

Rows of ladders fell from the enemy vessel and crashed down upon their own, giving way to lines of heavily armed men sprinting between decks. A parade of yellow and purple armor filled the deck.

Warriors of the Rhi Empire had arrived.

"For Maxoff!"

The Thorns of Pallala had armored themselves. Now wearing green and grey chainmail, the rest of their ranks hurried from below deck and made for the fray.

In utter disarray, Aypax took to his feet, revealing his beloved hatchet. Pungent smells of mildew and seawater assaulted his nostrils as he stared at the blade, taking a long moment of contemplation.

"Aghhhhh!" Julieta charged by and managed a kill before taking a hard slice to her forearm. Her wound gushed and squirted, the strike pushing her backward as groups of green and grey stepped into her vacant position, clashing with the enemy middeck.

Hendrix squinted, for it was all quite dark to see. One thing became clear, however: ropes. Perhaps ten swinging above. Loosely dressed warriors of Rhi dropped and landed on the deck behind. "To our rear!"

Julieta hustled for her young companion, though it didn't look good. Five men were upon him, but as these men drew closer, two arrows whizzed past Hendrix's cheek and found their marks within the necks of his attackers.

The bald man.

Hendrix glanced in his direction as Aypax thundered beside, cleaning up the remaining fighters with disturbing aggression.

"Find the tiny simian!"

That voice again. Closer now.

"Aypax," Julieta said, pointing. "Do you see him?"

Aypax focused. A beast of a man stepped over one of the ladders and boarded, pushing his own men aside. He wore a tight yellow helmet with an imposing purple plume. His plated armor was far more adorned than that of his soldiers, as was his longsword and yellow shield. Nearly seven forearms in height, his stature rivaled Aypax's. The man scanned his enemies, searching diligently.

"That is Consus-Rhi," continued Julieta. "Maxoff-Rhi's uncle and Bandano-Rhi's younger brother. He's tracked us since we fled the

Pallala countryside. This man is a true warrior, a man to be feared. You two must get off this ship, now!"

"This fight can be won," Aypax growled through gritted teeth, blinking.

"It cannot. There are rowboats down below. My husband died so you two could live. Don't spit on his grave." She turned and made for the fight, but the bald man grabbed her arm.

"He died so that we could live," he said in a northern accent. "Fighting now is the least brave thing you could do."

Julieta twisted free. "We owe the living our swords, not the dead."

"Little brother!" spat a shrill yet familiar voice. "Where are you?" Aypax turned with Hendrix, both shocked. Taryn was here. Her bellowing voice made itself heard above the commotion of battle. "Come to us now, and we shall bargain your punishment!" shouted the interim queen, now a warrior queen.

That voice. Aypax's insides rumbled. Yet this time, it wasn't his mind playing tricks.

"How is she here?" asked Hendrix.

"Hide yourself, and this entire ship dies on your account!"

Aypax quickly looked for Taryn.

Narrowing his swollen eyes, he recognized her green corset, the black boots and black coat. That silvery white hair and tail. Standing atop one of the ladders connecting both ships. "She's there, just beside the cousin." Aypax stepped in her direction.

"No!" Julieta grabbed him. "She's luring you! Look at her! She shan't leave Consus-Rhi's side, and we don't have the numbers to push them back. You'd never make it halfway."

The bald man did all he could to get a clean shot at Taryn, but the black night and cluster of bodies midship forbade it.

"Hendrix!"

Yet another voice, this time high and squeaky, travelled from the ship's portside, farthest from any violence. "Down here!"

Hendrix and company stowed their argument and hurried toward the source. "Sammy?"

They reached the portside edge of Maxoff's ship and gazed down over its rail. A small vessel floated beneath, hidden from Consus-Rhi's sight.

"Get yur asses down here! We gotta move!" Sammy's squeaky voice was welcomed as the chaos fought past midship. The Thorns of Pallala were beginning to give way; their fight wouldn't last much longer. "Hurry up!"

"Aye!" bellowed Sir Edmund Drake, in a deeper voice than his usual. He, too, was below, half his body hanging from a cabin window while helping Ava and Adora escape Maxoff-Rhi's burning ship. "Get down here before I change me mind!"

Hendrix locked eyes with Julieta, who finally agreed to accompany him. He whirled around. "Aypax—"

But Aypax was gone.

"No!" Hendrix shouted his loudest plea, though it fell upon deaf ears.

Aypax ran, hatchet in hand, void of fear and tactic. Forgoing armor of any kind, he sprinted through the struggling Thorns of Pallala, hacking his way past four warriors of the Rhi Empire.

"Aypax…" Hendrix watched him, tears pooling in his eyes.

"He's berserk," said Julieta.

"No," whispered Hendrix. *He's earning his place in the stars.*

The Rhi soldiers pulled back, turning their backs on the crazed Alyonian charging their way. Seeing this, Consus-Rhi took a side-step, revealing two archers behind him, arrows nocked.

Aypax never saw them, his eyes glued only to Taryn.

One. Two.

He stumbled, both arrows finding a home in his chest, neither quite piercing the heart.

Coughing more blood, Aypax held his charge.

The ten remaining Thorns of Pallala grew fearless, inspired by such daunting bravery. "A glorious death for Balo!" shouted one of them, hacking the hand clean from a man across him.

But Consus-Rhi's archers nocked again, releasing two more. Sharp tips punctured Aypax, his blood now pouring quickly. Much too quickly.

"Taryn!"

He ripped an arrow from his shoulder, but gazing ahead, the Alyonian lady stepped forward. And Taryn she was not.

What?

Aypax stopped, nearly falling. Silence befell the ship as the nearest Thorns were slaughtered behind him.

"An impressionist," said Consus-Rhi, calmly, some twelve fore-arms away. "The simplest, yet most effective tactic." The impressionist rushed back to the safety of her own ship as Consus-Rhi approached Aypax. Broken, the big Alyonian collapsed to his knees. "Where is the little simian?" asked Consus-Rhi.

Aypax glared up at Consus, his dying face enough to frighten even him. "Long gone…" He coughed, spitting blood on the man's boot before peering deep into his eyes. "As you'll soon be."

Consus-Rhi nodded. "Indeed, death awaits us all. But not tonight." He studied Aypax's hulking figure. "A great fight this might've been."

"Doubtful."

Cheers rang across the ship as Rhi soldiers finished the remaining Thorns of Pallala.

"Perhaps we'll find out one day in the warrior stars." Consus-Rhi sighed. "I truly hate this part."

"You and I both." They would be Aypax's last words. Consus-Rhi lifted his longsword and struck Aypax with lightning speed, piercing his heart, and closing his tired eyes forever.

55

HENDRIX

The Wooden Lie

Sir Edmund Drake eyed the hulking vessel above, grinning erratically as severed bodies plummeted down its wooded side. Cries of agony doubled with every blink as armored men struggled to the sea-foamed surface, maimed and desperate to stay afloat. A few minutes had passed since Hendrix and company scaled the ship's edge, quickly making their way down to Drake's vessel. Blocked by the much larger ship, their escape had been easily hidden. They'd boarded and been taken below deck, leaving Drake with the surrounding chaos.

An oar-boat made its way from behind Consus-Rhi's ship.

"'Tis done, Captain!" said one of the rowers. "We've set flame to their ship's rear, and without any rain, the flames are a'stickin'!" The pirateers laughed aloud as they boarded, ecstatic over their secret victory. "By the time that fire catches eye, it'll be too late!"

"What'a job!" Drake's voice rang out, harsher than usual. "'Tis the problem with sailin' such a large beauty. Ya can't see nothin below ya's!"

His pirateers chuckled further whilst Drake moved up a tiny ladder and gazed ashore. Droves of homeless fled their riverside tents to watch the ship's bloody battle; others raced toward Starsgard for safety. "Tynndale! Swing us around and start runnin' with the wind!"

DUST

* * *

Hours of silence and dread had crept by as Hendrix sat beside Julieta and the bald man. They'd been sent below to a compact cabin of rotting timber with a single desk of redwood in the corner. The trio grew nauseous from ceaseless bobbing, though this likely meant their ship had escaped to open waters.

"Sorry, I am," said the bald bowman. "It was a glorious death." He stood and knelt before Hendrix. "I am called Chu'a—"

"The captain'll see ya's up top," said a brawny pirateer, poking his head in through the door. "Don't dawdle."

Chu'a had meant to say more but held his tongue as his companions stood and made for the doorway.

* * *

Julieta led the way up a small hatch, pulling herself to the deck where Drake's entire crew awaited.

"Toss yur weapons to the deck," the pirateer spat, rusty shackles in hand. Twenty pirateers flanked him, bows or blades drawn and reflecting dim moonlight.

Hendrix gazed about; they had in fact escaped the Ratna River and now sailed open seas. "Sir Drake. I—I don't understand—"

"Shut yur mouth, boy." Drake's words dripped with acid, as if Hendrix had never been an ally at all. "Toss 'em."

The escapees did as asked, dropping Chu'a's bow and Julietta's sword to the wet deck.

"To the mast." Drake nodded toward a thick mast center ship, then turned to Tynndale. "Get the ladies."

Tynndale obliged as the crew shackled Hendrix and company to the mast. Hendrix looked for Sammy but found no sight of her anywhere. In fact, there wasn't much to see at all. Dark haze lingered

367

over rough waters, shadowing the eyes of angry pirateers. "Hey!" Hendrix yelled as Drake dug into his pocket, slowly pulling out the key. "Drake, wha—"

"Another word and I'll gut you." Drake wiggled his fingers, fondling the key.

"Tomorrow, you will not see," said Chu'a.

Drake grinned down at him. "I fancy me chances better than yours."

"Captain!" Tynndale arrived, forcing Ava and Adora up the same hatch, pushing and groping them from behind.

"Alive and well." Drake smiled, his blackened teeth matching the night. Pirateers jeered at the girls, each man sipping a canteen with one hand, wielding blades or bows in the other. Drake approached the sisters at his ship's rail, halting mere inches away from their faces. "Which of you is it? Who has the gift?"

The sisters averted their gaze. Drake lifted Adora's chin and looked deeply into her eyes, his own pupils nearly twice their normal size. "Not you."

Whoosh.

Drake pushed her overboard, then turned to Ava.

Splash.

"No!"

Ava tried to jump herself, fruitless.

Tynndale held her in place whilst Drake searched her eyes and skin. "The eyes," he whispered. "The wrinkles…" She did have a few wrinkles for one so young, barely noticeable if he weren't searching.

"Why?" Ava cried out, frantically searching the dreadful sea.

"It's you," hissed Drake, his voice cracking. "Bring her below." Drake walked toward the hatch, toward his own cabin.

"And, Tynndale, send a bird to Taryn Kaldor of Alyonia."

56

CRIMSON

Meddlesome

Harold stood behind a counter in his cabin's orange wooded kitchen, pouring a glass of something murky.

"Make it strong," said Crimson, seated on the main chamber's couch. The fire pit buzzed beside him, turning shadowed furniture red with light.

"Ain't got no weak shit anyway," replied Harold.

Their banter helped, but things were different now. No way around it. "Harold, I've no words."

Commander Harold walked two drinks toward Crimson. "How 'bout, 'Sorry for being a very wrong and very stupid cock'?" He took a mighty sip, savoring the taste and choosing his next words wisely. "I joke, I joke. Mate, if what those Thorns say is true, folks are after this girl, some in high places. I can't keep her here. Too many inspections, too many travelers. You need to take her up north when you leave in the morrow."

"Agreed."

"I didn't tell ya the worst," said Harold. "The reports, well, Balo save us. My reports read of men using the dust during combat."

Crimson set down his glass and faced his old friend. Thirty minutes ago he'd have slapped Harold for wasting time with such silliness.

"Kinds of things ya find in the books of old," continued Harold. "I needed ya to see their elder with your own eyes, but it's true, mate. Some of my best penned the report. They fled that battle with the tribes folk beneath us. Rest of the Thorns were slaughtered or scattered."

"Dust on the field of battle." Crimson felt even stiffer than normal. "Those books...we're talking thousands of seasons since they were penned? I thought them mere exaggeration. Everyone did."

"'Fraid not anymore." Harold downed what remained of his glass, swishing it around his mouth to invite a hot and sour pain. "The men of old, the Alyonian elders, seems they weren't fartin' around after all."

"The keys too? The maps, the Altar? It's all real?"

"Not a clue, mate. But by the stars, sure seems it." Harold leaned in again. "These new scouts coming through the Bight, the new inspectors? They seem different...meddlesome. I don't know, could just be in my head."

"Could be—"

Ding. Ding. Ding.

Bells rang out from the Bight's center towers. Harold grinned, satisfied with the coincidence. "Speak of shadows, and they shall appear."

Crimson stood and peered through one of the few windows.

"Commander Amos," said Harold, stealing a sip of Crimson's glass. "A full eight hours early and arriving in the thick of eve." Harold raised a brow, not so subtly patting himself on the back.

Crimson looked around. "How late is it?"

Harold referenced the distant moon. She was setting, but still high in the sky. "Like I said. Meddlesome."

* * *

Crimson followed Harold out the front door, his buzz immediately fleeing from bone-chilling winds and snow.

"Captain!" Lukon approached with a few members of Emerald. "Shall I arm the company?"

"No." Crimson gazed ahead, making out lines of Alyonians trotting down the snowy hillside on Naomiback. *Well dressed. Expensive furs and weapons. Even their Naomi are royally bred.* "They're Alyonians. Harold welcomes them."

Lukon calmed himself as Gable struggled out of a nearby cabin, still dressed in loose undergarments. "We got a fight?"

Lukon chuckled. "If we did, you'd already be dead."

More cabin doors flung open as the entire village roared awake, the bell tower singing overhead.

"Amos knows we're asleep." Harold spat. " Yet he sent no birds. Let's give him a cold welcome."

"Aye," nodded Lukon.

Harold led everyone toward his village entry, the same lane Crimson had guided his company down no more than six hours prior. "Evenin' chaps!" shouted Harold, reeking of sarcasm. "Were the birds too cold to give us a little notice, Commander Amos?"

The lead rider pulled back his green and gold hood, revealing a handsome yet rugged face.

"My apologies," said Harold. He turned to Crimson, whispering, "This isn't Amos." He straightened up and turned back to the unknown rider. "I was expecting—"

"Amos," said the lead rider. A rather imposing Alyonian, his left cheek had been branded with ancient symbols, his nose and ears pierced with tiny red crystals. Long white hair fell behind broad shoulders, nearly hiding a burn mark and longsword concealed by an obviously expensive scabbard. "Amos was reassigned. Taryn sent us instead."

"And you are?"

"Captain Grieves." Grieves' Alyonians were catching up quickly and forming impressive ranks for such a late hour. There were no less than one hundred, all well-armed and outfitted. "My papers." Grieves extended a sealed scroll with the unmistakable Kaldorian royal emblem atop.

"Quite a large lot for such an assignment," said Harold. "It'll take all three of my ships just ferrying you to the Lookout."

"I'm sure Emerald Company could use the rest," said Grieves. "You'll have the ships back within a few moons." Grieves looked directly at Crimson, not exactly asking for permission. "The assignment has changed, Captain. Taryn wants us on the field immediately. A new exploration campaign. I'm to lead this group no later than nova-rise. It's all in the papers."

Gable shot Grieves a dirty look. "I don't like him," he whispered.

"Ya don't like anyone," said Lukon.

Crimson also held Grieves' gaze, neither giving an inch. It wasn't long before he noticed the Alyonian beside Grieves. Even seated on his Naomi, this brute was the tallest warrior he'd ever seen. More unusual, however, was the ancient chest of wood strapped over his lap. He wondered what could be in such a chest. "If it's in the papers, it's in the papers," said Crimson. "Emerald Company will not be splitting sleeping quarters. After all, we could use the rest."

He turned and walked for Harold's cabin, leaving the visitors alone in the cold.

57

TAAIVETTI

The Red Sand Desert

"Do you believe in endlessness?"

Taaivetti's question rang more bleak than intended. The prince's injured eye had swollen shut, perhaps having lost vision entirely. His adrenaline had passed with the eve, rendering his broken leg unbearable. But to speak was to distract, and such distractions were necessary for survival.

"Endlessness?" questioned Zayn, one of the three remaining warriors of Hann. Their small group surrounded Taaivetti, painfully aware of two rising novas on the horizon.

Taaivetti struggled to answer. "Yes. Endlessness. Forever. The ability to never end…"

The three soldiers exchanged worried glances, each starving for a sip of water and in need of healing salves. "I suppose I do not, my lord. Everything comes to an end." Zayn moved toward his prince and handed over his canteen of water. "But our end is not now."

Taaivetti waved the canteen away. "You're wise, Zayn, for endlessness is not possible." The prince's whole body shook as he willed himself to cough, spitting up blood he couldn't afford to lose. "You see, everything that exists must begin. You and I? Sex. Same of our Naomi behind you." Another cough. "The sand beneath us?

Merely broken rocks. Nothing can appear from nothing. All things begin and end."

Zayn's worry doubled, for the prince seemed truly dazed. "Agreed, my lord. Please, drink."

Again Taaivetti waved off the canteen, snot falling from his nostril. "My father used to tell me that Balo was undeniable based on this…that all things must begin and end."

Zayn and the others stared at the prince, silent.

"For if endlessness were possible, and life had no beginning, we would have never arrived at this very moment in time. For time would stretch endlessly backward. Thus there must have been a beginning to our world, and if nothing can appear from nothing, then something must have created it…"

"What does this mean, my lord?"

"According to my father, that Balo created everything. That he started life and time itself. I used to believe that."

"But you don't now?" asked Yalli, a slender Alyonian facing imminent death. His armor had been chipped, his tail cut in two. There had been no time for a tourniquet, thus his tail's tip had become a scarlet mess of shredded muscle, hair, and sand.

"I don't know what I believe," Taaivetti said softly. "Father's logic is sound, but here I face the end, and the grand irony is it took death for me to realize…if endlessness is not possible, then how can eternal life in the stars be?"

The Alyonians waited for one another to answer, but in truth, none could.

"Perhaps there is no place amongst the stars," continued Taaivetti. "Perhaps there's nowhere for us to go. Perhaps all Father told me about Balo was a lie. Perhaps there is only death."

"Enough," muttered Zayn, somewhat shocked he was speaking this way to his prince. "We need only hold out a moon or two. We must trust in Rynn's forces. They'll no doubt have an apothecary.

We're a half day's ride, no more."

Taaivetti smiled, the first in ages. "You are good Alyonians. I can see it. Far better than I."

Again the group fell unsure. "My prince," mumbled the dying Yalli. "You are woozy. Drink or we will force water down your throat."

Taaivetti almost laughed but finally took a sip of his canteen. The prince looked around. If endlessness was possible, he felt it might just be this desert. Red sand stretched far as the eye could see in every direction, with no mountains nor hope of shade. This would end soon.

"*Caw.*"

The Alyonians looked up.

"An Askari?" said Zayn. "Yes!" He waved and shouted, jumped up and down. "There is hope yet, my prince!"

58

BANDANO-RHI

Spiraling

"Don't get soft now, Felix. Elo gives us all free will. Their decision was their own." Bandano-Rhi sucked down another leather wineskin, then dismounted a grand stallion.

Felix-Donro was already aground and knelt before three dead soldiers no older than twelve years. Felix's golden armor shined stainless, his face covered by a tight cloth. "The Ashland Empire must truly be desperate, sending boys this young." Felix stood, too afraid of the sickness to search the dead for any family papers.

"Of course they are." Bandano walked past the boys toward a series of desolate huts and houses. "The sickness halved their empire. It's a wonder they're fielding an army at all."

Army...

That struck Felix, for his adversaries had seemed anything but. Having conquered Coyo, Felix-Donro and Bandano-Rhi had already pillaged another three towns, each more helpless than the last. Felix surveyed hundreds of corpses, not one of which had retaliated with more than a chopping axe. Blood stained the grass and dirt, while bowels and waste plagued the air. The men had returned to the El-Road a short distance away, feasting and awaiting orders. Felix was unsure, but thought it possible they might not have lost a single man yet.

"Why they chose to meet us in this town is an even greater mystery," continued Bandano-Rhi, gulping another sip. He stopped at an open hut, peeked inside. *Still nothing*, he thought with one hand on his pommel.

"I would venture they were buying time, my lord." Felix arrived beside Bandano, wiping his hands on a wet towel. "We're a half day's march from the city of Ashland itself. If I were a gambling man, I'd bet we arrive to an empty town. Word of your war has likely reached every corner of Adria. If the Ashland Empire has any sense, they'll flee to the sea, or send for surrender." Felix knew the Ashlands would not surrender, for Bandano-Rhi had left that option off the table, even if unspoken.

"Do you know why the south became known as the Ashland Empire?"

"I do not, my lord."

"It is because long before you or I existed, their lands were ravaged by a great tree fire. Legend claims it burned for days and engulfed thousands of leagues."

Felix looked to a series of mountains and distant fields around him. Everything did appear rather barren.

"By the time the fire quelled, these lands were too far gone. They'd turned to ash." Bandano-Rhi finished a second wineskin, then scanned a darkening horizon as if expecting something to appear from the skies. "Elo punished them then, and he's punishing them now."

Felix cleared his throat. "I'll await your return at the lead carriage."

"Tell the wisemen to prepare their visuals. They foresaw a clear victory yesterday and today. I wish to know what awaits us next."

They foresaw ten thousand hardened warriors storming one hundred sickly farmers? Felix nodded. "Yes, my lord."

* * *

Adria's second nova had begun to set, yet Bandano-Rhi remained diligent. He hadn't left the sight of his most recent slaughter, nor planned to anytime soon. *You're here, I know it.* The emperor had searched every hut and home nearby, ever disappointed. He now sat amongst a dead crop field, his legs crossed beneath him, fingers clasped in prayer.

His army stayed put on the El-Road, never so much as sending a single man to Rhi's troubled and drunken side. They did note his letter, however, as he'd called for an ink pen and parchment some two hours prior. That letter sat beside him, for now.

Elo, show me the shadow god. Put it before me, and give me your strength, he prayed.

The wine had rendered Bandano-Rhi nearly senseless, but his prayers and mission remained intact. Both eyes closed, he ignored the stench and focused his ears on the answer he was sure would come. It never did.

House Rhi

Letter type: Nonurgent, Descriptive
To: Taryn Kaldor
From: Yours Truly
343 A.B, Bright Season, 104th Moon, Double Novas

The Next Phase

My sleepers are set. At our call, word will be sent to each garrison, and the great night will be upon us. I await signal.

An Addition

The shadow god eludes me. He flees knowing Elo protects my soul. The hunt furthers. I am near. I know it.

Bandano-Rhi

59

KORNILIOUS

An Unlikely Alliance

Kornilious had always loved the Splash Bottle alehouse. He had frequented the place as long as he could recall. Many a season had been spent here, each bringing new chapters to the same ordinary brick walls. Twenty tables, all made of wood and painted shades of pinkish-red, brightened the joint. Nights were lively, nearly always packed with patrons.

"The Master of Defense himself!" cheered his old friend Rexx, while shining a dirty mug behind a pink-tiled bar. "My congratulations."

Kornilious gave a not so sly nod, awaiting signal.

Rexx turned his mug upside down, then set it upon the counter.

Good, she's here.

Kornilious' drunken strides grew longer, his pace quickened. Passing crowded tables and flickering lights overhead, he soon descended a flight of stairs leading to an empty hall; this inevitably led to another and another. *The one place Taryn could care less for.*

"I was beginning to fear you wouldn't show," Tiannu Preters whispered from a half-open door to his left.

Kornilious peeked in to see a dark washroom and Tiannu

seated upon a chipped wooden chair, her feet propped upon a rusty sink filled with dishes.

Kornilious stumbled in and sat, nearly missing his chair. "Get on with it."

Tiannu reached behind the sink and pulled forth two mugs of ale. He accepted the gift rather cautiously. "If it's poisoned, let me know now so I can chug."

"I still need you, Kornilious. Besides, I could smell you from the hall. This will be, what, your tenth drink of the eve? The poison you've already consumed might do the trick by morn."

Kornilious shrugged. "Figured it might help me stomach the thought of a public announcement. I was wrong."

Tiannu studied his face. Intoxicated as he appeared, she felt quite sure he wasn't lying. Kornilious would take death before humiliation. "Our minds are so peculiar, aren't they? So easily molded to what we deem important. I suppose a member of parliament would truly believe humiliation to be worse than death?"

"Or perhaps death is simply overdue. Perhaps it's owed, even." Again Kornilious sounded true. He'd come tonight as promised, but clearly not in a state to negotiate.

A new tactic. "Do you remember the rainy season of 303 A.B.? That night you brought Crimson and I to this very establishment?"

"I do." Kornilious sipped his ale, reflecting.

"Crimson and I had yet to wed. But you knew—you *knew* what we'd become. Ever since you introduced us at the Lukonite Lake, you saw it in our eyes." Tiannu smiled at Kornilious, a genuine smile. "We owe you our marriage. By the stars you were different then, training and hunting with Crimson. And who was that beauty you were courting? You never closed your lips over her."

"Kyra."

"Ah yes, Kyra." Tiannu paused before she continued. "Crimson said you showed him something that eve. Your bracelet of promise? He said he'd never seen you so proud."

Kornilious sadly shook his head, disgusted.

"But who did you leave with? Whose bed did you wake up in?"

The Master of Defense slumped, this time covering his eyes as drunken emotion overtook him.

Tiannu leaned in close. "Taryn has always abused you, always ruined anything good to come your way, and I think you know it." Tiannu had witnessed Kornilious allow the unspeakable just one eve prior, but she sensed her old friend was still there. Somewhere. "Where is the Alyonian Kyra admired? The Alyonian we *all* admired?"

Kornilious gripped his mug so tightly it shattered. "There's a battle inside me. Like Taryn has something others don't, some sort of indescribable pull..." Shards of glass crashed to the floor as blood dribbled from his palm and fingers. "I know not to follow her, and yet I do."

"She has wonderful breasts, Kornilious. Your own desires are the only pull."

"I believe it to be self-destruction." He stared at the bloody floor and broken glass reflecting warped bits of his own image. "The things I've done... Somewhere deep down, I know I'm too far gone. I know the Bloody Perdition that awaits me. Seems she's the quickest ticket."

"How weak." Tiannu stared him down. "Our Master of Defense cannot master his own mind."

He bobbed his head with broken acceptance. "For what it's worth, I believed in her, in her vision for Alyonia. But somewhere along the way, she changed."

Tiannu took that in before setting her ale down. "Everything changes. How we respond is what defines us."

"I cannot make an announcement."

"I don't need you to. I've a far better plan."

* * *

"The story papers were perfectly executed," said Taryn, staring out of the impressive oval window in the infamous chamber of discourse. "The masses were gutted by the dance hall. Our time is ripe."

"Respectfully, my queen, I believe enacting new laws now would be pushing too much too fast," said Trakkonious from the oak table behind her. Five others surrounded him, precisely half of the High Council, four Novellusians and even one Vetusian.

"Oh, Bloody Perdition," said Orani. "And what do you know, Trakkonious of House...?"

"A house of great insignificance." Trakkonious bowed and grinned in Orani's direction. "But what I do know is this. If we're going to release such drastic laws so quickly, we must spin them in our favor."

"Agreed." High Council-Lord Preem stood and slowly walked toward an oak bar behind the table, silencing the others with his concurrence. "But how might we accomplish that? Alyonians love their damned bows."

The remaining High Council turned their eyes to Trakkonious, annoyed yet curious. "My thanks, High Council-Lord," said Trakkonious. "It is my opinion that we've been approaching this particular matter incorrectly from its inception. It is good that the story papers have shown the danger of bows and arrows to our caravans and...young ones. But we've merely appealed to one side of things in this manner: fear." Trakkonious joined Preem, then poured his elder a strong drink. "We must now appeal to hope."

Taryn turned her gaze upon the High Public Heed. "Go on."

"With the unfortunate news of Prince Taaivetti's death sure to arrive any moon now, I suggest we use the moment—and our new laws—to spur hope, not fear. Show our citizens that we are not coming for their weapons to burn them to ash or stash them away, but are instead requesting they be sent to Commander Bolden at once. Those against our confiscating of weapons will ironically be the first to volunteer them if they feel they're helping our soldiers in the desert. Bloody Perdition, after the news of Hann spreads, they'd likely join the fight if we asked."

Preem took a small sip, barely able to contain his smile. "Oh, how I've come to enjoy your company, Trakkonious of House Insignificance."

The duo laughed, forcing everyone to join.

"We pander to the warrior spirit by painting the prince killing Gorsh horde as one of historic power," Preem ventured, "and our new laws as points of honor."

"Is the horde not of great power, High Council-Lord?" asked Orani.

"It surely is, which means we need not even lie." Again Preem grinned.

"And what are we to do with the confiscated weapons?" said Orani. "We can't merely hide them after suggesting they'll be sent to the desert."

Trakkonious swigged his own drink now, having poured himself a proper glass. "Throw the weapons into the midline tides, for all I care. Toss them over the Five Falls."

Even Orani chuckled.

"All that matters is the way that we, and our changes to law, are perceived. Particularly before the news of Taaivetti's death spreads its inevitable fear."

Trakkonious walked to the window and stood beside Taryn. "My queen, our goals only work if the masses believe they are acting on their accord. The public cannot be forced, only deceived."

60

HENDRIX

Ashore

"Tynndale! Turn us with the bloody tides!" Drake's cry fought to be heard over the wind.

Hendrix's head whipped violently with every wave. His clothes and limbs were drenched, his hands tied to a soaking mast. Rain pounded the deck as monstrous swells splashed over rails on all sides. Drake's crew had battled the storm for near an hour, though this seemed only the beginning.

"Hold on!"

Drake's words were too late, for his ship had reached the peak of the tallest swell yet. His sullen eyes shut as the vessel tipped down and plummeted.

Crack.

The sound was unmistakable.

Drake's bowsprit snapped in two as the entire forecastle dipped under. Clinging to his slick wheel, he managed to stay clear of rising waters. "More buckets!"

Drake's craft resurfaced and ascended the next blue and white wall. Sprays of salty ocean assaulted everyone below him, each desperately clambering back up for air, each eyeing the next monstrosity looming above.

Tynndale did all he could not to swallow endless mouthfuls of water. Gazing up, he, too, could see the next wave. Twenty forearms overhead, at least. "No more water down the hatches!"

His orders went unheard, for the winds yelled louder and harsher. The pirateers held on for life, some having fallen into positions of anguished prayer, others drowning in booze.

"Drake!" yelled Hendrix. He watched the captain fight for control of his wheel with Tynndale. Yet try as they might, their rudder was powerless against the angry sea.

Tynndale's biceps felt like they would burst as he struggled against the soaked wood, his hands bloodied and slipping. "Current's too strong!"

"Stay calm!" shouted Chu'a, still tied beside Hendrix. "We live through this!"

Hendrix turned to him and Julieta, both shivering yet gritting their teeth with resolve.

"Down!"

Drake's words were finally heard, though it mattered not. The ship dipped over the next wave and plunged once again, bringing blasts of water too powerful to stop. Hendrix and company closed their eyes as several pirateers were launched overboard, gone forever. Gasping for air, Hendrix sought a plan. And fast.

* * *

Hendrix awoke to the soothing sound of waves breaking on a shore, though in seconds he realized the water was also dampening his cold and blistered feet. Lifting himself, he wiped both eyes and brushed sand from his drenched overalls. Wood and broken barrels lay scattered about, the only blemishes on an otherwise pristine beach.

All was quiet. Too quiet.

"You fell unconscious."

Hendrix whirled in the voice's direction. Chu'a sat behind him, as did Julieta and a waterlogged pirateer. "Is he—"

"Dead?" finished Julieta, still dizzy. "Yes." She poked the lifeless body. "I did what I could."

Looking about, some fifteen others lay face down on the sandy shoreline, all having suffered the same fate. *By the stars...* A few folk wiggled limbs, fighting for consciousness. Hendrix counted the survivors. Three pirateers, two scrawny shiphands, and to his surprise...Ava.

"Chu'a held you above water." Julieta stood slowly. "Swam quite a ways pulling you atop the wheel." She pointed to the soggy wooden wheel that had broken off the now-sunken ship.

Hendrix nodded his thanks to Chu'a, but could not remove his eyes from Ava. Her eyes were closed, but, thankfully, her chest rose and fell in a steady cadence.

"She will live." Julieta extended her hand. "Focus."

Hendrix accepted the woman's palm, standing. "The key."

Julieta lifted the key into view. "A tiny miracle." She nodded some distance down the shore, where Sammy stood on two legs, gazing out over violent waters.

"Sammy." Hendrix limped his way forward.

"He ain't been himself," chirped Sammy, still staring out. "Somethin' changed... I, I don't know. Before we went down, I took the key from him. I knew I needed to."

Hendrix nodded, slowly plopping down beside her.

"He's out there," continued Sammy. "Drake's a lot'a things, weak ain't one of 'em."

Silence claimed a long moment before Hendrix addressed the critter. "How'd you know which ship we were on?"

"After we freed Adora—" Sammy stopped, clearly recalling Drake's vicious actions. "I trailed you to Drill Bintonn's personal quarters. Pretty easy to find you from there, but they beat me to your rescue." Sammy nodded toward Chu'a and Julieta. "Speakin' of which, this yours?" Sammy reached into a small sack beside her, then withdrew Aypax's golden bracelet. It glimmered from the dim light of tonight's second nova setting over the sea.

"I, wow…thank you, Sammy. Thank you."

"It was easy, really. Drill's goons are tough, but no one expects me to be a pocket snatcher. Truth is, I'm no master thief, just an ugly critter most folks ignore 'til it's too late."

Hendrix sat with that, too broken to console. "And *The Wooden Lie*?"

"We sold her at the docks," said Sammy. "Figured Drill would torture names out of you, so Tynndale put her up for sale. Stupid buyers probably got raided the next day."

"Hunting birds shall return to the sky any moment," said Julieta. She'd trekked beside them, her eyes studying groups of dark grey clouds. "The storm helped, and the fires likely stalled them, but Consus-Rhi shall not yield. We must move."

Hendrix glanced around. No sign of Tynndale nor anyone he recognized. The sea had brought cold vengeance. "To where?"

Julieta knew not, though Chu'a was already pacing toward vast swamplands beyond the beach.

"There's a town deep in the swamp." Sammy finally turned to them. "Little shithole called RainRaven. They got floaters though. Couple'a big ones too."

"Do you know the path?"

Sammy's tiny eyes squinted for the swamp. "No, but they prolly' do."

A wooden raft showed itself through dense foliage, propelled by unusual folk oaring through marshy waters.

"Tourtoufians?" asked Hendrix.

"No one really knows." Sammy prepared to head their way. "Sure look it."

Look it they did. Two strangers, both short and fat, oared their rafts expertly. Sharing the Tourtoufian look, they, too, seemed half man, half lizard, though they looked more *frog* than anything, at least to Hendrix.

"Most folk call 'em 'big throats,'" chirped Sammy. "Ya know, on account'a their big throats."

Their incredibly large necks pulsed in and out with each labored breath. "Friendly?"

Sammy scurried toward the swamp. "Is anyone these days?"

Letter type: Urgent, Informative Commoner
To: Gable Stepenson
From: Josylinn Flynn
343 A.B, Windy Season, 104th Moon, Double Novas

My dearest Captain,

It is so much worse than imagined. These words cannot convey. I've seen things, creatures of legend, Alyonians from ancient seasons past. My dear, it is all true, all of it. I've seen the dust, seen it work.

Our old friend's involvement has been confirmed, and I've arranged to meet him this eve. Please do not worry, for I've swords in place should he come with aggression, but my heart tells me he will not. I've seen the old him, the one we grew old with. He will aid us against her, I know it.

She is murdering, murdering anyone with this knowledge, murdering anyone in her way. She comes for the keys, and fast. I've seen her beasts rip Alyonians to shreds. I've seen her red robes kill and maim. Worse, I've met her enemies, and they warn me of your danger.

You must find yourself, dear, righteously. Find yourself now... Seek Balo. Please.

My Next Steps

She's been there, to our very house of books.

The open road is too dangerous for our beloved, so I shall hide her for now. You must send for her immediately. But do not show yourself, for I fear that would end harshly. Be ever aware, I believe she is after you.

Things shall grow much worse here. In fact, I fear things shall soon grow unrecognizable. She's an expert, dear, with slaves in high places. She's winning. I will do what I can with the aid of her enemies. They're ancient, if you follow, and I wouldn't wish to face them. Rest well knowing they watch me.

Our beloved shall await your escort. If our home is empty, find her where we first kissed.

Yours

61

CRIMSON

Ice

Crimson couldn't believe the words he read. Fighting an urge to rip this parchment, he lowered the letter and stood.

"How bad?" Harold ushered three cups of hot water into his main quarters and sat beside Crimson. A few letters were laid out before him, most addressed to "Frost Bight" or "Commander Harold." But one addressed to Gable had snuck its way through rather curiously.

"'Makes bad look good' type 'a bad," said Gable, leaning against the balcony railing outside and watching three ships sail Grieves' Alyonians away. "But it makes Grieves and his lot damn clear. Makes a lot of these times damn clear."

Crimson remained still, his thoughts running amok.

"But that Tiannu…" Gable walked inside and plopped down by the fireplace. "She's wise. Knew anything addressed to Crimson might be intercepted. Gave herself a fake name and all."

Crimson stood, one hand squeezing his temple, willing the gesture to strike down another brain ache. "Gable, bring me Lukon and six others. Tell them to saddle and pack for a long ride."

Gable nodded, doing what he could to hide his displeasure. "I could accompany them, or take the journey myself—"

"No, you're too renowned in Alyonia. Lukon was only recently promoted. Sending him risks less eyes."

"Sending him to…?" asked Harold.

Crimson waved Gable toward the doorway, where the green cape departed quickly. "Harold, how much can we trust the Bight's scribes?"

* * *

An hour passed before Lukon pulled his Naomi to a stop outside Harold's cabin, ensuring his beast did not slip on slick morning ice. Dismounting, he appeared well rested in his green cape and thick brown furs, two hatchets crossing in his belt, a leather bag over his shoulder. "I'm going back?" Lukon knew not the mission but could sense its severity. "I do hope this to be a joke."

Crimson sipped another mug of warm water, leaning against a carved wooden statue of two Billow-Balo trees sculpted to converge and intertwine over Harold's doorway. "It's all here." Crimson extended a set of papers strung together halfheartedly. "Read them on your way out, then burn them." Next he handed a letter, his house seal embedded upon its top. "Give this to Tiannu the moment you find her. If Tiannu cannot be found, you are to locate my daughter and return with her. She'll await you at the Lukonite Lake."

"I don't like this, Captain." Lukon felt honored by the mission, yet something seemed awry.

"Nor I." Crimson pulled Lukon close and lowered his voice to a whisper. "I've arranged for a few of Harold's best to see you off, but once you hit the open, remove your green cape, and keep a constant eye for followers. Expect them. I've put you with Emerald's fastest riders; be swift."

"Crimson. What's happenin'?"

"Read the papers, Lukon. But read them on the road. You're wasting time."

Hooves pounded as six Emerald Company riders halted a short distance away, signaling their readiness.

Lukon nodded and embraced his captain. He turned to depart.

"Lukon...there may never have existed a more important mission."

"Then why aren't you going?"

"You'll see soon enough." Crimson broke from their embrace and nearly shoved him toward his Naomi.

* * *

Crimson and Harold walked down Frost Bight's primary lane, passing cabins and fisheries on either side. Thanks to last night's ruckus, there were more Alyonians awake than usual, most of whom had gathered outside drinking warm booze or heated water.

"Do you have any more ships?" Crimson asked.

"Two." Harold inhaled a long breath of fresh air. "Small, however. You and fifteen others on each, at most. And even then it'll make for dangerous sailin' in the Frozen Sea. That ice grows thick. Broken keels are common."

"We can't wait," said Crimson. "Every moment I'm away is a moment Grieves can better position himself. Set traps, spies, and make his way toward the"—Crimson couldn't believe he was saying it—"the key."

Even Harold felt silly indulging the lore. "We'll need a more personal connection, if you're to take this on. Dedicated transports, direct letters, that sort of thing."

"Aye. Even Alyonians, if you can spare them?"

"A few," said Harold.

"What will you do with the tribes folk? I can't bring them now."

"I'll have someone ferry them up the coast toward Ponca. Oar boats."

"Speak of dangerous sailing."

"Aye." Harold pulled out another cigar. "But it's the best they've got if you can't take 'em." There was a brief silence before Harold took to his smoke. "Might I suggest, however, that Nit'a could be of use?"

Crimson nodded, willing to entertain all options.

"As I said," continued Harold, "I've seen her do extraordinary things. She's a risk, no doubt. And Grieves will be all over you the moment you dock. But should your situation come to violence, I believe you'll be happy she's there."

"What of the mothers?"

"They care only of their elder. Nit'a's family is long dead. To be blunt, something tells me she'd rather go with you. Even against Grieves, her chances of survival are better."

Crimson nodded, solemn. "Prepare the ships. And bring Nit'a to your cabin."

62

HENDRIX

Zazz

Hendrix laid on his stomach, a thin blanket of wool draped over him. The covering had helped dry his limbs, though in truth, he'd merely wished to hide from facing the red-eyed Ava. She lay beside Hendrix, as did Chu'a, Sammy, and Julieta, all dreadfully silent, all draped in similar coverings.

"We saws the entire sinkings," said one of the island locals, oaring his way through swampy waters. He was the stockier of the two saviors. Tight green boots choked his thick calves, hugging a pair of loose brown overalls. Webbed hands and green skin hinted at Tourtoufian blood, but his large throat and many pockets of fat suggested otherwise. "The sea is a scarys place."

"That it is. You have our thanks," said Julieta, lifting her own blanket with gratitude.

The shorter local pointed toward a wooden bowl of mushed jam, wild rice, and water nuts. "No needs for thanks. Me names Boon, and this here's me brother, Babble."

"Pleasures," Babble said with a nod, helping row through a group of floating lilies. "You lot probably needs a place to sleep, yes?"

Julieta nodded. "And a large ship, if it pleases."

"It does, but we don't have any floaters ourselves, just our raft here." Babble tapped his wooden raft lovingly, rippling waves across buoyant flowers.

"We've coin," said Julietta.

"Saves it." Babble reached up and grabbed a low-hanging branch, skillfully turning his raft onto a connecting waterway. "You can sleeps with us free of charge. You'll needs your coin for big floaters. RainRaven has a few."

Hendrix peered over the raft's edge. Algae turned the water a putrid green, yet his nearness to the water itself reminded him of the Southbay, of his near rolling off Aypax's boat entirely. A sudden sadness struck but was short-lived thanks to a frightening brown snake sliding across a broken log protruding from the water's surface.

"Hendrix?" Julieta's whisper turned his attention as she mimed the unlocking of a door. "Once we've a ship, we'll have to make a decision. The Five Falls, or a long journey collecting the others."

She'd spoken in code, Hendrix knew. What he hadn't known was the option she'd put forth. *Destroy the key?* he thought. *The Five Falls.* He hadn't had much time to ponder his future since acquiring the key, though, admittedly, destroying the thing hadn't crossed his mind. It seemed an intriguing option, ridding himself of the responsibility and ensuring his adversaries never took hold of it. *But what if the keys are needed?* "Understood."

"I'd get under the blankets, if I were yous," said Boon. His slim vertical eyeball studied long strands of moss hanging from dying tree limbs overhead. "You don't wants to get bit by these bugs."

Heeding his warning, they ducked under their respective coverings, excluding Ava. She'd yet to return from tragedy, her mind wholly elsewhere. It wasn't long before swarms of critters buzzed, nearly blotting out the dwindling nova light.

"No stinging todays." Boon smiled at Ava. "You're a lucky one."

Hendrix resurfaced from the blanket, trying to distract his own sorrows with the setting nova; frogs, otters, and occasional lizard thrashing beneath green waters. Everything smelled of rotten eggs and wet clay, yet the terrain radiated its own type of beauty. "How far to town?"

"Not longs," said Babble. "A quick nap's time at best."

A quick nap sounded rather alluring. Against his better judgment, Hendrix closed both eyes and focused his still-pained ears on Ava's breathing. Slowly, he let their shared affliction usher in sleep.

* * *

Muted chatter slowly opened Hendrix's eyes.

Wow.

Their raft had traveled through boggy swamplands and into town. Now drifting down a section of swampy river that was littered with trash, they passed overwater huts on both sides. Wooden, water-logged, and many stories high.

RainRaven stretched far in both directions, with walkways and loosely hanging bridges overhead. Tavern windows flung open as fishers reeled in lines from rooftops and docks. Music danced through the air, as did drunken hollers from locals passing by on rafts of their own.

"Here's we ares," said Boon, using his oar to slow their pace. His green boot stepped out onto an eroding dock. "She ain't much, but she's ours."

It was a disheveled home, but Hendrix could tell there was care taken in its upkeep, even if the work was shoddy. New wood had been nailed upon old, each piece desperately holding on from storms past. Large beams gave the timber home a decent foundation, long plunged into the mud itself some ten forearms below the swamp's watery surface.

"I, uh, like your dock," said Julieta, avoiding rusty nails and splintery daggers of wood.

The dock functioned as a port for Boon's raft and the front porch to his home. The same went for his neighbors. These docks wrapped around back, where spiraling staircases led to most homes' second stories. "First floor is justs the fishery," said Boon. "Follows me up top."

Tying off to a wooden cleat, The Family followed Boon and Babble up the spiral stairs, inevitably making their way inside. Boon held a withering door as each guest shuffled in one by one until Ava finally moseyed by, carrying the posture of death. Boon's fat and hairless green face gave a rather dumb impression upon first glance, yet he possessed the foresight not to press her. "Make cozy over yonders, you lot will sleep here in me main quarters. Babble and meself will naps in the scullery."

Passing tables of fish guts, grains, and herbs, Hendrix moved toward a chipped window, ignoring Boon. His eyes drifted across the way, straight into the room of a home opposite the river below.

No…it can't be.

Katrin?

A red-haired Tourtoufian sat dull-eyed in a dingy chair, two men and an endless array of dalli-seeds beside her. Hendrix leaned against Boon's windowsill to get a better look, nearly tumbling out of it.

"Cawcawwwww!"

The noise was unmistakable.

Pattar.

Hendrix gazed up. The Askari circled RainRaven high overhead.

"Lots to see, I knows," said Boon, inviting everyone to sit. There wasn't much to rest on, however—a few chairs and disgusting blankets. "You's all rest up. Babble and me will find outs when the next big floater comes to town. We gots a lake about a half nap south'a here, that's where you'll find 'em."

The green-skinned brothers smiled and departed, seemingly

fine leaving strangers in their home.

"The oddest folk I've ever seen," mumbled Chu'a.

"The oddest *town* I've ever seen," echoed Julieta.

Hendrix's eyes shifted to Ava, who stayed silent as she wrapped herself in a blanket in the corner. His mind flashed back to the one responsible for Ava's sadness.

Drake.

It made no sense. Why would he do such a thing?

But Drake mattered not for now. Hendrix's potential discovery of Katrin had ensured that. Hendrix had one thing on his mind, and the memory of his dear friend demanded it.

* * *

Night fell quickly, for the second nova had set shortly after Boon and Babble's departure. Exhausted, The Family settled on sleep with rotating watches. Hendrix had requested the first, having snoozed on the raft ride in.

Almost, he thought, ensuring The Family was fast asleep and the decks below were clear. Peeking through Boon's window, the latter appeared true. Hendrix gazed to the stars. *Aypax, if you're up there, watch over them.*

And with that he left his friends and shimmied down the home's exterior. The smell of dead fish and rotting algae had intensified, as had the number of open windows. They were lit from inside, some spitting smoke and light out over the river.

Which door?

Hendrix counted his way up a few stories, making certain he would enter the proper building.

A short walk brought him to a flimsy bridge of wood and rope. Falling would end in water, yet still his nerves increased. Keeping his eyes on Katrin's window, he crossed the unstable bridge, stopping only to admire a breathtaking moonlight adorning all of RainRaven. He felt that *pull* once again…that strange yearning for something unknown deep within. Hendrix knew naught of the warrior stars, of the legendary comets and moons above. But staring out at them now, and with Katrin mere moments away, he was beginning to think that perhaps there was something more to his existence, that perhaps Aypax was wrong.

The front door came next. Like all the surrounding overwater homes, this one also had a front deck, but here, half had crumbled into the river below. Hendrix tried the door—locked. Wasting no time, he scaled the home's exterior like a spider to its web.

You can do this. His fingers clutched Katrin's windowsill, and slowly he lifted his face up and over.

There she sat, just as he'd seen her hours before. The dingy chair engulfed her tiny body, as did a humongous shirt of cotton, far too large for a lady so small. *Frighteningly small.*

"Katrin?" Hendrix said, climbing in.

She answered not, giving him time to survey the place.

Empty bottles of booze and clay tablets littered the stained timber floors, as did clusters of burnt pink poppies. A table of soiled undergarments sat in the corner, flanked by rolled up lamb intestine and tiny oiled papers. Positioned beside the undergarments, Hendrix imagined their use…

"Hello, love, leaves your coin on the table." Katrin's eyes fluttered, welcoming some semblance of awareness. "Comes here, love," she continued in a pained whisper. "I wants you."

The words forced Hendrix's focus back out the window. *Never mind, Aypax, if you're up there, just save her…*

"I'm readys." Still half asleep, she spread her legs and fidgeted with her undergarments.

Hendrix steeled himself and approached, grabbing her hand. "Are you called Katrin?"

Her bony hand escaped and gripped a dalli-seed from the adjacent table. She placed it into her open mouth as sensually as possible. "Am I what?"

An absence filled her voice, a void fueled by profound sorrow far deeper than any drug could conjure. Such an absence reminded Hendrix of his father during Taryn's younger moons, the moons when King Kaldor knew not how to help his daughter, how to erase the abuse she'd endured, how to wind back the clock so he could take better care of his little girl instead of allowing her to suffer under his watch. The many empty bottles surrounding Hendrix reminded of those King Kaldor would drain while drinking himself into inaudible stupors before violently striking Taryn, over and over, sometimes with greater and greater force. Hendrix knew this setting very well; he knew this behavior.

And so he knew…if this was Katrin, she was long gone.

"Are you called Katrin?" he whispered, choking up, and revealing Aypax's golden bracelet.

It took time—just how much Hendrix was unsure—yet her eyes did return. Her black pupils grew, showing ancient life of once-blue beauties. The lattice of red within them seemed to untangle as she blinked rapidly. "He…he…"

Hendrix placed the bracelet in her hands, then cupped her veiny fingers over its crystal. "Aypax loved you more than life. He spoke of you 'til his final breath."

"Aypax," she whispered, with the slightest form of a smile.

63

KORNILIOUS

Worth the Risk

"Why did you summon me so late?" Taryn sipped a glass of red wine, never taking her eyes from a sweaty yet well-dressed Kornilious. "You know I despise surprises."

"To apologize." Kornilious leaned in, ensuring the thirty or so customers surrounding could not hear. "I've been…frightened. What you showed me is admittedly off-putting. I needed time to digest."

"And?"

"And I was foolish." Kornilious hid behind a bite of meat and the high collar of his fancy blue doublet, feigning regret rather masterfully. "I doubted you. I should not have."

Taryn stared, assessing him. "Good."

* * *

Once you've entered through the rusty door, you'll find a tight hall with more doors on both sides. Pace five doors north, two doors west, then six stories up the hidden ladder.

Tiannu climbed, repeating Kornilious' directions along the way. Her gloved hands pulsated as she gripped a corroded ladder leading up a painfully narrow passageway. She'd climbed nearly six stories before—*There you are.*

The ladder ended a few forearms below a metal hatch, and just as Kornilious had described, a handle awaited. Tiannu took a deep breath, ensuring she kept one hand upon the ladder, then reached up and clutched the handle. She'd had little issues sneaking into the gargantuan Kaldorian manor, but Taryn's personal chambers…folly here would spell *death*.

As the hatch fell, she saw a carpet above, presumably hiding this secret passage. *Push the carpet north, but be sure to leave it precisely as it was when you exit.* Recalling such instruction, she pushed the carpet aside and ascended.

Balo, she thought, noting her surroundings.

Taryn's entire chamber was filled with candles—some on tables, some on shelves, others making love to the floors themselves. These candles came in all shapes and sizes, but most unusual, all were lit.

Tiannu paused at an archway leading to another room, half expecting someone lingering around its corner. Placing her hooded cheek to the stone wall, she listened carefully, but utter silence greeted. A lone window, with a couch beneath, rested opposite this room. Curtains blocked any potential outside eyes, though she did her best to avoid any openings, nevertheless.

Finally confident she was alone, Tiannu set off to find her target.

* * *

Taryn signaled for her third glass, maybe her fourth. Kornilious had lost count.

"Do you know the saddest thing about betrayal?" she asked, suddenly shooting her eyes into his.

Kornilious' insides burned, nearly lighting his heart aflame. *She can't know. She can't.*

Taryn simpered, keeping his eyes locked onto hers. "That it never comes from your enemies."

Kornilious held her gaze, identifying exits in his peripheral. "This is true—"

"Your beloved Trakkonious?"

Kornilious scoffed, though he listened intently.

"A traitor." Taryn put spoon to mouth, slowly enjoying the heat of her hot soup.

"What?"

"I know," she mused. "Never saw it coming. And I consider myself quite astute on the matter."

Her words lingered in the air like smoke. "How? What did he do?"

"Turns out he'd been writing back and forth with Aypax the Honorable. They grew up across the street from one another, a deep friendship, or something equally vomit inducing. Pathetic. Trakkonious hasn't shut up about our moving too fast with my plans. Now I know why." Taryn slid her hand across the table, placing it over Kornilious'. "He's held below in the catacombs. I'll let you deal with him in time. But for now, what say you take me home for the eve?"

Looking down, he could see her forearm fur slightly lifted, from he or the wine, he knew not. "We haven't finished." He gulped.

"I joined you for two things." Taryn drained the glass and licked her lips. "I'm done with one, and I can't have the other in public." Sliding back her chair, she beckoned Kornilious to follow, never giving him a chance for rebuttal.

* * *

Tiannu sifted through desk drawers and stacks of filed parchment, reading as fast as she could. *Not what I need, not what I need.* Moving silently, she passed Taryn's red couch and red robe strung atop a coat rack. She passed a box on the floor labeled *Taaivetti*. Pausing to inspect, she suddenly saw stagnant shadows of guards from a crevice beneath the main chamber door. *No time,* she thought, forgoing the box and making for the fireplace. Curiously—or maybe not, considering the source—a mound of charred parchment near the hearth was piled high as Tiannu's waist. She identified a stack of *The Prophetics*, awaiting a similar fiery fate. Oddly, Taryn's burn collection went far beyond *The Prophetics*. Tiannu noted various works of history, namely from the times of Queen Pallala, as if trying to erase the great queen's history all together, or perhaps the world's response to such a queen.... Some books were worn and torn, others burnt to crisps.

Queer as this was, Tiannu couldn't help but stare. Shivers tickled her spine as that feeling of being followed returned more powerfully than ever. Downright trembling, she gazed up, sensing something above.

But there was only a hanging chandelier.

Knowing time fought against her, she paced toward the kitchen and noticed another line of books, the largest standing out: *Lampede: Beasts of the Flame.*

Tiannu opened the ancient text, feeling some sense of dread from its mere touch. The pages were old and dirty, its stains more akin to blood than mud. Tiannu lost herself in the words, feeling a curious pull toward them. *Focus.* Setting down the book, a painting caught her eye. Moving back across the room, she studied a walled portrait. *Stralli?*

The painting depicted a horrific shadow god, tall and mighty, black as night. It looked down upon hundreds of worshippers. Some knelt at his feet, others erected an incredible temple of gold and marble. Dark clouds parted in the sky behind as red flames sprang from the ground beneath. Green smog filled the air.

Tiannu marveled upon a few winged beasts, seemingly freshly painted and out of place, flying in the background of the mural. They were massive beings of skin and bone. Things of nightmares. Things she'd just witnessed in reality. A few of these beasts chewed flesh, others screeched and descended upon the worshippers.

Footsteps sounded from outside.

Shit!

Tiannu tiptoed her way back to Taryn's room, keeping her eyes on the front door. Holding her breath, she dipped herself halfway down the escape route, then she saw them, a stack of letters resting beneath Taryn's bed. She'd missed them earlier, having tossed the wine-stained rug right over them. Reaching out, Tiannu lifted the top letter, puzzled by its sending name.

F ROM: *Yours truly*

She lifted the next, each coming from the same sender. Perhaps the context would help. Reading quickly, Tiannu's eyes skimmed like scattered lightning. Each sentence, each bar, each phrase more horrific. Piling them back to perfection, Tiannu had seen enough.

Pulling the carpet back toward her, she stole the letters, closed the hatch, and descended.

64

CRIMSON

The Frozen Sea

"These seas never grow on me, no matter how often we sail them."

Gable leaned against an old crate of wood and metal, presumably filled to the brim with supplies for a long stay at the Lookout. Two other crates flanked, creating a line in the center of their oar-ship. Silent waters and distant icebergs surrounded, as did grey clouds and the occasional spotted otter.

"Aye," said Crimson, also leaning against the crate. The captain would've normally responded more poetically, but not now.

"They'll be fine, Captain." Gable put a hand on his dear friend's shoulder. His warm breath created a cloud in the bone-chilling air. "You've done all you can in Alyonia, now we need ya here."

Crimson remained silent, his eyes to the rest of Emerald Company. Half sat atop chests positioned along the ship's edge, rowing with all their might; the other half awaited rotation.

"Captain," continued Gable. "What exactly is our 'here?' Do you have a plan?"

"We kill them all, then take the chest and find the damned key ourselves." Crimson lost himself in the Frozen Sea. "I'll declare a state of crisis the moment we arrive, giving Grieves no time to infect anyone with Taryn's lies. He knows not what we know, for Tiannu remains hidden. He'll take charge quickly, but can only get so far with our own brethren. I've commanded the Lookout as long as I can recall. We've five hundred loyal Alyonians. He commands half that."

Gable inhaled, looking more frightened than normal. "What if his soldiers are innocent?"

"Can't risk it. I suspect Grieves will take our best equipment and our fastest scouts, then move before we arrive. We'll have to track him with a large company. Supplies will be tough—"

"Captain, do you hear yourself? You wish to track our own with an army you've just convinced of our cause and slaughter them in open snow? Even if you could convince our brethren at the Lookout, Grieves' soldiers are far better armed. An open fight would not favor us, regardless of numbers. Please heed me for once."

"You've been heeded. Provide an alternative or we turn the snow red."

Gable straightened his tired posture, rubbed his gloves for warmth. "Assassination? Send a much smaller group. We know the Quiet Lands better than anyone. Grieves has never even seen 'em. A few good Alyonians with longbows, and the task is done."

"He'll have leaders beneath him. Kill Grieves and another rises."

"But how far down the chain of command?" asked Gable. "Are you suggesting the entire battalion knows their true cause? We kill the top ranks, the rest could fall in line."

Bang.

A slight but potent sound came from behind them.

Bang.

Gable turned and shoved his ear to the crate. "Bloody Perdition, what does she want?"

"Air," said a voice from within.

"She needs air." Gable pulled away from the crate. "Slits must not be wide enough."

"Good, I've been meaning to speak with her anyway." Crimson strode toward the crate door, conveniently guarded by two Green Capes. His nod moved them.

"Crimson?" Gable followed. "The plan?"

Crimson opened the crate door. "Red snow."

* * *

The brown furs of Crimson's hood nearly scraped the crate's ceiling as he entered. Stacked boxes surrounded, neighbored by barrels and bundles of hay. "Nit'a," he whispered, closing the door and welcoming darkness.

"I am here." She walked out from behind a pile of boxes, taking deep breaths and wiping tears from her cheeks. "Sorry, I am. The breathing is hard to do."

Crimson cracked the door, allowing a sliver of light and freezing winds to breathe cold but necessary life inside. "No need. Nit'a, I am quite curious of your recent seasons." He pulled forth a tiny package of dried meat, personally gifted from Harold. Shredding it open, he handed the entire strip to Nit'a, then sat beside her on a grain barrel. "Would you tell me what happened to your village of Haana?"

Nit'a tore the meat apart with what remained of her rotted teeth. "Yes." She nodded, smacking her lips and perhaps—*perhaps*—smiling. It was the slightest indention of dimples, yet such an action punched Crimson. If she could smile here and now, he, too, could endure.

"Please," he muttered. "Don't be shy."

"I was there not, when they attacked. But I have been many times before." She took another bite. "Black is their dressing, metal clothes and sharp weapons they bring. I have seen them come to many villages now, each time taking our young boys."

"What of the women?"

"They use us, usually over tree stumps or within their carriages, but they never take us with them. Our elders trade the boys and...our bodies, in exchange for peace, I think. But this is only my thoughts, perhaps not truth."

Crimson swallowed, his anger returning. "Have they ever been clothed in red?"

Nit'a thought. "Only at Haana. Two of them, with long braided hair. They came with those in black, but the two in red were like you, not me."

"Like me? You mean Alyonian?"

"Not our word for you, but yes. They rode on your strange horses and did no harm to anyone. They looked only around. Sniffed the air."

"How did you escape?"

"There was a fight. I hid inside as it raged. And then, the men in green and grey rescued me, said they had a place for my family. Next, I woke in that cave."

"What were the red ones after? The ones like me? Why sniff air?" His pressing seemed to scare Nit'a, but he had to hurry, for the damned brain aches were returning.

"My family."

"Because of the dust?"

Nit'a nodded.

"The village elder, is he a part of your family?"

Again she nodded.

"Your family, who else is left?"

"Just he, me, and my eldest brother, Chu'a. He left long ago, vengeance in his eyes and heart. I have seen him not for many sleeps."

Crimson reached for his temple, gritting his teeth against the growing migraine.

"You…" Nit'a began to quiver, slightly at first, yet gradually more severe. "You…" She stood and paced backward, terror filling her eyes.

"What?" Crimson forced an awful smile, doing all he could to quell her.

Too late.

The young girl's body shook, her limbs clattering like cold teeth as she dropped her meat strip.

"What?" Crimson watched her eyes move from his and slowly make their way just above him. He looked up at the crate's ceiling—the metal was warped and gross with age, but nothing out of the ordinary. "What?"

"Death hovers over you…a shadow god."

Crimson's eyes narrowed, his heart raced as the air grew even colder.

Trembling, Nit'a raised her hand toward him. "Give me *sustus*."

65

HENDRIX
RainRaven

Hendrix awoke on a gooey wood floor, head pounding from a night of hard use. Katrin had fallen into a peaceful slumber at the mention of Aypax's name, gifting Hendrix a few hours of free dalli-seeds. Mouth dry, eyes pink, he suddenly grew aware of how frequently his stupidity endangered him.

Oh no...

It was worse this time, for the snooze had threatened his entire group.

"Katrin? Katrin?" He tugged her oversized shirt.

But Katrin was dead. Hendrix slumped, more defeated than shocked.

Red hair fell beside her bony cheeks, which remained locked in the faintest form of a smile. The eve had turned her green skin pale, and yet the look of exhaustion was gone, as if life itself had returned to finally kill her.

Hendrix looked down. Sure enough, her hands were still wrapped around the golden bracelet.

Why...

Dishonoring the dead, he took back the valuable and nodded an apology to whatever star Aypax rested in. He'd intended on leaving it with her, truly, but there was no point anymore.

Pocketing as many dalli-seeds and poppies as possible, Hendrix made for the window. Stopping, he caught a glimpse of a letter. *The letter.*

Making his way toward the table it rested upon, he stared down at its wording. *I knew it.* Lifting the parchment, his eyes scanned back and forth, fighting tears. He'd been right. Aypax forwent Taaivetti and sent his own letter straight to Katrin.

Katrin, if this letter finds you, know that I follow shortly behind. My regrets have drowned me, made me who I am not. But I've found purpose in a little one. He reminds me of all that you and I might've had, all that we can still have. I shall make things right. I need but another chance.

Hendrix let the letter fall, struck with sadness and pride.

"Hold him down!"

Screams thundered from across the way. Hendrix ran to the window and looked toward Boon's wooden home.

Drake?

"Ahh!"

Boon's body tumbled across his living quarters, followed by an aggressive fight between Sir Edmund Drake and Chu'a.

With one last look at Katrin's body, Hendrix leapt through her window and descended quicker than even he thought possible. Scaling the bridge next, more screams and loud crashes echoed from Boon's home above. *Hold on, hold on!* Hendrix rushed to the spiral staircase before sprinting his way up and into the home.

Crash.

Chu'a flew across the room, shattering a shelf of bait and fishing lines. Hendrix paused in the doorway, frightened at the sheer strength of Drake. It wasn't right.

"Run!" beckoned Julieta from the room's corner. Leaning against a dirty wall, her hands were pressed firmly to her shirt, staining red with her own stomach's blood.

Hendrix shook. *No.*

Drake's eyes moved to him, yet they were assuredly not the eyes of Sir Edmund Drake. Dark-red and green, they'd become, lacking pupils entirely.

"Syntrilllllla…" hissed Drake. His voice sounded slow and whispery, yet so very loud. Deafening.

Hendrix plugged his ears as Drake lunged for him, grabbing and breaking a lampshade over the youngster's forehead. Glass shattered upon Hendrix's face, cutting him open and sending him to the floor.

"Syntrilllla…" uttered Drake, looming above.

"*Sehella rebuka, sehella rebuka!*" yelled Ava.

Drake screeched audibly, suddenly falling to his knees and shaking his head like an animal shredding flesh.

"*Sehella rebuka, sehella rebuka!*" yelled Ava yet again.

The group turned to her. Ava's grey eyes were void of pupils like Drake's. The remnants of powdery dust lingered beneath her nose, clinging to her upper lip as she focused.

"*Sehella rebuka, sehella rebuka!*"

Ava lifted her forearm toward Drake, exposing the ancient words branded upon her.

Hendrix stared in shock, blood dripping down and over his left eye.

Drake stood, his limbs contorting on their own accord. "Syntrillllllaaa!" He fell back, smashing a table before fighting to his feet. "Ahhhhh—"

"*Sehella rebuka, sehella rebuka!*" Ava stepped forward and placed her hand on Drake's chest, pushing with slight force.

Silence.

The room went utterly quiet for a full second.

A shadowy mist lifted from Drake's torso and lingered in the air above, ever screeching, "Syntrilllllllaaaaaa!" Hissing. Slowly, the shadow took the form of a slithering creature—half snake, half man, with clouds of green smog intertwining in and around a horrific face lacking eyes and ears entirely. The shadowy face had only a mouth and tongue, both black and stained with blood.

"*Sehella rebuka, sehella rebuka!*"

The shadow shrieked and twitched, fleeing the room in an aggressive whirl that shattered half of Boon's belongings.

Hendrix breathed deeply, sucking in each breath as if his last. He blinked through a veil of blood as he watched Ava crash to the floor. "Ava!"

* * *

"Agghhh!"

Julieta bit down upon a bloody brown rag as Chu'a finished stitching her painful gut wound. Having learned the technique from village elders in Haana, Chu'a weaved in and out expertly with a string of thin plant fibers attached to a needle he'd flattened from one of Boon's many fishing hooks.

Towel to his temple, Hendrix sat in the corner beside a quivering Ava, both unable to watch the gory operation. Ten minutes had passed as they tended to their wounds, each bearing an unthinkable fear and bewilderment. Boon and Babble had long left, seeking RainRaven's apothecary.

Drake remained asleep, having been tied down by dock lines and thick fishing nets, Sammy by his side. "And he'll be okay?" she asked. "You—you're sure?"

Ava could only nod, still coming down from whatever craze the dust had brought forth.

"Sweet maiden." Sammy gulped, wiping a few cuts of her own and staring at the bubbly drool leaking from Drake's mouth. "I've heard the stories…we all have, but…" Sammy couldn't finish. She merely placed her paw upon Drake's forehead. "I don't know what I'm supposed'a be lookin' for here. Just get better, Drake."

Ava chugged a glass of murky water, her fifth or sixth, before sighing with relief. "He shall return."

"So, what, you've done this before?" Sammy approached. "I don't understand. Where'd you even get the powder?"

"You do not wish to know."

Sammy stared at her. A smuggler herself, she understood. "This is why Drill wanted you?"

Ava sniffed, wiping snot and blood from her nose. "When I was little girl, Mother showed me the dust. A large bag she had, filled to the top. It was passed down from her many mothers before, a secret of our family's. Mother did many heals with the dust, mending cuts and bruises for those nearing death. But with time, word got out to all, and her appearance of the face changed."

Chu'a finished his stitch, then cut its tip and washed the wound's surface with a thick paste of honey and grease he'd concocted from the scullery. "With time," he said, "the changing of face happens to all who use the dust. I, too, knew a village elder who shared this same gift."

"Gift?" asked Hendrix.

"According to legend, there are seven gifts, and we all have but one inside us," said Ava. "True or false, I know not. But Mother's was healing, and mine is, well, I do not know how to say this."

Chu'a wiped his face. "Sight of the shadows, I have heard it called. The gift of seeing shadow gods. And, in some cases, ridding them."

The Family leaned in.

"As Mother's face changed and wrinkled, all of Gondol heard of the old 'witch,'" said Ava. "Frightened, the men searched high and low for her, but we fled to the mountains for a long while. Eventually, the men started killing our town's elder women, thinking maybe they were this witch. Whispers made way to Tourtoufa, and this Drill Bintonn sailed for our town, offering gold for the witch's capture."

Hendrix sighed. "By the stars…"

"My sister, Adora, then fell ill, and we did all we could to help. Father sold his everything, but still she burned red with spasms and sores, soon growing mean and violent. Mother tried to heal her but failed. This is when Mother showed me this dust and when I learned of my gift."

"You did…" Sammy pointed toward Drake. "That? To your sister?"

Ava nodded. "Yes. And the worse is, I shall never forget the shadow god that fled my sister that eve. It was the same shadow… the same we saw just now."

"Bloody Perdition." Hendrix swallowed, overwhelmed with fear and disbelief.

"Wait," said Sammy, "how did the Bintonns catch you all the way in Gondol?"

"One eve when we were still children, Adora never returned home. Instead, she feasted upon our neighbor's goats and pigs. The neighbors tried the killing of her, but she took their lives first, just as Drake tried tonight. The strength, the noise, the possession, it is same. I helped Adora rid the shadow god from within her, but the men of Gondol found our dead neighbors, found my mother, found everything… My father fled with Adora and I, rumors of our gifts following everywhere we went. Unescapable." Tears welled in her eyes. "We went south to Moro and lived a good life together for many moons. But eventually, local slave traders found us. We lived as Moronian slaves until one moon, the Bintonns came to Moro. You know of the rest."

Another silence crept through the fishing house, broken only by deep breaths and distant yells of RainRaven.

"If it pleases," continued Ava, "I must rest. I hurt."

66

TAAIVETTI

Hard Questions

The bird had come and gone, never bringing word nor letter, but instead circling overhead on occasion before disappearing entirely. False hope.

Sindria had carried Taaivetti as Zayn, Yalli, and the others trekked behind on Noamiback, desperately following the fleeting bird all day. But their trek brought only death. For the desert heat, countless wounds, and sheer exhaustion had eventually claimed the lives of all but Zayn and Taaivetti.

"It's not right," muttered the prince, laying against Sindria. A rock crevice extended overhead, shielding he and Zayn from intense novalight, but provisions ran thin, and their supply of water would last another moon or two at best. "I refused them. I gave them an order to drink and eat."

"And they refused you." Zayn eyed his prince. "They truly loved you. They traded their lives for yours."

"To receive the glory of the warrior stars."

"You dishonor them if you believe their motivations selfish."

Zayn was right, though Taaivetti knew his soldiers had been genuine when refusing their own share of water and forcing their canteens down his throat. It had cost them the ultimate price, but perhaps gained them ultimate honor. "No, I know their hearts," mumbled the prince. "They're greater Alyonians than I...as are you, Zayn."

Zayn ignored his prince, opting to keep his gaze on the mounds of sand piled over his fallen brethren. There hadn't been time nor energy for proper burials, but some homage had been paid, at least.

"Zayn," coughed the prince. "Come."

Zayn heard the severity of his tone. "Speak?"

Taaivetti dug into a bag attached to Sindria's side, then handed over Zo's bracelet. "Deliver this to Commander Zo's wife."

"No..." Zayn stared at the shiny item. "I've made my position clear. I shall not leave your side—"

"This is not only an order, but a threat," said Taaivetti, finding some will to stand on his good leg. "It is your final order, and the last you'll ever receive, should you decline." Taaivetti placed his blistered hand over the pommel of his sheathed sword. "I need this. Do not deny me my place amongst the stars. No help comes for us. That bird...rogue, random at best. We've no time and you know it." Taaivetti referenced his wounds. "My infection spreads...a few moons for me, I think. I must earn my place now, and dying for you is my best chance."

"I thought you no longer believed in the warrior stars? Endlessness..." Zayn stood, then tossed a bit of sand to see which way the wind blew.

"I know not what I believe, though I've seen things that are... undeniable." Taaivetti fell back, removing his hand from the sword. "Suppose I'll take precaution, just in case."

Zayn chuckled, then stepped out and surveyed the desert, the way his sand flurried with the hot breeze.

"Don't follow the winds," said Taaivetti. "They've been astray of late."

Zayn nodded, then took to securing he and Taaivetti's

remaining canteens of water. "Then what shall I follow?"

"Sindria."

Zayn stopped. "My lord...I cannot. I shall take my own Naomi, we've come this far—"

"She will not make it."

Taaivetti was right, and he'd already set the other Naomi free after their riders' untimely deaths. "I see." Zayn turned to his own Naomi and nuzzled the beast's mane.

"Yours will live," said Taaivetti. "Though next time you see her, she may carry a Gorsh atop her saddle."

That pained Zayn, though it seemed better than death by his own hand. Even with all his time in Hann's service, he lacked the stomach to kill his dear companion. "Hann is indeed the shortest distance from us."

"Undoubtedly. She would not make it to Commander Bolden, nor to the eastern docks with limited water. But Sindria... Give her drink twice daily, and ride her harder than feels right. She'll get you to the docks. Sail to Alyonia from there."

Zayn's head bobbed subconsciously as he walked toward Sindria and stroked her lovingly. "You know, I've been thinking about your conundrum, my prince."

Taaivetti stood on his good leg again, gave Sindria a long and affectionate hug, then backed away. "And?"

Zayn mounted Sindria, expertly becoming one with the large royal creature. "If endlessness is not possible, then eternal life in the stars is not either, this seems true... But upon reflection, I believe you've missed a critical point."

Taaivetti stood a bit farther away now, giving Sindria time to bond with her new owner. Sindria allowed the connection, though her eyes remained on Taaivetti. The look broke him.

"Your father said that since we've reached the present time, endlessness is impossible, and as such, time and life must have begun

somewhere. He then said that something must have created both…
But what I think you've missed, my prince, is that for something to
create both time and life, it must exist outside of them and be greater
than each. Perhaps this is the stars, Taaivetti. Perhaps they defy our
world's logic. And perhaps, their maker does too."

Taaivetti stared. "You will do great things, Zayn of Alyonia."

And with that, Taaivetti tapped Sindria's rear, and off she went
with a cry and goodbye.

* * *

Taaivetti stared up into the sky from his back, his body red and welting
with blisters. Inspired by Zayn, he'd fought toward Commander
Bolden's fortress, knowing he'd never make it, yet hoping for a
miracle. He'd fallen unconscious some time ago, just how long he
was unsure, but here he lay, awake.

"Taaivetti!"

"He's alive!"

Voices. Flashing novalight above. Blinding. The image of a
faceless serpent.

"Enough!"

The final voice rose Taaivetti to his elbows. "Sir Rynn?" he
mumbled, woozy, and unsure what was real with such constant
mirages.

"Aye," said Sir Rynn, leaping down from his Naomi.

An entire regiment sat behind him, each warrior clad and
mounted upon Naomi, each ready for battle. Strangely, however,
their force was a mixture of Alyonians and humans alike.

"It is good to see you, my lord," furthered Rynn. His tone was
pained, saddened. "I didn't expect you'd make it out of Hann."

Taaivetti reached out a hand. "Water."

"Stop wasting time," said an Alyonian behind Sir Rynn.

Commander Bolden. He, too, was mounted and clad in green and gold armor with numerous patches of accolades.

Sir Rynn shook his head obediently. "I'm sorry, Taaivetti..."

Bolden removed his helmet to wipe his sweaty face, revealing long white hair tied into numerous braids, each knotted at the end by a ruby-red ring. "We need to move. Her orders are clear."

And then Taaivetti understood. "Sir Rynn?"

Sir Rynn nodded, each shake of his head more shamed than the last. "She is the winning hand, my lord. She will unite us, and having served at Hann, I believe standing united with Rhi is our only true hope against the Gorsh. My love for you was always true. Still is."

Taaivetti fell speechless, then gazed up at hundreds of mounted warriors. Perhaps thousands, even. One by one, they looked away, not a soul wishing to meet their prince's eyes.

"The prince deserves a glorious death," announced Sir Rynn, sternly. "Bolden, you lead here and claim to be true with the sword. Give Taaivetti a proper send-off to the warrior stars."

Bolden dismounted and approached cautiously, knowing full well Taaivetti's battle capability, perhaps even in this state. Reaching for his leather handle, Bolden removed a longsword.

"There's no need," wheezed Taaivetti, doing all he could to simply speak. "I've already seen to my place in the stars."

Bolden stopped and studied the dying prince mere forearms before him.

"I request only to be buried at Hann upon its recapture," continued Taaivetti. "Swear to this at least, Rynn."

Sir Rynn swallowed. "We must bring her your head..."

A daunting silence befell the entire regiment. "I see." Taaivetti stood, struggling to remove his sword. "Get on, then."

Sighs. Hundreds. Not of boredom but uncertainty. Uncertainty in their decision now that its fruit demanded bearing. Half had followed Commander Bolden and Sir Rynn for coin, the others for the greater good and esteemed positions in Taryn's new army. Taaivetti's head had not been a known part of the deal...

Bolden stepped forward and easily disarmed Taaivetti with a single clash of swords. Pulling his silver blade back in a swift arc, he severed the prince's head from his broad shoulders.

67

KORNILIOUS

Fitting Ends

"Wow, wow…what a shame."

Taryn rolled over, removing herself from atop Kornilious. Their clothes strewn about the floor, they lay together on a bearskin rug inches from her ruby-red couch. The ever-busy fire pit crackled.

"A shame?" Kornilious breathed heavily, fighting a peculiar drowse. "I thought that was one of our best."

Taryn reached for what must've been her seventh glass of wine, then frowned. "Precisely."

Knocks sounded at the door, raising Kornilious' eyes, though slower than he'd expected.

"Come in," shouted Taryn. "We've finished."

And so the door swung open, giving way to Trakkonious in a perfectly cut white surcoat.

"My queen," he said, bowing deeply. "Tiannu did not make it far. We captured her shortly after the infiltration. Nothing from your quarters was found with her."

"Magnificent." Taryn stood, beads of sweat making her body glisten in the firelight as she left Kornilious on the rug below.

I see, he thought, realizing he was quickly losing control of his extremities. "Was it the wine? Or my boar, perhaps? Never figured you'd have the cooks tamed as well…" Kornilious rose to an elbow, struggling mightily below her.

"Well done." Taryn covered herself in a red robe hooked nearby. "It was the boar, indeed."

Three more Alyonians flooded the doorway behind Trakkonious.

"Stay outside, please." Taryn motioned her assassins away. "You too, Trakkonious. I need a moment."

Trakkonious bowed hesitantly, then led the others outside the door, closing it behind.

"They will draw eyes from sentries and anyone passing by," wheezed Kornilious. "Though at this point, perhaps they're all yours."

"No, you are correct. I will have to kill an onlooker or two by night's end."

"Then why leave them in the hall?"

Taryn strode to her window and looked out at the walkway of five hanging Honorable-Six bodies. They'd rotted, molting into half flesh, half bone. "Was there ever a way I could have convinced you to join me? Truly?"

She meant it.

Kornilious fought to his knees. "Does it matter anymore?"

"Not for you."

"Then you've grown even more selfish and deranged than I'd ever imagined." He let the words settle whilst spitting blood on the rug. "What good is defeating wickedness, if you become even more wicked in the process?"

Taryn kept her gaze out the window, perhaps unable to look at him. Kornilious' head slumped as red began to trickle from his eyes onto the carpet. His final breath was imminent. "Seems I'm crying blood," he joked. "But I don't see your tears for me, Taryn. Where are they?"

Finally, she turned to him. He looked a horror, seeping red

from mouth and eyes, foaming slightly around dried and purple lips. "Seems I'm unable, my dear."

Taryn opened her door and left him, stopping halfway out to speak with Trakkonious. "How best to inform the public?"

"Self-slaughter," said Trakkonious. "It's everywhere of late. The pressure overtook him, what with reelection and all. But fear not, Sir Kelterbury is ready to replace him. You were wise to set a beloved backup. I will arrange to show him what needs seeing."

Taryn nodded. "Good. Clean up, bring Kornilious home, and have someone report the tragedy. He's spent quite a lot of time in alehouses of late, make sure to include that in the story-papers."

* * *

Madison Preters walked down the dark and crowded streets of Alyonia, passing bakeries, inns, and woodshops. The city buzzed with life, from its southern farms to its industrious northern walls, but tonight, she found herself at Alyonia's heart, the Kaldorian manor.

Having waited hours for Tiannu's return, Madison had grown worried and set out to find her stealthy mother. But she'd failed. Her search had gleaned no more than anger at the sight of the High Council's many signs posted throughout the city:

HANN UNDER ASSAULT!
SEND YOUR BOWS TO PRINCE TAAIVETTI
AND OUR HEROES OF THE DESERT!

Perhaps worse were the overflowing collection bins positioned beneath such signs. Madison had passed no less than ten on her way, each accompanied by animated groups of Alyonians bickering beside them. Fights, screams, and drunken quarrels had arisen at nearly every bin. A great divide between citizens.

No matter. Ignoring such things proved difficult, yet finding her mother was of the highest priority. Stopping short of the Kaldorian manor's front arch, she caught sight of another sign across the street:

PRINCE TAAIVETTI FIGHTS FOR YOU. WILL YOU FIGHT FOR HIM?

The sign infuriated. Still, Madison's eyes lingered upon it, her mind slowly racing back to a memory.

* * *

"Madison Preters!"

A young Taaivetti marched his way into the Kaldorian manor kitchen, fully outfitted for a hunt. "You do have a home of your own, you know." The prince had winked at her with those ocean-blue eyes, as she recalled.

Madison blushed, as she'd been known to habit back then. "I very much prefer yours," she said and laughed.

"I think you merely prefer my brother." Taaivetti grabbed a plate of food from a table of white oak and shrugged toward Hendrix, who sat in the corner, stuffing his face with bread.

She grinned. "He's alright. I mainly come for the food."

Madison grabbed a piece of bread as a servant rushed through the kitchen carrying a tray with two glasses of dark booze. Stressed, he paced toward a set of large double doors and entered.

"Is that for the king?" asked Madison.

Hendrix nodded, equally vexed. "Has he left his study once all day?"

"What do you think?" Taaivetti went cold as the servant resurfaced with a look of fear across his face. "Hasn't left his study in moons. Balonian faith is one thing, but our father is obsessed."

"His actions don't suggest it." Madison grew sorry as soon as the words left her. She looked at both brothers apologetically.

"Worry not," said Hendrix. "You aren't wrong."

Taaivetti secured his rucksack and made for the door. "Are you ready, Hendrix? They say this could be the best hunt of the season. Clear skies are drawing out all kinds of beasts. Captain Crimson himself is leading. His caravan awaits us by the northern wall."

Madison rolled her eyes, having heard nothing but her father's excitement over said hunt for the past five moons. Even her mother had asked him to shut his lips.

"Almost, I'll meet you there." Hendrix did his best to subtly nod toward Madison, hinting at his brother's departure.

Taaivetti smiled. "Ahhhh, I'd no idea! My little brother, becoming a proper Alyonian!"

Madison gasped audibly. Hendrix too. "No…" she said. "No, Taaivetti, it is not as it seems—"

"There's no shame." The young prince laughed, having honest fun with them. "Hendrix is, as you said…alright. Have you two, well…?"

Madison's youthful eyes widened. "No! Of course not. Not yet, at least."

Hendrix sank into his seat.

"We've made a promise." Madison lifted her bracelet, reading *H.K.* "These signify our oath to save the deed for when we are wed."

"Bloody Perdition," cursed Taaivetti. "Want me to wed you now? I'm fairly sure the prince has such power—"

"Quiet yourself!" Hendrix stood and punched his brother, only to have Taaivetti laugh it off. The brothers wrestled by the doorway as Madison watched, grinning ear to ear.

68

HENDRIX

It's Messy

Hendrix entered Boon's smelly fishery, carrying a grey cup of water and a wooden bowl of mashed seeds. The room was nearly pitch black, lit only by RainRaven's nightlife slipping through dingy windows and crevices. "I'll just…leave it on the table here."

Ava laid upon a tangled web of fish nets, slowly waking from a long nap. "Then leave it." She yawned.

Hendrix remained, standing awkwardly in the doorway.

"Go on," she said. "You've more to say. So say."

Hendrix glanced upstairs, then gently shut the door behind him. "You said…" Still weary from events a few hours past, he set his food down on a box. "You said you hurt?"

Ava looked down, suddenly realizing.

Hendrix dangled a tiny bag of seeds. "Found them next door. I'd thought to use them tonight, but by the stars if anyone needs them…"

Ava sat up, her gifted tunic shining from window light above. Slowly, she managed a nod.

* * *

The seeds had taken root, stirring Hendrix's and Ava's nerves and manipulating their exhausted minds.

Hendrix banged his knee against a wooden box of worms and meat chunks.

"Shh," she whispered.

The high crushing his depression, Hendrix giggled from across the cluttered fishery. "I had to piss."

Taking a sip of murky water, Ava made room for Hendrix on the tangled nets.

"What you did…" He landed beside her. "I've never seen a thing like it."

"Life will show you worse yet."

"No, no, what you did was…miraculous."

"It was the dust, not I."

"Still." Hendrix slid a bit closer to her, scrunching the pile of fish nets. "It proves everything. Changes everything."

"Does it? I believe you knew this truth already, somewhere."

Hendrix thought about that. Perhaps his parents had embedded the belief so deeply within him that he'd never truly killed it. "Perhaps."

"What?"

"Such truths bring hard questions." Hendrix swayed, the seeds taking full effect.

Ava placed her hand beside his. "Speak."

"I can't help but wonder why such knowledge would make someone so…horrible."

"My mother used to say that great weight accompanies great power, and believe me, this knowledge is power. I've seen men change, seen them grow desperate and terrible for it."

Hendrix coughed. "My father…he was always hard, but he changed as my sister grew old. He became obsessed with *The Prophetics*; he became quite dark. Should he not have grown light from such knowledge?"

"When we are shown the truth, we have but two options. Run to it, or run from it. Both make life more difficult."

"Then what's the point?"

"When I discover, I shall tell you."

Hendrix chuckled, half covering his pain and uncertainty. "I'm sorry of your sister."

"She's been gone since Moro."

"How do you mean?"

Ava shifted in place, finally letting it out. "Losing my mother and brother was awful, but I have had life the easy compared to Adora. She was the older, see? And the prettier for a long while. Men had their way with her, and, well, we had one owner for some time, a wedded man who kept us away from his family. This man gave Adora child, a beautiful, ever crying child." Ava almost laughed at the memory, sharing Hendrix's tendency to distract. "This man's wife learned of the child and would not allow it to stay under her roof. She took the child to a mercy box and traded us to the Bintonns. Adora's mind has been gone forever since."

"I've...I've no words."

"Life seems to demand strength," continued Ava, "or the weakness to dull its pain." She grabbed another seed and placed it on her tongue, letting it sit a long while, ever keeping Hendrix's attention. "As I said before, we both hurt. We're both weak."

"I'm not weak—"

"I know of the key." Ava chewed the seed now, forcing it down.

"How—"

"I saw you below deck, with Julieta and the others. Heard you too." Silence. "What will you do with it?"

"I know not."

"At some point, Hendrix, you will have to start knowing." Ava moved a bit closer herself. "I lied before." She rolled up her sleeve and showed the horrific branding and scars. "'Twas not the Bintonns who branded me, but myself."

"Why? What does it mean?"

"'Tis Selmic, my homeland's second language. It means 'by light we rebuke you.'" She drew nearer yet, displaying her brand just beneath his stubbly chin. "It is from *The Prophetics* and carries terrible weight. Without such words, I've failed my gift in times past." Ava let that sit, flustering Hendrix further. "When I first saw you through the window that eve…I saw them, wrestling just above you."

"I don't understand."

"Shadows and light."

He swallowed, quivered.

"Light and shadow warred above you, Hendrix, as they have many times since."

And for the second time this eve, something did make sense, something deep inside. The pulls, the ear and brain aches.

"This shadow chose Drake, perhaps unable to infect you or Sir Aypax. I am unsure. My point remains, your time to be strong is coming, but in the now you are very weak."

"I'm not weak—"

Ava kissed his lips, igniting fires within him, a lust or passion he'd never known with Madison.

Her hands slowly pushed him down onto the net as she laid over him, staring into his eyes from mere inches above. "If I wanted to, I could kill you. This also makes you weak."

Hendrix took tiny breaths beneath her, his vision blurred by the high yet so very focused upon her. "Do you want to kill me?"

"No."

She kissed him once more, pressing into him. Rising, she slowly removed her tunic, revealing an entirely new world to Hendrix. "I want to stop being the bird."

* * *

Hendrix stepped back into his stolen overalls, concealing the giddiest smile of his young life. The smile faded quickly, however, as waves of guilt culminated in heartbreak. *Madison.* The deed had happened so quickly…and was *surely* aided by the seeds. It wasn't entirely his fault, he told himself. Besides, Hendrix felt death might come at any moment, such circumstances *do not permit my actions, but certainly—*

"I see." Ava had already reclothed in her loincloth beneath Julieta's gifted tunic. She now sat before him, saddened by his condition.

"What?" Hendrix took to his boots next, lacing quickly and avoiding her studious gaze.

Ava shrugged. "Your face shows the tale of two stories. The boys of good heart are always this way after making the love."

"Two stories?"

"Yes. One of greatest delight, and one of greatest sorrow. I always wondered why this was. But Adora eventually taught me."

He grinned. "Believe me, I've no sorrow."

"*Sorrow* is wrong word, perhaps, but still…" Ava pointed to where Hendrix's bracelet used to reside, to the subtle discrepancy in his skin's tan line. "You lied of this bracelet, and it is written on your face's second story."

"Perhaps my face's second story is unrelated."

"Perhaps."

Hendrix stepped toward her, torn by guilt and yet wondering if he would ever see his betrothed again. "I lied not."

Ava nodded and embraced him, pressing herself against his chest. "Good, for lies are one of the heart's many evils that open us to the pulls."

"The pulls?"

"Shadow and light, Hendrix. Shadow and light."

Hendrix gulped, feeling one now. "I don't follow."

"The worse we do in this life, the more vulnerable we become. When you feel the pulls, I hope you follow the true one—"

Ba-ba-ba-ba-ba.

A rhythmic sound, emanating low from the ground.

Boots. Countless boots upon wood.

Hendrix pulled Ava down to avoid windows as lines of Tourtoufians leapt onto Boon's front dock, then hurried their way up the home's spiral stairs.

"No…" Hendrix peeked out at the river. *Drill.*

"Little Kaldor!" shouted Drill Bintonn, stepping off a raft and onto the dingy dock. Twenty rafts floated behind him, pouring more Bintonns by the second. "Where's are ya'sss?" Drill's snakelike eyes found the first story window as Chu'a and Julieta's shouts rang through the home above.

"Bloody Perd—" Hendrix stayed low and searched, no routes of escape.

"What do we do?" Ava rummaged through the room's many barrels and cabinets for a place to hide, but they were all full.

Footsteps thundered down the stairs toward them as Hendrix raced to a rear window. "Come!"

"Ahhhh." Drill's voice yet again, closer now, hissing.

Hendrix saw the slender Bintonn standing outside the fishery window, staring right in.

Bang.

The fishery door flung open, its old and feeble hinges wholly ripped off.

"On the floors!" shouted one of the many Tourtoufians.

Subduing Hendrix and Ava rather easily, Drill's followers opened the window for him.

Sticking his long and skinny neck through, Drill smiled in Hendrix's direction. "There's he is." Reaching into his pants pocket,

Drill revealed Hendrix's little white book. "You left this backs in Starsgard. What kinda halfwit motha leaves her own house seal on something likes this?" Drill opened the book's cover and ran his wet fingers across the Kaldorian emblem. "Bintonns! This here be Hendrix Kaldor, the greats King Kaldor's son. And nowadays, runaway deserter for his queen sista. We's got some sailin' to dos."

69

CRIMSON

The Lookout

"By the stars, Captain, I'm glad you're finally heedin' my counsel. But me in charge of the Lookout? Sounds like you're plannin' on dyin' out there." Gable spat toward a patch of black ice just off the salted path of stone beneath him. Emerald Company hiked up a long and winding, shoveled path of stone. The path was hundreds of seasons old, and its stone was discolored from endless salt dumping.

Crimson trotted alongside, eyes glued to the salty path. He ignored Gable, as he had for some time. Instead, Crimson shifted focus to the frozen mountains ahead.

Reaching high enough to impale low-hanging clouds, the mountains' snowcapped tips remained hidden. What he could see, however, were the hundreds of caves in the mountainside above. Each cave had a thick black pelt hanging over its entry. The pelts flapped rapidly in harsh winds.

The largest cave was grounded not far ahead, a grand entryway into the mountain itself. The cavernous opening spanned eighty forearms high with icicles hanging from a jagged ceiling; no pelt could possibly cover it. The entryway was wide enough to fit Emerald Company, all three crates, and a group of wagons they'd acquired at the frozen docks a few hours prior.

"I get it, a shadow god is a scary thought." Gable waved to a few Alyonian sentries standing guard beneath the enormous entrance. There were four guards, each shivering and signaling to someone behind them. "But how am I supposed to convince the lads you actually saw one? Shit, Captain, I'm strugglin' to believe."

"You'll show them Nit'a, and she'll do the rest."

Gable inhaled, shaking his head. "And how many moons do I give you out there before I send search parties? Grieves' company could be two moons ahead already."

But this, too, was ignored as the duo led Emerald into the mouth of the mountain.

* * *

"Captain!"

"Look, it's Gable the great…lard!"

"Welcome home, ya sorry bastards!"

Endless voices berated as Crimson led his company up a twisting walkway within the mountain. The Lookout, as it had come to be known, was a series of spiked caverns stretching high overhead and covering an extensive footprint in each direction. Its chambers were peculiarly shaped, making its precise dimensions unknown, though it took even the quickest Alyonians a few moons to clamber from one end to the other. Caves could be seen everywhere, resembling a cluster of rooms at a lodge. Alyonians were scattered about, some drinking and eating at tables within their caves, others working diligently on woodwork, mining, or smithing. These folk weren't outfitted in furs, nor anything thick at all.

"Ahhhhh, finally." Gable removed his shoulder furs. The Lookout was positioned above a series of active volcanoes within the mountains, which yielded radiant heat to any caves near its surface. Outside, however, was a different story. "And me favorite little guys! Damn good to see ya's!" Gable pointed toward a shallow river twisting its way through the ground like a snake. Tiny shrimp and other critters scurried at its bottom. *Food.*

"They would be your favorite!" said Tattua, a muscular Alyonian with a white circle of hair that favored a helmet. Dressed in the Lookout's generic white tunic, Tattua matched everyone around, though his tall hair and green vine necklace set him apart.

Gable laughed. "Here it comes!" He embraced Tattua. "If it isn't the High Scout himself—"

"What news?" Crimson cut to it, foregoing shaking hands.

"I presume you mean the angry Alyonians dressed for a bloodbath?" said Tattua. Crimson nodded. "They passed straight through. Commander Grieves has the proper papers from Taryn. He claims you saw?"

Again Crimson nodded, though a bit sarcastically this time. "They took our finest equipment and three of our best scouts. Took our boot enhancements, damn near emptied our food supplies and canteens, even half our arsenal."

Gable and Crimson looked to one another, both subtly clinching their fists.

"I did what I could, but I'm outranked." Tattua tapped his tunic insignia: a longscope represented the Lookout, and a series of four stripes represented his rank. "Felt odd, mates. The whole of it. And now folks are askin' questions."

"Get me a hunting kit," said Crimson. "Longest bow we have and two birds with forged fur. A white cloak as well."

"Grieves sent the birds with forged fur out," said Tattua. "We've only mastered seven suits for the little guys. He took 'em all. Took the white cloaks too."

Crimson stormed his way toward a group of caves with firelight. Ladders rested at the backs of these caves, perhaps leading to neighbors above.

"Another thing!" said Tattua, following. "Grieves never asked for quarters of any kind. Not for anyone in his company?"

Crimson stopped and looked up at his own cave some five-stories above their position. A pelt draped over its entrance with a *C* painted atop. "That's because he does not intend to return."

* * *

Crimson shifted his heavy furs, now hot and desperate for comfort in such stiff, bulky layers. The cave around him was lit by a dim fire in the corner. Stones, Gable, and plates of shrimp shells surrounded. Seasons of Crimson's chalk drawings and poems rendered the surrounding walls a panoramic canvas.

The angry captain pulled back the pelt of his cave's entrance, giving view to two Alyonians operating a hefty longscope across the way. This scope was the largest at the Lookout, nearly eight forearms in height and fitted with the finest glass in all the realm. Another cluster of bodies surrounded the duo, taking notes as the longscope studied bright night stars. "Wish that thing could shoot," joked Gable. "Take care of our problem without sending you."

A trumpet sounded, signaling the arrival of a hunting or scouting party. Crimson ignored Gable and the trumpet, as he had most things of late. He elected to keep his gaze on a wooden table some distance in the cavern below. Alyonians circled the table, applying various adhesives to tiny suits of fur before forcing them upon a group of white birds.

"Captain?"

Crimson began dressing into an even thicker pair of boots. *If such shadows exist in Alyonia, by the stars, I must return to Tiannu—*

"Captain?"

Crimson finally came to, having lost himself in thought.

"Where is she?" asked Gable.

Crimson grabbed an enormous rug of wool that had been cut to resemble a cape. "The Green Capes are unloading our crates in cave thirty-seven. I've arranged a back room for her with Tattua. He knows everything."

"And if you don't return?"

"Show her to everyone. Bloody Perdition, show her to all of Alyonia."

"How many moons, Crimson? I need a number. I can't just leave you out there."

Crimson thought, sighing. "Ten."

"Ten moons it is."

Crimson picked up a well-crafted longbow. "I'll find him. No one can hide an entire regiment's footprints. Ten moons. If I'm not back, send aid. If he returns without me, I'm dead."

Gable extended his forearm. "We'll be ready to return the favor."

70

MADISON

New Laws

Madison Preters exhaled. *Kornilious too?* She watched a crowd of thousands follow Kornilious' lifted casket down the streets of Alyonia. *It must be connected.*

The awful news of self-slaughter had spread quickly through word of mouth and the story papers conveniently awaiting sale on every street corner. Respects would be paid on the morrow, once Kornilious' house protectorates had finished escorting his body to the realm's western waterfront. But for now, the Master of Defense would be remembered only by his colorful casket and the pained expressions of those escorting him.

Covering her ears, Madison could not recall a time the streets had been so loud, not even during the Peace Parade. Some groups had already fallen back into the inner city, growing twice as boisterous. Drinking and eating the local alehouses fresh of supply, they'd marched through alleys and fields drunkenly chanting for the fallen Master of Defense, the pride of many in Alyonia.

Madison saw further commotion at Justillian's Blades. Perhaps thirty Alyonians, mostly dressed in hunting or fishing gear, protested out front. "It is merely for the snowy season!" beckoned the new owner, desperate to calm his customers. "I've no choice! The High

Council decrees!"

Madison had never shot a bow herself, but she'd seen and heard the horrors they were capable of during times of conflict. Though it seemed conflict had reared its ugly head here at home more often than not.

Breathing her anxiety to the wind, she pushed past new signs calling for charitable aid to Taaivetti.

"Madison Preters!" yelled a familiar voice from across the street. "Little Preters!"

Madison turned to see Samswell Danson, owner of Danson's Pastries. He'd taken to the streets with a mobile food stand, pushing his wheeled table of goods to wherever the masses went next.

"Samswell!" she called back, waving.

"Can I offer you a Mussa? I know they used to be yours and Hendrix's fav—" Samswell paused, realizing. "I'm sorry. You've my apologies. Sorry—"

"It's okay." Madison paced toward him. "But I've no coin on hand."

Samswell nodded, disappointed. "No concern, anyway, don't think of it! I've done well today, I have. Stocking up, just in case."

"In case?"

Again Samswell had perhaps said too much. "I'll let your mother discuss—"

"Speak further."

Samswell bobbed his head rather flamboyantly, then noticed some fifty city guard approaching the chaotic masses. "Well, dare I say a shortage of profession and coin may be upon us. I've lived my fair share of seasons, I have. Something's in the air here, in the air, I tell you! Even the Master of Coin seems worried these moons. Nothing is free, even if they tell you it is, just remember that, little Preters! The coin must come from somewhere!" Samswell made his way down a corridor, waving his goodbyes.

Madison processed his words as ranks of city guard passed by. Trotting toward the inner city, their green and gold armor clinked with each step, their white hair bounced with every move. Exhausted, she decided to give up today's search and return home.

Two days without Mother. If she's not back by the eve, it's time.

LUKON

Lukon bounced atop a slick saddle whilst slowing his Naomi. Snow beat against his furry hood, ice stuck to his white mustache. Six others rode flank as their tiny group entered the northern gates of the Crossing. "Be ready. This is strange," he said.

Strange it was, for hundreds of Alyonians were gathered, all shouting angrily toward a wooden stage where two messengers passed out bundles of parchment.

"Please, please!" beckoned the messengers. "We did not stroke the pen ourselves! We merely deliver this news from the High Council."

The crowd roared louder, some descending into brawls. Lukon recognized a friendly face. "Nario!" he shouted, turning the southern gate master's attention.

"Lukon?" Nario pushed his way through the masses and reached up to Lukon's forearm. "Didn't think I'd see you for a few seasons yet."

Awed by the fierce commotion, Lukon accepted Nario's hand and dismounted. "You and I both. What troubles? I've never seen the Crossing so lively."

"Aye." Nario motioned toward the messengers. "The new Master of Defense is askin' for any and all bows and arrows. Hopin' to send 'em to Taaivetti. Apparently there's hard fightin' down at

Hann. Some folks are happy, others furious. Our smithies have been ordered to send all bows straight to Hann or the Bolden Barrier, so folks aren't happy if they're lookin' to buy."

"The *new* Master of Defense?"

"Aye." Nario frowned. "Kornilious...self-slaughter."

Lukon thought about Tiannu's letters he'd read on his way here.

"Wasn't a fan of Kornilious by any means," continued Nario. "But our warriors need better care back home. It happens every day, self-slaughter. He served our realm, he deserved better."

"Remind me, who was his high aid?"

"Sir Dyman Kelterbury."

Of course...one of the High Council's favorites. A lifelong politician can be easily controlled. Lukon nodded and eyed a smithy across the way. Its front door was locked, but nearly giving way to a second restless crowd. "Will you need our aid here?"

"No, no, you've my thanks. Town sentries will arrive soon, and this lot will break. The news is fresh, that's all."

"Understood." Lukon remounted, then motioned his riders to follow. "Was grand to see you, Nario. We're needed in Alyonia, but I suspect you'll see me soon. Stay safe."

MADISON

Madison unlocked her front door, slowly entering a quaint yet well-kept living chamber. Her parents had decorated with antiques and fashionably old trinkets, anything to evade the modern Alyonian style of minimalism surrounded by perfectly cut and perfectly painted wood. Yet even inside, Madison found herself unable to drown the noise from Alyonia's vibrant, nervous streets. These were strange times indeed.

"Mother?"

Still no sign of her.

Madison paced down a hall filled with Crimson and Tiannu's delicate paintings, even a few hung poems they'd written to one another. "Mother?"

Poking her head in the master chamber, Tiannu was not in her quarters either. Madison sighed, then took to her own quarters, quickly packing a travel bag with clothes from a dresser. She smiled, for the dresser's top was lined with items Hendrix had gifted her over their many seasons together. None more valuable than the secret deed to their little slice of land. Madison lifted the deed papers, imagining their life to come when all of this madness had finally ended. *If* it ever ended. Moving to the closet, she opened its doors.

"Aggh!"

A bloody body crashed down upon her, its pale and lifeless

limbs flailing through the arm holes of a red robe.

"Ahhhhh!"

Madison rushed to exit but smacked right into a humongous Alyonian, older than any she'd ever seen.

"Shh," whispered Jari, one finger to his lips, the other controlling her wrist. "We've taken care of them, but more may come yet."

71

BANDANO-RHI
Ashland

"Do you repent?" asked Bandano-Rhi calmly.

Five men, quivering and weeping, knelt before him in a valley of blood and wheat. Hundreds of bodies surrounded, painting the grain field dark red and assaulting Rhi's army with pungent smells.

His army, in fact, lined the El-Road behind him, covering their mouths from harsh smoke filling the hot air. The city of Ashland burned some eighty span north, a long ways off the El-Road. Its formidable walls were made entirely of wood. Now aflame, they exhaled choking smoke across the entire valley of carnage. Coughing and hacking, Rhi's soldiers sneaked sly looks in his direction, pleading for a swift exit. Tasked with keeping watch for potential counter-attacks, the large force knew one would never occur.

"Do you repent?" asked Bandano-Rhi, more sternly.

The first man of five shook, his hair jostling against warm, sweaty cheeks. "I don't know how…I don't believe." He inhaled the thick smoke, wheezed. "But I claim you, my lord. My master even, if it pleases—"

His head fell from scrawny shoulders, joining a pile of ten others nearby. An equal number of decapitated torsos lay dormant, spilling their insides to feed the field's critters.

Bandano-Rhi nodded to Felix-Donro, who cleaned his longsword with a rag. "Your precision impresses." Downing the last of the day's wineskin, the emperor knelt to eye level with the next prisoner of war.

"I repent! I repent!" The captive wept utterly. "Please, I'm true."

Bandano-Rhi studied his eyes. "I believe you. Rise and go."

The man rose and sprinted across the field of smoke and death, leaping over severed bodies along the way.

"He won't make it far," said Felix-Donro.

"If Elo wills it, he shall." Bandano-Rhi paused to search his surroundings. *Where, damn it, where are you...?*

It had been four long days since Bandano-Rhi sacked the heathen city of Coyo, and he'd killed countless unrighteous families at every lowly township since. Bringing such death to the forces of evil, he was sure their shadow god would show itself, sure it would come to challenge his light.

Show yourself. Nearly choking and coughing, Bandano-Rhi stared up into thick grey clouds. He turned and strutted to the next man in line. Three prisoners remained, two of which wet themselves uncontrollably. "Do you repent?" he yelled furiously.

"Go and hump your horse, Rhi," spat the prisoner, perhaps the only true Ashland warrior left. "You're a disgrace to the sect. Everything wrong with it."

His head rolled next.

"Please, please!" roared the final captives.

"I repent!"

"We repent! Praise Elo!"

Bandana-Rhi stepped to them. "Why?"

The prisoners trembled, reeking of urine and sweat. "I...I..."

"Why do you repent? Tell me." Bandano remained inches from them, forcing even his honor guard to avert their gaze.

"Because it is right!" voiced the braver captive. "We repent!"

Bandano-Rhi motioned to a supply servant, who ran fast as

he could from the El-Road with a canteen of water. "Listen carefully," said Bandano, leaning in close enough for his drunken breath to assault the final prisoners. "When Elonity dies, fear of a higher judgment dies. When fear of a higher judgment dies, morality dies. When morality dies, man is doomed."

The captives knew not how to respond, electing to nod in agreement.

"Go and preach this through whatever is left of your empire." Bandano-Rhi motioned them off into the field, sparing them.

"My lord!" Shouts from behind.

Bandano-Rhi stood to the sight of Cassius-Thrimm approaching. "I bring news, peculiar news."

"Speak."

Cassius dismounted and knelt. "Kornilious of Alyonia has died. Four moons ago, it seems. The new Master of Defense has...well—"

"Speak!"

"Withdrawn Alyonian forces from the Bolden Barrier. Reports claim that the great horde of Gorsh marches east completely free of retaliation."

Bandano-Rhi nodded, desperately attempting to understand why Taryn would allow such a move. *This is off plan... The Bolden Barrier was supposed to face the Gorsh.*

Cassius-Thrimm lifted a sealed scroll. "And then there's this. An Alyonian Askari delivered the scroll to your personal carriage, as if it knew your scent prior..."

Bandano grasped the scroll, quickly noting the sender was indeed *not* Taryn. It had been marked by one Tiannu Preters.

He opened the scroll and read slowly, his face contorting in a way Cassius had never seen.

"My lord?"

Bandano-Rhi exhaled, burying his anguish deep inside. "If this letter is to be believed, everything changes."

72

CRIMSON

Red Snow

Crimson forced his way through knee-high snow. His many layers of fur had been covered in thick flakes, blending him further with all that surrounded. White. Flat. Nothingness. For four nova-less days he'd transversed the infamously dark Quiet Lands, eyes ready for the bears and beasts of Dark Season legend. But they'd not shown. With the Bright Season looming, even the frozen Quiet Lands would lose a foot of snow to rising heat, and even the nastiest of jaws went underground for some great, yet unknown time.

Get yourself right, he thought, repeating Tiannu's words of wisdom.

Mountains loomed in the distance. Always. It seemed one could never near them no matter how long they'd trekked. Time warped here, or so it felt; for an hour's march through such harsh terrain yielded small and confusing gains. Crimson had scouted here aplenty, though he was admittedly reaching the boundaries of times past. Footprints and easily trackable remnants of Grieves' large company had led Crimson thus far, as had the Lookout's many wooden beacons planted every ten span. But the final beacon was upon him just ahead, then there was only the slope. *Balo, aid me.*

Crimson had feared this moment, though never voiced it.

Point C, as it had become known, the farthest point ever tracked afoot. Alyonian birds with forged fur had flown past such a point, but the infamous slope slanted the ground itself into a great canyon of black ice as deep and wide as the eye could see. Endless in every direction ahead, flanked only by the distant mountains that teased from afar. Stepping to the canyon's ledge, Crimson's insides roiled, pleading him to choose self-preservation, to turn back from whatever this was.

Height. Death.

Get yourself right.

Blood.

Hmm.

The spot was miniscule, yet Crimson's eyes could see sporadic spats of red outside a moonlit cave in the canyon below. The great canyon's descent was layered, dropping harshly at some points, merely sloping at others.

Can I make it?

The shadowy cave wasn't too far down from Crimson's position, and had obviously been accomplished by Grieves' company, judging by the many tracks surrounding.

The ice is torn and scratched nearly everywhere. I suppose Grieves took his entire company down.

A few ice axes remained stuck in the frozen drop-off beneath him, perhaps lingering from those unlucky enough to lose their grip whilst descending.

Why this specific cave? Could the map possibly be that detailed?

Crimson took to his pack and retrieved two ice axes of his own, then began a slow and quivering descent. The Lookout had grown rather astute to the art, sending Crimson off with spiked crampons and axes. Taking deep breaths, he chanced death with every smack of axe, ever making his way toward the frozen cave below, ever fearing if this lingering shadow god could intervene.

Where does its power end and begin?

The first descent was short, perhaps fifty forearms at most. Landing on flat ice, Crimson gathered his supplies and repacked. His crampons came in great use here, for the ground itself was black ice. Deathly slippery and hard to spot. The cave loomed ahead, with torn travel sacks and blood spots staining its exterior. He stopped, listened. A few steps to his right would put him within view of whoever rested inside this cave. No sounds came, however, no rustling nor crackling of fires. No murmurs of Grieves' presumably shivering company.

Retrieving a travel lantern from his pack, Crimson peeked into the cave, shocked by its raw size and emptiness, shocked by its horrid stench. The toothed ceilings stretched higher than he could see in such darkness, for vision ended some five forearms ahead of the lantern.

Silence.

Peculiar.

Kneeling, he shined his lantern upon the icy ground beneath. It was chipped everywhere, assuredly from a hundred crampons. Stepping in farther, Crimson made out more packs and items of travel: canteens, broken lanterns, swords.

Unsheathed...

Crimson watched his step, careful to maintain balance above the ice.

Why unsheathed?

The foul smells magnified, as did the clusters of items, most icing over already.

The bodies came next.

Crimson's lantern illuminated one at a time as his walk turned into a crawl. There were no full bodies, not a one. Torsos remained, as did severed heads and limbs, each in various stages of freezing. Then came the groups...mounds of limbs. The dead were everywhere, scattered across the black ice like a frozen graveyard.

A whisper. "Shh…"

Crimson whirled to it, his eyes wide.

Silence.

He remained low, then slid his lantern across the thick ice toward this whisper. The metal lantern came to a screeching stop, its light exposing a small mountain of bodies and limbs and one Alyonian concealed beneath them. *Grieves.*

Hiding below the dead, Grieves slowly brought a gloved finger to his lips, warning Crimson, then pushed the lantern away. Its metal shrieked yet again but was followed by—

"Eeeeeer!"

A sharp noise echoed through the cavern.

Crimson fell flat to his stomach, going still.

"Eeeeeer!"

Another cry. And slowly…

Bloody Perdition.

Crimson began to see eyes. Hundreds, then thousands. Some high within the cave, some low as the ice itself. Thousands of dreaded pupils blinked, staring straight in his direction.

73

TARYN

Torture

Sir Kelterbury's aged yet powerful voice boomed over the beach, over the hundreds of mourning Alyonians kneeling upon its chilled yellow sands. Standing atop a crab-ridden shrine of sea logs, he presided over Kornilious' sendoff.

"Lastly, I've known Kornilious Debauer for more than one hundred seasons, and never have I met a stronger Alyonian. Kornilious lived by a code of ethics and honor, one we must all strive to uphold. He lived to serve others, having spent his earliest days fighting for the realm and his latest serving its diplomatic wishes. Kornilious took no wife and no children, such was his great devotion to this land and the many tasks that come with a life of serving it. It is my life's great honor, and now my life's great work, to carry his legacy forward."

Sir Kelterbury nodded toward six of Kornilious' House Debauer protectorates surrounding his casket. On order, they lifted his box of rest and heaved it upon a wooden raft, then pushed it out to calm tides.

"You may now pay your final respects."

The kneeled crowd stood and made for the waterline, most holding tiny candles atop pieces of wood. At the foamy shore, the broken-hearted Alyonians pushed their sailing candles out to sea. Surrounded by a caravan of grieving flames, Kornilious floated past waves of unwelcoming breakers, never to be seen again.

* * *

The rain had ceased over Alyonia for four moons straight, yet the city's skies remained a cloudy grey filled with fleeting birds. Storms kept brewing overhead, ceaselessly bringing angry winds and the signs of hard rain, yet rain never fell. Shingles and woodchips covered the streets of Alyonia, as did leaves and branches blown in from the city's southern farms.

Madison stepped over a particularly large branch, shocked that any winds could carry it this far. The time was past darkest hour, rendering her black cloak effective. Clinging to the sides of manors, she slid her way through alley after alley, comforted by the knowledge of Jari and Cicero's stealth escort. *They're here, somewhere,* she thought.

"Jamos! Jamos!"

Madison searched for the voice, her travel bag flopping with each step.

"Jamos!"

An elderly Alyonian turned an alley corner, shouting in every direction. Her white hair had greyed with time, stretching so far as to tickle her hunched spine. "Have you seen a little one?" she asked Madison, frantically leaning over a wooden cane. "Perhaps half your height? He wears an old and blue tunic."

Madison kept her pace, passing by the teary-eyed elder. "I have not, but you've my sorrow and my best wishes to find him." Keeping one eye on the elder, she wondered if Jari had an arrow nocked somewhere nearby. *Just in case.*

She exited the city's thickest area, spitting her out into open fields surrounded by scattered homes of the wealthy. Alyonia's southern farmlands would begin soon, sprawling far in every direction and providing the darkest path of travel she required. *Almost,* she thought. *Almost.*

* * *

Taryn paced her way down the Kaldorian catacombs, running red nails across the same glass-cased Askari she'd once passed with Kornilious. His memory did linger, that much was true. Yet it came only in spurts of their younger moons, as if saving its guilt for childhood memories.

Loud noises echoed—violent at times, soothing at others. The halls now bustled with red-robed Alyonians, perhaps one thousand or more. Some bowed to the queen, others evaded and kept to their worktables. The life and presence of so many felt rather odd, for the family's secret catacombs had never known more than a body or two at once. But these were new times, times Taryn herself dictated. She kept her gaze fixated only upon a stone stairwell ahead.

Descending the stairs, she found herself in a much wider hall with barred cells on either side. Taryn passed them one by one, most filled with unconscious children or Alyonian prisoners of the highest degree. Even Brendann Brackwater remained, having been horrifically maimed since aiding Hendrix and Aypax in their escape.

Ignoring his cell and condition, Taryn came to the hall's end where a final chamber had been dug deeper than the rest, presumably below the Kaldorian manor's wine cellar. "You may stand down," said Taryn, approaching a guard outside the cell.

The guard opened the cell and stood aside, perplexed. "You're sure, my queen? Such a cell is saved for our most heinous offenders—"

"Do you believe I know not who rests inside?"

The guard shook. "Of course not. I meant no—"

Taryn extended her hand. "Leave me the dagger. I'll shout if my feeble limbs cannot handle the chained prisoner."

The guard unsheathed a small blade and gifted the queen before bowing and stepping aside. "I'll be a shout's distance."

Taryn waved him off and stepped inside to meet her target.

Tiannu Preters.

* * *

Madison sat upon pointed rocks, staring out at the Lukonite Lake's waterfront and willing herself to forget its wonderful memories past. Moonlight bounced off the lake's center, illuminating pine trees and sleeping critters.

"He shall show." Jari sat beside young Madison, his trained eye easily reading her. *Fear.* "Your mother left word to Crimson himself; he knows this is the place. Someone will come for you."

"What if the letter was intercepted?"

"It was addressed wisely." Jari patted Madison on the back of her dark tunic, its black coloring matching his own.

"I just, I cannot believe any of this."

"You are not alone."

Madison felt some comfort in that. Looking about, her eyes caught a few empty bottles of ale resting at the foamy shoreline, most broken or rehoused with algae and sea lice living inside. "What will you do with the letters she found?"

"Share them with all of Alyonia. Your mother's bravery must not be in vain. I'm merely sorry we couldn't protect her."

"How will you share them?"

Jari bobbed his head. "The story-papers, the High Council, I'm unsure. There are good Alyonians yet, this I do know, and they shall help."

"What of Bandano-Rhi?"

Jari grinned. "We sent him some of Taryn's more personal letters…letters she sent to Kornilious and others. Bandano-Rhi shall soon know Taryn is not a true believer in his god Elo, nor any god at that. He shall soon know he is but a stepstone in her great game."

A loud owl hooted in the distance before taking flight, dragging their attention. "How long do we wait?" asked Madison.

"Four moons at least."

"And if my father does not show by then—"

"I haven't thought that far."

Madison slouched. "It feels wrong, being here. I know it is what Mother would want, but I can't simply leave her there."

Jari nodded. "You aren't. You're giving Taryn less bargaining power. Leave your mother's escape to us. Trust."

"I trusted her. Look where that got me."

"It got you here safely."

Madison gazed down at her *H.K.* bracelet. "I grow tired of putting my trust in things that may not work out."

Jari looked her deep in the eyes, painfully aware of the journey she faced ahead. "Sometimes trust is only the first part of our lesson."

* * *

Taryn closed the cell door behind her, darkening the already depressing chamber of mud and clay.

Tiannu hung from a barren wall opposite her, bound at both wrists and ankles by rusty brown chains. Without circulation, her limbs tinged black and blue, and her bloodied face was swollen. Tiannu's sweat had hardened her white hair, which clustered and stuck to the many specks of dried red amongst her cheeks and forehead.

Assessing her prisoner's condition, Taryn deemed it time. "Your daughter has been captured."

Tiannu's eyes panned up, her very pupils wide from lack of light, broken from moons of abuse. "She'd be here, if so." Tiannu's tongue had been partially severed, rendering her voice rather quiet.

"On her way now."

"I've time."

"Perhaps not."

Taryn made her way closer, stopping an arm's length afar. "But our positions are clear. You won't talk until she's present, and I need little Madison for other matters, so we may leave her off the bargaining table. I'll make this simple. You came into possession of some very personal letters. I'd like to know what you've done with them."

The metal chains clanked as Tiannu shrugged, pained by the lifting of her shoulders.

"I see." Taryn stepped closer still. "I'll exchange your freedom for them."

"You'd kill me the moment I returned them."

"Have someone else return them. I'll kill them instead."

Tiannu thought. "To bargain with you is to ask the moon not to rise. A few hours would be bright, but eventually, the night would come."

"Do you know the worst part about having such weak enemies?" Taryn shortened the distance again, now a breath or two away. "It's that I can't do much to make their existence any worse than it already is. You, for example, have nothing worth taking." A short silence befell them as Taryn lifted the dagger into view. "So bargain we will not."

"Look at me. *All* of me." Tiannu paused to let Taryn take in her many wounds, the tiny rivers of red beneath her. "If your guard couldn't break me, you can't."

Taryn smiled a full-on grin. "Commander Grieves has taken your husband's life. His head is on the way to Alyonia. Taaivetti's too."

"I applaud your memory, but to keep track of so many lies may one day catch up to you. And thanks to your letters, it may come from the places you least expect."

Taryn nodded, somewhat exhilarated by a worthy adversary. Twirling the blade through her fingers quite expertly, she considered her next move.

Even Tiannu was impressed by her skill of hand. "Well done, but careful. Cut the wrong bloodline, and I'm gone forever with your letters."

"You place too much weight on mere parchment. Ah, just the same, there's a silver lining in our midst. What you've failed to realize, Tiannu, is that releasing my letters merely expedites my real goal."

"Which is?"

Taryn dug the steel into Tiannu's shoulder, then leaned in to whisper. "Something I want you alive to see."

74

HENDRIX

The Family

Hendrix sat beside The Family, each bound by golden shackles and leaning upon the brown walls of Drill Bintonn's personal ship, *Searcher*. Sir Edmund Drake lay before them, chained and unconscious on the cabin's splintery floor.

The cabin was breathtaking, nearly as pristine as Drill's quarters in Starsgard. Mounted trophies of animal heads lined the timber walls. Bent spears and dented swords also hung about, boasting prior hunts.

"He's moving," said Julieta, her cut forehead resting on Chu'a's bruised shoulder.

Drake writhed, then slowly blinked. "Sweet maiden, where am I?"

The Family stared, willing themselves to believe this was truly Drake.

"It finally happen?" Drake's voice returned, though it remained dry and raspy.

"Yes. Yes, it did," said Hendrix, tending to a lingering brain ache and a few raw wounds of his own. He sat opposite the room from everyone else, separated. "It did indeed—"

"They's up an movingssss," hissed Drill, pushing into the

room. No muscle followed; the slender Tourtoufian appeared alone for once. "Good, I was hopin' yous' wouldn't die just yet." Drill sat behind a table of white marble and pointed at Hendrix. "You's especially."

Hendrix swallowed, now aware of why he'd been separated. "I won't eat or drink."

"You wills." Drill nodded to a Tourtoufian in the corner.

The Family hadn't noticed him, but now they saw he was busy unraveling a bag of blades for various tortures. Satisfied, Drill removed the ancient key from a drawer and held it up for all to see. "I owe you my thanks, though. See, everything's I ever thought was true, everything's I ever searched for...you's proven to be a reality. And now that I've got one key, 'tis just a matter of times before I have 'em all."

"Good luck," scoffed Chu'a.

Drill grinned. "Don't needs it. See, when we reach Taryn, 'tis a simples trade. The Alyonian key for the boy."

"You're right," said Hendrix. "You need no luck for that, just a tall and skinny casket."

Drill led his torturous Tourtoufian to the door, then turned to Drake. "Speakin' of caskets, your littles dog wolf is up top. If the Alyonian dies, the pup goes too. Slowly."

The door slammed, leaving the family alone with Drill's threat.

* * *

"Drake," said Hendrix, breaking a grueling silence following Drill's departure. "Something has plagued my mind for some time. Now seems as good as ever."

The pirateer lifted his torso, finally able to move on his own accord. "Aye?"

"Before any of this, you spoke of payment for your aid in

463

saving Ava. A different kind of payment. What was it? Why did you help us?"

Drake coughed, buying time before coming clean and pointing at Ava. "Her."

Drake fought to a full sit and huffed. "When I was five, me mother gave me an eye patch, see? Some local apothecary said I'd be blind in me left eye if I didn't make it work double. I was a mere boy, though, and like every islander, I'd heard the legends of pirateers. So I loved that damned eye patch. Got good at fightin' and sailin', I did, grew up rough. And like all'a you's, me ma was murdered, and it changed me. I took pirateerin' to a new level, took to takin' back what life had stolen from me."

The Family leaned in, restrained yet captivated.

"I went dark," continued Drake, rambling to his point. "Took lives, I did... Looked men in the eyes, a few women even. 'Tis a vile thing to watch life leave eyes. Somewhere along the way, I brought that damned shadow forth. I see it in me dreams. The worse I do in this life, the worse it grows. The dreams, the aches. Drinkin' helps, but not for long. Bloody Perdition, maybe drinkin' only worsens it. In one'a me dreams, the shadow crawled across me chamber floor, see? Hovered over me. I felt it, felt it try to enter, try to become me. I been searchin' for a healer ever since."

Hendrix tried to shuffle forward, but the chains held firm in place. "But why use Aypax and me at all? Why not search for her yourself?"

"I saw the way she looked at ya, and I...I felt the strangest pull...like somethin' was draggin' me towards ya."

Hendrix and Ava exchanged a subtle glance.

"When the shadow started gettin' worse, Sammy and me sailed to Gondol and Contis, we did," said Drake, before nodding to Ava. "Saw your ma burned alive. Whispers of her daughters took over the towns, some folks sayin' they could heal twice as well as their mother, some sayin' you two could kill shadow gods by hand. I tracked you and your sister to Moro, then back to Starsgard, hopin' you might save me before me time was up. You've my apologies."

Another silence made room for the sound of waves pattering the ship's hull just outside their spacious cabin. Everyone glanced out of the cabin's many windows, yet nothing but a remorseless sea stared back.

"So what now?" asked Hendrix.

Julieta slid herself as far forward as the chains allowed, taking center stage among her broken peers. "We plan."

75

THE TARYN

The Taryn

Taryn stood before the largest window of her living chamber, her red robe hanging proudly from the rack beside. The robe's colors shifted from the light of crackling flames and candles spread about. The fiery sounds soothed, though not much could quell her annoyance regarding the frenzied protests in the streets below.

Taryn plopped on her ruby sofa, contemplating. Taaivetti's box sat beside her. Taryn could not look directly at it, as if greatly unsure, yet somehow pulled toward it.

Knock knock knock.

Taryn rolled her eyes and sighed. "Come."

Trakkonious entered, slyly shutting the door behind. "You summoned me?"

"Yes." Leaving the box, Taryn walked toward the window, studying her subjects and the warped, moldy rooftops of a few wooden manors below. "We must send word for Bandano-Rhi. I may even have to travel myself."

Trakkonious expertly hid his shock. "What has occurred, my qu—"

"What matters is that he can no longer be counted on. Not for the time being. We must send for new allies."

"Our withdrawal from the Accord has estranged them all. Perhaps Jordzilla or Myre might warm to us, but even these are slim odds." Trakkonious paced forward, carefully reading Taryn's mood. "If I may, my queen...you are off course. At every turn you ignore my counsel, and you're driving each stage of our plan much too quickly. Look at them all below."

Taryn did just that, watching her citizens fight and chant like an army of dissatisfied ants.

"If they're in such an uproar now, imagine when the news of Taaivetti's death arrives. There *will* be blood. Civil conflict, even. If you're not going to follow our stratagem, fine, but I surely hope you have a better path in store."

"Life is harsh, isn't it? And unexpected. So very unexpected."

Trakkonious nodded, puzzled. "Things are only unexpected if they are overlooked. What is your goal here?"

"Chaos."

Taryn waved him toward the door, dismissing him with the final parting word.

It took some time, but moments after his departure, Taryn's eyes found their way back to Taaivetti's box. Striding toward it, she ripped open the wood and stared down. A cluster of kingly items rested inside. Amulets, blades, scrolls, and trinkets. So very *personal*.

Then she saw it, perhaps the source of her strange pull, a bundle of parchment titled: *The Taryn*.

Lifting the bundle, she flipped back the first page...

House Kaldor

Letter type: Informative
To: Taaivetti Kaldor
From: Father
343 A.B, Windy Season, 85th Moon, Double Novas

My son,

The time shall soon come when a great burden must pass from my shoulders to your own. Before I join the stars, there are things you should know, things my father never told me, and things no father should ever face at all.

The priest who defiled your sister: Despite the many whispers of my lying, he truly did curse her name, the name of Lizabeth the Second. In an effort to protect her from the darkness he proclaimed, I changed her name by law. She hated me for this and thought I saw her differently, thought I lost my love for her. Not so, my son, not so... I merely saw what lurked inside her.

Upon discovering the priest's actions, I beheaded him, as you recall, but what I soon uncovered after, I withheld: Eros was the wrong priest, innocent. Your sister had burned the real offender alive, Priest Gypsis. She drew her actions on parchment. I've left the drawings in the back of this book. Taaivetti, to burn one alive at such a young age...unexplainable. I tracked her many eves, praying I had misjudged, but she always eluded me below our manor. That's when I met the Kaldorian Guard.

The guard are an ancient group, tracing back to our Alyonian elders. Yes, Taaivetti, the legends and dust are true.

The Guard changed everything, showed me the truth of this life, the depths of our own family's manor. There are rooms below our rooms, catacombs so deep the worms themselves do not dare. Pitch black. Horrid. *This* is where Taryn would go, 'tis why her skin dawns pale. We found the charred remains of Gypsis down below, along with our family's maps and chests, all dedicated to finding the three remaining keys. Because, my son, we've possession of one...

My search for the other keys began, and with it revealed the true purpose of the Lookout. The realm believes it is for exploration and a great search of unknown resources. Not so, Taaivetti, not so.

Eventually, the Kaldorian Guard opened my eyes to the seven gifts of the dust and to the horrors of our world's shadows. One eve, upon returning home from Preem's Ball, I saw one myself. I saw one inside my Taryn... I saw it in her eyes, my son. I struck her, desperate, yet the shadow-god remained; perhaps it only grew in strength.

Two of the Guard are twins, and they proclaimed to have expelled such a shadow from my beloved Taryn. But another called Jari said they did not. Jari proclaimed the twins themselves had gone dark, had lied to me. I never saw the twins again.

Time drew on, painfully so. I sent Jari and the Guard to find these traitorous twins. I spent countless seasons drowning in booze and books, desperate to help my Taryn, desperate to cover my own family from their cunning.

Taryn eventually seemed quite normal, and my readings hinted at such shadow gods fleeing with time. On the seldom occasions I asked your dear sister, she swore that she knew not of my madness, and with time, it became just that—madness.

This madness overtook me, festering and killing my marriage, my relations. I never told your mother, for I feared what might happen if I opened her up to such truths.

As I grew darker and more alone, I, too, began to feel the creeping shadows. I could see them on our manor walls, passing quick as the arrow flies. Hovering here and there... hiding...stalking. Soon I began to have dreams, the same dream every moon.

In the end, Taaivetti, I took your sister to the Forest of Balo, a grand walk and two moons of camping fit for a father and daughter.

We discussed this life, and I knew, I could see my baby was gone. When I pressed her, she swore to having no memory of going down below the catacombs, no memory of Priest Gypsis. She acted so normal, so precious, but it was not her, and I knew not how to help.

Jari never returned. None of the Guard did, and so I fear for them too.

I love your sister more than you can understand. Do not give up on her. She is in there, somewhere.

Raldor

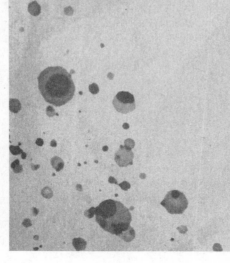

Taryn's fingers quivered, her legs shook. Dropping the bundle of parchment, the aforementioned drawings slipped out and fluttered to the ground like dead butterflies. Taryn caught one and glanced at the drawing: her portrayal of young Taryn burning Priest Gypsis alive.

Aghhhhhhhhhhhhhhhh!

Taryn fell to her knees and palmed her temple, Lizabeth the Second beckoning to come forth.

Helllllllpppppp meee!

The real Taryn screamed from within, louder than ever, yet silent to the world around. But she was coming back, this Taryn, this Lizabeth the Second by name. Shaking her head and smashing against furniture, she battled whatever shadow controlled her.

"Taaivetti!" she screeched in the childish voice, the voice that was, in fact, her own. "Hello? Is anyone here?" Pacing around, young Lizabeth the Second could not make out her surroundings. This chamber, the scary flames and parchment.

Wait, she thought.

These were Father's quarters. She was *trespassing.*

"Oh no."

Young Lizabeth the Second searched for a door, but nearly slipped upon the bundle of parchment beneath her. Gathering them, her eyes could not help but peek.

What?

It was impossible, surely...for the date itself was near ten years yet to come. And Father's words, his joining the stars.

Young Lizabeth the Second read on, something rumbling within her, pounding her intestines with every word as if beseeching her not to read any further. Yet the letter seemed clear; it was real.

Then the words echoed through her.

Do not give up on her. She is in there, somewhere.

And so it clicked, finally.

The words struck something deep within, some facet of mind and soul that young Lizabeth the Second had never been able to understand when coming forth in times past. But now, she was here, she was present, she was aware.

"Die!" young Lizabeth the Second shouted, but young Lizabeth's voice it was not. This voice belonged to Taryn, all twenty-five years of her.

The real her. The present her. Cognizant of whatever horrors and shadow gods lurked within.

Taryn rushed for the kitchen and made for a set of knives, stumbling and breaking her glass table along the way.

"Aghhhhhh!"

Sudden pains overtook her, forcing Taryn to writhe. Pushing through the pain, her eyes focused only on the knives, on the daunting task at hand.

"Dieeeeeeeee!"

It was the loudest she'd ever screamed, so loud in fact that footsteps thundered down the halls outside her chamber.

Crack.

Ughhhhh.

Pain. Unbearable.

Crack.

Taryn's bones contorted, breaking in two at her left elbow and knee. As if something deep in her very soul had control over her limbs. Tears fled her eyes whilst she forced herself to stand and fight toward the life-ending blade, toward what needed doing, toward the greater good. Gripping its handle she pulled as—

"Taryn!"

"My queen!"

Voices afar drew her vision to the door, which reverberated from constant bodies or boots fighting their way in. Blinking uncontrollably, Taryn dropped the blade, then released a guttural sound.

Her left arm hung limp, her left leg could bear no weight…and so she sat. The Taryn wisely sat.

Her door flung open.

"Taryn?"

Three house protectorates forced their way in, blades and bows at ready, eyes searching for an assailant.

"My sincerest apologies." Taryn smiled from her seat at the kitchen counter, her good leg swinging back and forth in an effort to show fair health. "Given the severity of late, I've accepted an invitation to lead the Kaldorian theater company in next season's rendition of *Death on Deadrock Isle*. My words shall not memorize themselves." Taryn smiled and gave the faintest bow.

"Understood, my queen," said the first protectorate, returning Taryn's bow.

"Aye, congratulations," said the others.

"My thanks." Taryn nodded, as if embarrassed to have been caught for such silliness. "Again, you've my sincerest apologies. What a fool I was to not yet inform you! Especially with such a dramatic scene to prepare!"

Her protectorates bowed before taking leave, doing all they could to keep her unhinged door standing upright. "We'll have the High Carpenter himself see to a new door at once."

"Excellent." Soon she was all alone yet again.

Almost.

Turning toward the countertop mirror, she stared at her reflection in its pristine glass. Her beautiful face had been replaced by an ugly, abominable thing…the red and green and nightmarish thing from within, the serpent with a star on its forehead and flames in its eyes, the king of shadows himself.

Stralli.

DUST

End of Book One

*"Art cannot change the world, but it can contribute
to changing the consciousness and drives of men and women
who could change the world."*

—HERBERT MERCUSE

Acknowledgments

To my mother and my family, for supporting and encouraging me to chase my dreams.

To my wife for putting up with me (just in general, but also through my writing).

To Don Pape, who took a chance on representing my work and my crazy ideas.

To Becky Nesbitt for believing in me as a writer and answering my many questions.

To Amy Kerr, for being the best editor in the business.

There are far too many to thank and acknowledge here, and for that I am blessed.

https://www.dustbook.shop/

Author Note

Lastly, I would be remiss to not mention SEALKIDS, the incredible group of superstars who have supported me for as long as I can remember. If you have a heart for helping veterans and their loved ones, please consider supporting SEALKIDS. Their information is below.

SEALKIDS provides academic support to the children of US Naval Special Warfare, especially those with developmental and learning disabilities. SEALKIDS assists with and pays for testing and diagnosis of disabilities, matches families with specialized tutors and therapists, assists families by providing advocates to address deficiencies in services and accommodations provided by public schools, and other needs that may arise. SEALKIDS provides full case management to ensure student success. Learn more at SEALKIDS.org.

About the Author

The son of a U.S Navy SEAL and 2012 Golden Gloves champion, Josh Plasse studied Homeland Security and Criminal Justice at Virginia Commonwealth University before moving to Los Angeles and dedicating his life to writing and filmmaking. With over fifty episodes of network television under his belt, (you may have seen him on iCarly, Grey's Anatomy, etc)! Josh has also penned and produced three feature films and two documentaries. His feature film titled *Ride*, was called "masterful" and "a rodeo movie like no other" by *Variety* and *Sports Illustrated*. He is responsible for raising over $50,000 throughout his multiple campaigns for veteran suicide awareness, and he currently resides in Nashville with his wife and two fur babies (dogs).